Praise for *Th*

Shortlisted for the John Creasey (New Blood) Dagger Award 2017

"A splendid read . . . handled with great skill . . . Bolton paints a portrait of the period with a confidence usually reserved for old survivors."

The Times

"An astonishingly accomplished debut."

Daily Mail

"A laser-sharp noir thriller."

Financial Times

"Brilliantly atmospheric and compelling."

Mail on Sunday

"Superbly realised."

Telegraph, Books of the Year

"Craine is not the usual maverick cop and his ambiguous nature makes this novel tick . . . Place and period are lovingly described."

Spectator

"Star-studded, deliciously dark noir."

Express

"Bolton spins a lurid tale of Hollywood after dark, complete with drugs, prostitution, and pornography . . . nicely mixing Hollywood glamour with backroom sleaze."

Booklist

"A skilfully written, atmospheric tale."

Literary Review

"Bolton has clearly done his homework on pre-WWII Hollywood . . . Bolton has imagination to spare."

Publishers Weekly

"This debut novel is good on the period detail, which never becomes mere iconography . . . a noir that provides a pleasant tour of Hollywood's golden age."

Kirkus

"It's one of those books which you pick up idly – and don't put down. I read it in a couple of days and I'm still thinking about a couple of the characters. Definitely recommended . . . There's a real pace to the story."

The Bookbag

THE SYNDICATE

Guy Bolton

A Point Blank Book

First published by Point Blank,
an imprint of Oneworld Publications, 2018

A CIP record for this title is available from the British Library

ISBN 978-1-78607-431-7
ISBN 978-1-78607-432-4 (eBook)

Typeset by Hewer Text UK Ltd, Edinburgh
Printed and bound in Great Britain by Clays Ltd, Elcograf S.p.A.

Oneworld Publications
10 Bloomsbury Street
London WC1B 3SR
England

For Laura

FRIDAY

Beverly Hills, Los Angeles
June 20th, 1947

He parked the car half-way down Linden Drive and went the rest of the way on foot.

The heat had been unbearable the past few days, but the man was wearing a long dark rain jacket with the collar up and hat pulled down low like he was braced for winter.

He was moving down the sidewalk at a pace he hoped looked casual. For the most part, it was quiet at night in these wealthy suburban roads, but then out of nowhere a series of limousines could turn up as people arrived home from the pictures or a supper club somewhere. He wondered what they'd make of him with his long coat and the trumpet case at his side.

The man continued down the curb, counting mailboxes as he went: 804 . . . 806 . . . 808. He stopped thirty yards from 810 and idled on the fringes of the neighbor's driveway. House 810 was a Spanish villa with two stories, but although the drapes were drawn, there was no light from inside and no sounds either. Good: they weren't home yet.

The man pulled back his sleeve and checked his watch. 10:20 P.M. or thereabouts; it was hard to tell in this light. The party was supposed to be back any minute now.

There were no cars on the neighbor's driveway and no signs that anyone was home, so he came off the sidewalk and made his way up the lawn toward the side of the house.

A fence separated the gardens of the two houses, but it wasn't more than six feet high and there was no barbed wire or security spikes. In the neighborhood where he grew up, people lucky enough to have backyards put broken glass on the tops of their walls. Beverly Hills was a far cry from Brooklyn.

The man checked over his shoulder to make sure no one was watching, then slung the trumpet case over the other side. He put his hands on the top of the fence and tugged. Flat and sturdy. It would take his weight. He was about to pull himself over when the bushes lit up around him.

He ducked instinctively. He stayed very still, craning his neck a little to see the road.

There was a car coming down this way. He saw his own shadow twist and bend across the fence panels as the car continued down the road. *They hadn't seen him.*

When he was sure it wasn't coming back, the man pulled himself up and over the fence and landed with two feet firm in a flower bed on the other side. He was wearing his old army boots but the soles were worn down and shouldn't leave traceable prints. He kicked at the earth around his feet just to make sure.

From his position the party's house was completely visible. There were four arched windows on the ground floor facing the lawn, each seven feet tall and more than large enough to see the living room inside.

He opened the trumpet case and unwrapped the cotton blanket inside, taking out an M1 carbine with a straight fifteen-round box magazine.

The shooter hadn't fired his carbine since the war. Most men in his business used Thompsons or short-barreled revolvers. The M1 was a .30 caliber semiautomatic weapon he'd fired countless times in battle, fitted with a sliding ramp-type sight that was adjustable for windage. Hardly necessary for these conditions. The living room windows were barely thirty yards away.

He waited, crouching in the bushes for what seemed like a long time, slowing his breathing, allowing his night vision to adjust and taking in his surroundings. He could hear distant traffic and the rustle of trees and bushes but little else. It was so quiet now he could hear his watch ticking.

He was starting to lose patience when he heard an engine echo from the other side of the house and a moment later the lawn was illuminated as a car pulled into the driveway and up into the open garage.

The man lay still. The engine stopped. He heard car doors opening and then the sound of talking. The unseen group entered the house through a side door, and once again there was no other sound but that goddamn watch of his.

He focused on the window to the living room. A light came on and two men stepped inside. They closed the door behind them. *They were alone.*

The shooter strained to see as the two men moved around the room. The first man was slight of build, with a cigarette drooping from his lip. *Allen Smiley.* The other man was broader in the shoulders and wore a pinstripe suit. *Yes, it was him. It was Bugsy Siegel.*

Jesus. Seeing his face was a reminder of the stakes involved.

Benjamin "Bugsy" Siegel: internationally renowned businessman, gambler and mobster. Almost mythical in his circles. Like a god.

The man rose from the bushes, lifted himself to one knee and raised the carbine to his shoulder. He checked his left foot was planted firmly, slowed his breathing and leaned his eye toward the rear aperture sight.

As his breathing became shallow and deliberate, he inched a little to his right until the barrel was directly facing the central window. Another car, but this time he ignored it. He was completely focused.

A girl came in the room with the third man. Ah yes, he remembered. *That* girl. He teased the sight over her pert nose before moving it over to her boyfriend. The two of them left the room giggling and drunk, and only the pair of mobsters remained.

The two friends were pouring drinks, playing music, laughing and talking. Moving targets. But as he followed him in his crosshairs, Siegel sat down on the davenport sofa facing the windows, moving out of his line of sight.

Dammit.

The shooter pulled his eye away and craned his neck for a better view. He could make out the edge of Siegel's shoe and the corner of a newspaper. He twisted in his spot, even sidling a foot or so to his left, but it was no use. The angle wasn't right. Siegel wasn't in shot.

He was half-hoping Siegel would stand up again but he knew there wasn't time. He'd have to get closer.

Twenty feet between the windows and where he was now was a willow tree. From that vantage point there was no way he could miss Siegel. But would he be caught running out into the open? Was it dark enough?

The shooter breathed in and out slowly several times and then pushed himself off his heels. A part of him had to accept that Siegel could spot him any second, but there was no stopping now. He ran at a crouch across the lawn toward the house, placing his feet quickly one in front of the other, trying not to make a sound.

When he reached the willow tree he stopped and looked ahead. The two men were preoccupied, talking between themselves. They hadn't seen him.

He was breathing hard now, struggling in the heat. He was worried they would hear his rasped breaths. There was no time to waste. He lifted the carbine again and pulled it firm into his shoulder.

Good, his line of sight was clear.

The pin was filed down to make the shots faster but after the first round he knew the recoil would ruin his aim. After the second he'd more or less be firing blind.

He found Siegel in his sights again, then moved his finger toward the trigger.

Slowly, with careful deliberation, he lifted the bolt and slid it back. His movements were firm and purposeful: too fast and the metallic click would be audible; too slow and the round wouldn't chamber properly and he'd have a stoppage. He heard the familiar sound of a cartridge entering the breach, then ran his finger down the slide to check the working parts had moved forward. Yes, it was correctly loaded.

The shooter pushed the safety off with his thumb, allowed himself a series of shallow breaths, then focused on the crosshairs.

He blinked. His body tensed. His eyes adjusted.

Siegel was still sitting on the sofa, a plume of smoke drifting from his mouth. The shooter lined up front and rear sights until the top of his crosshairs was nudging Siegel's head. He could see his teeth glisten.

An exhale of breath.

He counted to three in his head, then squeezed the trigger. Felt the resistance. Pulled past it.

He fired.

The noise and the recoil disturbed his aim but he found the target's center mass and pulled the trigger again and then two times more.

There was no need.

The first shot was accurate: the bridge of Siegel's nose caved in like a crushed soda can, blood and brain matter spilling in all directions. His left eye popped clean out of the socket.

The noise was deafening, almost disorienting. The shooter fired again, destroying a marble statue on a grand piano before lowering the barrel a fraction to adjust to the recoil. He fired four times more. Two rounds hit Siegel in the chest.

In barely five seconds he'd fired nine shots. He wasn't sure how many had gone wide but it didn't matter. Benjamin Siegel was well and truly dead.

When Tilda Conroy arrived at Siegel's house there were already six cars on the street, two patrol cars and the remainder unmarked sedans. None of them looked like press. *Good*, she thought. *I'm the first reporter on the scene.*

Neighbors had spilled out onto the edges of their lawns. It was eleven o'clock at night now and most were in dressing gowns. It was a natural inclination for people to rubberneck, and she could hardly blame them. They were living on the same street as one of the most feared mobsters in America.

She saw a black Pontiac at the curb. A suited man stood with the passenger door open, ushering someone in. Not the aggressive way cops push perps in; more like a chauffeur.

"Excuse me, are you with the L.A.P.D.?" she asked.

The man ignored her, too focused on whoever was inside to care about a female reporter. He pulled the passenger door closed and drove off at speed. *Who was inside the car?*

There wasn't time to dwell. She had maybe five minutes before yellow press photographers got here, and they'd be climbing fences and crawling through windows to get the pictures they wanted.

As Conroy walked up the lawn in heels several men in matching suits began moving in and out of the house, issuing instructions to uniformed offers. She didn't recognize them from the homicide unit. *Were they F.B.I.?* Seemed odd that F.B.I. agents would be on the scene so quickly, but then again, nothing was really unusual when it came to Bugsy Siegel.

The front door opened in front of her and a man was led out with an escort at each side. His shirt was speckled with dried blood and he looked distraught, but she recognized him immediately. He was a close friend of Bugsy Siegel.

"Mr. Smiley," she said, taking out her notepad. "Allen Smiley? My name is Tilda Conroy. I'm a reporter for the *Herald*."

One of the men in suits pushed her back, striding with Smiley toward another Pontiac further down the driveway.

"Allen. Tell me what happened."

"I shouldn't—I'm sorry. They shot him."

The two men hurried him along by the elbow. They couldn't stop Smiley talking but she could tell they wanted to.

"Shot who? Shot Ben Siegel?"

Maybe he was nodding or maybe he was shaking, she couldn't tell. "There was all this gunfire," he said. "My ears—I was right there next to him. It was like the room was exploding."

"Where is Siegel now? Is he alive?"

"I–I'm not sure. It looked bad. *Awful*."

Allen looked at her, then back at the house. One of the men stopped him from slowing down. "Get inside the car," the man said sternly.

"Who shot him? Allen, who shot him?"

They'd reached the Pontiac. The passenger door was opened and Smiley was pushed inside. "I don't know."

Conroy stood in the way so that his escorts couldn't shut the door.

"Was it a mob hit? Was Siegel shot by someone else in the mob?"

"I don't know—maybe. Yes. I think so."

"Who, Allen?"

That would be the answer Conroy would never get. Before she could ask another question, a man with a russet beard grabbed her shoulder and pulled her back.

"No press. This crime scene is closed."

"Wait a second." He didn't look familiar. "Are you Homicide or F.B.I.?"

The man was maybe a few years older than her – mid forties – but spoke to her like she was a child. "I won't ask you again," he said. "Step back."

"I'm a reporter for the *Herald.* I have a right to ask questions. Can you confirm whether Ben Siegel is dead or alive?"

The red-haired man ignored her, turning instead to his junior.

"This woman shouldn't be here. Get the uniforms to set up a perimeter." He pointed at different ends of the lawn before turning back to the house. "There'll be photographers all over the street in the next five minutes. I want barriers at the end of the driveway."

Whoever he was, the man disappeared back inside the house. He was right about the photographers. Local stringers would be here any minute. Headlights turned into the street—*that's probably them now*, Conroy thought.

But the two cars that pulled to a stop were police sedans. Captain Henson, head of Homicide Division, stepped out and put on his hat. In the other car she could make out more men in starched uniforms. They had white caps and gold trim on their livery: top brass.

The Captain saw her and sighed. "Tilda, get out of here."

She hadn't seen him in a while, and he looked like he was putting on weight. Sometimes she worried about his health and had to stop herself from caring.

"Captain Henson," she tried to say impassively. "Can you confirm there's been a shooting—"

Henson was already striding toward the house. "Tilda, this is a closed crime scene."

"I'm going to find out anyway. And you'd rather me than *Eyewitness*."

"Fine. There's been a shooting."

"I know it's Benjamin Siegel's house. Is that why the F.B.I. got here so quickly?"

"How did you know they were F.B.I.?"

She scribbled this down. "You just told me. What can you tell us about the shooting? Is Siegel badly injured? Is it a mob hit?"

But as she spoke a plainclothes detective and two uniforms came out of the house with a coroner. Captain Henson shared a few hushed words with the homicide detective from Central Headquarters before returning to Conroy. He was giving her an exclusive.

"He's dead?"

"Benjamin Siegel died instantly. We'll be releasing a statement first thing tomorrow, but all signs point to it being a mob-related killing. We'll have a full press conference in due course."

Conroy couldn't believe it. The most notorious mobster in America had been gunned down in his own home.

SUNDAY

CHAPTER I

Bridgeport, East California
Two days later

The dog whined.

He was an old dog, but that didn't make shooting him any easier. He'd been with them since the winter after his wife died and had spent most of his life on the farm. Jonathan Craine had never really been sure what breed he was. The people at the pound never said. He looked like a Black Mouth Cur but in piebald colors. Local farmers thought both man and beast were something of a joke in these parts. A city fella pretending to know how to work a farm. A dog that didn't even pretend.

"It's not fair," his son said.

Michael was standing beside him, stroking the dog's ears. He didn't look his father in the eye in case he could see he'd been crying.

"There's no other choice. We've been through this."

Craine took the Remington out of his hunting bag, and with the shotgun turned sideways pushed a shell into the loading flap. First time he'd ever used it, but he knew a twelve-gauge would kill the dog instantly at this range. Likely make an awful mess of it, too.

"It'll hurt him," Michael said.

"He won't feel it. It'll be quick. Instant. He's in pain, Michael, and it's only getting worse. This is the kindest thing to do."

Craine told the dog to sit and he did so. He was mostly deaf now but the routine was there. Rheumy eyes looked at him blankly. Despite their best efforts at grooming him, his coat was mangy and knotted. For the past week he'd vomited during the night and had blood in his stools. Poor dog hadn't left his bed in three days.

"Why don't you go back to the house?" Craine said. "You don't have to see this."

It had been a brutal June and the sun was penetratingly hot. Even the loose shirt he wore still clung to his back. Craine wiped his cheeks of sweat, then pointed at the house. "Go on, I'll call you out after."

Michael stood but didn't move.

The truth was, he didn't want Michael to see this. He was sixteen now and talking about going into the army. Men working on their farm had come back from the war with their stories, and Michael had got caught up in all their heroic bullshit. Craine had been the same at his age. Every young man thinks he needs violence in his life.

"I should be the one that does it," Michael said. "He's my dog too."

"No," he said firmly. "We've talked about this."

"I've fired it before."

"Shooting bottles isn't nearly the same thing. You shoot this dog, you're taking a life. You don't need to be mulling it over. Now step back, let's do this before he gets stressed being out here."

"Wait." Michael bent down and whispered something to the dog and rubbed his cheek against his snout. If the dog whined, he couldn't hear it.

"Step back," Craine said more gently now. "It's time."

Michael was upset but tried not to show it. He rarely got emotional in front of his father. "He's shaking. He knows what's happening."

"He's sick, that's why. It's this or much worse. Now get back, Michael."

Craine stepped a few paces to the side. The dog's forepaws came forward, trembling. "You stay," he said to him. "You stay there."

The dog knew it was coming. Craine pulled the shotgun into his shoulder and stepped around so he was behind the dog's head.

Craine pumped the forend to chamber the shell. Michael was breathing hard now, trying not to cry. He could see the tears rising in his eyes.

Craine aimed at the nape of the dog's neck where the spine met the base of his skull. His hand was shaking.

Michael stayed by Craine's side but turned his face away. Craine was glad for it.

Jonathan Craine thought about all the changes that had happened since the dog had been in their lives. About leaving the police department and moving out of Los Angeles. About learning what it meant to be a father without his wife. About the war, and all the death that had come to the world. He thought about the person he was now. This dog's life marked it all.

And then he fired.

They buried the dog in the same field behind their house. Michael seemed to take the task upon himself. If he ever slacked in his chores he didn't now. A two-month heatwave had left the soil hard and dry but that didn't encumber him. Michael dug like he was drilling for oil.

Craine had covered the corpse with a hessian sack so they didn't have to look at the gore, but the smell of meat was never far away. Flies that normally looked for moisture on damp lips and eyes had gathered in a frantic storm.

Craine was long accustomed to blood and innards. Years working as a homicide detective would do that to you. But his own emotions now took him by surprise. He wasn't sure if the salt in his eyes was tears or sweat. A few times he heard Michael sobbing, but it only made the boy dig harder. He would pant and groan with effort to cover the noise.

When the hole was three or four feet deep, Craine took Michael by the shoulder and told him it was deep enough.

They dragged the dog into the pit and together they pushed the dirt over until the body was covered. They patted down the dirt with the flats of their spades. There was no cross, but Michael had painted a stone white to mark his final resting place.

Afterward Michael brought his mass-book out and said some prayers. Craine wasn't sure what Michael was thinking about, but he thought about how long it had been since he'd taken a life. It wasn't something he'd ever wanted to do again. And yet it came so easily. No more than a squeeze of the trigger.

Killing was a strange thing.

Their farm was twenty minutes east of Bridgeport in a valley surrounded on two sides by the Sierra Nevada mountains. There was no police force to speak of, only the County Sheriff's office the other side of the valley. Crime was negligible, but that's what happened when you lived four hundred miles away from Los Angeles. It was one of the main reasons Craine had moved here.

The house itself had been built in stages. The core was an old farm building, which meant that the ceilings were low. It was a fraction of the size of his old place, but he much preferred it. There was space enough inside to find your own corner and a hundred acres to get lost in outside. He'd taken very little from his house in Beverly Hills. A handful of photographs of Celia and Michael as a boy. The rest he'd left behind.

"Figured we deserved pork chops," Craine said to Michael, trying to lighten the mood as they cooked dinner.

Michael smiled but didn't speak. That was enough for Craine. Michael was furtive in his conversations with his father, but the same could be said of Craine. They said a lot of things to each other without speaking.

Craine prepared greens as Michael cut potatoes. They worked wordlessly side by side. A ritual. Each of them left to his own thoughts. And yet both of them entirely together.

After dinner, Craine stood at the sink washing dishes, looking out at the fields. The farm was remote, even by rural California standards. They only got their R.F.D. mailboxes in the spring. It was considered a ranch but they had very few livestock. On one side of the house was a brown barn with a plank corral adjoined for their pigs and cattle to graze in during the day. They had four riding horses in a stable on the other side, and he could hear them nickering blithely.

Michael carried a coffee pot over to the table and sat down. "Can we start getting the paper now we've got our mailbox?" he asked tentatively.

"Alright."

"You don't mind?"

"I don't have to read it. You can leave out the crossword."

Craine didn't follow news events. L.A. seemed so chaotic and changeable in comparison to Bridgeport, and he had no ambitions to return. He liked the certainty of his life on the farm. The quiet routine. He had come to terms with the fact that he was a natural loner, and the long hours he spent in solitude suited his disposition.

When Craine came over with two clean mugs, Michael looked up from the checkered oilcloth.

"You mind if I head over to the Howleys' in a little while?"

"They invite you?"

"Penny's dad said it was okay."

"Alright, then."

Michael was keen on Penny Howley, their sixteen-year-old neighbor. They sneaked out most nights and met in the fields down by the lake. He wondered at what point he'd get a call from her father.

Michael stirred his coffee. "Recruiter came to school today."

Craine had been waiting for this conversation to come up again.

"You talk to him?"

"Yeah."

"He tell you that you can't join until you're eighteen?"

Michael lifted his chin. "Seventeen. That's in two months."

"Only with parental consent," Craine said. "And I'm not giving it to you."

Michael put his cup down. He stared at the table again. Annoyed.

Craine had always recognized that the war was necessary. But it was over now. He didn't want his only son to have his values upended, his moral inhibitions worn down so far that it felt nothing to kill a man.

"We talked about you going to college. You're smart, Michael. There's so much you can do. The army—it's dangerous."

Michael looked at his father directly. The eye contact was uncomfortable.

"Some of the other boys at school asked me why you didn't serve in the army. Said you weren't too old."

The question was direct, and he knew he had to answer it.

"I was still in the L.A.P.D.," Craine said calmly. "Then I had to testify for the F.B.I. I didn't have to enlist."

"But you could have done. Afterward."

"That business in Europe. In the Pacific. It wasn't to do with us."

"Of course it was. People died for their families. For their country. And I want to do my part."

"You can do more for your country than shooting at some other boy your age dragged into a war he never wanted any part of either."

Michael read comics about vigilante heroes. He didn't understand that there was nothing remotely romantic or divine about taking a life. It reduced someone to meat parts.

"I know *you've* killed men before," his son said hesitantly.

Yes, he had. But the burden of killing had left enduring scars. Their deaths were printed on his mind. "It's not something I'm proud of," he muttered.

Craine didn't want to discuss it any further but Michael couldn't let it go. "I don't get it," he said. "Everyone said you were a hero. So why didn't you go to war?"

Craine noticed a tremor in his hand and he took it off the table. He knew that sharing might help place what happened in perspective. He knew it was damaging to hold on to it. But he couldn't help it.

"I wasn't a hero, Michael. I wasn't then and I'm not now."

He picked up his cup and stood to put it in the sink. This conversation was over.

"Why don't you ever talk about it? About what happened after Ma died. About that investigation. About those men you killed."

Craine had never felt there was any point litigating the past. "What's to talk about?"

"People died. You . . . killed men. That must feel like something."

"What do you want to know?"

"What did it feel like?"

They say that when you kill someone, at first you feel elated. It was something Craine had never really forgiven himself for—for being happy about it. But then for a long time you feel shame and remorse. You try to rationalize it—*I didn't have a choice, it was him or me*—and then eventually you accept it. But Craine had never truly accepted it. Whatever had happened years ago had left him with an indescribable self-disgust.

"It felt—" He struggled to find the words.

The saucer on the table began rattling and there was a droning sound that at first he thought might be the pipes. But then the windowpanes juddered and he realized it was coming from outside.

"What's that?"

Craine lifted his head and listened.

"Earthquake?" Michael asked.

It sounded like a passing herd but without the rumble. And then he realized: it wasn't coming from the ground, it was coming from the sky.

"Airplane," Michael said, thinking the same thing.

"Doesn't sound like a duster." *Besides*, he thought to himself, *at this hour they'd virtually be flying blind.* A small part of him wondered whether it was a Japanese attack, but that didn't make sense. They were the only house for two miles.

The sound became very loud and the whole roof shook and then stopped as quickly as it had started. Craine's coffee cup rattled on the counter and he could hear the horses neighing outside. The plane was flying right overhead.

Craine went into the pantry and came back with the shotgun. When he returned, Michael was already by the front door.

"Where are you going?" he said to his father.

"Stay here."

Craine opened the screen door and stepped down off the porch. It was almost dark out but light enough to see it wasn't a crop duster. It looked to be a military plane, or one like it. The type he'd seen in newspaper headlines almost daily during the war.

The night suddenly lit up as a string of flares dropped from the sky on tiny parachutes. The intense pink light illuminated the whole farm, and as the plane turned toward them he realized they'd been circling because they were looking for somewhere to land.

The hairs bristled on the back of Craine's neck, as if his body knew the sound was an augury of something bad to come.

The plane landed in the fallow fields behind their house, the wheels creating tracks in the soil as it came to a crawl. The sound of the engine faded as the rotors slowed, and after a few minutes the main passenger door opened. A narrow air-stair unfolded onto the dirt.

Five men stepped out wearing rain jackets over suits and ties. There was little doubt that they weren't from these parts. Craine had sweat on his back where his shirt had stuck to him but now it turned prematurely cold.

Polished shoes made hard work of crossing the field toward the house. Two of the men ignited flares in their hands and the air lit up with a devilish glow, smoke trailing across the field like pink mist.

When they got within forty feet, Craine said, "That's far enough." He twisted the Remington to the side so it was visible from afar. He hoped they couldn't see his hands shaking.

There is a leader in any pack of males. In this case it wasn't the eldest or the biggest, but the only one smiling.

"Are you Craine? Are you Jonathan Craine?" An East Coast accent. *New York.*

It was unusual for visitors to arrive at the farm. The Howleys came by every few weeks or so to trade help or goods, but that accounted for most of their visitors. Not men in zoot suits with city accents.

An answer but without a nod. "I'm Craine."

"Detective Craine from the Los Angeles Police?"

"I'm not a detective anymore. Now it's just Craine."

The man held his hands open to show he meant no harm. He moved closer until there were only a few yards between them. Behind him, his men spread in a wide arc like they were in some kind of military formation. Under the smoky blaze they looked like ghoulish specters. By their age and build Craine thought they must be ex-soldiers. One of them even had a knot in his suit where he'd lost his forearm.

"My name is Samuel Kastel," the man said, taking in the property. Craine racked his brains but the name meant nothing to him. "We tried to call ahead, but you don't have a phone."

"What brings you here?"

"My employer asked me to meet with you. You mind if we come in?"

"I do mind."

Craine saw several of the men in suits open their jackets, and the light glinted off the metal of their pistol butts. *They weren't asking.*

He could hear Michael approaching behind him and Craine lifted his shotgun to his shoulder. He wished that boy had stayed inside like he'd asked.

"Tell your men to stay where they are," he said.

Kastel held his hand up for calm but the men were still advancing. Their flares wilted and two of them fell into darkness.

Craine aimed at Kastel. "I said tell them to stay where they are."

Finally, the man turned and patted the air and the others stopped. Another man lit a flare again; it kept Craine on edge.

"We're not here to cause you harm," Kastel said. "Only to talk. Why don't you invite me inside?"

"We can talk out here."

"My associates here don't need to come no further. But I'm hoping you'll invite me in for a cup of coffee."

The man Kastel took off his hat to reveal his face. He was younger than Craine by at least ten or fifteen years. Handsome, in his own way. But gaunt. Like his skin had been stretched over his skull. Something else. There were purple pockmarks on one side of his face and neck. Shrapnel scars.

Craine glanced to Michael, then back again.

It didn't look like they had a choice.

CHAPTER 2

Kastel's hands were spread like starfish on the table. Most of his "associates" remained outside, but behind him, a heavyset man in his fifties stood silently in the doorway. Kastel hadn't even thought to introduce him. He looked like Kastel's pet gorilla.

Kastel looked at Craine and then Michael in turn. He almost seemed amused by the situation. "You lived here long?" he asked.

"Seven years."

"I was fighting Japs, you were cutting corn." Kastel gave a humorless laugh. He had the same look as the young men Craine had hired when they returned from the war. Empty eyes. Constantly on edge.

Michael lifted the coffee pot from the stove. His hands were shaking so much he almost dropped it.

"Careful, there." Kastel half-stood and Craine's heart skipped.

Michael forced a smile. He poured them coffee from an enamel pot before taking a seat at the other end of the table. Craine wanted him in sight at all times.

"You know," Kastel said to Craine, grinning, "I've heard so much about you it's almost like we know each other."

"I wish I could say the same, Mr. Kastel. Would you care to tell me about yourself? And what brings you here?"

"I'm not from California. Although I came out here before the war." Craine noticed him touch his scars. "Worked for a man named Carell—you remember him? Chicago fella, tried to make it out in Hollywood. You recollect?"

Yes, Craine recollected. Carell had been a Chicago mobster working out of Los Angeles. He'd almost killed Craine. Almost killed Michael, too. Inwardly Craine had known all along that this had something to do with his old life in Los Angeles. It had cast a long shadow.

"Briefly," Craine said. "We met briefly before the war."

"Downplaying it. I heard you practically brought down the entire Chicago racket. Can't say you look like some big shot Hollywood detective now."

"As I said, it was a long time ago." Craine tried his best to hide his apprehension. "What is it you want, Mr. Kastel?"

Kastel put his coffee down and pushed it away. At last he stopped smiling. "My employer. He wants to meet you."

"Who is your employer?"

"That's not important. What is important, however, is that he asked me to come here and invite you to meet him as soon as possible."

Craine cast a glance at Michael. A flicker of concern crossed both their faces.

"I politely decline."

"It's not polite to decline an invitation."

"Why does he want to meet me?"

Kastel suddenly took his hands off the table. One hand went into his jacket pocket. It seemed to hover for a long time. Craine wondered if he was going to reach for a pistol but instead he brought out a pack of cigarettes.

"Smoke?"

Craine shook his head a small fraction. Kastel lit a cigarette and drew a deep lungful. "Didn't smoke for years. Service that got me hooked. Pack a day."

He pushed smoke out of the side of his mouth and leaned forward a little. "He wants to meet the famous Jonathan Craine. Or is it *infamous?* I always forget the difference."

"No, thank you. You can tell me who he is but my answer will be the same. I need to be here. With my son."

From the doorway, the thickset man took a step forward and for a second Craine thought he was going to hit him.

Kastel raised a hand. "Easy, Abe. Let's give Mr. Craine here a moment to reconsider. Maybe he needs to check his diary. After all, we came all this way."

The simian stopped still. Kastel maintained his steady smile but Craine could sense he was growing agitated.

"You tell your employer that I thank him for his invitation," Craine said, gripping the edge of the table and pushing himself up. "But I can't leave my farm or my son. Now, I'll ask you kindly to leave."

"We can't take off in the dark."

"Then you gentlemen are more than welcome to stay the night," he said tonelessly. "You can sleep in the bunkhouse across the way. Gets cold at night. We have blankets and cots for itinerant workers. But you'll leave as soon as it's light."

Kastel nodded. After a moment, he picked up his hat. He was still smiling but Craine could feel him stiffen in the low light.

"Very well. You're putting me in a bind, Mr. Craine. I can't pretend otherwise. My employer will be disappointed to miss you."

The wide man—*Abe*—left first. At the door Kastel said, "Thanks for the coffee. No doubt we'll see each other in the morning."

And then he walked out into the night.

Kastel's men went into the barn as instructed. It didn't have electricity, but Craine put out kerosene lamps and what blankets they could spare. He waited until he was sure the men were in the bunkhouse before bolting the front and back doors from the inside and closing the shutters on all the downstairs windows.

When the house was locked up and the downstairs lights were off, Craine went to see Michael in his room.

He tapped, then opened the door an inch. Michael was reading in bed. "Can I come in?"

"I'm reading."

He was a quiet boy but he had his mother's temper. Craine thought about that. No, that's not fair. He is the best of his mother and all that is salvageable from me.

"Wanted to check you were okay."

"I'm fine."

Craine stepped in with a tray. Michael's bedroom overlooked the rear of the house. You could see Lake Mono on a clear day.

"Brought you some ice water."

A peace offering. A welcome one in this heat. Michael took the pitcher and glass off the tray and pulled his legs up so Craine could sit at the end of the bed.

Michael's T-shirt clung to his skin in faint patches. He was becoming a man now. He was as tall as Craine was, skinny but with a breadth that warned he'd fill out. He imagined Michael in uniform. Holding his rifle. That boy would die for people he'd never met. He'd have no hesitation, he knew that. Could Craine say the same? Was there any cause he believed in enough to really die for?

None came to mind.

"Who were those men?" Michael asked.

"I don't know. They'll leave in the morning. Can't expect them to take off in that thing when it's dark. Besides, we're safe in here."

It was true. The house was a fortress. There was no way anyone was breaking in without him knowing it.

"What do you think they wanted?"

"I don't know."

"Are they dangerous?"

He didn't want to answer that. Instead he said, "If they wanted to cause us harm they would have done it by now."

Uppermost in his mind was figuring out who sent them. A part of him was curious, if not plain eager, to know what they wanted with him.

"What if they come back?"

"Then I'll tell them again."

"So you're not going with them?"

"No."

Michael nodded and said tentatively, "I was supposed to go over to the Howleys' tonight, remember?"

Craine could read between the lines. He wanted to meet up with that girl Penny.

"I think it's best if we stay here."

"But it's not late. I'll be back in an hour."

Craine glanced to the window. He didn't want to scare the boy but he couldn't let him leave the house. Reflecting on their argument earlier, he chose his words carefully. "Please. Stay here."

"You said they're not dangerous—"

"Please, Michael. Not tonight. I mean it. I don't want us taking any chances. They'll be gone in the morning."

Michael didn't answer, but Craine could tell he was frustrated. Changing the subject, he said, "This army thing. You want to talk about it?"

Michael shrugged and pulled a face. "You never want to talk. You never want to discuss. You only want to tell me what to do."

Craine's own father had died when he was young and sometimes he wished he could remember more about him. About what kind of father he was. He wondered if most men asked their fathers for advice on raising sons. Or whether that mystery was left to each alone.

"You have to understand, if something were to happen—" His explanation left his tongue stillborn. "Remember that after your mother—"

He faltered. He struggled to draw upon his emotions. They were rarely to hand when he needed them.

Craine stood up. "We can talk in the morning."

He wanted to say that he couldn't bear the thought of losing him. To tell him how proud he was of the person he'd become. How proud his mother would have been.

But he didn't. He'd never been able to express himself.

He left the room and shut the door.

* * *

The bedroom shutters were closed and the room was black. Years ago, Craine had been plagued by insomnia. But living out here, most nights he slept so deeply it was as if he would never wake.

Tonight was the exception. He knew instinctively that something wasn't right. That this exchange with Kastel wasn't over. Whoever they were, these men would likely be back in the morning and he'd have to negotiate with them a second time; they seemed acutely keen to return to wherever they came from with him in tow.

He thought of what Kastel had said about the Chicago Outfit. Those men he had killed.

Craine had never really got over what happened in '39. He had spent years untangling his thoughts about it. But he couldn't really remove himself from his acts, despite trying. When he walked around his farm the shadows of dead men followed him, waiting for night to come so they could whisper in his dreams.

And when he drifted to sleep now, they were here with him. The men he'd shot, staring up from the floor. Saying the same thing they always said: "Why did you kill me?", and Craine was clumsily explaining to them why it was necessary. Why he had to do it to protect himself. To protect his son.

The sound of the horses brought him to his senses. It didn't sound like neighing, more like a child's scream. For a moment he thought he was still dreaming.

He got out of bed and walked dazed to the window, brushing at his eyes. There was a tungsten glow seeping between the shutter slats. He couldn't even remember picking up the shotgun but it was in his hands and he was moving back to the bedroom door to check no one was in the house.

"Michael? Michael, wake up."

Craine went out into the hallway and found the darkness strangely comforting. Michael's room was barely five yards away, the bedroom door closed.

"Michael, you need to wake up."

No reply. Craine's hackles rose; he took one deep breath, then pushed the door open with the shotgun in his shoulder.

Michael's bed was empty. The sound of the horses was louder and there was smoke coming in from outside.

The window was open.

Craine came tumbling down the porch and could already see that his barns were ablaze. There was a smell of meat and burning hair and one of his horses came galloping past with its mane on fire. Another horse was rearing up, foaming at the mouth.

Ahead of him, Kastel's men held flashlights and burning torches made from cheap timber. They were holding their flames in the air like a lynch mob. Craine saw them shooting the horses as they passed; one of the mares fell to the floor, her neck in seizure, her hooves kicking up dust. The squeal she made unnerved him. Then the man Abe came forward and shot her twice in the head and she stopped.

Kastel was behind them. He had Michael, his hands tied in front of him. It was warm this close to the flames but Michael was shivering. His face was bloodied where he'd been struck across the cheek and one eye was swollen shut.

Craine began running toward Kastel but two other men put themselves in his path. He swung for the first man with the butt of his shotgun but although he made contact, the weight of the Remington knocked him off balance. It was enough to give the second man an opportunity to throw him to the floor and wrestle the shotgun out of his hands.

Craine tried to pull himself to his feet but the two men held him down. He began lashing out, but a series of punches to the back of the head left him dizzy. A kick to the jugular was enough to keep him still.

Craine drew breath and then more breath and then more. But he couldn't speak. His windpipe felt like it was choking him from the inside.

He heard Michael whimpering. "I'm sorry," his son kept saying. "I'm so sorry, Pa."

As if in response, Kastel kicked at the back of Michael's legs and the boy dropped and landed on his knees.

"Wait—"

But Kastel was already grabbing Michael by the hair. He yanked his head back with a twist of his arm and held a knife below Michael's throat.

Craine's heart began pounding so hard he could feel his whole chest move. "Please," he said, horrified, words rushing out in no order. "Don't do this—no, no. Please. Don't hurt him."

Kastel's eyes widened but there was no emotion in his voice. "This is you, Craine. You did this."

Craine tried to find Michael's face in the flickering flames and saw the terror filling his eyes. The boy was convulsing now, shaking hard enough Craine thought he might cut his own throat against the blade.

The large man, Abe, watched on, uneasy. Like he was trying to see how this might play out.

Craine couldn't swallow. He tried to form words. "I'll do whatever you want. Just let him go."

"It's too late for that," Kastel said as if speaking reasonably. "You weren't polite. I don't like that."

The Barlow knife was compact and short, meant for concealment, not utility. He pulled it closer to Michael's neck.

Craine looked at the knife and then at his son. There was nothing he could do now.

"Please," he managed. "I'll do anything."

Abe followed this exchange but didn't react. Craine looked at him pleadingly to help, but he did nothing.

"Like I said," Kastel smiled. "It's all too late for that now."

Kastel took the blade away from Michael's neck and moved it toward his wrists. For a second Craine thought he was going to cut the rope binds but instead Kastel grabbed at his fingers.

"No, don't—please, *don't*." Craine started to wriggle but the two men on top of him held him down harder, aware of what was about to come.

Craine watched helplessly as Michael's body shuddered with the pain of the blade cutting through flesh and bone. First he heard his son scream and then he saw Michael's hand erupt. Blood shot outward and Kastel threw two small finger ends into the dust.

Craine roared. Kastel stood upright, grinning. He used his boot to push the boy sideways. Michael slumped into his own gore.

"It's done," he said, wiping the sweat from his face.

Anger swelled in Craine's chest, filling him until he was bursting with it. He threw his head upward and his skull cracked into the nose of the younger man holding him. There was a howl and Craine felt the grip around his arms relax.

He was up on his feet now and running for them, paying no attention to the pain.

Kastel, seemingly aware that Craine was only a few yards away, turned his knife in his direction.

Craine half-expected to feel a bullet knock him off his feet but it was Abe who stopped him. Stepping into his way, the large man brought a piece of timber into Craine's stomach. The air rushed out of him.

Craine tried to keep moving but stumbled to the floor. Before he could move, Abe was on top of him. In another swift movement he had one arm around his neck, the other pinning his arms back. Craine tried again to wrench himself free but the large man was too strong. He couldn't even draw a breath. "Relax. For your own sake, relax," the big man whispered into his ear. "If you don't, he'll kill you."

Michael was on the ground, clasping his bloody hand, his teeth gritted, his screams dissolving into tears.

Craine froze. He had stopped moving, all resolve gone. He lay there with Abe restraining him. The barns were burning. Even with the blood swirling in his ears he could hear the horses braying all around him. There was nothing to do but stare straight ahead at Michael, ten yards away, crying and clutching his mutilated fingers.

There was violence in his life again. And there would only be more.

MONDAY

CHAPTER 3

The plane took off at first light.

Craine left his distraught son cradling his bloodied hand. Three of Kastel's men were left behind, the barns still ablaze and smoke filling the early-morning sky.

Craine massaged his temples with his fingertips. His eyes were puffy and tender to the touch. The adrenaline began to leave his body and his head started throbbing. He couldn't believe what had happened. What they'd done to his son.

He'd been frantically trying to think who had sent these men but deep down he knew. Before the war, he'd uncovered a Hollywood extortion ring that led all the way back to Chicago. There were arrests and federal indictments; there was a grand jury and newspaper headlines; many people had died along the way. A part of him had always believed his past would catch up with him.

Kastel was with the pilot in the cockpit. Abe was sitting opposite him, strapped into a narrow bench that ran the length of the plane. He wasn't as tall as Craine, but there was a mountain of meat under his coat. He carried himself like a dockworker or a logger.

"Where are we going?" Craine asked him. He had to shout over the engine. They'd already been flying for an hour. New York wasn't possible in a plane this small. And although he'd assumed they'd be flying to Los Angeles, after they'd taken off they'd passed Mono Lake to their right, which meant that they were flying southeast into Nevada.

"You're meeting a senior business partner in our organization."

Craine's suspicions were correct. Whoever it was that wanted to meet him, they wanted retribution. "Who?" he asked.

"You'll see soon enough. Won't be long now." Abe's eyes were dull in this light. They gave nothing away. He handed Craine a flask. "Won't help the headache, but it's all I got."

It was a small gesture but Craine took it. He winced as it burned his bleeding gums.

The large man stirred. He gave Craine a steady look, curious if not sympathetic. He must have been reading Craine's thoughts because he said, "I told them to take your boy to the doctor."

"Nearest doctor is a two-hour drive," Craine said.

Abe glanced sideways to be sure he couldn't be heard. "If they stem the bleeding he'll be alright." He held up a club-like fist and stuck out the two little fingers. "It was the top joint." He looked toward the cockpit. "Finger-shortening, he calls it. Told me the Japs did it in the war."

Their conversation was disturbed by the fuselage shaking. The plane yawed, tilting sideways as it began its descent through the clouds. A thin haze replaced the horizon until Craine looked down to see the faint shades of desert and realized they were flying over Death Valley.

Craine started to say something before the cockpit door opened. Kastel took off his earphones and twisted around in his seat. "Touchdown in fifteen minutes. Buckle up."

Craine leaned back in his seat as the engine whined and the plane dipped for its final descent. He squinted, trying to make out the small mass of buildings in the desert below. He noticed the neon colors and began to realize where they were headed. They were going to Las Vegas.

His stomach lifted.

When the plane taxied to a halt at the small hangar in the desert, two chauffeur-driven limousines were ready and waiting for them.

Craine was put into the rear of the second vehicle, their small motorcade driving silently down a wide road until he saw a sign directing them to the desert town of Las Vegas.

Kastel was in the front passenger seat with Abe behind the wheel, establishing his role as Kastel's second-in-command. There was a temptation for Craine to lash out. To try to throttle Kastel, but he knew there was no point. They were both armed.

Instead he sat in the back, overheating, staring out at the view, clenching and unclenching his fists. There was a scattering of buildings here, most of them construction sites, but he was too exhausted to wonder what for. His thoughts were a hundred miles away with Michael at the farm. The vision of cold steel slicing through his son's flesh made him angry like he'd never felt before.

"I hate the desert," Kastel mused, tapping the nose of his pistol on the dashboard as if to remind Craine it was there. "Take me back to the city any day of the week. I don't know how you can stand living in the middle of nowhere, Craine. You and your little farm, shut off from the world. Not much of a legacy, is it?"

Kastel was looking at Craine in the rearview mirror. He had a beatific smile on his face that made Craine hate him even more.

"They told me you used to be some crooked Hollywood fixer till you killed a few boys from Chicago. Put the rest of them in jail before disappearing off the face of the earth."

"It wasn't like that," Craine muttered.

But this wasn't good enough for Kastel. "Yeah? What about the Loew House shootings?" he said, swinging round accusingly. "That one even made the East Coast papers. Gave you a medal for killing Kamona, didn't they?"

Craine was surprised to hear a name that hadn't been mentioned to him in most of a decade. "You knew Paul Kamona?"

Kastel didn't answer, so Craine said: "Everyone's done things they're not proud of. You were a soldier—"

Kastel looked at Craine like he was white-livered. His right cheek was twitching. "I don't have trouble reckoning with the things I've done," Kastel said archly. "I was proud of everything I did for my country. Enjoyed every second. For men like me, that war was *our* legacy. That's something you'll never share in."

They'd been driving through scrub wasteland for ten minutes when a lit tower up ahead caught Craine's attention. As they drew closer, he began to see the outline of a wide hotel resort with landscaped lawns and palm trees. It loomed like a mirage. A pink neon sign above the entrance read: The Flamingo.

Most of the vehicles in the parking lot were Cadillacs or Lincolns worth thousands of dollars. An attraction board beside the entrance read ONE NIGHT ONLY: MARTIN AND LEWIS.

Craine's chaperones stopped below the pink neon sign and Craine was ushered out.

As they walked through the wide glass doors, two redcaps stood to attention. They'd been warned of their arrival.

A stucco-walled lobby brought them straight onto The Flamingo's casino floor. It was spacious and air-conditioned. The lighting was designed to accentuate the pink and green decor. A haze of smoke hung over tables for blackjack, poker, roulette and craps. Even though it was almost morning, each one was ringed by drunk and rowdy patrons in ballgowns and tuxedos. The room was loud. People were cheering, throwing dice and falling over each other.

Abe and Kastel led Craine past a group of men playing punto banco at a kidney-shaped baccarat table, their arms linked with those of women half their age. There was a strange electricity in the air, the players invested in the moment, foreheads shining with alcohol and anticipation.

A banker in a silk shirt and turnback cuffs swept a pallet over the green baize table and glanced in Craine's direction; he stopped, his attention caught by the man in the filthy coat and country clothes. Craine ran his hand through his hair. It was matted and filthy, caked with blood. He must have looked a sight.

To his right a series of glass walls gave a view of a swimming pool, and beyond it, a three-story hotel building surrounded by exotic trees and shrubberies. Craine tried to locate the exits, contemplating when might be the best time to run. Abe must have noticed, because Craine found him inches from his elbow, ready to grab him at any moment.

Their entourage didn't stop, moving through the casino floor at a pace, almost knocking over a woman in a cocktail dress carrying a stack of gaming plaques worth thousands of dollars.

Down a long corridor now. At different intervals were men in long coats with bulging pockets. No words were exchanged until they'd passed through a set of manned doors. Kastel looked at him sideways, issuing instructions: "When you meet our employer, you'll shake his hand. You will not raise your voice. You will not sit closer than within three feet of him. You make any attempt to touch him, there are four other people in that room who will make sure you regret it."

When Kastel pushed open the double doors to the suite, Craine saw for the first time the man who had requested his presence. It was a man he'd recognized from the newspapers. A man whose file he'd read many times at the L.A.P.D.

"You must be Jonathan Craine," he heard him say. "My name is Meyer Lansky. Thank you for coming to see me."

Meyer Lansky didn't look like a mob boss. With his small frame and blue sport shirt open at the collar, he looked more like an accountant or a lawyer on vacation. It wasn't what Craine expected from one of the most feared mobsters in America.

"You're a hard man to find, Craine," his summoner said after they had both sat down.

"That was the intention."

They were sitting at a table in a private suite with large windows overlooking the hotel's manicured gardens, but Craine felt like he was in a jail cell. Kastel and Abel were seated on a sofa facing the window. All the other men in the room were standing. There was a pecking order here.

"And you're a farmer now? You own a farm?"

Craine nodded. His body was aching and talking felt like an effort.

"Before the war," Lansky began, "you began an investigation that led to the downfall of the Chicago Outfit. The head of their organization, Frank Nitti, a brilliant, ambitious man, killed himself rather than go to prison. All of that, everything that happened—that was you."

Craine sat on his hands so Lansky couldn't see they were shaking. "You brought me here to kill me?"

There was a long silence during which Craine was almost certain someone would come up behind him with a gun to his head. But no one moved and no one said anything. Only Lansky spoke.

"No," he said. "I brought you here to help me."

Craine didn't know what to say. Lansky poured them both coffee from a tray with a folded newspaper on it. "May I ask: what do you know about me?" the older man said.

"Only what I've read in the papers."

"And what do they say about me in the papers?"

Craine shifted in his seat; each of Lansky's bodyguards matched his movements. "That you're a mobster."

"Mobster?" Lansky seemed more disappointed than surprised. "No, I'm not a mobster. I'm a businessman. I sell things to the honest citizen like any other businessman."

"So why did your men threaten to kill my son on my farm?" Craine asked.

Lansky shot a glance toward Kastel. For the first time, Craine saw a flash of anger in Lansky's eyes. "I'm sorry if you came here unwillingly. And I can only apologize for their actions. It wasn't at my request. Your son is safe."

He turned to Abe, who nodded to confirm this was still the case. Craine felt some of the weight on his shoulders shift.

"Do you know why you're here, Mr. Craine?"

Lansky was very considered when he spoke. There was nothing flashy about him. Unlike the other men in his outfit, he didn't have a Bronx Italian accent. His was harder to place.

"No one has told me anything."

"Then I apologize for dragging you here under such a shroud of secrecy. Please understand that there are people who wish me harm, and my security team have a hard task ahead of them. Now I'm going to be open with you. I have a mixed portfolio. But *our thing*," he said, emphasizing both words like it was an expression, "is gaming: gambling and hotels. You see, I like a fair game. A fair house. The games in my casinos are never rigged. That's why people come to my hotels night after night, week after week. The papers can say what they like about me, but my casinos are patronized by some of the finest people of the United States. Have you ever been to Vegas before?"

"Never."

"You gamble?"

"No."

"Me neither. Because in the end, the house always wins." He smiled, then swept his arm across the view. Craine looked at the full scale of the resort. An oasis in the desert.

"I'm a shareholder in several casinos, mostly in Florida or Cuba. And now I am a major investor in this hotel, The Flamingo. The rest of this town is a desert. Nothing but a few bordellos and card houses. But an associate of mine, a close friend, Benny Siegel, had been working on my behalf for several years to build this hotel. The first of many in Las Vegas. Did you know him?"

Craine stirred. Yes, he knew Benjamin Siegel. He knew him from his old life. A larger-than-life character popular on the Hollywood scene. Movie stars like Gary Cooper and George Raft were friends with him. Jean Harlow had been godmother to his daughter. But in the L.A.P.D. it was long known that Siegel was a senior figure in the Los Angeles crime world. Perhaps even the most senior figure.

"He moved to Hollywood maybe ten to fifteen years ago. I met him a few times before the war."

"Las Vegas was Benny's dream," Lansky went on contemplatively. "To turn this scrub of wasteland into a global entertainment mecca. To build *a city* out of nothing."

"Mr. Lansky, why are you telling me all this?"

Lansky turned over the newspaper on the table so Craine could read the headlines. On the left-hand side was a photograph of Benjamin Siegel. Beside it the headline read "SHOOTER KILLS BUGSY SIEGEL."

"I'm telling you all this because two nights ago he was murdered. And I want you to find the man responsible."

CHAPTER 4

"Tell me more about yourself, Mr. Craine," Lansky said, sipping his coffee. Craine noticed him push the newspaper away. He didn't want to see the photographs of his friend's dead body. Craine picked it up slowly, scanning the text. Benjamin Siegel had been killed in his home in Beverly Hills on Friday night. The address was barely half a mile from where Craine used to live.

"Before you were a farmer, you lived in Beverly Hills. Is that correct? You were married to an actress, the late Celia Raymond."

"Yes," Craine replied.

"And you worked for the L.A.P.D.?"

A pause. "I did."

"But really your job was as a fixer, of sorts. To hush up movie studio crimes. To protect movie stars from getting into trouble."

"That was a long time ago."

Lansky ignored him. "Benny told me once that you helped him. He'd been arrested and you got the charges dropped."

Craine nodded to him pro forma. "He had established a drugs run between Mexico and Los Angeles. Because he was friends with studio stars, I was asked to make the charges go away."

"That's how I heard it too. Maybe you don't know this, but Benny never forgot what you did. In fact, after that business with Chicago, Frank Nitti reached out to myself and my New York partners to have you removed." The last word didn't need explaining. "But Benny vouched for you. The request was waived."

"And this is why you're asking me to help you?"

Lansky nodded. "If Benny trusted you, I trust you."

"Mr. Lansky, I should be honest. I'm not sure how I could help. The police have more than adequate resources to investigate this murder."

"The police and the F.B.I. are convinced we did it. A mob hit, they're calling it. And the press are duly following suit."

"Can you blame them?"

Lansky put his coffee down and pushed the cup away as if he was disgusted. "They're jumping to conclusions without any of the facts, and not for the first time. I am not a violent man. I do not enjoy violence." He took a deep breath and went on, "I can't trust the police to do their job. So I'm hiring you to find the man responsible. You'll be recompensed accordingly."

"I don't want your money."

"Then you'll be a better return on investment than I'd hoped."

Craine was still coming to terms with what Lansky was asking of him. "Why me?"

"I need someone neutral. Outside the organization."

"There are private investigators. Pinkertons."

Lansky picked up his coffee cup again and his calm demeanor returned as quickly as it had disappeared.

"Not who understand Hollywood. And not who understand . . . *us*. Benjamin had friends in the movie industry. I need someone who can operate in those circles. Who can ask questions discreetly without drawing undue attention."

Craine did not belong among the Hollywood elite. And if he once had, he had lost his sole tie to motion picture pedigree and was no longer privy to its set.

"I haven't worked in Los Angeles for a long time."

"A man's reputation can take him a long way."

Craine sighed, considering the offer. If indeed it was an offer. "I know nothing about the case."

Lansky held up a hand. "There are people in our organization that you'll need to speak to. Abe—the talkative gentleman over on the sofas—will get you up to speed on what we know and make the right introductions. He'll be with you at all times. Kastel, you will stay with me."

Kastel looked frustrated, twisting his hat in his hands. "Sir—"

The senior man raised his voice. "I said, I need you *here*."

The seriousness of the situation Craine had found himself in suddenly dawned on him. He was being hired by one of the most senior criminals in the country to solve the murder of an ill-famed Hollywood mobster.

"Mr. Lansky, people in your line of work . . . your *business* are killed all the time. So why is this so important to you?"

Lansky cleared his throat. "I've known Benny for thirty years," he said thoughtfully. "We used to run around together thinking we were *shtarker*—tough guys. He was witness at my wedding. My closest friend, like a brother. We looked out for each other. We *always* looked out for each other."

Lansky caught himself ruminating, then he looked at Craine directly. "The police, the F.B.I. and the newspapers are all calling it a mob hit. I believe it isn't. I believe it was a personal vendetta, that he was killed by someone close to him. I want you to bring me the man responsible by Friday night. You have five days."

"Mr. Lansky, that's not a lot of time—"

"It's the time you have," the older man said without explanation.

Craine could hear himself swallowing. He tried to remain composed but firm. "If I do this, you'll leave me and my son alone?" he asked, his throat tightening.

"Agreed." Standing, Lansky held out his hand. "This is our contract. It means more than an army of lawyers. Do not break *your* part of the agreement."

After a long moment, Craine stood up and shook it.

"And if I do?"

Lansky squeezed Craine's hand firmly, then dropped it. "Then you'll read about your son in the papers," he replied before leaving the room.

CHAPTER 5

The roads out of Vegas were empty and hot. They went a whole hour on the highway without seeing a single soul. Craine was exhausted but he couldn't sleep. The scene of last night played heavily on his mind. He thought about Michael, and whether he was alright. And how he could secure his safety when the task ahead seemed impossible. He leaned his head back. His mind drifted.

Craine had never intended to join the Los Angeles Police Department; his career had grown out of a desire to do something useful when his ambitions to become an actor failed to materialize. Being a detective appealed to his romantic ideals, so his wife Celia asked M.G.M. studio head Louis B. Mayer to help her husband find work in the police department. Mayer played bridge with the Los Angeles mayor, and Craine's application was fast-tracked through City Hall. Within a month, he was attached to the L.A.P.D.'s Detective Bureau as the unofficially designated officer for all cases involving studios. Their man on the inside.

First across Vice and then, later, Homicide, Craine worked on assignments in Hollywood ranging from drug use to gambling, rape charges to suspected murder. But rather than seek arrests and charges, City Hall charged Craine to protect studio employees by any means possible: there were to be no convictions.

And even when Craine had turned his back on his role as a studio 'fixer,' he never considered himself a natural investigator. It was a young detective who'd cracked open the Chicago Outfit case. He'd merely overseen it to its tragic conclusion.

Craine must have fallen asleep because he woke, startled, as Abe exited the highway.

A mile down the road, Abe picked out one of two gas stations with a diner attached and pulled up by the last pump. A young man with a prosthetic arm came out of the shade toward them. A war veteran.

Abe turned off the engine. “Let’s eat,” he said.

“I’m not hungry.”

“You want to come in, you can,” he said, his voice clipped. “You want to stay, that’s up to you. Ain’t nowhere to run, here. And no one to help you, either.”

Abe got out of the car. He was top-heavy, moving slowly across the forecourt, handing the keys to the one-armed attendant before heading inside. Craine saw him pass a rack of newspapers on a stand. “SIEGEL KILLED IN GANGLAND SLAYING,” the headlines read.

Craine swallowed and could taste old iron in his mouth. He looked around. Nothing but desert and the odd coyote slinking through the shimmering heat. Without the air rushing past, Abe’s Mercury was sun-cooked, so hot that breathing was a struggle. Even the oil on the forecourt seemed to sizzle.

There were four other cars in the parking lot, but the other drivers barely noticed him. Everyone was heading somewhere. Craine wanted to call out to them. To beg them for help. One or two walked past and Craine looked at them imploringly but they didn’t look back.

He went inside.

The diner was a simple but clean establishment. Abe sat them at a booth nearest the back wall. That seemed to be important to him. Like he didn’t want anyone to approach them from behind.

The two men sat in silence, Abe studying a city map of Los Angeles that unfolded as wide as the table. A waitress with bleached, chin-length hair approached. She looked suspiciously at Craine’s bruises, like he might spring up and rob the place at any moment.

"Steak and eggs with a cup of coffee, please," Abe said. He glanced at Craine. "He'll have the same."

There was a boy in the diner about Michael's age. He was eating breakfast with his father. The elder man had his newspaper. The younger had his. But they seemed comfortable with each other. A family. He thought about where his son was right now and felt sick to the pit of his soul.

After their coffees had arrived, Craine asked the same question he'd been asking for hours.

"What will happen to my son?"

Abe spoke with a low burr, like his jaw didn't move as fast as his thoughts. "I told you before. Our men will stay with him at the house. They'll remain there for the duration. So long as you play by the rules, no harm will come to him."

"How can I trust you? Or them?"

"You can't," he said, slurping his coffee. "But I'd say you don't have a choice. As soon as you find Siegel's killer, you can go home. Argue all you want, but Mr. Lansky wants this resolved by Friday."

"It's a fool's errand," Craine said. "You saw the papers out there. Everyone knows it's a mob hit."

"It isn't."

"You tell me why it isn't. Because Lansky says so?"

Abe banged the coffee cup down. "Look, Craine. I don't know why Lansky wanted your involvement. But he did. My job is to take you from A to B. To make sure you do the job that's been asked of you."

"What are you, my driver or my jailer?"

"You're under my ward."

"So you're here to protect me?"

"Or to kill you, depending how you get on."

"Do you have a preference?"

"Not really." He slurped at his coffee again. "I go where they send me. I know a few people there but I don't know L.A. None of us do. Maybe that's why Lansky asked you."

"You don't think I should be here either, do you?"

Abe shrugged. "We used to wash our own laundry."

Craine stared at him. There was something primitive about Abe. Like a rudimentary drawing, sketched but unfinished. The only thing they seemed to have in common was a mutual lack of faith in Craine's abilities.

"Tell me why Lansky believes it wasn't a mob hit," Craine asked, sounding resigned.

Abe lowered his voice and held up three fingers. "There are three syndicates in America: New York, Chicago and Los Angeles. Lansky controls New York. Siegel controlled Los Angeles. And while that's been taken over by Jack Dragna, he's not considered a suspect. Too much to lose."

"And Chicago?"

"Aren't involved in California anymore. They've been weak ever since Frank Nitti killed himself. Their leaders are in prison, you and your F.B.I. friends saw to that. Besides, they'd never risk a move on Siegel when they're in a position of weakness. It has to be someone else. Which is where you come in."

Craine exhaled heavily. "What Lansky's asking . . . An investigation can take months."

"We have until Friday."

"Why? What else is going on? This feels more than personal."

Abe didn't answer.

Their waitress brought over their breakfasts. Craine didn't touch his at first. Abe ate inelegantly and quickly, working the food round the plate before pushing it into his mouth. "You should eat," he said when he was half-finished.

Abe was right. Self-pity wasn't going to help Craine. He picked at the breakfast steak. The salt hurt his blistered mouth but he started to feel better.

"I don't have the tools I need," Craine said when he couldn't eat any more. "I don't have the resources."

"Were you or were you not a homicide detective?"

"I have no jurisdiction. Why would anyone give me information?"

"You tell people Meyer Lansky sent you, you'll see the color drain from their faces. Then they'll help you alright."

Craine didn't reply.

Abe forked the last of his eggs into his mouth. "You decide where we go and who we need to see. But we don't talk directly to the police or the F.B.I. That's important."

"They'll already be involved. I'll need to read witness statements. Then there's autopsy reports. Ballistics information. Abe, I *have* to speak to the homicide detectives investigating—"

"No. Absolutely not."

Craine didn't hide his frustration. "I need all the help I can get. My son's life is at risk here. Kastel *mutilated* him."

"Oh, you're angry? Good. Anger gets things done. No one ever did anything with self-pity." Abe pointed his fork at Craine. "Dragna can get us in front of the people who were with Siegel that night, people close to him who might have reason to want him dead. And his girlfriend – Virginia. No one's seen her since Siegel was killed. We should try to talk to her, too. But you heard me right before. You *do not* involve the police or the F.B.I."

Craine rubbed his eyelids. He looked around desperately, as if one of the truckers in this diner might be able to save him from this situation.

"We don't know each other," Abe said, catching his eye. "But you should know this about me. If you try to run, if you do anything that puts me or my bosses in the firing line, you'll disappear."

Abe held his gaze to make sure the point had sunk in, then turned his head to call for the check.

For an L.A.P.D. homicide detective, a 40 percent clearance rate was a good year. The odds were already against him. And now he had none of the resources he would normally have access to. He was starting *tabula rasa.* A blank page. No information other than what was in the papers.

And then a thought struck him. Without police resources, newspaper reports were his best assets. They would give him witnesses and leads; crime scene photographs and updates from police press briefings.

When the waitress came over, Craine asked her if he could buy a newspaper.

"Sure." She shrugged, chewing gum.

"You keep Saturday's papers, too?"

She checked her watch. "Delivery comes late this far out. Probably still out there. Which ones you after?"

"All of them." Craine noticed her pencil and pad. "And can I borrow your pencil for a second?"

She looked at his bruises again. "If you give it back."

"Absolutely."

Five minutes later, they pulled back onto the road and Craine sat silently in the passenger seat, scouring the headlines for information on Siegel's death.

When Craine worked in Hollywood, the major West Coast broadsheets reported objectively on newsworthy events, but like most nationals leaned toward political bias when it suited them. City Hall would pressurize publishers to make sure Los Angeles didn't seem soft on crime or overwhelmed with mob shootings.

William Hearst's *Los Angeles Examiner* ran the headline "BUGSY SIEGEL MURDERED." Subheadings added, "Rubbed Out in Beverly Hills in Hail of Bullets," and "F.B.I. Brought in for Mob Slaying." Craine pored over the report, highlighting key facts with his newly acquired pencil.

"BEVERLY HILLS, Calif., June 21—Benjamin Siegel, 41-year-old gambler and one-time New York mobster, was slain on Friday night by a fusillade of bullets fired through the living room window of his Beverly Hills house.

"Police Capt. Henson said an unidentified gunman fired several shots shortly after Siegel and friends Allen Smiley and Charlie Hill returned from dinner at Ocean Park Beach, and fired through the glass doors.

"At least four shots entered the body of Siegel as he sat reading the paper on a divan. Working alongside the Federal Bureau of

Investigation, the L.A.P.D. reported that Siegel was pronounced dead on arrival. Both Charlie Hill and Allen Smiley were said to be in shock but otherwise unharmed. They have not been available for comment, but police and F.B.I. believe this to be a mob assassination. Siegel has spent millions of dollars building The Flamingo Hotel in Nevada and unnamed sources stated that 'his investors were unhappy he'd gone over budget.'"

Craine knew he had to talk to Smiley and Hill to find out exactly what had happened and if they'd got any sight of the shooter. He remembered Allen Smiley as a "sporting figure," better known as a low-level gambler. Charlie Hill's name didn't mean anything to him.

Editorials of most other local papers tallied with the *Los Angeles Examiner* report, suggesting Siegel had been murdered by New York mob associates but keeping the details of the crime itself vague. As he compared stories in different papers, Craine could spot the news items taken word for word from the police briefing.

Yellow press dared to call Siegel "the Al Capone of California." They'd managed to get photographs of the living room where Siegel was shot but offered little detail on the crime itself. They stated that motive for his murder was likely due to his hotel ventures in Las Vegas, but their sources were both unnamed and questionable.

The Hollywood Enquirer, the city's biggest trade newspaper, didn't mention Siegel at all; owner William Wilson's trade view column seemed more preoccupied with outing communist sympathizers within the motion picture industry.

It was the *Los Angeles Herald* that caught Craine's attention. They were the only paper to note that Siegel's girlfriend Virginia Hill had not been interviewed by police and was unavailable for comment. Unlike Hearst's papers, the *Herald*'s reporter outlined the crime in specific detail and attacked police refusal to share information on Siegel's whereabouts on the day of his death. The article highlighted that Siegel had been shot with a .30 caliber military M1 carbine. The weapon interested Craine. Not a submachine gun, the mob's usual weapon of dispatch. A soldier's weapon.

Crime reporters didn't always get a wide berth from the police when Craine was a lieutenant, but this one had done their homework. The reporter even had a quote from Smiley at the scene, saying: "I was right there next to him. It was like the room was exploding."

Unlike the other broadsheets, the *Herald* also quoted unnamed sources stating that Siegel had been with movie star George Raft earlier that day. Raft's omission from other papers made sense to Craine—studio publicity teams would have lobbied the press to avoid mentioning Raft's name to protect his star image. Which meant that the *Herald* wasn't toeing the party line.

Craine looked at the columnist's name: *T. L. Conroy.* The name rang a bell but he couldn't put a face to it.

Craine felt the car slow for the first time in an hour. The roads were getting busier. He looked up and a sign announced LOS ANGELES—10 miles.

He was entering the belly of the whale.

CHAPTER 6

The *Los Angeles Herald*'s budget meeting was held in the City Editor's briefing room every Monday at 10 A.M. It covered the day's news, but its main focus was what was going to be featured in the week's papers.

The flatplans for tomorrow's edition were laid out on the table. A horseshoe of two dozen senior reporters surrounded the City Editor as he rolled through key items. Tilda Conroy was the only one not smoking.

"The Chief Printer has set up a new block for the front page," he announced. "To confirm, the lead story tomorrow will now focus on the Taft–Hartley Act going into effect. Tom, I want four hundred words on why last year more than five million blue-collar Americans were involved in strikes."

The Taft–Hartley Act was a controversial labor bill that imposed limits on strikes and required union leaders to declare that they had no ties to the Communist Party. The country was divided on union strikes in America, but the *Herald* was broadly supportive. In fact, Tilda Conroy had always wanted to work at the *Herald* because it was more liberal and metropolitan than most nationals.

The City Editor stared across the office. "Anything else?"

Conroy cleared her throat. A row of cigarette cherries turned in her direction. She was one of only three women in the room, the other being the editor of the Homemaking section and a secretary taking minutes. "The police are briefing the press tomorrow on the latest with the Siegel murder."

"Unless there's a suspect, omit it entirely. I don't want us to repeat ourselves."

Homicides were tedious from a news perspective. With most crime locating itself below the poverty line, Conroy had a habit of linking murders to wider social issues, something the City Editor was less than fond of. But Siegel was a national celebrity, one with ties to major figures in Hollywood.

"Sir, it's got interest on both coasts. Updates on the case are—"

The City Editor stared her down. "I said we omit it entirely," he snapped.

The room fell silent. Most of the men were staring at Conroy over their cigarettes. "Now," he said more quietly, "I had breakfast with our esteemed publisher this morning. He asked me if we're going to do a report on the crime numbers. Can you cover it?"

Less a question and more a demand. Crime had fallen in the last two quarters, which in City Hall's eyes warranted front-page news. They wanted Los Angeles to be seen as a safe haven for real estate investors.

"I'll get right on it," Conroy said with muted enthusiasm for writing another police puff piece.

"Good. Anyone else?"

A wave from the back. "Howard Hughes is preparing to fly his 'Spruce Goose' flying boat."

"We have pictures," the Pictures Editor added.

"Fine. Column on page four. Two hundred words."

Teddy Kahn, the Political Editor, raised his pencil. "One of my press agents tipped me off that Jack Warner, Harry Cohn and Louis Mayer will be testifying to the House Un-American Activities Committee."

"H.U.A.C. are in L.A.?"

"That's what he said. Apparently the F.B.I. has got them worried about the studio unions. 'Communism infiltrating the pictures,' et cetera. It's a closed hearing but they're holed up at the Biltmore Hotel."

The City Editor considered this. "Cover the hearings," he said decisively. "I want five hundred words on page six. Make sure you get pictures, and see if you can get a statement from Mayer or Warner."

Conroy noticed Teddy Kahn look at her and sneer. He was a braggart and a male chauvinist and they'd never seen eye to eye. He rolled his eyes whenever she spoke. Wolf-whistled when she walked past. She'd gotten used to it but that didn't mean she'd learned to accept it.

"Is that everything?" the City Editor asked the room.

His secretary leaned forward and whispered something into his ear.

"What?" he barked. "Oh, we have some news. Teddy, you sly dog. Ladies and gentlemen, today is Teddy's birthday."

The political reporter grinned.

"Do we have a cake?" All eyes turned to the women in the room. Conroy had never baked a cake in her life. "No?" he asked, glancing at Conroy. "Well, we'll get some donuts sent up. Teddy, you'll have to make do with a rousing chorus of 'Happy Birthday.'"

When the conference broke up, Conroy followed the City Editor to his office, a small glass-walled suite overlooking the City Room.

After she shut the door he said, "Don't you question my fucking judgment in the budget meeting again, Conroy. It's fucking disgraceful."

Most men refrained from swearing in mixed company, but his tone wasn't aggressive, merely part of their informal rapport. He was the one that first suggested her for the crime desk.

"Sir, can we at least discuss it?"

He sat down behind his desk and prodded his finger at a pile of galley proofs. "I decide what goes in the paper, not you. No, don't sit down. You're standing."

"I'm sorry, sir. But I can't understand why you're pulling my story on Siegel."

"People are *bored* of Siegel. It's a mob hit. There's no conspiracy. There's no story because we'll never know who did it."

"We could dedicate resources to finding out who—"

He broke in before she could finish. "It's not your job to find the killer or postulate on suspects. Why don't you write about that wannabe actress raped and killed in Echo Park. She'd signed with Paramount a week ago."

"The *Examiner* are covering it," she said dismissively. "There's nothing new."

"The *Examiner* are covering it because it's tragic and sad and that's what people want to read about. They even got a great spread on the latest Paramount picture."

The City Editor was a gun dog. Easygoing to a certain point, but hardly prone to sleeping by the hearth. He was results-driven.

He lit a Chesterfield. "Let's just say City Hall is less enthusiastic about coverage of Siegel's death than you are. You already ignored me when I asked you not to mention Siegel's ties with George Raft."

Mobster Benjamin Siegel had several friends in Hollywood when he was alive. But now that he was dead, no one wanted their names mentioned next to his. As always, the newspapers depended on keeping the studios onside.

"Siegel met with George Raft the day he died. It was relevant. We have a duty to satisfy public interest in the case—"

"Drop Raft. No rowback, but don't mention him again."

"Sir—"

He spoke to her like a Dutch uncle: "Save yourself the filibuster, Tilda, the *Herald* isn't on a liberal crusade. Classified revenues are down and we have a duty to our advertisers, most of whom are studios who don't want their contract players dragged into a murder that's nothing to do with them. Siegel's connection to Hollywood is a delicate subject. You understand what I mean?"

Of course she did. It meant that no one wanted the fourth estate to highlight mob presence in Los Angeles. This wasn't going to be another New York or Chicago. L.A. didn't need its young reputation tarnished.

"We're not an ivory tower," he said plainly. "We're a business whose business is giving people news stories so engaging they're willing to pay to read them. So find me *engaging* and I will support your endeavors."

"There are new facts about the Siegel case we can still cover as the investigation unfolds."

"Facts can be listed!" he exclaimed. "Like a directory. Murders today: three. Hit and runs: six. Thefts: twenty-two. Any idiot can write that. I want the *Herald* to stand out."

Conroy wasn't sure where he was going with this. "How do you mean?"

"Tell me: what about Siegel is worth reading about? Worth *paying* for."

Conroy had been looking into Siegel's background for months. She chose her next words carefully: "The F.B.I. are in such a state over the unions that they're neglecting organized crime. I have a source who tells me New York and Los Angeles syndicates supposedly run three-quarters of U.S. bookmaking and narcotics rackets between them. Las Vegas was their combined project."

"You have my attention. Go on."

"We've known for years that different cities have different rackets. But now they've become organized. They've joined together to turn Vegas into a hub of gambling entertainment—a city. They're paying people off left, right and center to make it happen. Siegel was too unruly, so the mob had him killed."

The City Editor didn't scoff but he wasn't convinced. Las Vegas was little more than a dusty desert stop with a population of ten thousand. "Vegas? A *city*? Conroy, I get it, celebrities can afford to fly to that little dirt town so they can flutter and have a good time. But why would anyone else?"

"They're using Hollywood movie stars to promote rapid growth. They're trying to turn their rackets into legitimate businesses. The mob are hoping millions of Americans will fly there each year."

"And why would they?"

"For the entertainment and all the trappings that come with it. Gambling. Prostitution. Narcotics. Nevada's regulatory laws are considerably more lax."

The City Editor began nodding, making small grunts to himself. He left a cigarette in his ashtray but lit a fresh one. He smoked four packs a day.

"Kill the murder story. I don't want pictures of Siegel bleeding on the carpet. I don't want toe tags from the morgue. You're not going to find the killer."

Conroy was confused. "But sir—"

"Stop talking. This is my talking space, okay?" He exhaled a plume of smoke over the desk. "I don't want to read about the murder. I want to read about the man. Use Siegel's murder as a jumping board for this bigger story. 'Nationalized crime.' "

Conroy tingled. *Investigative reporting.* Far from shutting her down, the City Editor was offering her an opportunity and they both knew it.

"I'll get right on it."

"Get me something for Saturday's edition."

"Saturday? That's not a lot of time."

"You'll lose interest as the investigation wanes. By the time Siegel is buried, the mob will be forgotten. I want it out on Saturday."

"And you'll promise to print it?"

"I'll give you a six-hundred-word feature in the weekend edition."

Conroy's eyes lit up. "Eight hundred words."

"Seven."

"Seven, and I include photos."

"I would have thrown in the photos anyway," he said with a smile. "Siegel always wore nice suits."

Conroy beamed. "Thank you, sir."

"Don't let me down. Find out what Siegel was doing in Vegas. Look at his New York ties. Avoid focusing on this city's criminal element and I'll let you write what you want."

Conroy felt a pang of excitement. "Yes, sir."

"But be discreet," he warned with the end of his cigarette. "And get sources to back it up. We need quotes."

"What about the police investigation?"

"Keep tabs on it. But avoid conjecture." He waved his hand in the air as if shooing away a fly. "Now get out of my office."

Conroy hovered. "Sir, there was something else. You remember the conversation we had a few weeks ago?"

The City Editor ran a palm over his face. Nothing needed wiping. "Oh, *that*."

Last month, after years of working on the same salary, Conroy had asked for a pay rise in line with her male colleagues.

"Conroy," he said, choosing his words carefully, "I got your job approved by the publisher because you were fiscally suited to the role."

Fiscally suited. He meant she was cheaper than a man.

"Teddy Kahn is paid three times my salary. I earn less than Ed Seymour, and he's a junior reporter."

"We've had two dozen veterans return to the paper. Several of them worked on the crime desk before they were drafted. I have to think about how your position is regarded by other staff members."

Conroy tried to hide her frustration, which only made her more annoyed with herself. She shouldn't be embarrassed. It didn't matter that this was a liberal, progressive newspaper. Her time was worth less than her male peers'.

"Tilda, I'm sorry. Really." In a voice that was meant to sound sympathetic but instead was only patronizing, he added softly, "A two-tier pay scale is always going to exist here. Now I've got you on the crime desk, not the society column. You can't ask for much more."

Conroy tried to look thankful. But she wasn't at all.

CHAPTER 7

It was almost noon when they entered the fringes of Los Angeles. A cirrus cloud stretched thinly across the sky, the midday sun scorching the asphalt. Entering Downtown, Craine noticed the city seemed both busier and faster than he remembered. From every direction came the sound of cars.

They passed west, and Craine could see the scale of growth that had happened since the war. Everywhere there were new buildings and roads being built, the web of boroughs that once existed now a gigantic sprawl. It looked the same and yet somehow so different from when he lived here. Like the gold rush had been and gone and now there were two million more people left to fend for themselves.

Abe didn't say where they were going, only that it was a short drive. He pushed through the gears, the engine straining as they crawled their way through the pell-mell of traffic.

"I hate this place," Abe grumbled. "Came here a few years ago. Winos in New York are lucky to survive the winter. Here the worst thing they got to deal with is walking to the beach." When Craine didn't say anything, he looked over. "How long since you been in Los Angeles?"

Craine didn't answer. Couldn't even bear to look at Abe.

Abe looked over. "I said—"

"A long time," he snapped back, anything to keep him quiet. "It's been a long time."

"You miss it?"

For Craine, returning to Los Angeles was like dragging a knife through an atrophic scar. It would never matter how much it had changed; the minute he arrived it was like 1939 all over again. This was the place where the best and worst years of his life had been spent. His marriage. His entire career. The city where his son was born and his wife was buried. A lifetime he'd left behind him.

"No," he said. "I never missed it."

By 1 P.M. they were driving down Sunset Boulevard, not far from where he used to live. Abe pulled in and Craine recognized the newly painted façade of the Beverly Hills Hotel. It was as familiar to him as an old pair of shoes.

With its chandelier-hung ballroom and open-air swimming pool, there was nothing inconspicuous about the Beverly Hills Hotel and Craine wasn't sure why his East Coast sponsors had chosen it. When he was last here you'd see Carole Lombard or Jean Harlow playing tennis; Will Rogers and Douglas Fairbanks were usually drinking by the pool after a day of polo. He was thinking of them when he realized that they were all dead now. Lost in their prime.

They pulled into the curved driveway but a passel of photographers was swarming outside the entrance doors and the parking lot was full of press vans.

Craine recognized a few of them. Aging stringers still paying the bills by working for the gutter press. The types of lowlifes who sneaked through the gates of his old house to take pictures of his dead wife being loaded into a morgue truck.

Abe pressed the horn, but before they could push through the photographers darted forward and started taking pictures. Bulbs erupted as a small, frail woman came out of the hotel escorted by two men in white lab coats. They were heading into a private ambulance at the bottom of the steps.

". . . Judy! Look this way, Judy!"

". . . Miss Garland, how are you feeling?"

". . . Judy, can you tell us what happened?"

The photographers kept together in a tight Roman phalanx so that they couldn't be manhandled by the hotel security guards. Craine spotted Judy Garland as she was ushered through the rear ambulance doors. A shawl covered her face and bandages were wrapped around both wrists. They were stained where the blood had come through.

War didn't kill movie stars, Craine thought. *They did that all by themselves.*

Abe left the car with a valet and the two men walked toward reception. Porters were taking luggage from well-heeled guests in pressed sport jackets and summer frocks. Craine and Abe looked like they'd stumbled out of the dust bowl.

The manager shook both their hands firmly when they entered the reception lobby.

"I do apologize for that commotion outside, gentlemen. I trust you've had a pleasant journey. It's so good to see you again after such a long time, Mr. Craine," he said, noticing only now Craine's odd dress and bruised features. "I'll have someone see to your bags."

"Don't bother," Abe growled, holding up a small battered holdall. "I can carry this myself."

The manager tried his best to hide his distaste. "Then I'll have you taken up to your suite without delay."

At the elevators, Craine noticed several men loitering in the lobby. They were wearing double-breasted pinstripe suits. They looked over and then walked out, making a show of tilting their hats in Abe's direction.

"Friends of yours?" Craine asked.

"They're here to tell me they know we're here," Abe said. "There's a man we need to go see before we do anything else. Jack Dragna. I'm hoping he can help us."

Their two-bedroom suite must have cost several hundred dollars per night. A balcony overlooked the Los Angeles Country Club to their right and Sunset Strip to their left. Directly below was a lengthy swimming pool bordered on all sides by wealthy couples keen to sunburn. Latino attendants straightened the chairs and picked up used towels; white-jacketed Negro waiters were on hand with trays of iced tea.

Abe tipped the redcap, then locked the door and pulled the chain across.

"You're in that room," he said, pointing to a set of double doors. His own room was on the opposite side.

Craine felt at a loss knowing that his son was at home at gunpoint, and here he was, a click of fingers away from a champagne cocktail.

"You always stay in these types of hotels?"

"Not in the old days," Abe grunted. "Things are different now. Old man even has us keep our receipts. Let me know when you're ready to go."

When Craine moved toward his bedroom, Abe said, "Oh, we had some clothes ordered for you. Told the tailor you were tall and skinny."

Craine went into his bedroom to find a tailor-made suit folded on the bed and two fresh shirts with starched collars.

His thoughts were everywhere, so he forced himself to go through his case triage: without access to homicide reports, he needed to gain access to the crime scene, which wouldn't be easy. He also needed to talk to Allen Smiley and Charlie Hill, the two witnesses who were with Siegel the night he died. Finally there was Siegel's girlfriend, who was conspicuously absent.

He tried to focus on what he knew so far about Siegel, but he was so agitated that he wanted a shower to clear his mind. He caught his reflection in the bathroom mirror. His shirt was stiff and stained with perspiration. His face was swollen. But his head had stopped hurting, which was something.

The hotel provided mouthwash but no toothbrush. Craine poured himself an inch into a tooth glass and swilled his mouth. Everything hurt. When he spat, his saliva was stained with blood.

In the shower the hot water found its way into cuts and grazes. The pain receded but he couldn't wash away the thoughts. He saw Michael whenever he closed his eyes.

Craine sat in the basin of the bath with his head in his hands. If the last twelve hours hadn't fully dawned on him before, they did now. An image of Kastel with his knife to Michael's throat came into his head and Craine felt his knees shake. Mobsters were holding his son to ransom, and if he couldn't find the murderer of a man he barely knew, he and his son would both be killed.

When Craine got out of the shower and started putting on his new suit he began to feel angry. At Kastel. At Lansky. And at Abe. He was reminded that even if he did find out the identity of Siegel's killer, there was no guarantee that his son wouldn't be murdered. That this man Abe wouldn't think twice about killing him, too.

He was dwelling on the situation he'd found himself in when he heard the phone ring. The telephone for the suite was outside Abe's room and he heard Abe pick it up after three rings and the sound of his low voice muttering into the receiver. Craine put his head to his bedroom door, but by then the conversation was over. He heard Abe go back into his bedroom and close the door. Then a few seconds later he heard the shower go on in Abe's room. And with the sound of the water came a sudden recognition.

This was an opportunity.

Their suite had an open living room that separated the two bedrooms. Craine made his way across the room to Abe's door and tapped gently. No reply.

He strained his ears but there was no sound from inside. Only the noise of the shower from the bathroom.

Craine wasn't sure what exactly he was doing but he wanted to take control. His heart started beating faster. *Could he take Abe hostage, trade his life for his son?*

Craine entered but the drapes were drawn and the room was dim. In the half-light he could see that the bed was empty and the bathroom door was shut. Abe's holdall was open on the bed and Craine went through it quickly. The bag contained five rolls of dollar bills as big as his fist, a Charga-Plate and a strange-looking leather wallet. He opened it and there was a photograph inside: a group of soldiers in their late teens or early twenties. But the photo was not what Craine was interested in.

He found what he was looking for on the chair by the bed: Abe's pistol. The Savage Model 1915 wasn't manufactured anymore and it must have been all of thirty years old. It was as unpolished and brutal as its owner.

The shower was still running and the bathroom door was shut. Craine took the Savage out of its holster and checked that it was loaded. He hadn't held a pistol in years and the metal was foreign in his hand.

He tingled.

The door handle to Abe's bathroom turned quietly, the latch barely audible. Craine pushed the door open slowly and steam billowed out. He stepped inside with the pistol outstretched and moved toward the shower curtain.

The water was so hot Craine could barely see through the eddying steam clouds. As his hand reached out for the shower curtain he felt movement behind him, then an arm wrap around his throat. The arm pulled him backward and Craine felt something sharp press against his neck.

Craine could smell Abe. Could feel his hot, smoky breath on his ear.

"In the sink," Abe said.

Abe didn't threaten Craine—he didn't need to. Craine dropped the Savage in the sink and held his arms out.

Abe's voice was quiet, a low grumble like an idling engine. "We're meeting Jack Dragna in thirty minutes," he said. "I suggest you get dressed and meet me downstairs."

The condensation in the mirror cleared and Craine could see Abe had a towel around his waist. He was wearing an open shirt with the collar unattached. The barber razor he had to Craine's throat glistened in the reflection.

Craine felt lightheaded, like there wasn't enough air in the room. He tried not to swallow. "Alright," he whispered.

Abe lowered the razor and picked up the Savage. He left the room and Craine retched into the sink, standing bent over the enamel, gathering his breath. He hadn't cried in almost ten years and the tears didn't come now. But after several deep breaths did nothing to stop him from shaking, he wrapped his teeth around his forearm and wailed.

CHAPTER 8

In the car they didn't talk about what had happened. Abe spoke to Craine as if it had never occurred, talking casually instead about their meeting with Dragna and who might be there.

Jack Dragna was a name that was familiar to Craine, even if they'd never met in person. Although he didn't move in motion picture circles, Dragna had run gambling and prostitution rackets when Craine lived in Los Angeles. What Craine hadn't understood was that their presence in Los Angeles warranted an introduction – a 'blessing,' Abe called it.

Abe's responses to his questions about Dragna were intentionally vague and obfuscated, but Craine managed to establish that Dragna worked under Siegel in Los Angeles and had now, by default, become head of the Los Angeles syndicate, answerable to Lansky in New York. For Craine, that was motive enough for Dragna to want Ben Siegel dead, but he knew that accusing a mob boss of murder would be a delicate proposition. Particularly as he might also need Dragna's help to find Smiley and Hill, the two men with Siegel that night.

The meeting had been arranged at the Bel Air Country Club, an exclusive golf club that had Bing Crosby, Spencer Tracy and Fred Astaire on its members' roll. Craine had never been a member himself, but years ago his diplomatic skills were required when Howard Hughes got into a lawsuit with the owners for landing his plane on the fourteenth fairway. After that he got a free pass to use the club whenever he liked.

After a valet parked their car, a man called Harvey Sterling met them at the entrance and shook Abe's hand several times.

"Good to see you," he said enthusiastically. "Come inside, come inside."

He was young, late twenties at most, but scarring on his face made him look older. There was something familiar about Harvey, but Craine couldn't place him.

"Harvey, this is Jonathan Craine," Abe said by way of introduction.

Harvey shook his hand and something in his look implied he recognized Craine too. "Yeah," he said. "Heard of you. That Lilac Club business."

Whoever he was, Harvey's facial scar made Kastel's look like acne. There was a dent in his jaw where the skin had been pulled together and the coloring was lighter than his cheeks. Craine sometimes had to remind himself the war left half a million Americans dead but many more wounded.

Abe had been more willing to tell Craine on the drive over about Harvey Sterling. He was a friend's son. Harvey had worked in New York and Chicago before he was drafted into the army during the war. Afterward Lansky helped set him up in Los Angeles and got him a job with Dragna. Abe said Harvey was a good guy to know, given that times were tense. A middleman they could rely on.

The Bel Air clubhouse was filled with sotted men in pastel polo shirts drinking at the bar. Silver buckets were crowded with upturned bottles of Laurent-Perrier and golfers were now supping greedily on balloons of brandy. It was barely 2 P.M.

They followed Harvey down a long, carpeted corridor and Abe and Harvey made small talk.

"Wife good?" Abe said to Harvey. "Kids okay?"

"Lucy's doing good. Eldest is almost four."

"He's four?"

"Shore leave baby. Didn't even see him until he was sixteen months. Now he's got a little sister."

It seemed strange to see Abe being friendly. The smile was even stranger. He could talk so affectionately about small children, when last night he'd helped Kastel abduct his son. Craine was almost glad when Harvey moved the conversation on. "How'd you get here? Train?"

"Caught a flight. We've been in Vegas." Harvey looked perplexed so Abe said, "You know about Ben Siegel, right? You know why we're here?"

"Yeah, yeah," Harvey said vaguely. "Tough break. Everyone's shaken up about it."

The corridor brought them to a private dining room overlooking the green. When they got within a few yards of the door Harvey stopped still and held his hand out. "You want to eat after?" he asked casually. "Sure I can arrange a table."

Abe took the Savage pistol out of his shoulder holster but neither man batted an eyelid. "Thanks," he said, handing over his weapon like it was a set of car keys. "But I think we got some errands to run."

"I don't like surprises, Abe," Dragna said in a thick Italian accent after they'd made introductions. He gestured emphatically when he spoke, his horn-rimmed glasses rising up each time he puffed out his cheeks. "Lansky should have warned me you were coming. Especially with this ex-cop of yours."

Jack Dragna was in his middle forties and looked like any other club member in the building. Polo shirt, flannel trousers. The give-away was a series of rings on both hands.

"He meant no disrespect."

Dragna addressed Craine for the first time. He wasn't comfortable with him being there. "And you, Mr. Craine. I understand Lansky sends you here to discuss Ben Siegel?"

Craine was careful to tread lightly. "Meyer Lansky has asked me to review the circumstances of Siegel's murder. I need to know if you know anything about the shooting."

"He'd like to know if I did it, you mean?"

Abe said, "Rumor is you've taken over Siegel's assets."

Dragna reared back on his chair and threw up his arms. "Am I running the wire service? Of course I am. I was running it with Benny before. Now it's mine. Lansky has an issue, he can come visit me. But I've told Lansky myself and you can tell him again, I had nothing to do with Benny being knocked on the head."

Abe went to say something but Dragna held up his hand. His monologue continued unrelieved: "Despite our difficulties, I admired the man. Benny was good for business. And first and foremost I'm a businessman."

So everyone keeps telling me, Craine thought to himself.

"What can you tell me about Vegas?" Craine asked, changing direction.

"Why are you asking me this? You can ask Lansky."

"I want to hear your perspective."

Jack Dragna rolled his eyes and swiped a hand under his chin. "A few years ago Siegel got this crazy idea to build Vegas into some kind of gaming city. This is a tiny little dirt town miles from anywhere with nothing going for it except one thing."

"Gambling is legal."

"Exactly. Benny got the money from Lansky and his New York friends and then he wastes millions of dollars trying to turn sand into diamonds. The cost of capital is rising, the timing of receipt was all wrong. No wonder his investors were becoming frustrated."

"What are you saying?"

Dragna held his arms open, palms out in front. He shrugged for extra effect. "I'm saying that the overall economics of his Vegas venture no longer made sense and Siegel had to go. Lansky had more motive than anyone to see the back of him. Now he'll have to sell the place to make his money back."

Craine leaned forward, both hands flat on the table. He didn't have time to be anything but completely candid with Dragna. "I fully appreciate men like yourself and Lansky have a healthy paranoia about the motives of your competitors. You believe he might be responsible. He believes in the possibility of your involvement. Now you're adamant that you didn't have anything to do with Siegel's death, and he is too."

Dragna grunted. Craine spoke to him like he was arbitrating with a D.A. prosecutor.

"My reading of your position is this: you've indirectly benefited considerably from Siegel's death. You're consolidating your position in the market. Mr. Lansky will look more favorably upon you and your assets if you assist in my investigation."

"You're bargaining, Mr. L.A.P.D.?"

"No, I'm simply trying to be transparent. Because we both know it makes good business sense."

"I'm not convinced you're not a stalking horse. Lansky sending you in to ask questions when really he's trying to find an excuse to take over my organization. I'm well aware Mickey Cohen is waiting in the wings."

Clearly, he had no idea how Craine had become involved in this scenario. He wondered why Abe hadn't told him.

"That's not the case," Abe said before Craine could say anything.

"Good. Because I have no intention of sitting back and watching Rome burn."

Dragna leaned back in his chair and cooled. "But I have no plans on poking Lansky in the eye either. He and I have done business together for many years. As a sign of respect, if you need cars, weapons, contacts, you only need to ask. In Los Angeles, you are my guests."

Craine nodded toward the newspaper. "Siegel was killed at his house in Beverly Hills. I'd like to see how he died. Accessing the scene of the crime would be invaluable to my investigation. Is this something you can arrange?"

"Paying off cops? What good could that possibly do apart from encourage more police to turn up on our doorstep?"

"This is purely about understanding what happened to Siegel. We're not interested in drawing attention to you or your organization."

Dragna made a face that said he was unconvinced. "I don't like it. What else?"

Craine's directness was motivated by urgency. Every second counted. "We need you to help us locate Smiley and Charlie Hill. They were both at Siegel's house that night. It's absolutely critical we speak to them."

"No one knows where Smiley is. He was interviewed by the F.B.I. after the shooting. After that, who knows? Maybe they still have him."

"What about Charlie Hill?"

"Don't know him. He doesn't work for us." He waved his hand in the air. "Some kid, I think. Virginia's brother. Not important."

Craine wasn't going to write off Charlie Hill so easily. Like Smiley, he was a person of interest. He needed to speak to him.

"You mentioned Virginia. Siegel's girlfriend?"

"Virginia Hill. Crazy, but hardly a killer. Besides, she's been out of town for weeks. No one's seen her. I think Smiley could tell you more. I barely knew her."

Abe was less forthright than Craine. He respected Dragna, or he was afraid of him. "Mr. Dragna, I think what Craine is trying to say is that it will benefit all of us to stop the F.B.I. from investigating. And Allen Smiley and Charlie Hill may know something important."

Dragna thoughtfully lit a cigarette. As he did so, his men followed suit. The room calmed.

"I'll have Harvey help you track them down." He held Abe's gaze to make certain he understood the conditions. "But while you're here, you'll let us know your movements: where you stay, where you go, who you talk to. You tell Harvey everything. Call it a courtesy."

Abe went to say something before Craine spoke up. "In return, you'll use your contacts in the police to get us access to Siegel's house."

Dragna stared at him. "It will cost me."

"Call it a courtesy."

Dragna laughed. "I can get you into the house. You give me three hours. We have enough cops on our pad that you shouldn't have any issues."

"Thank you."

Dragna was sitting in a brass-studded leather chair. He leaned forward.

"But if you bring the F.B.I. to my door, I'll make sure Lansky regrets ever coming to Vegas."

"We'll do our best."

"I wasn't asking you, Craine. In Italy, there are gestures for everything. But there are no gestures for please. Remember that."

A threat. Add it to the list, Craine thought.

They left in silence, Harvey and two other men escorting them to their car. They didn't talk for a long time, but when they were on a quiet stretch of road Abe said out of nowhere, "You can be very persuasive."

Craine wound down the window and looked at the city he'd tried to forget about. "Dragna doesn't know how I came to be involved—"

"No." When Craine didn't say anything, Abe asked, "You think he did it?"

"Dragna? No."

"How can you be so sure?"

"I can't be. But I've seen enough guilty men to know that he isn't one. You think we can trust him to help us?"

"I don't think he'll kill us if that's what you mean," Abe said, his eyes on the road.

"And Harvey Sterling?"

"Friends with my son. They were in Omaha together. He's a war hero. I trust him with my life."

Craine thought of the photograph in Abe's bag. "You have a son?"

Abe didn't reply. Instead, he said, "Harvey said he'd call us when Siegel's house is accessible. It'll be some time tonight. I say we head back to the hotel and wait for his call."

Craine was frustrated. It was like Abe didn't appreciate that he wasn't simply investigating a murder. He was staking Michael's life.

"So I'm supposed to go back to our suite and sit there playing with my thumbs?"

"You do whatever you need to do."

Craine pinched the bridge of his nose. The first twenty-four hours after a murder are the most critical in any homicide investigation. After that, witnesses' memories became fuzzy. Suspects destroyed evidence, ditched their cars, left the city or at least worked out solid alibis. They needed to take advantage of the fresh chaos caused by the murder.

Siegel had died three nights ago and they were barely getting started. He had no intention of resting on his laurels until they could access the crime scene or Smiley and Hill turned up. He was still missing essential information on the case: Siegel's movements the day he died; his business ties; people close to him who may have wanted him dead.

Craine stared out the window, trying to stop his thoughts from going over and over what had happened at the farm. He was living in a strange limbo. There was a clear task in front of him, but every time his mind took a step back he was reminded of the stakes involved. *Where was Michael right now? Was he safe?*

They passed a newsstand and he caught the headlines. Mostly it was about labor unions. A few stories about studio strikes and the threat of communism in Hollywood. Nothing new on Siegel. Which meant the police hadn't got any leads.

A new route came to him with a sudden urgency. He couldn't speak to the L.A.P.D. and he didn't have the time or resources to work this case alone. He needed the best source of information he could get hold of. Out of nowhere he made a decision.

"I need you to drive me to the Civic Center."

"What's there?"

"The offices of the *Herald*," he said. "I need to speak to T. L. Conroy."

Craine wasn't sure what he might gain from talking to a crime reporter, but some plans aren't well thought out. Some are simply a frantic stab in the dark.

CHAPTER 9

When Craine was at the L.A.P.D., he used to go to the *Herald* almost weekly, persuading the crime desk to drop their stories about reefer-smoking actors and drunk studio execs caught up in hit-and-runs. Reporters were poorly paid and most were happy to oblige for a few bottles of Bollinger at the Cafe Trocadero.

The City Room was an open office, and he'd forgotten how loud it was. The hard sound of typewriters and phones ringing, people shouting across the floor to be heard. They passed row upon row of desks facing the same direction, each adorned with an Underwood typewriter, a rotary telephone and litter of typesheet.

"Excuse me, where's the crime desk?" he asked a cub reporter running past with a stack of papers.

"Far corner. Near the mail tubes."

The crime desk had been relegated to the back of the office beside a loud pneumatic mail system. Abe hung back as Craine approached the barricade of desks surrounding various mug shots and crime scene glossies pinned to a board.

"Can I help you, sir?" a colored clerk asked. Her voice was loud over the clacking sound, almost a yell.

"I'm looking for a man called T. L. Conroy. He works here on the crime desk."

The clerk glanced to the woman next to her. Whoever she was, she didn't look up, engrossed in her work.

"T. L. Conroy is occupied at present."

"When is he free?"

"Most of our crime desk are in meetings for the morning," the clerk said. Her clothes and hair were immaculate; her desk clean and ordered. "You work for the L.A.P.D.?"

"No."

"Who are you then, sir?"

"Concerned member of the public."

The clerk arched a penciled eyebrow. The woman hunched next to her looked up and studied Craine from behind a pair of round spectacles. "Relax, Alice. I'll talk to him. I'm Tilda."

"You work for Conroy?"

The woman was maybe Craine's age or a few years younger; she had short, untidy brown hair and frown lines in her forehead from where she'd been concentrating. She didn't seem too happy to be disturbed.

"*I'm* Tilda Conroy," she said with a look that said this wasn't the first time someone had mistaken her for a man.

He held up his hands apologetically. "I'm sorry. My name is Craine. I was hoping to ask you a few questions about an article you wrote. Can I buy you a cup of coffee? Lunch, perhaps?"

"I'm busy and besides, I've eaten." She waved toward her desk, where beside several scraps of paper sat a half-eaten orange and a Whiz bar wrapper.

"Please. Five minutes. I'd like to talk to you about Benjamin Siegel's murder."

This caught her attention. "You know something about Siegel's murder?"

"I have information that might be useful to you."

Tilda Conroy took them to a quiet office where they could speak without being overheard. It seemed to be of concern to her.

You could see the entire newsroom through the glass partition. A factory floor of men pecking at typewriters with cigarettes hanging off their bottom lips so they could write without taking breaks. Everyone had two or three empty coffee cups within reach.

"Did you know Benjamin Siegel?" she asked as soon as the door was shut.

"A little."

"How did you know him?" She took out a notepad and perched on a desk.

"I'm sorry, but I'd rather you didn't quote me."

"Fine," she said, putting the pad away. Craine noticed she had ink stains on her blouse.

"I knew him casually many years ago. We weren't close friends."

"Do you have any information about his death? Is there something you want to share?"

"No. Not exactly."

Conroy stared at him. "You're not willing to go on record. You say you knew Siegel but you don't want to go into how, and now you're telling me you have no information on his murder. I hate to put you on the spot, but why are we talking?"

He could see her disappointment. Like he was one of those people calling up claiming to know who murdered the Black Dahlia. She went to stand and Craine said, "Actually I was hoping you might be able to answer a few questions of my own. In exchange, I might be able to help you too."

"Are you a private investigator?" she asked. "Because I don't work alongside Pinkertons."

"I'm not a Pinkerton. I promise. And I'm hoping this can be a mutual exchange, if you'll answer a few questions for me first."

She sat back down but made a show of checking the clock on the wall. "Questions about what?"

"First, why are the F.B.I. involved in a local murder?"

She shrugged. "Congress has given the F.B.I. new federal laws to fight racketeering and gambling. Their involvement isn't surprising."

This was news to Craine. The F.B.I. had never involved themselves directly in homicide cases when he was at the L.A.P.D.

He went on. "George Raft saw Siegel earlier in the day. None of the other papers mentioned it. You did. I'm assuming studio publicity teams—"

She nodded as he spoke. "They did the rounds. Tried to get my editor to remove any mention of George Raft. Didn't want one of their top actors associated with a mob killing."

"Do the police have any leads?"

"It's notoriously difficult to find suspects in mob-related murders," she said diplomatically.

"Are they sure it's a mob-related killing?"

"Have you spoken to the homicide unit about this?" she asked, making another show of checking the wall clock.

"I haven't."

She smiled weakly. "Then perhaps you should speak to the police press department. Or I can give you the name of the primary detective in charge."

"Have they done a formal press briefing?"

Conroy exhaled. "They released a statement to the press on Saturday afternoon. But we're having a full briefing tomorrow."

"Your article—it impressed me. Are you privy to information the other papers aren't?"

"I should hope so."

"You were on the scene?"

"Yes."

"And you saw Allen Smiley and Charlie Hill?"

"Well, I saw Allen Smiley. Hill was leaving when I got there. Why do you ask?"

Craine answered with another question. "You got a quote from Smiley. You've spoken to him?"

"I spoke to him at the time, briefly. Haven't been able to contact him since."

"Do the police suspect either Smiley or Hill?"

"Charlie Hill I don't know, but Smiley and Siegel were close friends and when I saw him the night of the murder, he looked pretty shaken up. The F.B.I. took them off our hands but both were released without charge. Which indicates neither man is a suspect."

Craine went to ask another question before Conroy stopped him. "Wait. My turn. This isn't a mutual exchange of information. What is it you can tell me that I don't already know?"

I know almost nothing, Craine thought. "What if I told you it wasn't a mob killing?"

"I wouldn't believe you, for a start. And I'd ask you how you came to believe that."

Craine hesitated. *What did he really have?* "I have sources close to the deceased." He tried to sound convincing. "Privileged access."

"What kind of access?" she asked with an air of suspicion.

He nodded through the glass partition toward Abe, who was idling by the pneumatic mail system. He looked fascinated by the technology.

"Through him. He has connections." As if on cue, Abe leaned forward, staring at the row of metal vacuum tubes like a cat watching butterflies. He jumped as a mail canister popped out.

"Oh, congratulations," the reporter said drily.

He tried to appease her. "If you help me now, I promise to pass on information when I get it."

"What's your angle here?"

"Let's say I'm an interested party."

Conroy weighed up Craine's response before quickly listing off her demands: "I want to know more about his Vegas venture. I want to know who the real owners are, and how Siegel was connected to the New York crime rings. If possible I want interviews with Siegel's investors and associates. On the record."

Craine hesitated. Press attention was exactly what Lansky wanted to avoid. "That's not something . . . that's a little difficult."

"I see. *Difficult.*"

"Is there something else I can—"

"No, Mr. Concerned Citizen. I'm afraid you've got no stock to trade. So I think this conversation is over." Conroy pushed herself off the desk and held out her hand officiously.

Craine was frustrated. She was bargaining and he'd come up short.

"Pleasure to meet you, Mr . . ." She paused and glanced at her empty pad. She couldn't remember. "*Graham*?"

"Craine. Jonathan Craine."

His name seemed to catch her off guard. He wondered if it still meant something, even after all these years away.

"Have we met before?" he asked.

"No," she said firmly, holding the door open. "We've never met before."

CHAPTER 10

Dragna wasn't lying. When they pulled into Siegel's street in Beverly Hills a little after 8 P.M., the two uniformed officers whose job it was to guard the murder scene simply got in their black-and-white patrol car and drove off.

Craine was more than familiar with the machinations of bribery in the L.A.P.D. But his experience had always been in the higher echelons. The City Mayor calling the Chief of Police for a favor; the studio asking the D.A. for leniency. He'd never really appreciated that bribery also worked from the ground up, too.

"Police usually so amenable to payoffs?" Craine asked.

Abe looked at him like he was crazy. "People do what they need to do to feed their family," he said.

Linden Drive was adjacent to Sunset Boulevard, a premier location with mansions on both sides: French chateau, Spanish colonial, English Tudor. Craine used to come to parties here, first with Celia and then with Michael as a child when their social life moved away from movie circles and closer to parents at Michael's school. The memories of Saturday barbecues or Sunday brunches drifted by like passing cars.

Abe drove past Siegel's house, then parked fifty or so yards down the street. In rougher parts of L.A., neighbors would be stood in their windows with cups of coffee, content to spend their evenings watching vehicles come and go, nosing in on other people's business. Not here. Here people locked themselves away, pretending to themselves they were the only Tuscan villa on the street.

Siegel's front door was unlocked, but both men checked through the windows before entering.

The house was spacious, with an open-plan hallway leading on to a kitchen-diner that took up most of the heart of the house. It reminded Craine of his old place in Beverly Hills. Large rooms leading on to to even bigger rooms. More space than a family could ever fill.

"You been here before?" Craine asked.

"Never."

"Big place."

Abe shrugged. "At the end of the game, the pawns and the kings go in the same box."

It was evening now but Craine didn't flip the light switch. Even in the half-light they could see the wide hallway was covered in bloodied footprints where crime scene technicians had moved in and out of the house.

They found the living room at the end of the hall, police tape covering the doorway where the crime scene had been duly processed and closed. Craine pulled down the paper tape carefully and turned the door handle with his shirtsleeve.

The living room wasn't visible from the street, so Craine could turn the light on. He picked his way around broken shards of window glass, taking an inventory of what was there: a piano in the corner; a fireplace that looked like it had never been lit; a record player and an expensive range of long-play records. French windows overlooked a backyard, but the glass in one of them was broken; except for some police tape, the room was open to the elements. Finally he saw the floral sofa in the center of the room he recognized from the newspaper front pages. A giant bloodstain was the last of Siegel.

"What do you think?" Abe asked. Craine noticed him check his watch and log the time.

There was a strong metallic smell from all the gore but other than the bloodstains and broken glass, the rest of the room looked oddly pristine. Nothing out of place. Like a show home that had undergone a brief but acute trauma.

"Looks the same as the photographs in the paper," Craine said. "I'll need to take a closer look. You can see the shots came through that broken window. Siegel was on this sofa here." Craine pointed at one of the sofas and drew a line with his arms. "From the angle of the holes in the wall you can see the direction of fire."

Craine noticed Abe check his watch again. "Are we in a hurry?" he asked.

"I don't know what Dragna paid them but you normally get an hour."

"You've been in this situation before?"

"Uh-huh." Abe didn't expand. "I'll check the rest of the house."

Abe left the room and Craine felt relieved. In the pictures, detectives walked around the room talking to their partners, chewing over facts. But he had always preferred to work a crime scene alone.

Knowing that he would only get one chance to survey the crime scene, Craine's approach was methodical and unhurried; he moved around the room in an outward spiral, noting salient features, filtering out others.

There were two tumblers on the coffee table in front of the sofa, both still with whiskey in them and one with dried blood spray on the outside. The papers had said that Smiley was sitting with Siegel when he died. So where was Charlie Hill when the shooting started?

Craine went over to the sofa and crouched so he was eye level with where Siegel would have been sitting. Leaning on his haunches, he lifted the sofa cushion between thumb and forefinger. It peeled away where the blood had pooled and congealed. The back of the sofa was sodden and stained with the debris of murder. Siegel must have emptied several pints of blood here. He looked around: blood had painted most of the furniture and wallpaper within a two-yard radius. One round must have severed one or both carotid arteries. There wasn't even the barest suggestion that he could have survived the shots.

Craine closed one eye as if he was aiming down a barrel and looked at the direction of spatter on the wallpaper behind. There were bullet holes on the back wall but they were tightly clustered. Given the direction of fire was consistent, it didn't look like there had been more than one shooter.

The accuracy was impressive, even at this limited range. Whoever did the shooting knew what they were doing. Like a soldier. Police ballistics had identified the weapon as an army carbine. Could the F.B.I. compare the projectiles against registered military weapons?

Craine closed his eyes and tried to picture the scene, imagining the moments that preceded the shooting. Siegel sitting on the couch reading a newspaper. He has a glass of whiskey nearby. He's talking with Allen Smiley, a little drunk. He doesn't see the lone shooter creeping up through the garden with a rifle raised, drawing a bead on Siegel and pulling the trigger.

Siegel probably never even heard the bullets. Or felt them. A thump in the head and then blackness as two rounds tore through his brain.

Imagining it all made Craine shiver, but already he'd drawn some basic conclusions.

It wasn't a crime of passion. It was a lone shooter. Possibly military.

Abe came back into the room, bringing Craine to himself. "Doesn't look like anything's been taken. You done? Don't have a lot of time."

"We need to check the bedrooms," Craine said.

From the living room they went upstairs, where a landing led to a long corridor with two doors on either side.

The first two rooms hadn't been touched. No boot prints; no blood; no fingerprint dust.

The third was the master bedroom, the room where Siegel slept. Abe had a flashlight and swept the beam across the room, but there was nothing untoward. Framed photographs on bedside tables. A few watches on top of a dresser that looked to be of high value. The wardrobe was partly open and he could see a row of tailored suits, mostly houndstooth check, and a few chalk-stripe flannel sports coats. The belongings of a very wealthy man. Craine didn't envy any of it.

The room at the end of the corridor was a guest bedroom, but something stopped Craine in his tracks. This was different: ruffled sheets, a few bed cushions thrown onto the floor. He looked closer at one of the pillows on the bed. There was light powder on it. *Was that makeup?*

"You found something?"

Ignoring Abe, Craine picked up the pillows one by one, checking them over. He picked one of the cushions off the floor and brought it to close to his face. The faintest smell of perfume.

But it was something else that confirmed his suspicions. On the carpet: a single earring.

Craine was running through a new scenario in his head when there was an engine sound from nearby. Two pairs of headlights swung into the driveway and the room lit up, their silhouettes sliding across the wall.

Craine's watch read 8:50 P.M. They were back early.

Rising to his full height, Abe stood chest out, suddenly alert. He reached inside his jacket and took out his Savage.

"We have to go," Craine said.

They backed out into the corridor, trying to avoid their shadows. When they were half-way down the stairs, Craine saw in the glass panels around the front door a set of shadows moving outside. There were voices barely a few yards away.

"The kitchen," Abe whispered.

Moving quickly now, Abe led Craine into the kitchen, using his pistol to point at the back door.

Without discussion, they went outside and began running across the lawn toward the back fence. *A man in middle age, climbing fences in Beverly Hills. This isn't how I saw myself spending early retirement,* thought Craine.

Once at the car, Abe got behind the driver's wheel. They drove off slowly, both of them staring at the side-mirrors in case they were followed.

After they'd turned off the street, Abe said, "In the bedroom. You saw something."

"An earring," Craine said.

"So?"

"So the police and the press have said that there were two people in the house when Siegel was killed."

"Charlie Hill and Allen Smiley."

"Exactly. Allen Smiley was downstairs with Siegel. But Charlie Hill was upstairs. You saw the bed. I think he was with a girl."

"The police said there were only two witnesses."

Craine nodded. He felt something. The excitement of a lead.

"Why would they lie?"

"That's what we need to find out."

Abe didn't say anything. Craine noticed he was shifting his head to look at his rearview mirror. His shoulders arched.

"What is it?"

Abe waited deliberately before answering. "We're being followed."

He was right. In his side-view mirror, Craine could see a set of headlights bearing down on them.

Abe turned off Sunset Boulevard. The wrong direction. "Hotel's right there."

"We don't want them knowing where we are."

Nothing was said. They passed another two blocks, Craine checking over his shoulder, scanning the road behind. He couldn't make out anything more than the two beams twenty yards back, never closer, never further away.

"Still there," he said, facing forward.

The beams flashed twice and Abe tensed his hands against the wheel.

"Police?" Abe asked.

Craine focused on the car in the side-view mirror. It wasn't a black-and-white. There were two men inside, but their faces weren't visible.

"I said, is it police?"

He didn't want Abe to do anything rash. "It's not marked," he said as calmly as he could manage.

Craine could see a series of questions forming on his frown.

"F.B.I.?"

"Could be," he replied, but they both knew his answer was the affirmative. "Pull over."

No reply.

They continued driving with Abe looking at his mirrors and Craine looking at Abe. After several seconds Abe banged his fists against the wheel and pulled up on the side of the road.

The car slowed to a stop behind them. Craine and Abe glanced between the rear- and side-view mirrors but the other car's headlights blinded them. All they could see were two silhouettes as they exited onto the street on either side.

The two figures kept apart from one another as policemen are trained to do, one with his hand on a pistol belt and the other circling round to the driver's door with a flashlight.

Abe reached into his inside jacket pocket for his Savage.

Craine grabbed his hand and Abe gave him a feral look in return. "Don't," said Craine.

Abe firmed his grip on the pistol and began to pull it out of its holster. Craine could see the figures behind them getting closer.

"Please, Abe. No one needs to get hurt."

Abe made no sign he agreed.

Through the glass, Craine could see the two men had slowed, their pace faltering. One of them was beaming the side of the car. First their license tags, then the coachwork. The second they saw Abe's hand on his pistol they'd start shooting.

"Let me handle this. Don't turn this into a firefight."

The men were so close now. The beam lit up the interior. When the man with the flashlight was no more than two yards from the door, Abe grunted and put his hands back on the wheel.

"You better know what you're doing," he said.

The lead man approached the driver's side and Abe rolled the window down. The man pointed the flashlight on the ground. He didn't lean down but they were close enough that Craine could see his face.

His heart sank.

It was someone Craine hadn't seen in several years. He looked the same in many ways: russet beard, red hair creeping out from underneath his hat. He was remarkably lean and polished for a man in his early forties.

"Jonathan Craine," F.B.I. Agent Redhill said without hiding his surprise. "I thought you'd retired."

CHAPTER II

They had coffee in a hash house half a mile away, probably the only diner in the area. Craine and Redhill sat in a booth by the window. Outside, two other F.B.I. agents were standing beside Abe's car in the parking bay.

"So what have you been up to, Craine?"

Emmett Redhill and the District Attorney's office had taken Craine's case against the Chicago Outfit to the grand jury. They hadn't seen each other since Craine's deposition. But while his attitude toward his civic duty might appear uncompromising, Craine wasn't sure he trusted Redhill. Yes, he'd helped him arrest key members of the Chicago Outfit, but he'd also used Craine and his son as bait in the process. He'd put their lives at risk.

"Been a while," he went on. "Last I heard you'd left the L.A.P.D. and moved out of the city. What did Hoover call it? Oh, yeah. 'Disgrace dressed up as heroism.'"

Craine's face didn't react.

"Siegel dies, I half-expected a little war to break out. When I hear Lansky's in Vegas with a contingent, I figure it's only a day or so before they're in L.A. Then I hear a mob man is visiting Dragna with some stranger. Never thought it would be you."

Redhill looked toward the window. Abe was staring straight ahead with his hands on the steering wheel like he was waiting at a traffic light. "Interesting company you've found yourself in. Abraham Levine."

Craine hadn't actually known Abe's full name.

"I knew I'd see him here," Redhill went on, his spoon scraping circles in his coffee cup. "You know much about him? Lansky's hatchet man?"

When Craine didn't reply, he said, "The files we have on him could fill a library: key member of what the press coined 'Murder Inc.', chief suspect in the murder of sixteen men, implicated in four others. Even went to trial a few times, but they never managed to secure a conviction. That was back in the thirties, but doesn't seem like time has mellowed him much."

Craine felt a creeping discomfort. Redhill took advantage of it.

"He carries a pistol around with him but mostly he likes to use his hands. A guy he worked for tried to sell him out. Abe killed him"—Redhill made a show of clutching his hands together—"But only after he'd finished with his wife. Dragged her out of her house into her backyard where her kids could see. Then he beat her to death with his fists. Imagine the scene, Craine. Imagine doing that to a woman.

"Another guy he kidnapped, wrapped in a coal sack and buried alive. Another he strung up in a butcher's fridge till he froze to death. The next morning when he went to see him he was still breathing, so he hacked off his head with a cleaver. You don't believe me, I have photos. The things I could tell you about him, Craine. A man like that, he's what keeps me up at night. But sure, you drive around with him. You go to work for him."

Whatever tricks Redhill was using had the desired effect. Craine was breathing faster. There was no avoiding the visceral reality of who his new companion was. Abe was a slaughterhouse worker dressed in a suit and tie.

"We could never get a conviction," Redhill said, returning to that coffee cup and spoon. "For years. Then finally when he found out his son died in Omaha he went into his local bar and beat three Chinks half to death. Figured they were Japs. He did fourteen months in Sing Sing for that." He snorted. "Lawyers got a reduced sentence because he said they'd provoked him."

Abe's criminal history, shocking though it was, didn't come as a huge surprise. But this was news to Craine. Abe's son had died. Would it ever be possible, despite their differences, that they shared something, too? That a man like that—a vicious murderer—might understand Craine's situation as a father?

"What'd you think of Siegel's house?" Redhill said, stirring still. "You get a good look?"

There was no point reacting to Redhill's bait. In interrogations, the mistake suspects made was saying anything in the first place.

"I'd ask you why a retired police detective is breaking into the crime scene of a renowned criminal, but I think Abraham's presence here explains enough. What I can't understand is why you're working for them. Especially after what happened. You even killed a few of them, didn't you? So why the change of heart? It's the money, isn't it? You're missing the studio work."

Craine waited until Redhill was finished with his little speech before he asked, "Who was the fourth person at the house that night?"

That stopped Agent Redhill stirring.

"What fourth person?"

Craine had chosen his moment. "There was a girl. You didn't see her? Or you're pretending she wasn't there."

Redhill said nothing. Craine knew he was thinking about whether or not to answer. He pushed his saucer away.

"You're hiding something," Craine said.

Redhill didn't like being accused. "You're not an investigator, Craine. You never were. You were a fixer. You cleaned dishes, and even then you couldn't help but break a few. How many people died after that Lilac Club fiasco?"

Craine didn't answer. The two men sat there, breathing.

Redhill put his hand in his jacket pocket and held out a card. When Craine didn't take it, he dropped it on the table. "I don't know what the syndicate has on you but if you need me, I can help you. But I should be upfront: if you get in our way—"

He didn't say any more. The waitress passed and Redhill waved for the check. "I've got this," he said.

Abe drove them the two miles back to the hotel without discussing what had happened. Craine couldn't stop thinking about what Redhill had told him about Abe. About the things he'd done.

"He's an F.B.I. agent. Emmett Redhill," Craine said when they were within sight of the hotel. Abe spread his hands on the wheel and Craine noticed the callouses across both knuckles. "I didn't tell him anything," he added.

Abe nodded. "You have enough reasons not to," he said plainly, less a threat than a reminder of the risks involved. "He tell you about me?"

It was Craine's turn to nod.

"The things people tell you. The things people put in the papers. It wasn't like that." Abe paused, then muttered, "Not for the most part."

"He said your son died," Craine said when they pulled into the hotel parking lot. "In the war."

Craine heard Abe take in a few shallow breaths. The look Abe gave him might have shown understanding of Craine's situation. But equally it might have shown nothing. They didn't talk about it again.

Tilda Conroy lived alone in a courtyard apartment complex on Sierra Bonita Avenue. She'd been married once, but they'd met a little late in life. She was thirty-two when they wed, thirty-four when she lost their baby and thirty-five when he died in an army training accident.

Sadness was a little bag she carried around with her. Sometimes it was heavy, sometimes it was light. But it was always there.

Conroy ate a light dinner and went to bed early like she almost always did. She was in the middle of a dream where her late husband was asking her over and over why the baby had died, when she heard the sound of the telephone ringing and then her husband telling her to answer it.

Conroy woke up. The phone was by her bed. She picked it up so quickly she knocked over her glass of water.

"Hi—hullo." She turned on the side lamp.

She heard static down the line, then a man's voice say, "Tilda Conroy? I'm sorry it's late. It's Jonathan Craine."

She swore, then realizing who it was pulled her sheet up as if he was in the room. *Craine.* Seeing him yesterday, she felt like she'd seen a ghost. After his movie star wife died, he'd disappeared for most of a decade, only to turn up at her office today unannounced. She wondered if he blamed her for what happened to Celia Raymond. She wondered if he *knew.*

"How did you get this number? Are you following me? Are you paying off someone in my office—?"

"You're in the telephone book."

Conroy pulled tissues from a box and tried to mop up the water. She was still reeling from her nightmare. "Oh. Sorry, I didn't . . . What time is—?"

Craine wasn't listening or wasn't interested. He seemed in a hurry. "I've seen the crime scene. The information you've been given is wrong. There were three other people at Siegel's house that night. Three witnesses."

"What do you mean?"

"Allen Smiley was downstairs with Siegel. Charlie Hill was upstairs with a girl."

"What girl?"

"That's what we need to find out."

"Wait a second. How have you accessed the crime scene?"

"It doesn't matter. Did you see a woman at the crime scene when you arrived?"

Conroy thought back to Friday night. To the car she saw driving off just as she arrived.

"No."

"Then she'd left before you got there. Were the F.B.I. on the scene before Homicide?"

"Hold on. I don't understand—why would the police not release to the press that there was someone else in the house that night?"

Craine asked her again. "Did the police arrive before or after the F.B.I. got there?"

Conroy tried to recall. She was still half-asleep and her memory wasn't clear: "There were F.B.I. agents on the scene when I got there . . . and some uniformed officers and a primary detective. But the Captain arrived after."

"I don't know why, but I think the F.B.I. are hiding her identity. I think that they've taken over the investigation because this thing with Siegel touches people in delicate positions. They're protecting someone."

"You're making sweeping accusations. Charlie Hill or Allen Smiley could clear this up—"

"No one has seen them."

"Smiley's been seen with George Raft," Conroy said. "But I can't get to him."

There was a pause, then Craine said, "You sure?"

"I'm sure. Got a lead on it this afternoon. But his publicist won't let me anywhere near him. Says he's working on a picture."

This seemed to be important to Craine. He was silent for a second before he asked, "You know an Agent Redhill?"

Conroy propped herself up. "I met him on Friday and looked him up. He's the new S.A.C. for the F.B.I.'s Los Angeles Field Office. The Bureau don't flaunt their positions, but I know he's Hoover's inner circle. They've been expanding because they're worried about communism in Hollywood."

"Redhill is across the Siegel murder. At the briefing tomorrow morning, you're going to ask Captain Henson why the F.B.I. have taken over the investigation. Then you're going to ask them to confirm who was at the house when Siegel died. If they don't mention a third witness, they're lying."

"Assuming that you're right about the woman being there."

"I am," he said with irritating assurance.

"And why should I do any of this?"

"Because if I'm right, then the F.B.I. are keeping information from the press."

"I mean, why should I do this for *you*?"

"I'll share everything I find."

"So what?"

"Given what I've worked out in less than twenty-four hours, I'd say it was a good deal."

Conroy thought about this. She couldn't understand what Craine's motivation was. No one she'd asked had any idea he was back in town. They looked at her like she was crazy when she said she'd seen him.

"Why do you care who killed Siegel? Who are you working for?"

"It doesn't matter."

"Of course it matters."

"Conroy," he said without answering, "do we have a deal?"

She exhaled. "Fine."

"I'll call you after the briefing."

"Wait, I want to know—"

But it was too late. Jonathan Craine had already hung up.

TUESDAY

CHAPTER 12

Craine didn't sleep that night. The ceiling fan stirring steadily did nothing to curb the city heat, and the night unfolded in a kaleidoscopic fever, his memory and imagination playing tricks on him, repeating the moment where Kastel severed Michael's fingers over and over again in his head.

At some point in the night he went into the bathroom and saw that his entire body was clammy, varnished with sweat. He threw water on his face and tried to clear his head.

Craine's farm was part of the eastern slope of the Sierra Nevada mountains near Yosemite. Unlike Beverly Hills, the nights were cool and they rarely had trouble sleeping. But once the sun was up, the days were so hot that sometimes weeks went by and barely any work happened on the farm other than grazing the horses and praying the fields weren't scorched.

When Michael was on summer vacation, they'd happily pass whole days sitting on the porch reading books. Michael had friends from school but he seemed content to spend his free time with his father. The two of them would go riding early in the morning or sometimes borrow a boat and head down to the Twin Lakes to go fishing. Their relationship had grown that way. Not in long conversations or emotive exchanges, but rooted in the silent afternoons that they shared over many summers.

Craine thought over what Redhill had told him about Abe, and wondered what kind of relationship he'd had with his son. But it was hard to fathom that the butcher sleeping next door had ever cared about anything or anyone outside of his organization, family or not.

The sun started rising, and Craine heard the sprinklers go on and not long after that the first sound of cars on the road. With sleep eluding him, he went back into his room and began cataloging everything he knew so far about Siegel's murder.

Benjamin "Bugsy" Siegel had been shot at his home on Friday night with a military carbine fired from the garden. Smiley was sitting next to him but Charlie Hill was upstairs with an anonymous woman. When the F.B.I. arrived, the woman was gone or they had her removed. She might have been an actress under studio protection. She might have been someone's wife. She might have been a mob stooge. Whoever she was, Craine was convinced that she held the answer to Siegel's murder.

Solving a crime was like solving a crossword puzzle. You couldn't always figure out the clue you wanted. But if you answered the questions around it, you'd find enough letters that the answer became obvious. Finding the identity of the unknown woman was the clue that ran right down the middle. The one he needed before everything thing else fell into place.

Charlie Hill was still nowhere to be found, so to track her down, Craine needed to speak to Smiley. And if what Conroy had told him was true, the actor George Raft would know where he was.

There was a knock at the door and Craine came out to find the maid entering with a trolley stacked with coffee and hotplates. Abe was standing there in his dressing gown. He tipped her, then laid the food out on the table.

"You eating?" he asked without looking at him.

"I'll have something," said Craine.

The two men shared nothing else in this unexpected morning routine. Craine still wasn't hungry but he'd need all his energy to focus. He sat at the dining table and picked at his breakfast, assigning urgencies to what needed to be done as he ate. Abe read the paper, glancing up at Craine curiously every few minutes but otherwise leaving him alone.

Getting access to one of Hollywood's biggest movie stars wasn't easy. Craine put in an hour's work on calls to old studio contacts who could help locate him without asking questions. Most were bewildered that Craine was in touch; but those who remembered him didn't want to make small talk. After their initial surprise, they simply passed him on to the next person who could help as quickly as possible. He located George Raft in six phone calls.

Some reputations outlived careers.

CHAPTER 13

The press briefing was held inside the L.A.P.D.'s Central Headquarters. Captain Henson addressed the room a little after 10 A.M., flanked by senior personnel from the police and City Hall. There were maybe fifty reporters there. Siegel was a nationally known figure, and the back of the hall was standing room only. Surrounding Conroy were representatives from the major West Coast dailies and several faces she recognized from the Chicago and New York press.

"Good morning," Captain Henson began. "I'm joined here by the Chief of Police and Assistant District Attorney, and we want to thank everyone for being here today."

There were several other men at the front of the room who Henson didn't introduce. Conroy recognized the man with the red beard from the night Siegel died: F.B.I. Agent Redhill. He had a commanding appearance. Regulation haircut. Government-issue smile.

A flashbulb went off unexpectedly and Henson flinched. "As the Chief of Police and the Mayor have also stated, we're using any and all resources to work this case and locate Benjamin Siegel's murderer, an investigation that includes interviews with witnesses close to the victim and a thorough examination and analysis of the physical evidence. This case is only four days old and continues to evolve, so certain details will not be given out at this point. I will say that the L.A.P.D. are working as part of a team that includes the F.B.I., who are assisting in this investigation. No autopsy or ballistics tests have been completed, and at the moment, while we still believe this to be a mob-related murder, no suspects have been charged."

His address was greeted with a wave of raised hands. Conroy didn't move an inch. Don't ask the first question. Ask the last one. The one they've missed.

"One at a time," Henson said firmly. The new Captain, well practiced in these briefings, gave a firm nod to the *Examiner*, a more police-friendly paper.

"Where are Allen Smiley and Charlie Hill? They've not been seen since the shooting."

"We have spoken to both Mr. Smiley and Mr. Hill, who gave written statements shortly after Friday's shooting. They're not considered suspects, and I can confirm that they're not in police custody. I have no information on their whereabouts."

Interesting, Conroy thought, crossing this question off in her pad.

"Did Smiley see the shooter?" a reporter near the front asked.

"Understandably, Mr. Smiley was shaken by events but nothing he said indicated he could identify the shooter, no."

"What about Charlie Hill?"

"Likewise, Mr. Hill has fully cooperated with us but could not offer us a description of the shooter."

A few murmurs. Conroy was thinking about what Craine had said. About Charlie Hill being upstairs with a woman.

Henson pointed to someone else.

"Have you had any word from Mr. Siegel's girlfriend, Virginia Hill?"

Henson's expression didn't change. "We'll be actively speaking to anyone who was close to Mr. Siegel as and when they're available but I'm not going to get specific on who that includes."

Another hand went up. Yellow press. "Is it true George Raft and Humphrey Bogart were drinking with Bugsy Siegel only hours before he died?"

Muted laughter, and Henson made a show of rolling his eyes. "We're still working on a timeline of the day of Mr. Siegel's death, but no information we have right now suggests their involvement whatsoever."

More murmurs across the room. A second hand went up, then another.

"Captain Henson," said Conroy firmly, raising her hand for the first time.

Several heads turned. Some reporters never got used to hearing a woman's voice in the briefing room.

As Henson's eyes found Conroy, he seemed to sigh. Maybe because she'd become known for asking difficult questions. But maybe also because the police captain and Conroy had their own separate history outside of these four walls.

"Mrs Conroy," he said with as little emotion as he could manage.

"Can you confirm that there was no one else at Siegel's house that night?"

"You mean other than Smiley or Charlie Hill?"

"There are rumors that there was a third person at the house that night. A woman."

Conroy could see her question had thrown Henson. She noticed him glance to Redhill and then back again. The F.B.I. agent remained as stiff and starched as his collar.

"As I've noted several times," he said, "there were only two other people present at Benjamin Siegel's house the night of his murder – Allen Smiley and Charles Hill, both of whom have been interviewed by officers from the police department and the F.B.I."

Conroy was watching Redhill, trying to figure his place in this. With his slim-fitting suit and athletic poise, he looked like the stockbroker to Henson's faded door-to-door salesman. There was something untrustworthy about him.

"Does that mean the F.B.I. are taking over this investigation?"

The Captain took his time to run through his answer in his head before replying. "I am not going to respond to any further questions about the role of the F.B.I. in this investigation. No inference should be taken from this."

"Captain, what—"

"Mrs Conroy, I've answered your questions," said Henson, moving swiftly on to the next set of hands.

"God, Conroy. Give it a rest," the reporter from the *Examiner* muttered.

No one else in the room had any interest in her enquiries, preoccupied as they were by Siegel's ties to the motion picture industry.

"Can you tell us more about Mr. Siegel's connections to Hollywood . . .?"

"Is George Raft going to be questioned . . .?"

"Who is taking over The Flamingo?"

"Is this related to the Flamingo hotel?"

There was a final volley of questions before Captain Henson stepped away from the plinth, but Conroy wasn't listening. She was mulling over what Henson had said about the third witness. Because if Jonathan Craine was telling the truth, then the police and the F.B.I. were lying to the press.

After the briefing, the reporters were herded out, talking to and over each other. "Drink? Lunch? Both?" Conroy heard one of them say.

Most of the other L.A. crime reporters were friendly with each other. They liked huddling in bars, bragging about the stories they'd covered. It was a boys' club culture and Conroy was never invited.

Conroy saw Agent Redhill speaking to the Chief of Police at the back of the room. Captain Henson had left in a hurry, two uniformed officers leading him to the elevators up to the homicide department before any of the press could probe him further. She wanted to talk to him.

The corridor was already crowded with reporters and photographers, so Conroy took a side door that led to the stairwell and ran up four flights to the Detective Bureau.

Wide windows on the stairway looked over City Hall. It was a striking image, a pillar of power. But for Conroy, the building had for years also been a physical representation of the corruption that was embedded in Los Angeles' government. An inkblot on the city.

She arrived in the Detective Bureau flushed and out of breath. Normally, crime reporters were barred from the homicide department but Conroy had made a habit of coming up so often that most detectives in the bullpen barely batted an eyelid. Besides, she'd been smart enough to befriend the steno pool. She took Captain Henson's secretary out for lunch every fortnight, and she was there smiling at Conroy when she reached the Captain's outer office.

"He already told me not to let you in. Said to tell you he was unavailable."

"Is he?"

The secretary glanced sideways in both directions. "He's got a meeting in ten minutes, but he's free till then." She stood up and picked up her handbag. "Tell him I was in the bathroom."

Henson visibly tensed when Conroy entered. After his divorce, he'd asked her for dinner and they'd gone out a few times. She liked him enough, but she knew it was only her loneliness and his persistence that made her say yes. She'd ended things after only a few weeks, but their working relationship had remained awkward ever since.

"Tilda, if you think the brazen manner in which you sneak into the Detective Bureau gets you points in my book, you are most definitely mistaken. How did you get in here?"

The Captain's irritation was lightly worn. Whether or not he still held a torch was irrelevant. She knew he respected her, begrudgingly.

"I think your secretary's on a bathroom break," she said casually. "Wanted to ask you a few things."

"Look, I appreciate you do a great service to your readers. We're all highly indebted," he said drily. "But just because you carry a press card don't think you have any place in my office."

"I don't often ask for help."

"Infrequently and yet still too often," he said with a grunt. "You take advantage of our . . ." he struggled to find the word, "friendship."

"I have a few more questions about Siegel."

Henson spoke quickly. Like she was wasting his time. "Cause of death, injury from G.S.W. Weapon was a military carbine but Ballistics have not matched the projectiles. No other physical evidence. What other questions could you possibly have at this point?"

"Are you comparing the projectiles against military service records?"

"The F.B.I. runs the Fingerprint Factory. They'll be liaising with Washington, not us."

"But you're not mentioning it to the press. Why? Because City Hall doesn't want their heroes seen in a bad light?"

He didn't answer, but they both knew that was the case. No one wanted to admit that many American G.I.s had returned from war with an entirely different outlook on the sanctity of life.

"Is that all?"

Conroy paused to check the door was shut. "What do you know about a man called Craine? He was a police lieutenant before the war."

The question seemed to throw the Captain. "*Jonathan* Craine?" His face stopped moving. "He's here, in Los Angeles?"

"He used to work here, didn't he?"

"A long time ago. What about him?"

"He seems to have a vested interest in finding out why Siegel was killed."

Henson's eyes flickered. As if his mind was elsewhere. Combing through the past, perhaps. "Be careful what you share with him. He's not a detective anymore. At least, not in this bureau."

"He believes that the mob didn't kill Siegel. That someone else is responsible."

"You and I both know Benjamin Siegel had a wide circle of friends. And a wider circle of enemies."

"He also believes that there was a third witness in Siegel's house that night. A woman."

Henson pulled a face. "Ridiculous."

"Can you say with certainty that he's wrong?"

"Look, I get it. You're under pressure to get headlines. But I was on the scene thirty minutes after the shooting—"

"—You arrived after I did."

"What are you saying?"

Conroy spoke carefully: "What if someone else was upstairs when Siegel was killed but was never questioned by the L.A.P.D.? Do you have anything to say to that?"

"Oh, come on, Conroy. That's absurd."

There was a temptation to think Henson was withholding information. But from her current vantage point, the Captain didn't seem to be lying. Which meant that he simply wasn't aware. Conroy changed tack. "Why are you letting the Federal Bureau take over this case?"

"They haven't taken it over, we're working hand in hand."

Conroy went to write this down. "What role are they playing?"

"Put your pad away, I'm not telling you the split of responsibilities. The L.A.P.D. and the F.B.I. have cooperated in several high-profile cases over the past few years. This case is no different."

His words rang hollow. Conroy knew from insiders that the L.A.P.D. and F.B.I. had never much enjoyed working in parallel.

A pause. Then she realized. "You're happy to let them take over. Why?"

Henson spoke quietly. "You know better than anyone that Siegel's murder isn't going to get solved. This file will be left open, two dozen glossies and an inch of report sheets that people in this building will be poring over for years to come with no discernible outcome. We will never know who did this. So you can bother me all you want, but remember this: the only thing I care about is making this case disappear as quickly as possible so we can focus on the seventeen other homicides this city has had this month. *Those* people deserve to have their killers found."

Henson was a man well at odds with the headlines. But he had a point. *Did Siegel deserve to have his murder solved any more than anyone else?*

There was a tap at the door. His secretary.

"Agent Redhill wants two minutes before you head to your meeting."

"Tell him I'll be out shortly," Henson said, gathering a set of files on his desk. "And now that you're done with your 'bathroom break,' will you be so kind as to escort Mrs Conroy out of the building?"

The secretary gave Conroy an apologetic look and closed the door. "Yes, Captain."

Henson picked up his tower of folders and moved toward the door. With the handle half-turned, he said more softly, "Tilda, I'm telling you because you're a reporter and you have access to this information anyway: Siegel was building hotels in Vegas using mob money. He'd way overspent, leaving his bosses millions in the red. Someone high up in the mob wanted him killed, and so he was. The mob like a good bloodletting every few years. Keeps everyone on their toes. That's your story."

"Can I quote you?"

"All of this is off the record."

"You know when you say 'off the record?' If you say it *after* you've told me, it doesn't actually count for anything."

"Still stands."

"And if I put it in?"

"Then you'll be printing a retraction. City Hall is only across the street, remember. And your boss still plays golf with my boss. Don't think for a second you're tightening the rope around anyone's neck but your own."

He was right, of course. Up in the higher echelons, it wasn't so much what you knew as who you knew. And his boss had a better handicap than her boss.

CHAPTER 14

Abe drove them across town to Culver City, where George Raft was supposed to be working on one of the M.G.M. soundstages.

Craine was wary of setting foot on M.G.M. turf after everything that had happened before the war. Of all the studios, Metro-Goldwyn-Mayer was the one that had played such a significant role in Craine leaving Los Angeles. It represented everything he'd come to hate about this city.

But Michael was his priority now. Everything else was merely a distraction. They needed Raft to help track down Allen Smiley and besides, if anyone knew Siegel well in Los Angeles, movie star George Raft was one of them. It was Raft who had introduced Siegel to the Hollywood scene in the first place. They were boyhood pals, Raft told people. He was frequently cast in gangster roles, and being acquainted with a widely recognized mob man lent him some credibility.

When their car approached the studio gates they found themselves stuck at a human barricade, their path blocked by crowds of men and women holding placards. There must have been hundreds of them there, chanting and shouting. It was as if the heat was firing their anger.

"What's going on?" Craine asked.

"Strikers," Abe said. "Ain't you been reading the papers?"

Not if I can help it, Craine thought to himself.

Abe didn't wait for an answer. "Union trouble a few years ago made the East Coast papers. Tear gas. Water cannons. 'Bloody Friday,' they called it."

A short line of cars—strike breakers—were trying to get into the studio lot but the picketers were blocking their way. Craine looked at the placards hoisted in the crowd. 'RESPECT THE PICKET LINE' one said. 'FAIR WAGES FOR FAIR WORK' said another.

When Craine helped pull down the Chicago Outfit, the case was based on their extortion of the movie studios. Under Frank Nitti's guidance, they'd taken control of the unions and begun blackmailing the studio heads. Now, with Nitti gone and his cohorts in prison, there was no one to keep the unions in check. Carnage had been unleashed.

"Come on," Craine said. "I know another way in."

As they turned the car around, Craine heard the sound of sirens from inside the lot and four security cars pulled up by the gates. Craine saw the bulldog figure of Whitey Hendry, M.G.M.'s Head of Security, shouting orders to his detail to push the crowds apart and let vehicles in. In response, the picketers began rocking cars from side to side, trying to turn them over. Others jumped on roofs and started shouting abuse at the M.G.M. police.

The Hollywood dream machine was facing a civil war.

The picture was called *Down by the Docks*, and the roll sheet said it starred George Raft and Humphrey Bogart, with Lauren Bacall in a supporting role. It wasn't clear what the picture was about, but the set was some sort of dockyard and Raft and Bogart appeared to be playing characters audiences would be familiar with. The scene saw the two actors in trench coats arguing over whether the "cargo" was going to be loaded onto the ship. It ended with both men blasting each other, Raft getting down on one knee and clutching his side before Bogart finished him off.

It was hard to believe now that George Raft was once the bigger star. But he'd made some bad choices. Passed on *The Maltese Falcon.* Rumor was he'd passed on *Casablanca*, too.

Abe preferred to wait outside, but when the director yelled cut, a passing best boy took Craine to where George Raft and Bogart were sitting. Raft saw him coming, but if he was surprised he didn't show it. He whispered something to Bogart and Bogie looked over with a raised eyebrow.

"Jonathan Craine," Raft said, approaching with his hand outstretched. "The ghost who walks."

Craine wouldn't call Raft an old friend but they'd always been friendly. For a movie star with underworld ties, there was very little underhanded about him.

"What's it been? Eight, nine years?"

"Close enough."

George Raft left Bogart talking with the director and took Craine across the lot, filling him in on all the recent strike action.

The M.G.M. lot was huge. A small town in itself. Miles of paved road connected the soundstages, office buildings and exterior sets that ranged from Tarzan's jungle to Andy Hardy's cul-de-sac. Through all of this Abe remained twenty or so feet behind them, looking for shade at every opportunity.

"So you want to ask me about Benny?" Raft asked once they'd made small talk.

Craine nodded. "You don't look surprised to see me."

They were walking down the alleys between the soundstages. Raft seemed to be taking him toward the General Dressing Rooms buildings. Craine rarely wore hats, but he wished he had one now. It was like the sun had slipped from the sky. Like it was hanging right above them.

"Lansky told me somebody was coming. 'Somebody discreet,' he said. Still, didn't figure it would be you."

"He explain why?"

"Said he's looking into who killed Benny. Tell you the truth, I was a little surprised. I kind of figured it was one of Benny's New York investors who did it."

"That's what the police are telling the press. But Lansky is adamant they didn't do it. As is Jack Dragna."

The actor nodded but his face said he wasn't convinced. Raft was upset, that much was clear. "Well, somebody did."

"I know studio publicity teams are trying to deny it, but you saw Siegel the day he died, didn't you?"

Raft nodded, checking no one else was in sight. "I saw him for lunch. Didn't see him for dinner. And to be clear, I wasn't there when he was killed."

"Who else was with you?"

"It was only the two of us. He left to see Allen Smiley and some other friends."

"Charlie Hill and a girl. You didn't see them?"

"No, sorry. Never even met Charlie before. Didn't even know there was a girl with them."

Craine exhaled, disappointed. He'd been counting on Raft knowing who their missing girl was.

"How did Siegel seem when you had lunch? What was on his mind?"

"Ben? I mean, he was under a lot of pressure. His investors were unhappy. He'd been stressed about it."

"Unusually so?"

"Is it unusual to be worried when you're one guy building a whole town in the middle of the Nevada desert and your sponsors have a history of running their business with less traditional methods?"

"Have you been to The Flamingo yet?"

"As a matter of fact, Lansky wants me to go Friday."

Friday, Craine thought. "What's happening Friday?"

"Lansky said he had some important guests arriving. He's got a bunch of big names in town going. Pulling out all the stops."

Instinctively, Craine looked over his shoulder at Abe. There was a reason Lansky had given him a Friday deadline to find Siegel's murderer that Craine wasn't privy to.

They'd reached the Star Suites apartment complex. The directory sign outside said the apartment owners included William Powell, Clark Gable and Spencer Tracy. When they stopped outside, Raft said wistfully, "I'll miss Benny. People said a lot of bad things about him, some of them true. But he was always good to me. We came from nothing. Made our way from the cellar to the penthouse."

"George, I should tell you that we got a lead last night on Allen Smiley's whereabouts. Apparently you know where he is."

"Yeah, I figured somebody would hear about it." Raft sighed and looked up to a window two stories above. There was music coming from inside, and several loud voices. "You'd better come upstairs." He glanced at Abe. "Both of you. But I can't promise he'll be happy to see you."

CHAPTER 15

The Star Suites were lavish apartment units built to allow actors to get dressed and unwind between takes. In practice, they were scene to many a drinking session on the lot.

When they went upstairs, Craine could hear music coming from down the hall, and then a door burst open and a woman came out of the room propping up a man.

The woman was Katharine Hepburn. The man was Spencer Tracy, M.G.M. movie star, heartthrob and filthy drunk. As he brushed the wall with one hand, the aging Tracy knocked a wall light with it, sparks flying.

Hepburn had to use all her effort to prop him up. "Keep walking, Spence. Let's go."

Hepburn must have recognized Craine because she lowered her gaze. She was dragging Tracy down the corridor to his own suite. She managed to open his door one-handed, but as she pulled him inside, Tracy looked up and his eyes caught Craine's.

"Wait, is that Craine? Hey, Craine, where you been? You back on the payroll? Hey, help me get a divorce. Help me get a divorce so I can be with Katie—"

Hepburn unhooked his arms from the jamb and dragged him inside. The door slammed without another word being said.

Spencer Tracy had been M.G.M.'s biggest box office draw for years, but away from the cameras he went on week-long drinking binges. Craine had seen him down bottles of whiskey like it was iced tea. When he joined M.G.M. they even organized his own personal doctor and driver to take care of him when he passed out drunk. That had been Craine's job for years. Ferrying stars home with M.G.M. security before some stringer took a photograph of them being sick on themselves at eleven in the morning.

Inside, Raft's suite was no different. A round table of motion picture actors sat drunk and rowdy, shouting over each other as they tried to play bridge.

Through the haze of cigar smoke Craine saw Robert Mitchum in profile. Beside him was Clark Gable, drinking from two different bottles of beer. The years had taken their toll on M.G.M.'s fading champion. He looked heavy and worn. Like he'd given up on life.

Facing the door was a silver-haired man at the card table, sucking on a cigarette with short, sharp drags. He was unshaven and jangle-nerved, shocks of hair peeling out from his scalp in all directions. Allen Smiley.

"Raise you fifty, Mitchum," the man said, louder than he needed to.

"Fellas, I hate to ruin the party, but we're going to need to break this up," Raft said, to much dismay. Smiley looked around the room as the others stood up. He seemed confused.

"What's happening, George?"

"Allen," Raft said, "these guys want to have a word with you."

Allen looked at Craine and Abe. It took a second for him to register what was happening, then he stood up so quickly the chair flipped back. His feet were frozen in place but he was swaying like he was on a ship in a storm.

Craine looked at Abe to stop him from running, but realized he too was shocked. This was the Hollywood no one else ever saw. Not the polished close-ups and the winning smiles. Not the tuxedos and the red carpets. It was the hedonistic days of drinking on the studio lot. Reviving yourself with bennies after all-night drinking sessions so that you could pull yourself together for the cameras before returning to the bridge table an hour later.

* * *

Allen Smiley was either coming down from a high or coming up from a downer. Craine saw him swallow several pills dry from a small bottle in his jacket pocket.

"What's going on?" he said to Raft. To Abe. To anyone. "Why's everybody gone? Who's he?"

"He's Craine," Raft said. "He's helping us."

When the contract players had filed out, the room suddenly fell silent. Like they'd been brought together in their own vacuum.

Raft took a seat on the sofa and lit a cigarette, as if this conversation was nothing to do with him. Allen was sitting at the poker table and Craine had pulled a chair toward him so they were only a few feet apart. Abe remained standing behind Smiley with his arms folded.

"Hello, Allen. Can I call you Allen?" Craine spoke to Smiley like he was talking to a child or a patient.

"Sure. That's my name."

"I was hoping we could talk."

Smiley's eyes darted in different directions. A shaky hand ran through his hair. "Have we met before?"

"No, Allen, we haven't." *I've met so many versions of you*, Craine thought, *anxious man with a secret.* "My name is Jonathan Craine. Do you know who I am?"

"You're the man people talked about. The husband of that actress who died." Smiley leaned closer, almost to get a better look. "You're the man who makes problems go away. That's what Benny called you."

"Then you know why I'm here."

Smiley pressed down on his knee to stop it from shaking on the spot. "You need to help me. I think people are trying to kill me. They think I betrayed Benny. I would never do that."

"I am going to help you, Allen. But to do that, I need you to help me."

"Can I have a drink?" Allen looked between all three men, clearly intimidated. "My nerves—"

"Let's have a drink after. I want to ask you a few questions first. I've read the papers," Craine said, "but I want to hear your side of things.

I don't need every detail but I want you to go over the main facts. Try to speak slowly and clearly." Craine's voice was calming rather than condescending. When Smiley nodded, he added, "Try not to repeat yourself, Allen. And if you can, start at the beginning."

When people lie, their stories are short, incomplete and inconsistent. They jump around. They have gaps they can't explain. But when Allen Smiley recounted the night Siegel died, the details he included varied but the story stayed the same. Almost immediately Craine was convinced he was telling the truth.

Smiley had met Siegel earlier at Jack's restaurant in Ocean Park. Siegel's girlfriend Virginia was in Europe on vacation and Ben wanted a night out with old pals. Ben was mostly his usual self, Smiley said, but underneath he seemed worried. The Flamingo Hotel in Las Vegas was his baby and it was losing money fast. He was worried he'd upset his investors.

Smiley explained that after dinner, two friends of Siegel's joined them for drinks. Craine tried to hide his anticipation.

"As I said, Virginia is in Paris," Smiley said when Craine probed him for who they were. "But her brother, Charlie Hill, came out. He and Benny get on—" He corrected himself. "He and Benny *got* on well. And Charlie had a girl with him."

Craine could hear Abe's feet shift behind him. Raft lit another cigarette. Even Craine felt his heart thump harder.

"What was the girl's name?"

Smiley said, "I don't know."

An inward sigh. Craine thought he heard Abe mutter under his breath.

"Try to remember, Allen."

"I can't. I'm sorry. It's all a blur."

Abe stepped forward aggressively. Craine held up his hand. "Think, Allen. What was her name? How did Charlie introduce her?"

A long pause, and then, "I can't—I can't remember," Smiley stuttered. "I'm sorry. I've seen him with lots of girls. Every time I see him, a new girl. We didn't really get introduced. She was blond, young, early twenties. That's all I remember."

Few people taught themselves to deflect and fabricate so efficiently Craine couldn't see it. Smiley wasn't lying, but that didn't make it any less frustrating.

Craine exhaled. "Tell me what happened after dinner."

"We drove back to Siegel's but we were drunk. When we got in the others went straight upstairs. I was relieved, you know. I wanted to have a drink with Benny. Catch up. He'd been so stressed with everything, I wanted to see how he was doing."

"Then what happened?" This from Abe, clenching his fists one after the other.

"We had a drink, sat down. We can't have been in the house more than a few minutes when—"

As Smiley began to detail the moments of the shooting itself, he became increasingly distressed. At different times he began shouting, only for Craine to calm him down again gently.

"I'm sorry," he said, his voice tightening, the words squeezed. "I'm just . . . I just can't believe it. I was inches—*inches*—away from being shot. I saw Ben puckered. One minute there, talking to me. The next instant his face was a pincushion. His eye . . . *Jesus.* One of his eyes . . ." He looked at Craine disbelievingly. "It popped right out. Fell on the floor in front of me."

Hearing Smiley talk reminded him of all those years ago when men had come into his house firing guns, trying to kill Craine and his son. Suddenly it made sense why Smiley seemed so scared.

"I'm sorry you had to see that," Craine said empathetically. "That must have been hard for you." He let Smiley compose himself. "What about the shooter? Did you get a look at him through the window?"

Smiley made a face. His teeth were chattering. "No, no, of course not. It was so dark."

Craine went over everything again at a slower pace, trying to find inconsistencies or fresh details in his story. He gleaned nothing new other than that each time Smiley spoke about the moment Siegel was killed, he seemed genuinely shocked. He didn't look like someone who had arranged for his friend to be murdered.

Craine returned to the two other witnesses there that night.

"Do you know where I can find Charlie?"

They'd been talking for most of an hour. By now Smiley's agitation had been replaced with lassitude. He looked exhausted.

"I haven't seen him," he said, tilting his head to the ceiling and blinking several times. "Not since the F.B.I. took us away for questioning."

F.B.I. agents. Interesting, thought Craine.

"The F.B.I. spoke to you? All of you?"

"Yeah, I think so," Smiley said, nodding. "It was dark. I was drunk. I saw them put Charlie and the girl in one car. Then they put me in another. They drove us all down to their offices to ask us questions. But I only told them what happened. Nothing about Siegel's businesses. Nothing about us."

Something about this bothered Craine but he wasn't sure what. He was still information-gathering, and for the moment his main priority was finding Charlie Hill and this unknown girl. It was good to confirm she was there but he couldn't understand why the police hadn't revealed her identity to the press. Why would they hide her? He needed to speak to Conroy.

"You said Ben had been having a tough time in Vegas. Was there anyone he was particularly angry with? Anyone he was concerned about?"

A long pause. Smiley stiffened, like he'd misplaced something and was trying to recall where he'd left it.

"There were people Ben had upset," he confessed, although it wasn't exactly news to anyone, present company no exception. "In Los Angeles. In New York." Smiley began crying. "My friend. Somebody killed my friend."

"Who had he upset, Allen? Who?"

Smiley stopped, remembering something. "Well, there was one person in particular. I remember it was a big deal at the time. Billy Wilson."

"William Wilson? Wilson who runs the *Enquirer*?"

"Yeah, him." Smiley sniffed.

William Wilson was one of the most powerful men in Hollywood, a colorful figure who owned *The Hollywood Enquirer* and a string of nightclubs on the Sunset Strip. In the past he'd had his own connections with the mob.

"A lot of people don't know this but Wilson owned half the Flamingo at one point," Smiley told them. "A while back Ben told me he and Wilson had got into a big argument. He'd bought Wilson out and it didn't go down well."

Craine turned to George Raft. "This true?"

Raft shrugged sheepishly. "Rings a bell. I won't know any more than Allen."

"All I know is they had an argument," Smiley insisted. "Please. I told you everything. I promise."

Smiley had his head in his hands and was rubbing his face. Craine realized he wasn't going to get anything more out of him until he'd sobered up.

"Wilson still based in L.A.?" Craine asked Raft.

"Oh, yeah," the actor said. "*Hollywood Enquirer* has been listing names of people round town he thinks are communist. Popular guy right now. But he's still here."

Craine considered this. William Wilson was a mercurial character, used to getting his own way. But did that make him capable of cold-blooded murder?

Less than a quarter-mile away, in a private screening room on Lot 1, Louis B. Mayer was watching a color screen test of movie star Lana Turner. The director had filmed several takes for their upcoming version of *The Three Musketeers* for Mayer to review. He was supposed to be looking at lighting and makeup options, but for some reason he was struggling to concentrate. He had a lot on his mind.

As head of M.G.M. Studios, Louis Mayer was the highest-paid man in America, but his fortune hadn't made him happy. His marriage had failed, costing him his house and a $3 million settlement. He and his eldest daughter were estranged. And this year looked like it would be the first year ever that M.G.M. would make an operating loss. Movie budgets had become too high. The era when men like Clark Gable and Spencer Tracy ruled the box office was drawing to an end. And now Judy Garland, the little girl who had single-handedly given him the greatest motion picture of his career, was lucky to be alive.

Judy Garland was one of the things his ex-wife had brought up several times when their marriage was in trouble. Margaret had always loved Judy, and he knew she'd never really forgiven him when it became clear she had a drug problem. Other M.G.M. actresses had died of overdoses in the past, and she'd tried to warn him Judy was at risk. She said he had mistreated her, which only made him angry. He told Margaret time and time again that it wasn't his fault. Or his responsibility. He wasn't Judy's father. He was her boss.

Thinking about their arguments left him feeling glum, so Mayer tried to focus on the screen tests.

Lana Turner was a considerable investment and it was crucial that they get her first color picture right. Just because she was a movie star in black and white didn't mean audiences would fall in love with her in Technicolor. He'd seen the same thing happen when the 'talkies' came in. Many of his top silent stars disappeared overnight because audiences found their voices funny.

Lana was M.G.M.'s biggest starlet, and audiences flocked to her movies despite her tumultuous love life. She had a way of picking men who treated her badly. Gamblers and club owners. He was worried she'd find herself in the mob crowd that so many of his contract players found so intriguing.

He thought about that Bugsy Siegel character. Mayer didn't know him well but they mixed in the same social circles. He'd approached Mayer recently about sending some of his stars to his new hotel in Vegas, where they could gamble and whore away from public scrutiny. But Mayer remained worried about rubbing shoulders with mobsters. And with F.B.I. Director Hoover turning over every pebble in Hollywood trying to find communists, it was the wrong time to be drawing attention to themselves.

The door opened and a figure entered the fringes of the cinema screen.

"Mr. Mayer?"

Mayer lifted a hand in the air. Behind him the projectionist stopped the film and the lights came up.

Whitey Hendry, the head of M.G.M.'s private security force, stood in front of him with his police-style cap in his hands. He was in his fifties now but he still cut an imposing figure.

"Sorry to disturb you. Ida told me you were here."

"What's the latest with Judy?"

"It's confirmed it was a suicide attempt. She's in Las Campanas."

Suicide? What a disaster. "The sanatorium?"

"Dr. Fulton says it's the best place for her. She'll be there another week or so."

"A week? *Jesus.*" Judy Garland's latest picture *The Pirate* was already delayed and over budget. She'd been ill for 100 filming days out of 135. Gene Kelly had the potential to be a big star, but Mayer knew they had a bust on their hands if they couldn't get her to finish her scenes.

"I heard press were outside the hotel. Why didn't our security take her through the back?"

"They weren't there. She was taken out by a medical team and the hotel staff," Hendry said hesitantly. "All our men are occupied with strike action at the gates."

Mayer sighed and ran a hand over his bald spot. "We have the H.U.A.C. hearing tomorrow. Make sure this doesn't hit the press. Any of it."

"Sir, something else." Hendry glanced at the projectionist's booth and lowered his voice. "Clark Gable told me he saw Jonathan Craine earlier. He was talking to George Raft on the studio lot."

Mayer paled. *Jonathan Craine.* After eight years he'd thought that he'd never hear from Craine again. The man who blamed Mayer for his own wife's suicide. The man who'd shot dead his closest confidant. The man who'd tried to destroy everything Mayer had spent his career trying to build.

"Craine? Are you sure? Was Gable drunk?"

"Sir, Gable was adamant."

Mayer ran a finger round his collar. He felt a little sick.

"Who's he working for? I thought we buried the story about George Raft and Siegel being friends."

"The *Herald* didn't follow suit. It's in the public domain."

Mayer slapped his legs. Clark Gable's wife Carole had died in a plane crash a few years ago and Gable had never really got over it. He'd turned to drink. Mayer couldn't be sure he wasn't seeing things.

Mayer balled his hands into fists. "Find out whether what Gable told you is true. Talk to George Raft. And for God's sake, if it is then I want to know what the hell Jonathan Craine was doing on my lot."

CHAPTER 16

Tilda Conroy was at her desk, battling paperwork, ignoring memos from the copy editor that she needed to turn her articles in.

Most mornings consisted of going through her own notes on city-wide homicides and trying to decide what was interesting enough to warrant typing up. The crime desk managed obituaries, too, but Alice usually wrote those. Alice also scoured national court cases and flagged anything of interest to Conroy that might make a good story. Between them they usually wrote a thousand words a day.

Every day repeated itself. The story you handled yesterday disappeared completely and then you started again.

Conroy had never had a problem with getting her stories on the page, but the briefing earlier had shaken her. She'd barely typed a single word since she'd got back to the office. While she wasn't sure if Craine was telling the truth about the third witness at Siegel's house, there was a distinct lack of noise in this case that still bothered her.

Alice was typing up Conroy's shorthand notes from the police press briefing. Conroy hadn't told her anything about the anonymous girl yet.

"Alice," Conroy said quietly, "did the police release any of the witness statements on the Siegel case? Neighbors on Linden Drive?"

"Not that I've seen." Alice stopped typing. She looked around to check no one was watching. "Friend of mine at Central told me the witness statements were never typed up by the steno pool."

"Really? Why not?"

She shrugged. "Were told not to. Any notes taken by uniforms or the primary detective were handed straight over to the F.B.I."

Conroy thought about that. The murder of Benjamin Siegel had the hallmarks of a major case. And yet the police and F.B.I. seemed to be doing all in their power to make it disappear. No special detail of detectives assigned. No regular statements to the press. No uniformed patrols canvassing every street within a mile.

Conroy checked over her shoulder and lowered her voice to a whisper. "Alice, at the press—"

"Speak up. Can't hear you."

Conroy made a face and brought a finger to her lips. "Inside voices, Alice."

Alice rolled her eyes. "Oh, Lord."

They bickered, but the two women had learned to rely on each other. Despite being her senior, Conroy had a lot of respect for Alice. She had hands-on experience on the crime desk of the Associated Negro Press in Chicago. Conroy had hired her as a clerk on the crime desk because she didn't just want someone to type up her notes, she wanted someone with an investigative mind. They both knew that Alice was overqualified. But they also knew that opportunities for black women on a white newspaper were almost nonexistent.

She beckoned Alice closer. "Alice," she said quietly, "after the press briefing I spoke to Captain Henson. He said that there were two people at Siegel's house that night. Allen Smiley and Charlie Hill."

"So?" Alice mouthed.

"So," said Conroy, glancing in both directions, "I also spoke to Jonathan Craine last night. He was adamant there was a third person at the house with them. A *woman.*"

It was Alice's turn to pull a face. "You going to trust that guy Craine over Captain Henson? And what were you doing meeting him?"

"He called me."

Alice looked at her with a troubled expression. "I don't trust this Craine. After he came in, I asked around. You know who he is, right?

Used to be married to that actress Celia Raymond. Rumor is he killed her."

Conroy knew full well about Craine's wife. It was one of her first assignments, a sensationalistic piece for some yellow rag. She'd been younger then and foolish with it. She didn't have the journalistic integrity she had now, and the repercussions of her actions had always stayed with her. It was something she'd never truly forgiven herself for.

"I know what happened with Celia Raymond," she replied, not wanting to talk about it. "And he definitely didn't kill her."

"Well then, he covered up her suicide. And he killed those mob men."

"Enough gossiping, Alice." Conroy could feel herself going red. "He also helped bring Frank Nitti in front of a grand jury. The Chicago extortion trial. That was him, too."

"Well," said Alice, "all I know is before that he used to work as some kind of fixer for the studios. Took payoffs to get charges dropped. Corrupt cop. I don't trust him one bit."

As she spoke the phone rang and Alice picked it up. "Crime desk." A pause as Alice made a dramatic face. *It's him,* she mouthed.

"Why hello, Mr. Craine," she said with exaggerated courtesy. "Very nice to hear from you. Let me see if she's here."

Alice was shaking her head like this was a bad idea and Conroy should absolutely not take the call.

"Pass it over."

No way, Alice mouthed.

Conroy held her hand out and Alice reluctantly gave her the phone.

"This is Conroy."

No introduction. "Did you speak to Henson?" Craine asked.

Conroy demurred. "I'm sorry, but there was no third witness. Henson said so."

"He's wrong," Craine said.

Conroy was starting to think Alice was right. "Mr. Craine, you've got nothing to corroborate—"

"Charlie Hill had a woman with him. Smiley confirmed it."

Conroy stopped. This changed things. Alice was fixing her with a glare, so she twisted her chair sideways and spoke quietly into the receiver.

"You've spoken to Allen Smiley?"

"I'm with him right now."

"Tell me exactly what he said."

"He said Charlie Hill was there that night with a girl but that the F.B.I. took her away before the police got there."

Maybe Conroy wasn't sure she trusted Craine, but she couldn't pretend she didn't think he was on to something either.

"Okay," Conroy said, "let's meet."

Alice puffed out her cheeks and shook her head. She picked up her coffee and left. She didn't offer Conroy one.

They met at Herbert's Drive-In Restaurant on the southeast corner of Beverly and Fairfax. It was Conroy's suggestion, probably because she didn't want to be seen with Craine in a public restaurant. Or maybe in her own way she felt safer in her car. A lone woman meeting a strange man. He couldn't argue with that.

The building was easy to find. A twenty-foot pylon said HERBERT'S in vertical letters. The drive-in was circular so cars could park around its neon-ringed roofline. Diners were supposed to remain parked and eat inside their cars. Abe drove them there, arguing all the way that Craine shouldn't be telling the press any more than he had to. But somehow his protests seemed empty. Craine knew this investigation had his attention.

When Conroy's car pulled up she motioned for Craine to get in. Abe remained in his Mercury. In the back seat Allen Smiley was sleeping off the worst of his hangover.

A server in a red striped shirt and white paper cap came over and they ordered coffees. They sat in awkward silence until the server came back with their order.

"I didn't realize who you were yesterday," Conroy said, pouring several sugars into her coffee. He counted four.

Craine had several reputations. He wasn't sure which one she meant.

"The Chicago extortion ring," she went on, blowing on her cup. "I followed it to trial. A justice in the Beverly Hills court told me it was the catalyst for a serious shift. Major criminal players went to jail. Frank Nitti killed himself. Then afterward, you disappeared."

Craine didn't say anything. It was never something he felt particularly proud of. "I got the ball rolling, that's all."

"I've been covering stories in and around the Hall of Justice for most of ten years. We need more police like you."

He sipped at his own coffee. "I don't remember seeing you. Surprised we haven't met before."

He thought he saw her flush red but it might have been the heat. She shifted in her seat and changed the subject.

"The L.A.P.D. have said they're working alongside the F.B.I., but when I got to the crime scene on Friday it was pretty clear Agent Redhill was running things."

"Who else was there when you got there?"

"Primary detective and a few uniforms. Captain Henson and the Chief of Police arrived not long after I did."

"Chief came out?"

"*Everyone* came out. District Attorney was there not long after. High-profile name like Siegel gets killed, it puts City Hall into a tailspin. Los Angeles is booming. No one wants it to be seen as a turbulent crime city like New York or Chicago."

There was a fly in the car and it was buzzing across Craine's face, desperate to get out. He knew the feeling. He opened the window an inch and the fly escaped. Across the parking lot Abe's Mercury was still there. He was conscious of the time.

"Your interest in Siegel. Is it the murder? Or something else?"

Conroy thought about that before answering. "I cover a lot of homicides and court cases. More in a month than I could count. With

Siegel's murder, I have the chance to really get into the story. His connections to the underworld. The *nationalization* of crime. I believe The Flamingo Hotel is part of a bigger plan. A hotel casino built by a range of investors to turn Las Vegas into a mob city. But I think Siegel went over budget, and so his New York financiers killed him. He owed them money."

Their intentions weren't aligned. Craine wanted to solve the case; she wanted to report on the mob, something at odds with his employers. He glanced toward Abe's car and knew he had to be careful what he told her.

"Let's assume Siegel's New York connections are not directly responsible for his death," he said tentatively. "Who else do you think might be involved?"

She pursed her lips. "He had hands in so many businesses. There's a potter's field out there. Besides, in the end it won't even matter who is credited with the fatal shot. The shooter is probably a satrap. There's someone bigger behind this."

It didn't make Craine feel any better. It could be absolutely anyone in America, she might as well have said. "What about Virginia Hill?" he asked.

Conroy nodded. "His girlfriend? No, she's been in Europe the last week. No one's heard from her, but while she could have ordered someone to assassinate her boyfriend, it doesn't really ring true."

Craine felt the same. He'd already ruled out a crime of passion. But he still wanted to talk to her.

"I'm going to talk to Billy Wilson," he said. "Allen Smiley told me he was an investor in The Flamingo Hotel."

This seemed news to Conroy. She rested the coffee cup in her lap.

"The owner of *The Hollywood Enquirer* was involved with Ben Siegel?"

"Appears so."

Conroy stared at the window for a beat. "Wait a second. To connect a man like Wilson to Ben Siegel is huge. I've spent years working on this. Most people think that crime rings are little rackets. Wily gangsters running gambling dens and bordellos. But if a Hollywood mogul is partnering up with a mobster, it shows how much they've scaled up, how rooted they are in the system."

Craine had always known that different mob groups—*syndicates*—had existed in American cities. He'd dealt with the Chicago syndicate directly. But the idea that they had consolidated their power outside of their own cities and begun to take over America—to *nationalize*—this was an entirely new concept, even to him.

Craine looked sideways at the Mercury again. He was beginning to think Abe was right to be wary. Getting Conroy involved was drawing too much attention.

"You've published articles?" he asked.

She rolled her tongue around her gums instead of saying no. "My editor feels that now is the moment. To use the Siegel case to highlight how deep this runs. Wilson's involvement helps me prove that they've tried to legitimize. That it's not a racket, it's an organization."

"Do you have any proof of this?"

"Stories from different people. All secondhand. Nothing corroborated or substantiated enough that I can print. That's where you come in."

"I have to be careful."

This time it was Conroy who glanced over at the Mercury.

"How affiliated with them are you? I don't understand your role, Craine."

"I'm sorry, but I can't go into it."

"How do I even know we're on the same side?"

"You don't," he said. "But I'd say it's pretty clear we have common interests."

The rebuff frustrated her. She took a gulp of coffee. "For whatever reason, you can access people I can't. *Smiley. Raft. Wilson.* I'm looking for sources on Siegel's ties to the underworld and it seems to me you might be able to help."

"In what way?"

Conroy considered what she was about to say, sipping at her coffee before continuing: "You share with me everything you find out. In return, I'll keep you across police briefings and any new information relating to the investigation. Are we in agreement?"

Craine thought about this, but there wasn't much to argue with. In truth, he needed her help more than she needed his. Anyone with her resources was an invaluable asset.

"Okay," he said, "but you'll not mention myself or anyone I'm associated with by name unless they say so."

A pause, then, "How can I trust you'll fulfill your end of the bargain?"

Craine wound down the window. He waved toward Abe's Mercury and the big man got out and went to the passenger door. When he opened it, Smiley stepped out, using his hands to protect his eyes from the sun.

Conroy squinted. "Allen Smiley?"

To say Abe had been less than enthused about Smiley talking to a reporter was an understatement. But on this Craine had been adamant: they needed Conroy onside. Smiley would talk to Conroy about the night of Siegel's death and nothing else. But he'd tell her everything he knew about the shooting. It was the only way they could persuade the reporter to share information with them.

Craine got out and held the door open for Smiley to get in next to Conroy. "Consider this a gesture of mutual cooperation," he said.

Conroy spent most of the afternoon typing up her notes from her conversation with Allen Smiley.

The first challenge had been persuading Smiley to talk in the first instance. Naturally, he was intimidated by talking to a national newspaper in connection with a major murder story. He'd also been given warnings by Craine and his associate. But Conroy had made a human connection and he responded to it. She told him it was his opportunity to tell his side of the story, knowing that any minute the police could change their minds and list him as a primary suspect. If anything, refusing to talk might implicate him later.

Smiley was strung out, seemingly coming off a drugs binge. He was emotional and difficult, hesitant to go into too much detail about Siegel's Vegas plans; he also refused to mention anyone by name. Even when Conroy probed him about names she already knew—Lansky, Jack Dragna—he was coy. And while Craine had explained to him the principles of 'off the record' and 'reporter's privilege,' Smiley made her repeat over and over again that his name wouldn't be used in any of her articles.

So instead they agreed a few basic ground rules. Everything he told her was off the record and anonymous, meaning he couldn't be directly quoted or named. He would be a confidential source.

For the most part, Smiley's story offered little she didn't already know and when it came to the missing woman, his descriptions were vague and unhelpful: *She was young... pretty... She seemed nice enough... all these kids look the same to me.*

But before she dropped him off at a taxi rank, Smiley told Conroy something that stuck in her mind. He said that when the uniformed police first arrived on Linden Drive there were neighbors on the street. One of them was screaming that she'd seen the shooter drive off. Seen the man running down the street, even.

This bothered her. She remembered what Alice said about the steno pool not typing up witness statements. *But how could the police ignore this?*

There was a tenet in journalism that Conroy had always adhered to. 'If your mother says she loves you, check it out.' It meant that reporters should treat all leads with a degree of skepticism, no matter if the source seemed trustworthy. She remembered her old editor drilling it into her: double-check everything; verify what you can; act with caution.

And here was the dilemma. The City Editor had asked her to ignore the investigation into Siegel's murder and focus on his ties to

Hollywood and the underworld. But her best access was through Craine, and he'd bargained with her.

Whether she trusted he could meet the terms of their deal or not, she knew she had to follow up on any leads she had if she was ever going to get the inside scoop on Wilson. Assuming, of course, that Craine was connected enough to speak to a Hollywood tycoon like William Wilson in the first place.

CHAPTER 17

Before he'd had a son of his own, William Wilson had endured endless friends' children's parties. The trick was to treat them as work social events. You arrived as late as politely permissible, bought the little princess Chutes and Ladders and played good ol' Uncle Willie as best you could. Then you mimed your best to "Happy Birthday", clapped when the cake came out and promptly hit the gin fizz so you could talk to such-and-such from the studio about who was fucking who in Tinseltown.

But recently all those friends seemed to have disappeared. He'd had children late in life, that was true, but you'd think those years of service would have counted for something. Now here he was, hosting a hundred screaming juveniles for his son's birthday and hardly an old pal to be seen.

Wilson was sipping at a cola in the kitchen, feeling sorry for himself. Behind him, his young bride was hiding from his ex-wife by icing a birthday cake she'd spent all morning baking. Managing ex-wives was something of a skill of Wilson's, a byproduct of having so many. Four, at last count.

"Fonda make it?" he said, loitering but not helping.

"He sent a lovely card," she said, to appease him. "Said he's filming down in Mexico."

"Mexico? I heard he was in Ciro's two nights ago. What about Flynn?"

"It was his birthday yesterday. Besides, you *really* want Errol here?"

Wilson sighed and got himself another cola. It wasn't simply having children later, of course. In addition to several supper clubs, Wilson owned Hollywood's biggest trade newspaper, *The Hollywood Enquirer*. A few months ago he'd listed a handful of screenwriters he considered 'un-American' in his paper, given a few other names to Hoover's boys of Hollywood players he suspected of being communists. He thought he was doing a service for his country. But then suddenly he found himself with more enemies than friends. People like Burt Lancaster, Humphrey Bogart and Lauren Bacall used to come to his clubs all the time. Now they wouldn't even answer his calls.

"This H.U.A.C. thing has gotten out of hand," he said, stepping out of the way as his wife pushed candles into the icing. "Everyone's getting their noses out of joint."

"Well, honey, some people aren't as *American* as you are." She frowned. "Is that another cola? You've had three already."

Seven, but who was counting.

Wilson walked back into the garden. Two dozen children were swarming around the fountain. Cost him a fortune, this party. Three clowns, a magician and an elephant he'd borrowed from the *Tarzan* set. Wilson thought the elephant rather suited his garden, with its grand cupola, Roman columns and palm trees. A little lavish, but then again, so was the house. It had 25,000 square feet of living space. A dozen bedrooms and as many bathrooms. A dining room capable of seating up to eighty. He was pretty sure he had the most opulent house in Los Angeles. Or at the very least in Bel Air.

His son was standing alone, watching two other boys throw elephant shit at each other. He looked up at him with a frown on his face.

"Hey, kiddo. Having a good time?"

"I guess."

"Your stepmother made you a cake."

"*Mom* made me a cake."

Wilson looked over to the other end of the garden. His ex-wife's cake had three tiers and Dumbo marzipan figurines. It was a work of art.

"Well, let's do both. When your mother leaves, we'll bring out the other one. But let's keep that between you and me."

His new wife came outside, loitering at the doorway.

"Billy. *Billy*," she hissed.

She better not bring out that cake, Wilson thought. "What is it, sweetheart?"

"There's a man at the door, wants to see you."

"Cary?"

"No, not Cary. I don't know him. Security let him in. Says he's an old acquaintance."

Wilson's ears pricked up. He didn't have acquaintances. He had people he liked and people he didn't like, and the feeling was usually mutual. Rarely did someone fit into a middle category.

"What acquaintance?" he said when he'd reached the kitchen.

Wilson looked past the door to see a silhouette of a man hovering in his marble hallway. He exhaled sharply.

"Hello, Billy," said Jonathan Craine.

Wilson didn't say anything. He didn't have to.

They talked in Wilson's study, a double-height open space styled like an opera house. A pair of red velvet thrones overlooked the garden, but Wilson sat them away from the window. Evidently he didn't want anyone to see them talking.

"Sorry to disturb you at home," Craine said, sitting down. "Birthday party?"

Wilson had poured Craine a drink but it would sit there untouched.

"My son's," Wilson replied, before adding somewhat proudly, "we have an elephant."

Craine had been to parties here years ago. The French-inspired interior was decorated throughout in white and gold; the exterior was modeled after an eighteenth-century palace. Everything was gilded. Nothing about it was subtle or tasteful.

"So, you're on a farm now. I didn't know. Figured you for a shut-in. You and Howard Hughes sorting peas and wiping each other down with tissues up in the Hills. You enjoying country life?"

Craine tried hard not to react. He couldn't tell Wilson about Michael. Knew he couldn't mention the circumstances that led to him being here. "Suits me," was all he said.

"Staying in town long? Come down to The Troc for dinner sometime. We can gossip about old times."

"I'm passing through."

"I forget, it was your wife who was the social butterfly. You were always more of the reclusive moth. Shame. I was out with Cary and Errol a few weeks back. You hear about Judy Garland? Apparently she's gone crazy. Walked off *The Pirate* half-way through filming. Now she's in a sanatorium. What a hoot."

Wilson almost seemed glad to talk to someone from the glory years. When Craine was working as a fixer, Wilson was usually at war with one of the studio heads. Which meant that Craine was like the middleman between the Hatfields and the McCoys.

Craine didn't waste time getting to the point. "I need your help, Billy. Benjamin Siegel was murdered a few days ago. I wanted to ask you about it."

Craine let the silence settle. He was trying to see how he'd react. Whether he could sense him panic.

"You working for the L.A.P.D. again?" the press baron said, running a finger along his waxed mustache.

"No. A third party."

Wilson frowned. "So if you're not working for the police," he asked, "who sent you here?"

Craine was hesitant to answer but knew that Wilson wouldn't cooperate otherwise.

"Siegel's business partners."

This seemed to take Wilson by surprise. "So, you're the New York crime syndicate's emissary?"

"I wouldn't call it that."

"*Semantics*, Craine. You're working for them. Their little errand boy."

William Wilson spoke to everybody the same, which was to say badly. When Craine didn't answer, he said, "My, my, what circles you're moving in now. I preferred the old Craine. The Hollywood bogeyman. You know Errol Flynn would tell little ingénues stories about you before tucking them into bed at night."

Craine let him speak. You didn't need to interrogate Wilson. You simply allowed his enthusiasm to get the better of his discretion.

"How is old Lansky? Let me guess, he told you he was in the leisure and hospitality business. He give you that little speech about being a businessman? They act like bean counters but they still carry knives in their socks. I assume he ordered Siegel dead personally."

"They didn't kill him. Despite what the press are saying, the people I'm working for believe that someone else is responsible."

"*Please.* Mob men kill each other. It's their favorite pastime."

"But that didn't stop you going into business with Siegel, did it? You're hiding your involvement, but I know you had shares in The Flamingo. I hear you had a falling-out over it. Someone might think that was enough to find motive."

Wilson looked up. "Are you here to ask me questions or sling ridiculous accusations?"

"All I want to hear is your side of events."

Wilson could see Craine studying him. "I didn't kill him, Craine. But I won't deny we were involved together."

"Then tell me how. Start from the beginning."

After several sips of cola, Wilson explained that before the war he'd decided to build a casino resort in Nevada. An avid gambler, he wanted somewhere he and his Hollywood pals could go and entertain themselves without repercussions from the police. Air travel was cheaper; air-conditioned cars and better roads meant driving out to Vegas for the weekend suddenly didn't seem so ridiculous.

"I sell a few clubs," he said, playing with his soda bottle, "put up a million, but it's not enough. Not for real quality, you know? Not for the first time in my life, the banks won't lend to me. So I'm out looking for investors and Siegel approaches me. He's interested, he says. We have lunch, we talk. I know he's '*from New York*.'" Wilson stressed the three words more than he had to, patting the air with his hand. "I'm not an idiot, I knew he came with baggage."

"But that didn't put you off? After everything that happened, Billy."

"Don't preach to me, Craine. I'm familiar with intimidation and violence. Chicago were the ones that expressed interest in Vegas in the first place." Wilson rubbed his knees. He was referring to his involvement with Chicago racketeers before the war. It started a chain of events that led to Craine leaving Los Angeles and Wilson narrowly surviving being thrown off a hotel balcony by Outfit hoodlums. "Took me a year to walk after what they did to me. I'm lucky I'm here to tell the tale."

Wilson exhaled. There was a hint of regret in his tone. "I was desperate, and Siegel seemed legitimate. Says he has money, and he does—he comes good. I keep one-third of The Flamingo and retain control over construction. Siegel takes another third and the rest comes from his friends in the right places. They're silent partners."

Wilson sighed dramatically. Craine finished his sentence for him. "Only soon they're not so silent."

He nodded. "When I build something, it's to budget. But what does Siegel know about building hotels and casinos? Soon he's asking for all this ridiculous stuff: 'Move that wall here,' he says. 'Has to be like this.' Except he's not asking, is he?" Wilson shook his head. "Siegel, he's a loon. Once he's decided he wants to be involved in hotels, it's all he wants." Wilson looked outside. Craine saw two French poodles and an Indian elephant running loose across the garden. "No one is as dogmatic as a convert," he grumbled.

"Did you ever meet his girlfriend?"

"You mean Virginia? Of course! She was stealing from the hotel fund. Probably still is."

Craine shifted. This was news. "How much?"

He shrugged. "Thousands. Hundreds of thousands."

"You know for sure?"

Wilson was enjoying the opportunity to gossip. "I know for certain money kept going missing from the budget. I know for certain she was off to Switzerland every month with more suitcases than she needs for a weekend. Oh, she's an absolute darling is Virginia. And now she's disappeared. Probably knew she was on the list."

Craine had previously ruled out Virginia Hill. But this changed things. He wondered if Conroy or Dragna could help him get in contact.

"What happened with the hotel?"

Wilson rubbed his eyelids. "The hotel. *Christ.* Do you know why they call him Bugsy? Because he was crazy as a bed bug. When he got mad, he would shout and scream and God only knows what. Next I hear he's fired all of my men and torn up the blueprints. Then he needs even more money. Wants to buy my third, cut it up and sell it on."

"When was this?"

"This is a year ago, last June. I go into a stockholders' meeting with my attorney, and we have it out. He tells me he's buying my shares at half their worth."

"This conversation. Where did it take place? Vegas?"

Wilson shook his head. "Siegel had an L.A. office where we would meet. It wasn't under his name but a company within a company within a company."

"You remember where it was?"

"Even remember what it was called. 'Nevada Projects Corporation.' Bradbury Building in Downtown. Told you these mobsters like to pretend they're real businessmen. A '*corporation.*' Ridiculous."

Craine made a note of the address. It was a well-regarded commercial building on South Broadway. Not the type of place he expected a mobster to set up a business, even if it was a front. Conroy hadn't mentioned it. Neither had Dragna or the press. It was a lead he needed to follow up on.

"What happened next?"

"*Next?*" he exclaimed. "Next he was threating to kill me."

"He said that?"

"He said enough. I walk out. I leave my attorney to it and give him my shares. I take a plane to Paris and have a few weeks away from the whole thing."

"You let the syndicate take it away from you." Craine left it as a statement of fact and not a question.

Wilson's face turned as red as a firecracker. "He threatened to kill me, Craine."

Wilson had reason enough to kill Ben Siegel. He'd strong-armed him into selling his shares. He'd ruined his Vegas dream. But Craine wasn't sure he was the type of man to go through with it.

"You know the F.B.I. might consider this motive for you to kill him."

"Maybe they will, but I didn't. Sure there were times I wanted him dead, but I could never do something like that. Say what you like about me, Craine, but I'm not a murderer. The gangsters kill each other, I don't."

Craine nodded. He had gleaned enough information to know that Wilson's guilt was doubtful. He was right—it took a certain type of person to order murder, and despite his faults, Wilson wasn't built like that.

Craine was about to leave when Wilson said, "I always wondered if Siegel might get killed. In many ways I'm glad I got rid of The Flamingo when I did. But then . . . I was so close, Craine." Wilson sighed, lost in his own soda-induced reverie. "It wasn't just a casino. I could have had a whole town. A city. I believed in what we were trying to do." He sighed. "People laughed at us but Benny and I, we shared a vision."

Ten minutes later, with no more information to glean, Wilson walked Craine down his two-hundred-yard driveway to a set of gaudy gates. It seemed like a gesture of friendship, but maybe Wilson simply wanted to make sure he'd left.

"I don't envy you. You're on a hiding to nothing, Craine."

Craine didn't need reminding of the stakes involved. He'd been tempted to tell Wilson about Michael, but he knew publicizing it might only put him in more danger. Particularly with a tattler like Wilson.

The security guards he'd known from years back were still working there. They opened the double gates. Abe's dusty Mercury was parked at the end of the cul-de-sac. This was the most exclusive of districts and he'd told Abe to drive around for thirty minutes so people didn't call the Bel Air police to have the car removed.

"Appreciate you talking to me," Craine said.

"Figure I owe it to you. I said a few things about your wife when she died. Things I regret—"

"Printed them, too."

"Then it's the least I can do. Besides, bet you a thousand bucks you never find out who pulled the trigger."

"I don't gamble," said Craine.

Wilson scratched his mustache again and smiled with big teeth. "I think that's maybe why you and I never really got along."

CHAPTER 18

Tilda Conroy had never been to Linden Drive before Siegel's murder. Had barely been in Beverly Hills other than for parties she used to go to when she was young enough to be invited. Her usual milieu in crime reporting—drug murders, auto wrecks and robbery-homicides—tended to stay south of Santa Monica Boulevard.

She was hoping the affluent of Beverly Hills would be forthcoming with information on Benjamin Siegel but suspected they wouldn't want their names associated with a mob death. The houses here were like small castles. The owners were prominent surgeons, oil tycoons and the Hollywood elite; they were probably never too happy to have found themselves living on the same road as a notorious criminal in the first place.

She parked further down the street and canvassed door-to-door.

No one answered at the house next to Siegel's, 808.

809 were away in Palm Springs when Siegel died.

The couple at 812 heard the shots but didn't get out of bed until they heard sirens.

The woman at 811 changed everything.

She was maybe late twenties, willowy, with milk-white skin and fine blond hair recently cut. Everything about her clothes and look was intentional. She had a bandage across her nose, and ushered Conroy inside before she could even say why she was here. By the time Conroy had explained that she was writing an article on the murder of her mob boss neighbor it probably seemed rude to turn her out.

"I'm sorry," she said, touching her nose instinctively. "I wasn't expecting visitors."

"You had an accident?"

"Corrective surgery," she said, with emphasis on the first word. "Rhinoplasty." She smiled but her dimples strained. "It's nothing, really. Please. Come through. Can't leave you out in the heat like that."

Rhinoplasty, Conroy thought. Fancy word for a nose job.

Conroy looked around the hallway. A coffered ceiling and period appointments, the embodiment of old Hollywood glamor. Framed silent movie posters lined the walls. Awards statues were gathering dust on a dresser.

"You work in the industry?"

"My husband. He was an actor. He's in the other room. Come through."

Conroy was offered iced tea by a Mexican maid and brought into an antique living room with portraits of dogs and a sofa that looked like it was fluffed on the hour.

"My husband's first wife's tastes," she said, noticing Conroy take in the place. "I'm redecorating the whole house."

"It's quite something."

In the corner by the window was a man in a wheelchair. He had a slack arm and his head was tilted down on his chin. He looked to be sixty or so. Seeing him caught Conroy by surprise.

"I'm sorry, I didn't realize—"

"My husband. He had a stroke last year," the woman said, a little less sadly than you might expect.

"I hope I'm not bothering you? I really appreciate your time."

Conroy made the effort to be polite, courteous and well presented. If you're walking into people's homes, good clothes and clean shoes always made people more relaxed about having you in their personal space.

"Please take a seat under the fan. I find it's the coolest place in the house. My children are outside, but I can't bear to be in the heat."

She was gesturing a lot, between the fan, the seat and the back yard, anything to draw Conroy away from her nose.

"I'll bring them in as soon as it's dark. I'm sure you think I'm mad to worry, but the thought of something happening to them—"

"I understand."

"You have children?"

"No."

"Oh." She seemed excessively surprised. "That must be awful for you."

I have a career and friends and a life, Conroy wanted to say, but didn't. The latter two weren't necessarily true, either.

She held up her notepad. "You mind if I take notes? I wouldn't want to misquote you."

People were far more willing to let you quote them if you asked to take notes than if you brought out a Magnecord recorder the size of a suitcase and jammed a microphone under their chin.

"Okay, yes. I don't see why not."

"Would you mind telling me your full name, please?"

"Foster. Cay Foster. Cay with a 'C.' My mother chose it because—"

She stopped. She was staring at the odd shapes and lines on Conroy's pad.

"What is that?"

Conroy held up her pad, to be transparent. "Shorthand. It's a way of writing faster."

Unlike cursive, shorthand relied on symbols to record words phonetically. Conroy could write almost two hundred words a minute. Plus, because it looked like hieroglyphics, people had no idea what she was writing.

"I should say my husband and I are very private people. I'd rather not be named." She touched her nose. "Or described."

"You won't be, you don't have to worry," Conroy reassured her.

Cay Foster. 2 children. 20s. Nosejob, she wrote down.

"Can we talk about the night of the shooting? You said at the door you saw the whole thing. I was really hoping you could walk me through what happened that night."

"Well, it was pretty late, at least for this neighborhood. Around ten thirty, I suppose. My husband was in bed and I was downstairs alone. I was about to go upstairs and then I heard people arriving at Mr. Siegel's house."

Conroy was nodding and smiling. There was always lots of nodding and smiling. It helped build rapport.

Cay Foster went on: "My children were asleep, you see, and their bedroom looks over the front lawn. Cars in the driveway can disturb them and I have a heck of a time getting them back to sleep again. My youngest really struggles—"

Conroy kept her on the subject in hand. "Mrs. Foster. Did you see who was in the car?"

"No, but there were a few of them, I remember that."

"Did you see exactly how many?"

"No, I'm afraid not. But I could tell there were a few of them. They were drunk, I'm sure of it." There was a lot of emphasis on the word *drunk* and she looked at Conroy's pad as if to say that she should write that down. "Anyway, Mr. Siegel wasn't there much but when he was it was awfully loud. Parties until four or five in the morning. I went over once to ask them to turn it down and that girlfriend of his came out. I forget her name."

"Virginia Hill."

She touched a lash at the edge of her eye. "Yes, *her*. Anyway, she more or less threw me off her porch. The language from that vile woman."

Conroy steered her back to the night in question. "So, that night. Friday. You heard the cars and you went outside?"

"Not exactly. I opened the door to check on the noise. But that's when I heard the shooting. It was so strange. The exact moment. Like me opening the door had set something off. I thought maybe it was fireworks. Early ones for Fourth of July."

"There were several shots?"

With her pad on her knee, Conroy made detailed notes as she spoke.

"Yes. Ten, maybe. But I was inside by then. As soon as I figured what it was I ran right back inside and locked the door."

She pointed to the window where her husband sat, as if he were on lookout. "There. I watched it from there. I wanted to go up to check on the children but it was all so fast. I wanted to be sure he wasn't running this way."

"Did you see the man firing?"

"I'm not sure—not exactly. I saw a man running down the lawn onto the sidewalk. He had a guitar or a trumpet case in his hand. And that's when I knew for certain it wasn't fireworks. Because you meet jazz players and musicians, sure. But *not* in Beverly Hills."

"What happened next?"

"There was a car further down the road. He got right in and drove away."

"There was a driver?"

"No, he got in the driver's side."

Conroy was fizzing with excitement. Her pen was furious on her pad.

"Did you get a look at him?"

"I guess."

"Could you describe what he looked like?"

"He wasn't a Negro. Pretty sure he was white."

"How tall do you think he was?"

"Average, I guess. Not small."

"Did you see his face at all? Or his hair color?"

Cay Foster leaned back, patting the cushion beside her. Like she was testing it. "It was so dark. He was wearing a coat. A hat."

"What about the car?"

"Blue." She hesitated. "Or dark green. I'm sorry. It was late."

The details were so vague Conroy had stopped even writing them down.

"Could you tell me the make of the vehicle?"

"All these automobiles look the same to me."

Conroy tried not to show her frustration. "Could you tell whether it was a new car? A new model?"

Production of new automobiles stopped entirely in 1942. Manufacturers made trucks, airplane engines, guns and tanks until the end of the war. It meant cars were usually brand new or rather worn. Few were in between.

The young woman puffed out her cheeks. "I couldn't say. One of those cars you see around all the time. Maybe a Packard, I don't know. Wait, a friend of mine has an old Nash. Ten years old. Looked similar, as it had one of those yellow number plates you don't see much anymore."

"The same?"

Mrs. Foster rubbed her fingernails against each other. "It was all so fast."

There were over half a million cars in Los Angeles County. A blue or green Packard or Nash probably accounted for a quarter of those.

They went through the story a few more times but Conroy gathered nothing new. She went to wrap up the interview, but Mrs. Foster had a few questions of her own.

"Most of the newspapers are saying it was a gang thing. Was it because of his *business*?" That last word spoken quietly but pronounced with exaggerated mouth movements. "They're saying it was an assassination. Or at least, that's what the police told me."

"And you spoke to the police the night of the shooting?"

"Of course. I spoke to them that night and then again the next day."

Conroy was wondering who had hidden her statement and why. "The same men?" she asked.

"The first night it was men in uniform. They only asked if I was okay and if I'd seen the shooter. The second they wore regular clothes. Different men. Federal Bureau, they said. They asked more questions."

"And you told them about the car?"

Mrs. Foster bit her lip. "I can't remember. I think so. Maybe. They didn't seem interested." She finished her iced tea and glanced at the clock above the fireplace. "I suppose I better get the children in. Gabriela will have made them sandwiches, and I'll need to supervise or the whole thing will be a mess. I guess that's something you'll never have to deal with. Maybe that's a positive."

Conroy held her tongue until they reached the door. "Thank you for your time, Mrs. Foster." Then, unable to help herself, she added, "I hope your nose gets better. Looks awfully swollen."

Conroy waved at her from the driveway but Cay with a 'C' was already slamming the door shut.

If you're building a case, you want a combination of different kinds of substantive evidence like fingerprints and ballistics. But the most efficient way to solve a murder investigation is to locate a witness. So why were the L.A.P.D. and F.B.I. ignoring the only person who claimed to have seen the shooter?

"We know the F.B.I. lied to us," Conroy said to Alice in a hushed voice. "They knew there was a woman at that house who they're denying was ever there."

Alice arched an eyebrow over her coffee cup. "Assuming Craine and Smiley aren't lying to you. Or plain wrong."

"Assuming they aren't." Conroy nodded. "But even if they were, now we know the F.B.I. had a witness who could identify the getaway car."

"Maybe they thought it was a blind alley."

Conroy shook her head. "It didn't look like a blind alley, there was enough detail there to pass as truth. Juries trust civilian witnesses. Why would they cut corners like this?"

Conroy had shared all her findings with Alice since she'd returned from Linden Drive. The City Room was factory-styled, an open floor in a regimented layout with editors' offices on all sides. A private conversation was impossible by design, so they were huddled around the coffee station, whispering between themselves.

"We don't know they're not following up on it," Alice said.

"Then what reason would they have not to tell the press? They could have put a bulletin out asking for the public to come forward. There'd be a deluge of tip-offs and anonymous calls. Even if they knew most of them would be a waste of time, why not put it out there?"

Alice sipped her coffee, nodding in thought. "So they're hiding something."

"I think so."

"But even if they are, you've got no license tags," Alice exclaimed. "Sure I could speak to the D.M.V., but all you have is a *green-possibly-blue-possibly-Nash-possibly-some-other-car* description. That's every other car in Los Angeles. How you going to find the murderer with that?"

"Look, I think Craine's right," Conroy said. "I think the F.B.I. know who did it or are intentionally preventing anyone else from finding out who did it. I think they want the public to believe it was an unsolvable mob hit."

Alice tilted her chin toward the City Editor's office. "You told me we weren't to follow the investigation."

"Yes, but I need the type of access Craine can get us. And to do that I have to have something I can offer in return. Besides, either way this is proof that the mob are embedded in government. There's a chance they're paying off the F.B.I."

Conroy went to pour Alice more coffee. Alice demurred, pulling her coffee cup back. She picked up the coffee pot labeled "COLORED" instead.

"Oh, Jesus, Alice. Drink from this one. I don't care."

"Easy for you to say."

Alice checked no one was watching, then let Conroy fill up her coffee cup. When she sipped it, her face looked disappointed. "Tastes the same," she muttered.

"Whether Craine's right or wrong," Conroy mused, "we're on to something with this car. And yes, the description is vague, but what if we assumed that the shooter was using a stolen vehicle? We could talk to the D.M.V., track down the list of stolen vehicles this last week."

"Too many assumptions. Everyone's making assumptions. First Craine, now you."

A subeditor walked past and they both stood still. When he'd passed Alice looked at her squarely. "You need to be careful with Craine," she warned. "Man like that will get us both into trouble."

Alice turned to walk back to her desk and Conroy noticed a few people were watching. More concerned about sharing their coffee jug with Alice than whatever they were talking about.

"Alice, can you try our friends at the D.M.V., see if they can get back to us tomorrow morning?"

"Where do you think I'm going?" Alice called back.

CHAPTER 19

A self-proclaimed "veteran of this kind of business," Abe petitioned that they go to the Bradbury Building in the middle of the night when no one was around. Craine disagreed, adamant that every hour counted. He couldn't handle another day with no progress. Eight o'clock was the compromise, so they decided to drive back to their hotel for a few hours before heading back out.

Craine was disheartened, trying to untangle the knot of what happened the night Siegel died. The F.B.I. had hidden the identity of the missing girl. Virginia Hill had been stealing money but was in Europe. Charlie Hill had disappeared off the face of the earth. Friday's deadline was fast approaching, and he had no tangible leads other than the location of Siegel's old office. He was reminded of Sisyphus and his rock. Every step forward was three steps back.

He knew that trying to deconstruct and dissect all the different variables wasn't helpful. He needed to let his mind relax. Step back from the problem in front of him. There was an expression Michael liked: "*The harder you cup your hands, the easier the water spills.*"

But of course, thinking about that only made him miss his son. He wanted to know that he was okay. That someone had taken Michael to see a doctor. But he knew that wasn't possible. Even if Abe let him, they didn't have a telephone at his farm. He had to trust that what Lansky told him was true. That he would be looked after. He had to have faith and concentrate on Siegel's murder.

They returned to the hotel to find the staff setting up for an evening function. A stage was being constructed in the Rodeo Ballroom, and round, white-covered tables were being laid with silverware and crystal glasses.

Wanting to check in with Lansky, Abe crossed the lobby to the telephone booths. Craine approached the reception desk and asked the manager if there had been any messages, hoping that Conroy might have an update for him.

"As a matter of fact, I believe there's a package for you, Mr. Craine. If you'll give me a minute."

Craine idled at the desk but when he turned around Abe was waving him over, holding out the phone.

"This is Craine," he said when he was sure no one was in earshot.

The voice belonged to Kastel and Craine could feel his mood sour. "Answer all questions with yes or no answers, nothing more. Answer truthfully but do not mention anyone by name. Do you understand?"

A pause as he digested, then, "Yes."

The voice went quiet and there was static until another voice came on the line. Lansky.

"You know who this is?"

"Yes."

"Are you any closer to understanding what happened?"

"No." Craine exhaled.

"Time is ticking. Do you have any leads?"

He didn't have the missing witness. He didn't have Charlie Hill. He only had an office building. He was shaking his head but he managed to say, "Yes."

"Are the right people helping you to get what you need?"

His eyes involuntarily looked to Abe. "Yes."

"And you've not involved anyone we asked you not to?"

Craine was hoping that Abe couldn't hear the question. He knew he was wary of Tilda Conroy's involvement but without police resources, they had no choice.

"No."

The questions were beginning to frustrate him. Craine felt a sense of urgency Lansky didn't share. "What about my son? Please. I want to know he's okay."

The phone went quiet. Kastel came back on the line.

"I told you, yes or no answers only."

"No more games. You tell me he's alright."

"Hand me over to Abe. Now."

Craine moved his head away from the receiver and Abe took it from him. He heard him muttering into the phone with his back turned. "Yes. Everything is good," he muttered. And then a look at Craine, "No, no one."

He knew Kastel was asking him if anyone else was involved. He wondered why Abe was protecting him. But before he could dwell on it, Abe frowned. "What package?" he asked, his eyes widening. There was something unsettling in the force of his reaction.

The package.

Abe called after him but Craine had entered a trance. He went back over to the desk, where the girl at reception was already expecting him.

"Mr. Craine." She smiled courteously. "Your package—it arrived this afternoon."

It was an envelope, but it wasn't flat. There was something soft inside. The writing across the front was a childlike scrawl. His name and the name of the hotel. The stamp said Bridgeport.

Craine felt suddenly sick, but by now Abe was running over.

"Craine, don't open it. Craine."

Craine had arched his back and was walking to the exit, the envelope clutched close to his chest. Abe was almost upon him. "Please, Craine. Don't open it."

Ignoring him, Craine's trembling hands tore at the seal. He ripped open the manila paper and looked inside.

He might have gasped but the noise that came out of his mouth wasn't so easily described. Later he wouldn't remember whether he'd fainted then or if Abe had simply grabbed hold of him, but he recalled feeling weightless, his legs no longer able to hold him up.

"It's alright," Abe said into his ear as Craine's face creased in all directions. "They're the ones from before. It doesn't mean anything. No one's touched him. They're trying to scare you. That's all. It doesn't mean anything."

But the dusty finger ends inside the envelope meant everything to Craine. There was no way they couldn't.

They buried the envelope at Westwood Village Memorial Park a few miles west of the hotel. It was the cemetery where Craine's wife was laid to rest, and he pulled at the turf around her grave until he'd made a hole deep enough. It was the only thing that seemed right in that moment, but seeing her headstone only made things worse.

Celia Raymond. Loving Wife and Mother.
1904–1938

He'd lost a wife to this city and now it threatened to take his son, too.

Craine put his head in his hands and covered his eyes. And then they were shut.

And he was there. *The funeral.*

January, 1939. There were a few words said but no readings. She had no eulogy. Not because she didn't deserve one. He simply couldn't bring himself to speak of her.

He and Michael had stood on either side of this headstone. They didn't look at each other. Didn't share a word. Michael didn't shed a single tear. An eight-year-old. Able to contain his grief in that moment. The strength that would take. The bravery. There was no doubt who was the better man.

Burying his wife was the worst day of Craine's life. But not because of Celia. It was because once the coffin was lowered and the ground covered in soil, he'd driven his son back to boarding school. They didn't talk about what had happened. Didn't speak of any of it. Craine left him at the school gates with nothing more than a cursory wave. Michael watched as Craine turned around and drove away. He wouldn't see him again for four months.

The shame of that parting had never left him. Of abandoning a small child mourning for his mother because he was too selfish to share his grief. He'd never forgiven himself for it. Couldn't even begin to.

Michael was mute for much of that year. The voice that later returned was different from the one before. Changed forever. Not any deeper. Only quieter. He would never be the talkative child he'd been growing up. Now every word came only when needed. And every one was dripping with sadness.

They didn't grow close through talking. Or through sharing. It happened slowly, over time. Being in each other's company. Helping each other. Craine would help with homework. Michael would give a hand on the farm. It was a project they shared, and every year it developed they grew closer. They both knew the farm was their memorial for Celia. And neither of them left it for any longer than was necessary.

Staring then at his wife's gravestone, Craine knew. That when Michael talked of joining the army Craine wasn't only worried about losing him to war. He was worried about being left alone.

It was dark by the time they left, and Abe drove them to a diner in Downtown, around the corner from the Bradbury Building.

Electric fans were a nice respite from the night heat, even if Craine wasn't really hungry. He ordered a club sandwich and a cup of coffee but it sat mostly untouched as Abe worked through several plates of meat loaf. It was a diner he used to go to with Michael before catching a picture, and in a strange way being there made him feel closer to him. Like he might come in any minute and ask if they were still serving apple pie.

"Doing okay?" Abe asked when their food arrived.

Craine didn't reply. Of course he wasn't okay. "We have nothing," he said despondently. "We're no closer to understanding who killed Siegel than when we left Vegas."

"What did Wilson say about the Bradbury? You think he's throwing you off his scent because he's guilty?"

"It wasn't Wilson." Craine sighed.

"You don't like the fact that a man in fancy clothes and a big house might also be capable of making arrangements."

Craine pushed his plate away.

"Their falling-out was a year ago. He wouldn't have waited this long. I know Wilson, and I can only imagine him doing something like that in a fit of rage, and no one stays angry that long." He looked at Abe and said pointedly, "Not everyone is as capable of killing as the people you work for."

Abe ignored him. After a few minutes' silence, he said, "So what's in the Bradbury? His office?"

"Probably nothing. We should be focusing on finding Charlie Hill."

"Harvey is working on it," he reassured him. "They'll get him, I'm sure of it."

Craine was frustrated: he was pursuing a lead that might go nowhere when the priority was tracking down the missing girl. But making jibes at Abe wasn't going to help him. For his sins, he was the only person helping him save Michael.

"I'm sorry about yesterday," Craine said, changing the subject. "Your gun."

Abe exhaled with what sounded like a strained sigh. "What were you going to do? Shoot me? Take me hostage?"

"All I care about is making sure my son is safe."

Abe tried to use a tone that said he was sincere. "Nothing good will come of you resisting this," he said. "There's no out. I'm not here to hurt you, Craine. I'm here to help."

"Are you? Because I feel like there are things I'm not privy to."

"Like what?"

"George Raft told me that he's going to Las Vegas on Friday."

Abe didn't nod, but his face said that didn't surprise him. He lit a cigarette from a pack he'd left on the table.

"What's happening on Friday, Abe? Why does Lansky want me to find Siegel's killers by Friday?"

Abe filled his huge chest with smoke. "They were close. Friends."

"That's not enough. What's happening on *Friday* that's so important?"

Abe raised a finger and signaled for coffee. When the woman behind the counter was out of earshot he said, "Lansky is meeting potential buyers. He wants to put on a good show."

"Who are these buyers?"

Abe didn't respond, so Craine said, "Abe, Lansky said that you'd help me with my enquiries. Well, this is something I need to know."

The large man flicked ash on the table. "People are flying in from different cities. I'm sorry, Craine, but it's not relevant. I told you, it's not our organization that's responsible. So focus your attention on this Bradbury thing. And you need to be careful talking to that reporter. I didn't say anything, but if Lansky finds out that we gave her Smiley he could get mad."

"We both told Smiley not to give his name or any details about your organization."

Abe scratched his bulbous nose. In this light Craine could see it had been broken several times at the bridge. "Still. It's asking for trouble."

"Abe, I understand you're trying to be discreet. But Conroy has information that could really help me. Help *us*."

Craine emphasized that last word. It was a way of telling Abe that he was involved in this too, now. He wasn't merely Craine's driver. He was part of this investigation.

"The police—"

"Are not going to be involved."

Craine appealed to his reason. "It's the F.B.I. who are leading this investigation. They've pushed the L.A.P.D. to one side. Which means we could persuade them to help us—"

"There will be no contact," Abe grunted. "Most of Dragna's men have been arrested at different times. They're not going to want us to have anything to do with the L.A.P.D. I don't trust cops. At all. None of us do."

"I was at the L.A.P.D. for ten years, Abe."

"Yeah, but you were on the pad, weren't you? Not a real detective. A hatchet man, like me."

He stubbed out his cigarette. Any compassion he'd shown to Craine had passed as quickly as it had arrived.

"Come on," he said. "Building will be empty by now. Time to go."

CHAPTER 20

It was after nine when they got to the Bradbury Building. Abe had wanted to break in but Craine was insistent it would only draw attention from the police. Instead they tapped on the gated doors, where a security guard in his sixties ran a flashlight over each of them in turn. Ten dollars and the promise that they were Pinkertons was enough to convince him to let them inside.

Despite its low-key exterior, the building had an extensive Victorian atrium with a glass skylight five stories above. There were six offices on each floor, all surrounding the central foyer.

"You have the keys to the offices?" Abe asked the security guard when they'd emerged through a brass swing door into the lobby. In front of them was a marble staircase with wrought iron railings projecting in every direction. It reminded Craine of an Escher painting.

"'Course I do. I'm the night guard. Gotta have the keys."

The building was dark, sparsely lit by a line of dim wall lights. Craine blinked, letting his eyes adjust. He had to squint to read the names of the offices on the board in the foyer. None of them said *Nevada Projects Corporation.*

"Mr. Siegel's office is on the fourth floor," the night guard said to him. "I'll take you up."

"What kind of businesses you got here?" Abe asked the old man as they crossed the tiled floors toward a birdcage elevator.

The night guard swayed as he walked, like he'd just stepped off at port and was still finding his land legs. His skin, clothes and hair reeked of old alcohol. "I dunno." He shrugged. "Insurance companies, real estate, import-export. All types."

When Craine was last here, it mostly housed offices for prominent doctors and dentists. Rita Hayworth was a big star now, but Craine remembered her as a teenage Margarita Carmen Cansino. Columbia Pictures thought she looked too Spanish and exotic, so they anglicized her name, dyed her hair red and put her through electrolysis to raise her Latina hairline. Craine had to come here once when one of the doctor's assistants had started talking to the press. A hush job. He thought about what Abe said when he'd called him a hatchet man. It was true—he'd never been a real detective.

"You been a private investigator long?" the night guard enquired when he'd shut the elevator cage and pulled the manual lever.

Abe humored him. "Most of my life."

"You ever take photographs of cheating wives?"

"All the time."

"What about cheating husbands?" he asked apprehensively.

"That's my specialty," Abe said.

The old man looked worried. He rubbed his scalp. "Only, most people who visit Mr. Siegel's office aren't like you."

Craine wasn't sure what he meant by that. "Who are they, then?"

The night guard shrugged. "A.F.T.R.A., and S.A.G."

Abe said, "Sack?"

"*S.A.G.*," he corrected. "*Actors.* You know, like normal people but with the volume turned up. Mr. Siegel's offices are for the Extras Union."

Abe and Craine shared a look. This wasn't what they expected. What connection did a mob man have with an actors' union?

"You don't have offices for the Nevada Projects Corporation here?"

"No."

"Sure?"

"'Course I'm sure. I'm the night guard."

Craine followed this through. "How often was Siegel here?"

"He didn't come here very often. Still, I was sad to hear about him being killed. I guess when you're friendly with gangsters . . ."

"When was the last time you saw him?"

The old man picked his nose. "Oh, I'm not sure when exactly."

"Days, weeks or months ago?"

"Months, I guess. No wait, last week. No wait, it was last month. Hundred percent."

An exchange of glances. Abe looked like he could slap their new friend, and Craine would have given him his blessing.

They reached the fourth floor and the night guard led them toward an office in the corner. It was after business hours and most of the lights were off. Another line of dim wall lamps cast ghoulish shadows through the filigree ironwork.

Thumbing a key from a jailer's ring set, the night guard opened a pair of double doors into an office suite.

The interior office had a backlit glow. Brown bookcases lined the walls, but it was mostly empty, with desks and telephones that looked completely unused.

At the back of the room was a smaller office. Stenciling on the glass said TREASURER.

"Mr. Siegel's offices. He's the Treasurer, I believe."

Treasurer. Benjamin Siegel was a man of many trades, Craine thought. Treasurer wasn't one he expected.

Craine asked, "Do you have the key?"

The old man's eyes turned up to the right. "No, not to this office."

Abe raised an eyebrow. "You said you had a key?"

"I said I have a key to the office suites," he said, gesturing to the door they'd come through into this corridor. "I don't have a key to his private office. Never have."

"Jesus Christ," Abe muttered.

"No need to be getting hostile with me. I'm only the night guard."

Abe started to say something before Craine held his hand out. He took the night guard's flashlight and probed the beam against the door.

"The door's been kicked in," he said with a sinking feeling.

All of them stopped talking.

Abe took out his pistol and Craine suddenly felt like he wanted one too. He'd never much liked carrying a weapon. But the odd occasion you needed one tended to make up for the others.

Abe padded closer to the door. He peered quickly through the glass and, when he was sure the room was empty, pushed through and went inside.

Streetlight from the window came in sideways though the blind slats. It was enough to see that the office had been ransacked.

"We're too late," Craine said. "Someone's gone through the place."

The guard stared at the mess and scratched at his scalp. "Oh, dear Lord." He let a second pass and then added, "Janitor doesn't come till the morning. Better not expect me to sweep this up."

Craine could sense Abe raising argument, but stopped him. He addressed the night guard. "Who else has access to the building?"

"Everyone who works here has their own key."

"When was the last time someone came in here?"

He looked put-upon. "Hard to say."

"Estimate."

"I was here the whole time," he said with little enthusiasm.

The search had been clumsy. The filing cabinet was about the only thing still vertical. Everything else had been upturned, opened and emptied. There was no way the night guard wouldn't have heard.

To the old man he said, "There's no way men got in here tonight without you hearing. Must have taken an hour to turn this place over."

The night guard didn't look at them. He backed toward the door. "I don't know what you're talking about."

Abe pointed his Savage at him, lifting it to the man's eyes. "Stop bullshitting us."

The man put his hands over his eyes. "Are you really Pinkertons?"

"We work for the mob," Abe said.

"You're lying to me."

"He was lying to you before," Craine said. "Now he's telling the truth."

The old man took a step back with such a dramatic turn that Craine half-expected him to clutch his chest and fake a heart attack.

"I don't know what you want. I can't help you—"

"Yes, you can."

"I'm only the night—"

Abe cut him off. "*The night guard.* We remember. Start talking. My arm's getting tired."

The old man danced every time the pistol wagged in his direction. "A man came at seven," he blurted out. "Gave me twenty dollars and told me to take a few hours off. I'd been here twenty minutes when you two rolled up."

Craine was tempted to grab him and shake him. Instead he said, "Who was he?"

"I don't know."

Abe stepped closer. The man froze.

"I'm telling you, I don't know. He didn't give his name. Could have been anyone. Was dressed like you."

Ignoring him, Craine ran the flashlight over the floor. He picked up different files spilled across the carpet. "Try and find anything with Siegel's name on it," he said to Abe. "Or the Nevada Projects Corporation."

Abe knelt and the two of them began to sift through the files. The old man loitered without helping. The effort of bending down seemed too much.

Different letters had different headers. Some had a Nevada logo on them. Some had 'Extras Union' written across the top. There were invoices, receipts and memo upon memo relating to God only knew what. But after ten minutes, Craine gave up. There were hundreds of papers here, thousands maybe. It would take days to go through every single one.

Abe stood up. "Loan sharks bust up a place like this," he mused. "Seems funny a burglar would."

Craine almost ignored him but then mulled that over. Abe was right.

"Why toss the room over?"

"What do you mean?"

Craine clarified: "When you search for something, you do it systematically. You move things to one side, go through them, then move on. This seems amateurish. Unnecessarily so. If they'd have wanted accounts they would have taken all of them. Why throw the files everywhere?"

Their conversation was interrupted by a hum from outside. Mechanical movement.

"What's that?"

They followed the night guard back through the office to the fourth-floor landing, where the wall lights gave them an oblique view of the central atrium.

There was a clank and a whir. The sound of oiled metal moving, and then they could hear the elevator sheave on the top floor begin turning. Craine squinted and saw the counterweight drop and one of the metal birdcages on the ground floor begin to rise.

Someone was coming up.

The three of them stood in silence at the balustrades, staring into the darkness. The elevator was maybe fifty feet away.

Second floor. Third.

The cage elevator stopped on the fourth floor, exactly opposite. It was too dark to see through the metal grilles and the door wasn't visible from this side. *Was it empty?*

There was an echo from somewhere. It had a metallic edge to it.

Abe looked to Craine. "Is it police?"

"No." Police announce themselves. This wasn't the L.A.P.D.

They stood silent and motionless, each waiting for the other to move. In the end it was the night guard who moved first, pointing his flashlight in the elevator's direction.

"Who's there?" he said.

"Lower the flashlight," Abe said.

"He's right. Put it down." Craine put a hand on his arm but the old man pulled it away.

"I got a right to do what I want. I'm the night guard," he said, waving his flashlight. He had his free hand on his gun belt, groping at the butt of a revolver that looked like it hadn't been used in twenty years.

"Who's there?" he said again, but as he did so two of his teeth seemed to fall out of his mouth with most of the contents of his head. Then the bullet report came to them like a match strike a split second after.

The building echoed. The old man fell sideways, landing on the tiles with a heavy thud. There was a moment of confusion, as if neither of them were exactly sure what had happened, and then Craine and Abe dropped to the floor.

More bullets followed, separating the air. Office windows behind them cracked, then blew inward. Craine swore but it came out as a rush of loose vowels. *This is it*, he said to himself.

Craine looked to Abe and saw his mouth was moving. He was trying to tell him something but Craine couldn't hear it over the blood throbbing in his ears.

It took a long time for his adrenaline to wipe away the shock and give his body what it needed, and then everything came back in a sudden surge, bringing his senses alive.

"I said, are you hit?" Abe was shouting. He had the Savage in his hand. He cocked it and pulled the hammer back.

Craine's face was warm. There was blood on his face but it wasn't his. He wiped his cheeks with his sleeve.

"I'm okay," he may or may not have said out loud.

Abe didn't reply. He was scanning the atrium for any sign of movement.

Craine could see the night guard lying on the floor, emitting a fleshy moan. He tried to crawl over to him but there was blood everywhere and his elbows and feet slid uselessly on the tiles. When he finally reached him he could see the old man's chest was rising and falling, blood spurting out with each gurgled breath. He was groping at life.

Craine put his hands round the night guard's throat and felt the artery pumping blood through his fingers. In the darkness it felt like warm water spraying from a faucet leak.

"Help me . . ." the man was gasping. "I'm dying, I'm dying, I'm dying." And then with a choked whimper, "I'm sorry, Marie. I'm so sorry . . . I don't want to die."

Craine tried to locate the burst artery. Found it. Pinched his fingers hard, trying to stem the blood flow, but by now the old man had stopped talking.

Another shot came and he recoiled, the man's blood lacing across his face as his fingers loosened. Craine tried to concentrate, knowing that this man would die in the next thirty seconds if he didn't stop the bleeding.

Abe was in a crouch now; he cut along the edge of the balcony and scrutinized the empty blackness with his pistol. Straight-backed, assured, the pistol seemingly homing in on danger. He was acting unthinking.

He glanced toward Craine. "He's over there. Do you see him?"

Craine picked up the direction in his eyes. He wanted to stand but his knees were shaking too hard. He kept his hand on the old man's neck as he tried to look for the shooter. His eyes darted in different directions; he saw movement where there wasn't any.

A loud bang and the building lit up. Craine's position suddenly felt very exposed. Bullets splashed across the darkness, two or three sparking off the scrollwork a few inches away from Abe.

"Get the gun," Abe shouted, firing back with remove. "Get the guard's gun."

With one hand tight around the old man's neck, Craine unholstered his snub-nosed revolver. The grip was warm and wet with blood. Turning, he used his thumb to pull the hammer back and pointed it toward the darkness.

Abe was scanning the atrium. From his vantage point he couldn't get a shot. He shifted sideways and fired. Sparks came off the railings.

He fired again. The noise was disorienting, like you couldn't tell where the fire was going to or coming from. But in the strobe light, Craine saw a silhouette moving down the balcony to the staircase.

"He's on the third floor," Craine said. He straightened the night guard's pistol and aimed at the moving figure.

"If you see him, shoot, goddamit," Abe shouted.

Craine pressed his forefinger against the trigger but didn't fire. He felt a cold chill like he'd entered a locker plant.

"I can't see him," he said half-convincingly.

A second later and the gunman disappeared, swallowed by the darkness. There one moment, gone the next.

Craine dropped the revolver and listened for the night guard's breath. Air was bubbling out of him but otherwise he was silent. From downstairs there was the sound of footsteps echoing against the tiles as the shooter made his way to the ground floor. The firing had stopped.

Seconds passed. Then minutes. They remained stock-still in the darkness, ears pricked for sounds of movement.

Nothing.

Abe cautiously leaned over the balustrade and stared up and down the staircase. After what seemed like an age, he came over in a crouch. "He's gone."

"Are you sure?"

"I'm sure. But we have to go," he said, composed but firm. "Police will be here any minute. Grab as many files as you can and let's get out of here."

Craine looked to the night guard. His remaining teeth were chattering together like pebbles. His windpipe sounded like a paper bag blowing in the wind.

Craine gave Abe a defiant look. "He's still breathing."

"He won't be much longer."

An understatement. In the half-light, Craine could see the old man's eyes had turned up, already clouding over. He was in the final death throes.

"We can't leave him here," Craine said, drawing in short, shocked breaths. "He's dying."

Abe grabbed him by his jacket. Craine went to protest but he lacked the strength to argue with him. The old man's body had stopped moving. His heart was no longer pumping and what blood there was, was already cooling. Craine felt something in him sink.

Abe looked at the night guard, then at Craine. "He's dead," he said.

CHAPTER 21

Craine drove them back to the hotel, Abe in the passenger seat, reloading his Savage pistol in case they were followed.

It had been years since Craine had driven through L.A., but he pushed through the gears as fast as he could, trying to remember the quickest route back to Beverly Hills. It was after eleven now and the roads were empty, nothing to disturb them on their way but potholes chafing against the tires.

"He was definitely dead, wasn't he?" Craine asked, his mind questioning itself.

"He was dead."

The answer didn't satisfy him. He needed to debate it. "We should have waited. Called an ambulance."

"For what, Craine?" Abe said a little testily. "He was dead, I told you. No good would have come from waiting around for the police to arrest us."

Craine kept driving but it wasn't until they reached West Hollywood that he noticed Abe was clutching his arm.

"What is it?"

Abe gritted his teeth. "Nothing."

Craine saw something glisten on Abe's shirt. Blood. "You're shot? Jesus."

"Caught my shoulder. I didn't even notice at first."

Abe brought his hand out and Craine could see it was slick with blood.

"We have to get you to a hospital."

"No hospitals." Abe was adamant. "Police will be all over the building by now. They'll have an A.P.B. out within the hour."

"You need a doctor."

The big man winced with the pain. "No. Get me back to the hotel. We'll take care of it. Dragna will have somebody."

"Keep pressing on it." Abe looked at him like Craine was speaking the obvious. Clearly this wasn't the first time this had happened. "What was that back there? Felt like an ambush."

"I think whoever ransacked the place saw us go in."

"Which means they want to stop us from piecing together their motive. Whoever killed Siegel didn't do it for personal reasons. Lansky's wrong. You don't sneak up through someone's garden with a rifle unless it's an assassination. Now whoever did it wants to make sure we don't find out why."

But Abe wasn't listening. He took a deep breath and tilted his head back like he was falling asleep.

Craine was starting to worry he'd slipped unconscious when Abe muttered, "You could have fired back."

"What?"

"I saw you. You had a moment you could have fired but you didn't."

Craine thought about answering but Abe had already turned his head away. Besides, a part of him knew Abe was right. Craine had got buck fever when it mattered most. But it wasn't the fear of dying that had stopped him. It was the fear of killing.

There was some kind of party going on at the hotel; press hounds were huddled outside taking photographs of young ingénues in cocktail dresses and men in tuxedos as they slid into limousines and headed home. They were probably in their early twenties but looked like children playing grown-ups to Craine—middle age did that to you.

The valet didn't ask questions when they pulled up at the front steps, but Craine could see him notice his shirt was caked in blood when he opened the driver's door. Abe had his rain jacket draped over his shoulders, one arm pressing firmly into his shoulder underneath. His face was pale and clammy and the valet only had to take one good look at the passenger seat to notice the bloodstains on the upholstery. That was the thing about these types of hotels. You paid extra for discretion.

They entered the hotel's circular lobby and walked straight past reception to the elevators. The gala was in the Rodeo Ballroom but guests were cavorting in the lobby or running out toward the swimming pool. Flashbulbs popped as photographs were taken of different groups of celebrities. As they weaved through the party, Craine spotted comedians Al Jolson and Jack Benny cracking jokes, but they were too soaked with champagne to notice the two men dripping blood across the marble floor.

A waiter was wheeling a drinks trolley past them and Craine dipped his hand into the ice bucket, wiping the worst of the blood off his face. The cold water kept him alert.

Abe was becoming unsteady on his feet and Craine had to prop him up by the elbow. The weight of the man almost made him buckle.

As they reached the elevators, a woman wearing mink and diamonds walked past and frowned at them but she was looking too tipsy to care much.

Craine summoned the elevator and watched as the brass arrow above the doors crawled around the dial. Fifth floor. Fourth. Somewhere behind them a band was playing swing tunes. There was something faintly ridiculous about the two of them waiting here casually with blood at their feet as the tuxedoed throng around them whistled and cheered.

The elevator opened and Robert Mitchum and Henry Fonda stepped out. If they recognized Craine, they pretended not to. Craine managed to get Abe inside and pressed the button to their floor repeatedly until the door began to close.

A young couple came toward them, kissing and laughing, the elevator the only thing between them and their bedroom. The man grabbed the elevator door before it shut but as he did so he noticed blood on Craine's shirt and looked at him. The girl caught sight of Abe slumped inside the elevator and let out a tiny shriek.

"He's had a few too many," Craine said. "Best you get the next one."

There was a maid's trolley parked in the corridor on their floor and Craine grabbed several white towels before dragging Abe into their suite.

The big man practically keeled over as soon as they entered and Craine had to half-drag him across the tiles to his bathroom.

Inside, Craine lowered him onto the floor and propped him up against the bath. He took off Abe's jacket so he could see the full extent of the bleeding. The whole left-hand side of his shirt was shiny with blood.

Abe's breath had become raspy and uneven. Craine loosened his shoulder holster to help him breathe and the Savage clattered onto the bathroom floor.

There was a moment then that he realized this man was at his mercy. He could leave Abe here to die. Or grab the gun and shoot him. Craine had every motivation to hate this man, and yet for whatever reason he felt a sort of kinship with Abe. Or maybe he simply knew he needed his help if he was ever going to save Michael.

Craine went to pick up the Savage and then felt Abe's hand grab his wrist. He fixed Craine in a stare but his eyes were unfocused. Maybe he trusted Craine wouldn't kill him or maybe he no longer cared, but they both remained completely still before Abe's hand went slack.

"Call Harvey," Abe muttered. "He can send somebody."

"How do I get to him?"

But Abe's eyes were closed now. He started mumbling, "Is Joseph here? Where's Joseph? Did his ship leave already?"

Craine realized he was talking about his son. He wasn't sure what to say.

"Abe," he said softly, "I need you to tell me how to contact Harvey."

Abe was fast losing consciousness. Craine slapped him.

"Abe," he said. "Wake up. Abe."

Abe didn't respond, and Craine started to panic. "Abe," he said. "Tell me how to contact Harvey. Wake up, I need to know how to contact Harvey."

Craine's chest fluttered. He slapped Abe hard across the face again. When the big man didn't react, he slapped him twice more, harder now.

"Abe!"

Abe's eyes opened, startled.

"What? *Jesus,*" he slurred. It was almost as if he was drunk. "Stop hitting me, Craine. What do you want?"

Harvey Sterling arrived within the hour, by which time Craine had managed to stem the bleeding with towels. The bathroom floor was smeared with great brown arcs where he had made a poor effort to wipe up the blood. It lent a certain absurdity to proceedings.

"What took you so long?" Craine asked when he opened the suite door.

"Relax, Craine. I brought somebody to help."

Behind Harvey was a man with a medical bag who looked like he'd only recently been woken up.

"This is Dr. Fulton."

There was something vaguely recognizable about him, but Craine had felt that a lot the past few days.

"Take me to him," Dr. Fulton said without further introduction.

Craine led both men into the bathroom and Fulton wasted no time in getting to work. Without saying anything, he placed a stethoscope over Abe's chest and moved it from the heart to the lungs.

"Breathing is shallow," Fulton said. "But there's no bruit and no liquid in the lungs."

Nothing in the way the doctor acted implied this was new to him. From the relaxed fashion Harvey let him go about his work, Craine surmised this wasn't the first time he'd done this.

"What's his name?" Fulton asked.

Craine told him, and the doctor clicked his fingers in front of his eyes and tapped his face. "Abe, can you hear me? Abe?"

No reaction. Abe was unconscious.

"Help me take his clothes off."

Pressure from the towels had helped stem the blood flow, but now the blood had clotted and dried it clung to the fabric of Abe's clothes like glue. They had to peel his shirt and pants off of him.

Abe's figure was no less imposing in his underwear. There were small pink and brown scars dotted across his chest like cigar burns; he had a looping knife welt that ran from the bottom of his rib cage to the center of his belly. Craine thought of the brazen way Abe had faced the gunfire tonight; it crossed his mind that Abe was the type of man who might in other circumstances have been a war hero and not a hired killer.

Fulton examined the entire body with his fingers before focusing on the bullet wound itself. It was like a side of raw beef open to the bone.

As the doctor worked, Harvey lit one cigarette from another. His face betrayed nothing. Like this was any other night.

Dr. Fulton took his time, working through a routine, speaking as if an assistant was taking notes: "Looks like a ricochet," he said. "Single entrance wound to lower deltoid. No damage to underlying structure. Wound is relatively clean, considering. No gunpowder embedded, no damage to anything but tissue immediately surrounding the wound."

Finally, he addressed the others directly. "Help me move him onto his side."

They heaved Abe sideways and Fulton examined his shoulder blades.

"Bruising located at the rear of the trapezius muscle but no exit wound. No bone fracture and no interior bleeding either. The bullet avoided major nerves and blood vessels. He's a lucky man."

Nothing felt very lucky about the last few days.

"You can lay him flat again."

They lowered Abe onto his back, using towels to prop his head up. Craine could hear Abe's internal organs bubble and groan but his facial features were still.

"He's lost some blood," Fulton said. "He won't need a transfusion, but I'll set him up with an I.V. I'm going to clean and dress the wound, but that's about as much as I can do."

"He'll be okay?" Craine asked.

"Look at him," Fulton said, for the first time revealing his human side. "It'll take more than a bullet to the shoulder to finish him off."

"No exit wound?" Harvey asked. "You mean the bullet is still in there?"

Fulton nodded but didn't take his eyes off the wound. "The projectile is resting in the muscle mass. Removal is harder than it looks, particularly given our current"—he looked at the pile of bloody towels—"circumstances. We risk too much injury to the surrounding tissue. If we leave it, the projectile should work its way toward the surface over the coming weeks. Or it'll get walled off and stay put. It's not doing any damage where it is."

Dr. Fulton stood up and laid out different items from his medical kit on the bathroom countertop. They left him to clean and dress the wound and went into the other room.

Harvey poured them both drinks, then asked in detail what had happened at the Bradbury Building, each time circling back to what the shooter looked like.

"I didn't see him," Craine said.

"What about Abe?"

Craine sipped at his glass and his throat burned.

"No. As I said, it was dark. It could have been anyone."

"You said there was a security guard. Could he identify him?"

Craine was staring at his whiskey, deep in thought. His mind kept replaying the shootout over and over. He felt sick about what happened. There was an image of the night guard's desperate last breaths he couldn't get out of his head. He kept thinking about him calling out for help. Could still smell his irony blood. "He's dead," he said.

By now the police would be at the Bradbury Building. They'd find the night guard outside the ransacked office. Chances were they wouldn't connect it to Siegel until the morning, but as soon as Captain Henson heard about it he'd join the dots. Craine thought about the night guard again and wondered if he had any family and if they'd been notified.

"I think it was Charlie Hill," Harvey said. "We got a lead he's been spotted in Downtown. He never left Los Angeles."

A tingle of hope. "Can you find him?"

"Leave it with me," Harvey said. "I've got all my guys on it."

After maybe thirty minutes, Fulton came out of the bathroom, drying his hands with the last of the clean towels.

"He needs to change the gauze daily. I've left some antibacterial drops he should apply morning and night." The doctor opened his case and held up a small glass bottle. "These for the pain. Two, four times daily."

"What should I do with him?"

"Leave him in there. I've set him up with a saline drip, but you should cover him with blankets. Keep him warm."

"Will he be okay?"

"If he wakes up in the morning, almost definitely. If not, he's probably dead." He gave a dry smile. "But I feel good about this one."

When they got to the door of the suite Harvey said he'd be in touch. Dr. Fulton didn't go to shake Craine's hand, but he did say, "You look pretty tired. You sleeping much?"

When Craine didn't reply he said, "If you need something, I have pills to help you sleep. Then a whole range of options so you're up and alert the next day, too." As if turning into a salesman, he added, "I do all the stars, you know."

And then Craine remembered where he'd seen him: outside the front of the hotel, guiding Judy Garland into the back of a private ambulance.

WEDNESDAY

CHAPTER 22

Craine spent the rest of the night going through the files they'd rescued from Siegel's office, hoping to find something relating to The Flamingo.

Clearing a space in the living room, he placed the papers in different piles according to company, date and subject matter. There were receipts for building works dating back two years. Planning applications and correspondence with contractors about cement. Requests to change architectural designs at late notice. Demands to import European furniture and hire internationally renowned chefs.

Within the piles of papers, Craine also found correspondence relating to Siegel's cover business, the Extras Union. At first he pushed them aside, separating the wheat from the chaff. But as the sheer number of bank receipts and transfers added up, Craine started to realize that these papers shouldn't be ignored. His focus on The Flamingo had distracted him. There was a different kind of paper trail here. One that connected Siegel's union to a range of studios across Hollywood. And the sums involved were considerable.

Before long, Craine had connected outgoing purchase orders from the Nevada Projects Corporation to invoices and receipts relating to the Extras Union. He circled several figures and dates. Last year, the union had amassed payments from the studios of almost $920,000. That very same amount had then been paid out to various contractors for The Flamingo Hotel.

Craine was no accountant but he went through the figures several times, checking invoice dates against each other until he was sure he was on to something. Because as far as he could tell, Benjamin Siegel was receiving large sums of money from motion picture studios and then using that money to fund his Vegas venture. But the key question remained: what were the studios paying him the money for?

At 4 A.M. Craine checked on Abe. The man's breathing had settled into a deep rhythm and there was more color in his cheeks.

He went back into the living room and poured himself another drink. His mind began wandering. The adrenaline of the past few hours was too much for his threadbare veins and he began to feel exhausted. He bent down to go through the papers one more time but before he knew it he was laid on the floor, his thoughts drifting from the present to the past few days. Michael. Kastel. The night guard. And then to the central question: *how did I find myself in this situation? Yes, of course. By my own actions all those years ago. All of this is my fault.* He blinked several times and then his eyes closed.

He dreamed of Celia's old movies. And then the movie was real and his dead wife was asking him over and over again why he'd let those men hurt their son.

You never stop feeling a failure when you hurt someone to despair.

When Conroy arrived at the office that morning, Alice was waiting for her by the elevators.

"You need to go to the briefing room. Right now."

As she spoke the City Editor opened the briefing room door and beckoned her in. Behind him was Captain Henson in full dress uniform. But it was the second figure in the room that concerned her. The man in the charcoal-gray suit and black tie. F.B.I. Agent Redhill.

Henson didn't waste any time when they'd sat down at the briefing table. There weren't any pleasantries, introductions or even explanations. He cut straight to the point.

"Last night there was a shooting at the Bradbury Building. Do you know anything about it?"

"No," Conroy said truthfully. "Was anyone hurt?"

"A night guard was shot and killed outside of one of the office suites on the fourth floor. Looked like a robbery."

Conroy wasn't sure what this could possibly have to do with her. "Thank you for letting us know," she said. "We'll write up the story in time for the evening extra."

"Don't be smart with me, Mrs Conroy."

Conroy looked at Redhill, then back to Henson. "Does the F.B.I. typically investigate robbery-homicides?"

Henson answered for both of them: "The office belonged to the Extras Union. Unbeknown to us it was owned by one Benjamin Siegel."

He let his words rise and then fall in the air. The mention of Siegel was important. *Was Craine involved at all?*

"I had no idea."

"Really? Is anything I'm saying sounding familiar to you?" he asked.

"No. Nothing."

"Because I should warn you that sitting on evidence—"

"She's answered the question," the City Editor said.

Henson seemed angry with Conroy. Like he'd taken this as a personal slight. "I can subpoena you if necessary. Both of you."

Conroy looked to the City Editor. He nodded to her in a way that said he was in her corner.

"I don't know anything about this shooting. The first I heard of it was less than a minute ago. From you."

Redhill spoke up. His voice was low, with a Midwest accent. "Captain Henson has informed me that you've been in conversation with a man called Jonathan Craine."

Conroy shrank in her seat. "We've spoken briefly."

"*Jonathan Craine?*" the City Editor said, speaking for the first time. "He doesn't work for the L.A.P.D. anymore, does he?"

"No," said the police captain. "But he's expressed interest in Siegel's murder. Hasn't he, Mrs Conroy?"

Tilda tried not to blush, but that was the thing about blushing—you didn't get to choose when and where it happened.

"He asked me a few questions. I assumed it was to do with his previous involvement with the extortion ring."

Redhill said, "We believe Craine may be working on behalf of Siegel's mob associates to disrupt our investigation."

So it was true, Conroy thought. *Craine was working for the mob.* He didn't seem the type of man to work for violent gangsters.

"Have you been in contact with Craine since we last spoke?" This from Henson.

"No," she lied, hoping he couldn't read her eyes.

Redhill stared at her, then looked to Henson. He nodded.

"Thank you for your cooperation," Henson said.

Both men stood up.

Redhill looked at the City Editor. Addressing the man in the room, he said, "Thank you for your time." He turned to Conroy, then nodded out of courtesy more than respect. "Mrs Conroy."

The City Editor waited until both men had cleared the floor before he started grilling her. Conroy explained everything she knew to date. She told him about Craine asking questions relating to Siegel; she told him about Siegel's connection to Wilson; she told him about the missing witness.

"Did you speak to Henson?"

"Yesterday."

"And what did he say?"

"Denied it."

"Then maybe Craine is wrong. You've got no corroboration, no witnesses to—"

"I got it corroborated. By Allen Smiley."

"Siegel's friend?"

She nodded. "He was there, confirmed that there was a girl at the house. He didn't know her name but she was with Charlie Hill. When the police came she was whisked away."

"By whom?"

"That's where it gets tricky. Potentially the F.B.I."

"*Potentially* the F.B.I.? Redhill will deny it unless we can get it backed up. Has Smiley told you about Siegel's political connections? Or his New York investors?"

"I'm building trust."

"Build it faster. I assume you got quotes."

Conroy's face squeezed together. "Nonattributable."

"God *dammit*." He banged his hand on the table. Hitting things was part of his personality but the briefing room was large and empty and the sound echoed. She knew why the City Editor was frustrated. It wasn't so much that he didn't trust her judgment as he'd have to justify to the board why a woman had been given carte blanche. This profile needed to be bulletproof.

Conroy had cut corners before. She didn't want to fall into that trap again. "I'm sorry, sir. We talked about terms of use and Smiley was adamant. He has a right to privacy."

The City Editor had refrained from smoking in the presence of the government men but now he lit up freely.

"Conroy, I want to bring on Teddy Kahn. He's covering H.U.A.C. and the union strikes. He's got good connections inside the agency."

Teddy Kahn was the *Herald*'s political correspondent. She'd worked with him before and found him arrogant and overbearing. "Wait, you can't kick me off."

"He's more experienced in these matters. You'd be staying across the story but in a lesser capacity."

"Sir, please. This is my story. I've been working on this for months. Smiley is *my* source. So is Craine."

"I don't care what they say, Jonathan Craine is a nobody that was once married to a somebody. Not enough to hang your coat on."

"You gave me this profile. I've got the sources, not Teddy Kahn."

The City Editor picked up a red pen and tapped it on the table so hard she thought it might break. Reporters used blue ink. Editors used red ink. It was a reminder of who was in charge.

"Fine. I'll give you two more days. But I'm not going to allow you to turn a murder case into a national story without attributable quotes.

Keep digging. But for God's sake be careful what you share with Craine. We don't know who he's working for."

Jonathan Craine woke with a gasp like he'd been drowning. There was the sound of banging on the door. Panic was quick to set in. *Maid service didn't knock like that.*

Slowly he rose to his feet, as if they might kick open the door at any minute. He'd put Abe's Savage on the glass coffee table and he picked it up and checked it was loaded. The chamber still smelt of cordite.

"Who is it?" he said quietly.

No answer.

Craine put the muzzle to the door and slowly turned the latch. Then in one quick movement he twisted the handle and opened the door an inch to see who was in the corridor.

Tilda Conroy.

"I brought coffee," she said chirpily. "You decent?" She frowned when she saw what he was wearing. He hadn't changed. His shirt was stained with dried blood and perspiration. She took a step back.

"Oh my God."

"It's not what you think."

"The Bradbury Building . . . did you kill that man?"

"No," Craine said.

She shrank further away from the door.

"Tilda, we didn't kill him. I promise. But someone else did. Now come inside."

When Craine ran through exactly what had happed at the Bradbury Building, Conroy seemed a little shocked. It did nothing to assuage Craine's guilt. She sat down on the sofa and kept checking over her shoulder like someone might be creeping up behind her.

"I need you to keep an eye on police reports," he said. "See if they run ballistics."

She thought for a moment. "I'll talk to my contacts. See if anything comes up that can be compared to Siegel's house."

"Different weapon," he said. "This man was firing a pistol, not a carbine."

"But you think it was the same man?"

"Logically, yes, but I can't be certain. I didn't get a positive I.D."

"And that pet bear of yours, he didn't see him either?"

"Abe? No."

Her eyes frisked him, looking from the blood on his shirt to his hands.

"That's the night guard's blood?"

He nodded, although it might have been Abe's. He wondered how soldiers could stomach it. Not just the stale irony smell. But forgive themselves for what they'd seen and done.

"When Captain Henson came this morning, he was with the F.B.I."

"Redhill?"

"Yes," she said. "They've realized the office was Siegel's and they asked me about you."

"What did you say?"

"As little as possible." She took a breath, then said, "They told me you're working for the mob. Is that true?"

Craine looked at his hands. The dried blood was peeling away but it was still there. *How could he deny it?*

"It's not how you think," he said.

They heard a sound and Abe came out through his bedroom door wearing one of the hotel bathrobes. 'Beverly Hills Hotel' was stenciled on his chest pocket. He'd drawn it tightly enough that you couldn't see the bandages.

Craine was almost relieved to see him up.

Conroy looked from Abe to Craine. "Wait, he's staying here too?"

Abe said, "Don't worry, I didn't hear anything."

"How you feeling?"

"Like I've got a helluva hangover." He sniffed the air. "Coffee smells good. Let's order breakfast."

Conroy's mouth was agape. Abe glanced at her, then picked up the phone. "I'm hungry as a bear."

It was almost amusing to see Abe and Conroy in the same room together.

Here was an educated woman, curious and bright and entirely unfamiliar to the caliber Abe was used to. He eyed her with suspicion, a foreigner he couldn't trust, and the feeling looked mutual. Abe's gravelly voice seemed to put Conroy on edge; Craine even noticed her visibly lean back whenever he spoke. It was like a Pit Bull and a Siamese making their acquaintance.

As Craine continued to work through the material he'd taken from the Bradbury Building, the other two went back and forth on who might be responsible for killing Benjamin Siegel. Everyone Bugsy had ever met or been associated with seemed to be a suspect. They debated and argued, accused and defended. They agreed on only one thing: they were no closer to knowing who had killed Siegel and why than they were two days ago.

"This wasn't on us," Abe insisted when Conroy returned to the idea that this was a mob killing. "I told you. We have hierarchy. We have rules."

Conroy was already shaking her head. "On what proviso?"

He looked at her like she was speaking in tongues.

She rephrased. "On what *basis*? Because the head of your outfit told you?"

Abe stared at his feet and shook his head. The very idea of talking to the press had bothered him immensely from the get-go and Craine knew allowing Conroy to be here made him uncomfortable. "It wasn't on our orders," he growled. "*Period*."

"So what if this wasn't sanctioned? There are a dozen reasons why they could have had him killed."

Craine had been silent up until now, poring over files, trying to separate them into piles. For the first time he lifted his head and said, "Actually there are usually five reasons people commit murder."

He had their attention. The room went quiet. Craine held up an open hand and counted them off. "Money, jealousy, revenge, protection or because you're being paid to do it. And that last one circles round to the others."

The other two stared at him and then at each other. They waited for Craine to explain.

"Money," he said, holding up the first finger. "Everyone assumes Siegel was killed because he was overspending on The Flamingo and owed his investors money. But if that's the case then we'd know about it because the investors would have needed Lansky's buy-in."

Conroy glanced at Abe. "You're both making a huge assumption."

"Agreed, but we can't return to it until the others have been ruled out. Which leads me to jealousy. That is, Siegel's other partner in the trade: Dragna."

"Jack Dragna? The gangster?"

"Dragna's wanted Siegel's business for years," Abe said, looking at Conroy suspiciously. "The race wires have huge value."

It would be easy not to credit Abe with much of a brain, but he had experience Craine and Conroy didn't have and with that came a level of knowledge that was crucial to this investigation. Craine only hoped he wasn't keeping things from them.

"But would he risk killing Siegel and taking what's his without approval from the New York syndicate?" Craine asked. "I'm not sure."

Conroy spoke up. "Who else? Chicago?"

"Wilson told me they were interested in Vegas years ago," Craine said.

Abe was steadfast. "There's been no war between Chicago and the L.A. or New York syndicates for ten years. And their leaders are all in prison. Even if they did send muscle to L.A. to kill Siegel, Dragna would have heard about it. You saw how quickly they knew we were in town."

"That doesn't preclude the possibility." When Abe looked at her blankly, she said instead, "They could have still done it."

As Abe mulled that one over, Conroy said, "What about revenge?"

"William Wilson," Craine said, counting off another finger. "Siegel strong-armed him into selling his shares at a price Wilson had no say over. But again, I'm not convinced."

"Would a newspaper guy really have the stones to kill a mob guy?" Abe said. He had a point. "What about his girlfriend, Virginia Hill? Maybe she got tired he was sleeping around."

"She's still a suspect," Craine said, nodding. "But I don't buy this as a crime of passion. And either way, she was out of town. So even if it was on her orders, we still need to find the shooter. And we still need to find the missing girl."

"I've got a lead on the shooter's car," Conroy said. Both men looked at her like she'd struck oil. "You were right. The F.B.I. are hiding something. Witness gave a partial description. I'm speaking to the D.M.V."

"And I'll speak to Harvey," Abe chimed in. "Remind him we need Charlie Hill."

Craine nodded, satisfied. Every lead counted. This felt like progress.

Conroy stirred. "So what are we left with?"

Craine held up his thumb. The fifth and final. "Protection."

"I don't get it," Conroy said. "Protection from what?"

"What if Siegel was killed because someone was worried about what he knew? We have someone ransacking Siegel's office. Someone willing to cover his tracks by killing us. And because of what?"

He passed invoices and receipts from the Extras Union between them. It had taken him hours to decipher exactly what they related to, but he wanted to demonstrate evidence.

Abe said, "What are these?"

"Payments from all the major motion picture studios," Craine explained. "Monthly bank transfers made directly into Siegel's account at the union. He then used that money to subsidize building The Flamingo."

"Because he was over budget?"

"Exactly. The paper trail isn't clear, but it's clear enough."

"I don't follow," said Conroy.

"What if Siegel wasn't killed over Vegas? What if he was killed because he was strong-arming the studios into paying him off? Say, for example, he'd picked up the reins from Frank Nitti and the Chicago Outfit."

Conroy frowned but she was nodding. "It's the same trick they tried years ago. Paying off union heads to avoid strikes. Ever since Nitti killed himself and his associates went to prison, the studios have had major union troubles."

Craine chimed in. "So maybe Siegel stepped in and decided to extort the studios himself. They pay him to get the unions back in control. He uses that money to fund The Flamingo, knowing he's way over budget and under pressure to complete from his investors."

Conroy said, "What you have here—this demonstrates the sphere of their influence. If they're getting payoffs from studios, it's not only Wilson they had leverage over. Siegel had several of the most powerful figures in Hollywood under his thumb."

"But why kill him?" Abe said.

Craine noticed Conroy tilt her head back. She ran through her train of thought. "Hoover has asked the F.B.I. to investigate communism in Hollywood. Maybe whoever was paying off Siegel suddenly got cold feet. Maybe they were worried the F.B.I. would realize what was happening. The timing isn't coincidence, there are private H.U.A.C. hearings this week."

Abe looked confused. "*Hew-ack?*"

"The House Un-American Activities Committee," Conroy explained. "They're looking at communist penetration in Hollywood studios. The whole town is riled up about it. The studio heads are all under intense scrutiny by the F.B.I. Mayer and Warner are being questioned at the Biltmore Hotel as we speak."

"Today?" Abe asked, and Conroy nodded.

"So the studios have reason to want Siegel out of the way," Craine said. "Which means that one of the major Hollywood studios could have arranged for Siegel to be killed," he added with finality, saying what they were all thinking.

Conroy looked at Craine. "What you're suggesting is very . . ." There were several words she could have said but didn't. *Contentious. Foolish. Dangerous.*

"I know," he said. "I'm not sure if this is the end of the string. Or the beginning of it."

Were men like Jack Warner and Louis Mayer above killing a man? Craine wasn't so sure. But he needed to find out.

The situation had shifted on its axis. They were no longer looking at Siegel's connections to Las Vegas or the criminal underworld as motive for his murder. They were looking at his ties to the motion picture industry.

CHAPTER 23

Louis B. Mayer was still ruminating over his divorce. Over what it had cost him to lose a wife, emotionally, professionally and financially. He was dwelling on the check he'd signed over to Margaret—the most expensive divorce settlement in history—when the chairman addressed him for the second time.

"Mr. Mayer," the chairman repeated, "I asked whether you have observed any communist infiltration into the motion picture industry since you've run M.G.M. Studios?"

Mayer's attorney nudged him. "Mr. Mayer?"

Mayer blinked and realized where he was. "Sorry, can you repeat that again for me?"

"Mr. Mayer, I'll remind you that this committee has the support of F.B.I. Director Hoover, who strongly believes that motion picture labor groups have been infiltrated, dominated or saturated with the virus of communism. I'm asking you whether you believe this to be true?"

Mayer cleared his throat and addressed the panel with his rehearsed answer. "Like others in the motion picture industry, I have maintained a relentless vigilance against un-American influences, and to the best of my knowledge I can't speak of any communist infiltration."

In a closed hearing at the Biltmore Hotel, Louis Mayer was facing a subcommittee of the House Un-American Activities Committee. An anti-communist fervor had swept the country and now it was aiming its sights at Hollywood. They'd been quizzing Mayer for almost two hours.

The chairman went on with his questions: "Several studios including yours have faced mass picket lines from the unions, which according to the stated intent of their leaders were designed to prevent by physical force anyone from entering the studios. Would you say that is an accurate assessment?"

"Yes, it is." Actually it was an understatement. Disney workers dressed as Mickey Mouse were picketing picture houses. Strikes at Paramount and Warner Brothers had broken out into full-scale riots. Mayer had used his own studio police force to break apart strikers only this week and then had his publicity team stop it from reaching the press.

"And have you encountered the same problems at M.G.M.?"

Mayer chose his words carefully. "We have faced only minor strike action in the past."

The jowly chairman asked, "Would you say strike action at M.G.M. was less problematic than at other studios?"

Mayer leaned forward and poured himself a glass of water. The Biltmore was where they typically held the Academy Award ceremonies each year, but this meeting had been held in one of their wood-paneled meeting rooms. He was seated at the end of a long, polished table directly across from the stenographer. He wondered if she was noting down how many gulps of water he was taking.

"Yes."

"And why do you think that is?"

Mayer wasn't sure how to answer. In truth, he'd brokered a Faustian pact with a certain underworld figure to ensure M.G.M. wouldn't face continued strike action. Frustratingly, that partnership had come to an untimely end last Friday.

"It would be difficult for me to say," he answered vaguely. "We cannot be responsible for the political views of each individual employee. And yet I do believe that M.G.M.'s values have always been inherently *American*."

The panel of three looked at each other, unsatisfied.

The hearing was interrupted by the door at the back of the room opening. Whitey Hendry, head of M.G.M.'s security, came in. He handed Louis Mayer a folded piece of paper; on it was a simple note scrawled in pen.

Room 736.

The man had scribbled his surname below.

Craine.

Mayer let out a deep sigh. So it was true: the prodigal son had returned.

Mayer whispered something to his attorney, who took the opportunity to address the committee: "This hearing has been in session for two hours," he said. "My client would like to request a short break."

Mayer shut the door very quietly when he entered, as if someone was asleep.

To Craine, Louis Mayer wasn't simply the head of the largest movie studio in the world. Their relationship was personal and complex. When City Hall had Craine act as their Hollywood liaison, it was Mayer who Craine worked with most often. Craine's own father had died when he was young and for a long time he looked for mentor figures. Louis Mayer was one of them.

Craine's wife Celia was an M.G.M. star and Mayer had always been there for them, the doting uncle who furthered both their careers, inviting them to family parties, helping them buy a house and even sending his own private doctor when Michael contracted measles as a child. So naturally, Craine had spent years trying to pay him back in some way, looking for his approval. It was like his self-esteem was factored around pleasing him.

But like his real father, there was a lot unsaid between the two men. When Celia became addicted to opiates, Mayer suddenly and without warning canceled her contract. She'd killed herself a few days after, and with Mayer's encouragement, Craine had pretended to the public that it was an accident. That she'd overdosed and slipped in the bath. He'd never forgiven himself. And he'd never forgiven Mayer either.

"You look tired, Louis," Craine said when Mayer entered the hotel room. "Is it H.U.A.C. or the strike action that's wearing you down?"

Louis Mayer didn't take a seat, almost as if doing so would commit him to actually being here in this moment. *If I stand here, I can deny ever being in this room*, his body language said.

"These are closed hearings. It's not public knowledge I'm here."

"And yet I know."

It wasn't a coincidence that Craine had chosen a hotel suite. He could have gone to Mayer's house or even his office at M.G.M. But he wanted to meet Mayer in no man's land. Somewhere he wasn't comfortable.

"I can't talk long," Mayer said. "They want me back this afternoon. I told them I had a lunch meeting with Jimmy Stewart. Seems to be the only man in Hollywood not on their shit list."

Even in older age Mayer was not a quiet individual. Bombastic. Animated. Colorful. But somehow he didn't seem himself. Like the fire in his eyes had petered out.

"I heard a rumor you were back," Mayer went on. "I didn't really believe it. 'No,' I said, 'Jonathan Craine is retired to the middle of nowhere raising pigs.'"

Mayer noticed the sheaves of paper Craine had left on the bed. They were upturned but it didn't stop Mayer from staring at them.

"Do you know why I'm here?"

"If I knew why you were here I probably wouldn't have come." Mayer stood square to face him. His hands were by his sides in tight fists. "I suppose some studio is scared their writer or actor is getting thrown under the bus. That's it, isn't it? You're back on payroll."

"This isn't about the hearings. I'm not working for any studio or the L.A.P.D. I haven't worked for them in years."

Mayer's eyes wrinkled, struggling to suppress his surprise. He almost looked relieved. "You have my attention, now what do you want?"

Craine got to the point. "A New York businessman called Meyer Lansky asked me to find out who killed Benjamin Siegel."

"*Lansky* asked you to look into Siegel's murder?"

Mayer looked somewhere between perplexed and amused. He had the advantage, and he enjoyed it.

"The head of the New York mob asked the pig farmer to find out why his man in California was killed?"

"The press are pointing fingers at his organization. Lansky doesn't want the attention. Particularly from the F.B.I."

A frown split Mayer's brow in two. "Did he seriously believe you were once one of L.A.P.D.'s finest? Even before the war you could hardly call yourself an investigator, Craine. You were a journeyman policeman at best. Now you're the underworld's best boy."

Craine had no intention of rising to Mayer's bait. He'd be happy to suspend his ego as long as Mayer kept talking.

"They've asked me to find out who killed Siegel. That's all."

"Then why am I talking to you in a hotel room, Craine, when downstairs I'm supposed to be in a hearing that threatens to arrest half the actors and writers on my lot? I'm Julius Caesar, turning to face down my enemies before they can stab me in the back. Bugsy Siegel is hardly top of my agenda."

"No, but it'll be top of *their* agenda when they see your name in the *Herald* this week."

Mayer waved his hand in the air. "I didn't associate with Siegel," he said evasively. "I didn't invest in his Vegas ventures and I never went to his hotel."

"But you did know him. Very well."

Mayer glanced at the bed. "You have something—lay it out. I have nothing to hide."

Craine turned over the papers, revealing a sample of the account files he'd found at Siegel's office. Mayer scrutinized them, his short fingers pushing them over the bedcovers. It wasn't his shoulders that fell but his whole body.

"It'll never make the press. City Hall won't touch me."

"Maybe. But would the committee like to know that you were paying off Bugsy Siegel for years to avoid union trouble?"

Some silences were hard to read. Not this one.

"I told you, this is a closed hearing."

"And yet there are photographers and reporters lining up outside the hotel. Besides, rumor is they'll be public hearings in a few months. Paying off the West Coast press is one thing. But the fourth estate isn't so easily swayed in New York and Washington."

Mayer gave Craine a sulky look. "What is it you want to know? Siegel—he was a gangster. A *mob* man. What does it matter who killed him? *I* didn't."

"There are people out there who want to know who killed their friend. And so far, I'd say this here is enough to give you motive for doing so."

"*Bullshit.*"

"You were paying off Siegel to keep your unions quiet. If H.U.A.C. ever found out, Hoover would personally close down M.G.M. It's *enough.*"

Mayer tested the bed with both hands as if to sit on it, but didn't. He was unstill.

"It wasn't like that," he said. "After Frank Nitti killed himself, Siegel must have been in my office two weeks later. I had no intention of doing business with him."

"But you did."

The older man exhaled. "Everyone is worried about the communists. I needed a way of keeping my unions stable. This hearing—it's only the beginning. Like you said, it's going public and it's going national."

"I've spoken to Billy Wilson."

"Then you know what the *Enquirer* has been saying. And it's got H.U.A.C. in a stir. Now their attention is on the studios. It's not about the pictures. None of my productions could ever be labeled red propaganda. But they want public figures to make examples of."

"Your stars?"

Mayer nodded, raking his hand through thinning hair. His face tilted away into memory. "The morass we've found ourselves in. It threatens to shut us down completely."

"So Siegel offered a solution?"

"It wasn't a decision I took lightly." Mayer almost seemed to be justifying it to himself. "I had no interaction with him on a day-to-day basis. I loaned him money, that's all. Plenty of other people loaned him money. The only difference was, we all knew we weren't getting it back."

"And in return he used his influence to keep the unions in check?"

Mayer nodded. "That was the limit of our engagement. It was worth it to keep Hoover off my back. At least before all this H.U.A.C. nonsense. Oh, the *irony*." He looked at Craine. "I've had dealings with men I wished I hadn't before, we both know that. But I had nothing to do with Siegel's death and that's the end of it. You've got nothing on me but a few account receipts."

Mayer was right. There was no smoking gun. No conclusive evidence. No persons caught in flagrante.

"Why did you ally yourself with the underworld, Louis? After what happened before?"

Even though both men knew Craine would have more, Mayer went through the papers and then rolled them up. He had no intention of anyone seeing them. And he had no intention of saying anything else.

"I could ask you the same question," he said, moving to the door.

Craine had been unsure whether to tell Mayer about Michael. But the history between them had to mean something. "They have my son."

Mayer had one hand on the door handle. He didn't turn around when he asked, "They have Michael?"

"Yes."

Mayer didn't say anything. He left the room.

* * *

Afterward, when he took a taxi back to Beverly Hills, Craine felt at a loss. He was too tired to be angry, but the truth was that all of his lines of enquiry had gone nowhere.

Craine could visualize Siegel's murder. He could see the shooter creeping up through the back garden and killing Siegel in his house. He could picture the weapon. He'd probably even come face to face with Siegel's killer last night.

But nothing had brought him any closer to understanding who that person was or what their motive for killing Siegel could possibly be.

There were only two potential leads remaining. The missing witness and the shooter's car. And Friday was only two days away.

When he got to the hotel, Abe answered. He was dressed now, his jacket in one hand, the Savage in the other.

"Harvey called," he said. "They've found Charlie Hill."

CHAPTER 24

Conroy's major break came a little before lunch, when Alice returned from the D.M.V. and handed Conroy a carbon sheet that went for several pages and was many hundreds of lines long. 'CALIFORNIA DEPARTMENT OF MOTOR VEHICLES' was written across the header.

"Blue and green vehicles," she said, flicking the paper with her finger. "Packard and Nash."

"Good work, Alice." Conroy scanned the list. She flipped through the pages and frowned. "Wait, there are too many here to count, let alone call."

Alice took a pencil and used it as a pointer. "But I've underlined the ones that were stolen in the last week. And I double-underlined the ones stolen Thursday or Friday. That leaves forty."

"Forty cars were stolen *last week*?"

"And that's not even unusual."

"That's still a lot of leads." Conroy was contemplating how long it would take to track down and call forty irate car owners when she remembered something from her conversation with Cay Foster. "Wait a second. What else did she say . . .?"

Conroy slipped a piece of candy in her mouth, then went through her notepad until she found what she was looking for.

"*Here.* She said the license plate was yellow."

Alice shrugged. "They're yellow this year."

"But she said the car wasn't new. It was prewar."

Alice didn't say anything so Conroy explained, "Until recently, license plates in California have been yellow letters on a black or blue background."

"Going back how long?"

"Well over a decade. But then in thirty-eight and forty the California Department of Motor Vehicles issued all-new license plates with black lettering on a yellow background. Which means our car is most likely a 1938 or 1940 model."

Alice bit the side of her cheek. "Explain that again for me. After you've made me another of those white-people coffees."

Twenty minutes later, Conroy and Alice had worked out that of the forty cars that were stolen in the last week, only fourteen were prewar. And only nine were '38 or '40 models.

It took less than fifteen minutes to work through the list between them. Of the nine, two didn't answer. Five of the remaining seven matched the description entirely, but only one of those was stolen the night before the shooting.

The owner was a Mr. Webb, and when they called his home number his wife answered. They could do a background check on the owner but nothing from their conversation suggested they might be complicit. Mrs. Webb was a mother of two and her husband worked as a technician for Warner Bros. He'd finished work late after filming and gone for drinks with members of the crew. As far as she was aware, the car was stolen from the parking lot of the bar at approximately 11 P.M. last Thursday.

Had he sold it to the shooters? Possibly, but it felt unlikely. *And was he where he was when he said he was?* Maybe not, but in truth the details didn't really matter. In fact, the information they had suddenly seemed useless. They had details of the stolen car, including the age, model and license plate, but none of that was relevant if they couldn't find the car itself.

"We have a lot of information here."

"Yes," agreed Alice.

"But none of it gets us our automobile."

"No," agreed Alice.

Conroy tilted her chair back on its rear legs and popped another piece of candy in her mouth.

"You're the shooter," she mused. "You know you have a hot car. You haven't removed the plates and you know that the police might be looking for your vehicle. You commit a murder where you've driven right up to the target's address on a well-lit street. So what would you do with the car after? Would you keep it?"

"I could do with a new car," Alice said. "Mr. Hickerson's been promising to get us one since the war."

"Alice—"

"I guess I'd sell it or I'd dump it," she replied with a shrug.

"Exactly," Conroy went on, playing this theory out. "And anyone in Siegel's circles is unlikely to need the money. So they ditch it on the side of the road, or they drive it out of Los Angeles."

Alice was biting her lip. "Why take the risk it's spotted? You said yourself it connects them to the scene of the crime."

"What, then?"

"Take it to a car wrecker."

Conroy's stomach tightened with excitement. Alice picked up the telephone directory and pulled her telephone toward her.

"Is it 'S' for salvage or 'W' for wreckers?"

"Try 'A' for auto wreckers," Conroy said as Alice began flipping through the yellow pages. "And I'll make us fresh coffee."

Conroy practically skipped her way to the coffee station. They were no longer skirting the edges of this investigation. They were at the center of it.

The road to Pasadena took them past miles of concrete sidewalks and telegraph poles, a sprawling wasteland of billboards, pharmacies, garages and Chinese laundries.

"How's the shoulder?" Craine asked when he noticed Abe grunting every time he turned the wheel.

"No better for you asking after it," came the reply.

They came off the highway shortly after the Colorado Street Bridge and pulled up outside a row of old warehouse buildings. A sign outside said CAR REPAIR, TIRES, LAUNDROMAT.

On the outside, their destination looked to be a disused foundry or metalworks factory. Craine almost asked if they'd got the right address. But when they went inside Craine saw that the building had been converted into a giant office floor filled with men and women manning telephones.

"Siegel's race wire service," Abe muttered when Craine looked at him for an explanation. "It's Dragna's now."

The floor was loud, people talking quickly into receivers and scribbling numbers down on paper dockets. Craine had heard years ago that an illegal wire service existed in Los Angeles. It relayed horse race results from tracks around the country directly to gambling houses in L.A. Controlling the wire meant by proxy controlling gambling at a national level. The financial rewards were unthinkable.

"Where's Harvey?" Abe asked a man manning several telephones.

"Through the back. He's expecting you."

Abe took them through into a back room where Craine could see Harvey Sterling wiping his hands with a dark cloth.

"Hill through there?"

Harvey nodded. His face was wet with sweat like he'd been grafting. "Come through. But I warn you, it ain't pretty."

Abe and Harvey walked toward a metal door, speaking quietly between themselves. There was something undeniably clannish about the two of them, with contempt for anyone and everyone not born within four square blocks of where they grew up.

The room was a disused laundromat, filled with industrial-sized drum washers and steam pressing machines. At the far end a man he assumed was Charlie Hill was tied to a metal ceiling pipe. Fluorescent strips hummed above him. It turned the blood on the floor black.

Years of homicide work had hardened Craine. But seeing what men were capable of doing to each other never failed to make an impression.

Charlie Hill was stripped naked. His chest was peppered with cigarette burns, his torso covered in blood blisters and his face was so misshapen that his own mother would have struggled to identify him. Trussed like that with his clothes stripped off, Hill resembled something you'd see in an abattoir.

"That him?" Abe asked.

Hill looked horrified when Craine and Abe entered. Like new recruits were being brought in for a fresh round of beatings.

"It's him alright," Harvey said. "He was hiding out in a motel. I found this on him."

Harvey took a pistol from a metal side shelf. Abe raised it to his nose.

"Been fired recently," Abe said, looking at Craine.

"I didn't shoot it," Hill blurted out from the end of the room. "I swear to God."

Harvey took a drag of his cigarette and Craine saw Hill's Adam's apple bulge with sick anticipation.

"Let me go," Hill screamed, pulling at his restraints. "Let me go. I didn't do nothing, I swear it."

In response Harvey simply strode over and punched him in the stomach so hard that blood and vomit spurted out of Hill's mouth.

"Then why did you run, you piece of shit?" he yelled.

Harvey began thumping Hill's cheekbone with short sharp jabs, like a butcher hammering meat. There was something workmanlike in his approach to torture. It had the ease of a ritual. Craine wondered if there was a limit to the pain a man could handle.

"You had Siegel killed," he said between jabs. "Then you went for these two at the Bradbury, didn't you?"

Hill was winded. "I didn't . . ." he managed through choked breaths. "I didn't."

Harvey wiped sweat and saliva from his lips. He seemed to be enjoying the intimate brutality. "You're lying," he said through gritted teeth. "Now you can keep lying or you can admit what you've done."

Craine looked at Abe to do something. When Harvey glanced back to see if he wanted a few rounds himself, Abe signaled to let Craine come closer.

"Fine," Harvey said. "But there's no point going easy on him."

Craine moved slowly, like he was approaching a rearing horse.

"Charlie? Charlie Hill?" he said softly when he was a few feet away. "Charlie, I need to talk to you."

Hill grimaced and tensed, waiting for the blow. "I didn't do it," he said, blood dripping from his nostrils. "I didn't kill him."

"I'm not going to hit you, Charlie. So I need you to calm down."

Up close, he could see Hill was young, barely out of his teens. Maybe only a few years older than Michael.

"Charlie, my name is Jonathan Craine. Meyer Lansky sent me."

Hill had a bulbous lump pressing down on his right eye. He had to swivel his head so he could see who he was talking to. "Please," he said. "Tell them I can't take any more."

Craine looked to Abe. "Get him down."

Harvey stepped forward. "What are you doing?"

"Look at him," Craine said. "He's not going anywhere. I need him conscious."

Harvey lit a cigarette in protest. He did nothing as Abe took out a small knife from his pocket and cut the ropes holding his wrists to the ceiling pipe. Hill slumped to the ground.

Craine was composed but firm. "I'm not here to hurt you, Charlie. All I want is information. But I'll warn you now: you don't want to lie to these guys. That would be a mistake."

Hill took long, deep breaths like he'd been drowning. "Please," he said, coughing and retching. "I don't know who did it. I'm not working for anyone, I swear."

The pain in his body must have registered because Hill began inspecting his wounds like a confused infant that had fallen over.

"Don't look at the blood, Charlie. Look at me."

"They're trying to kill me."

"Then tell me what went on and I can help you take care of your situation."

"I'm sorry. I keep saying I'm sorry."

"Don't apologize. *Explain.*"

The ceiling tubes flickered and Craine had a momentary respite from looking at Hill's face. He gave the poor boy a minute to gather himself.

When Hill had steadied his breathing, Craine asked, "What happened the night Siegel died? I want you to tell me everything that happened after you met Ben Siegel at Ocean Park. I want you to take your time. And I want you to tell me the truth."

"Okay," Hill cried like a child to his mother. "Okay, I promise."

For the most part, Hill's version of events was consistent with Allen Smiley's. They'd met in Santa Monica, then come back to Siegel's for drinks. When they got to the shooting, Charlie said that he'd been upstairs at the time with a girl he'd taken out. They heard the shots and ran downstairs to find Smiley screaming at them to call the police. The F.B.I. had arrived a few minutes before the police did, but Charlie Hill and his girlfriend were whisked away in an F.B.I. car before he could talk to anyone from the L.A.P.D.

When Craine asked him who the girl was, Hill offered a vague response. Craine didn't probe it any further. You keep the secrets till last.

"Let me ask you something," he said as if they were old friends. "Where is your sister? Where is Virginia?"

Craine tried to find Hill's eyes. To see if he was hiding something.

"I don't know," he said earnestly. "Europe. Paris."

"When did she leave?"

"About two weeks ago."

"Why hasn't anyone heard from her?"

"I don't know. Honestly. I don't know."

Behind them, Harvey muttered something but Craine held up his hand for silence. He didn't push Charlie any further. Virginia Hill wasn't the destination of this conversation. The mysterious woman at Siegel's house was.

"The girl you were with . . . who was she again?"

Hill looked down. He didn't want Craine to see him dissembling. "I told you. Some girl I met. She's not important."

"Where is she now?"

"I don't know."

"Have you seen her since?"

"No. Not really."

"Not really?"

For the first time, Craine could see the boy reaching for answers. His body language changed.

"Tell me the truth, Charlie. Who is she?"

"Some girl I took home. That's all."

"Tell me about her. Tell me everything about her."

"I've told you."

"I don't think you have," Craine said calmly. He didn't draw on anger or aggression. He didn't need to.

"I have. I have, I swear."

"Come on, Charlie. Tell me. Tell me so I can make sure these men don't hurt you again. How did you meet her? What was her name?"

Craine went on like this, drawing on lost habits, every question designed not only to probe but to destabilize, to shake Hill's calm until the information dropped out of him like coins from a piggy bank.

"Now these men will say you're lying to me, Charlie. But I think you've simply made a mistake. She wasn't a one-night stand, was she? You liked her, didn't you? You're protecting her because you have feelings for her and don't want her to get in trouble. That makes sense. That's something we'd all do in your position. So, were you lying? Or did you make a mistake?"

"I'm sorry," he said, his voice phlegmy. "I–I made a mistake."

"Go on, Charlie."

"We've been together a few months," he finally admitted. "She's a nice girl. A nice, sweet girl."

"Where did you meet her?"

When Charlie didn't reply, Craine heard either Harvey or Abe step forward behind him. He held up a hand again but more firmly. They stepped back.

"I'm not here to hurt you. And I'm not here to hurt her. But if you don't help me, I can't help you. Either of you. That's the bottom line. I don't need to spell it out in black and white. They'll kill both of you. They'll bury you in the desert if you don't help me find out who killed Siegel. You understand? You understand that, right?"

Hill began crying. Most people carried secrets around with them; they were desperate to unburden themselves.

"She works for Virginia," he said at last, the words coming out in a release of tears.

"As what?"

"Personal secretary," he sobbed.

"Doing what?"

"She picked up her dry-cleaning. That kinda thing. Benny paid her." There wasn't bluff in his voice. He genuinely believed it. "But they were friendly, too. Like sisters. Virginia, she was good like that."

"What's her name?"

He waited for a moment, then said, "Please. She's nothing to do with this."

"We're not going to hurt her."

"She's just a kid. A sweet kid who happened to be there at the wrong time."

"We're not going to hurt her, Charlie. But we need her name. And we need to know how to contact her. Tell me, Charlie. Whisper it."

Charlie Hill would tell Craine everything he needed to know. All of it without Craine ever lifting a hand against him. This was Craine's gift. Not investigation. *Confession.* He didn't hold you under the water. He swam you out to the deep and let you drown yourself.

CHAPTER 25

Her name was Joyce Mills and she lived in Downtown L.A. Her address was only a few blocks away from the Bradbury Building, although there was nothing to prove that wasn't a coincidence. They'd left Charlie Hill in the comforting presence of Harvey and were speeding south down the Arroyo Seco Parkway.

"What will happen to him?" Craine asked when they'd passed through Highland Park.

"Who?"

"You know who. The kid."

"I told Harvey to take him to the hospital."

"He'll be lucky if he's still alive tomorrow."

"Had it coming," Abe burred.

Craine looked at him. "He didn't do it."

"You don't know that."

"He said he didn't do it."

"So what? Everybody says they're innocent."

"But nobody can lie well enough I can't tell. Beating him to a pulp like that was never going to get you answers. At least, not truthful ones."

Abe gripped the wheel tight in his hands. Craine heard his palms on the leather. "You can frown and quiver and curse our methods all you want, Craine, but there's violence in you as there is in me. Don't pretend you're any different." When Craine didn't respond he said, "You know why Kastel hates you so much? Because he had an uncle once in New York. A man called Paul Kamona." Abe didn't need to expand on the connection. They both knew it was a man Craine had killed many years ago. "You see? Doesn't matter who you are, there's no telling what a man will do when his back's against the wall."

"It's not the same. For Christ's sake, Abe. He was a kid. Probably not even old enough to drink."

Abe shook his head. "For a long time I said I'd only kill people that needed to be killed. The ones that deserved it got it, and that was that. But then you start bending the rules. And pretty soon there ain't no rules at all. Only what needs to be done."

They crawled past billboards telling them that a new picture called *Crossfire* was playing in theaters. The tagline said: *Hate Is Like A Loaded Gun.*

It was Abe who suggested they didn't knock on Joyce's apartment door. He worked out which floor was hers and instead had Craine call her apartment from a pay phone across the street.

"You speak to her," he said. "I tend to scare 'em off."

Craine was so apprehensive about finally finding their missing witness that he struggled to get his nickel into the coin slot.

The phone rang several times before anyone answered.

"Hello?" A girl's voice. Soft. Young.

"Joyce?"

There was a pause and then that young voice seemed to age. "What do you want? I did everything you asked."

"Joyce. My name is Jonathan Craine."

"Who are you?"

But evidently Joyce didn't want to know the answer because as soon as she said it she hung up.

Craine called again. And then a third time, and a fourth. She answered only when it was clear he wasn't going to give up.

"If you don't stop harassing me I'll call the police."

"I'm not whoever you think I am."

"I can see you. You're across the street."

Craine looked up to see a set of drapes twitch.

"Meet us at Clifton's Cafeteria in twenty minutes."

Abe was staring up at the window. He wondered whether she could see him. "If you don't," he added, "I'll tell Jack Dragna you were with Siegel the night he died. And his men don't call in advance."

Smiley was right about her having blond hair. What he didn't say was how young Joyce was. Or maybe it was seeing her without makeup. She looked like a little girl. Young enough to be his daughter. And so small and fragile now she was sitting next to Abe. Craine wondered how this timid child ever came to be mixed up with a bunch of killers.

"I'm sorry but I don't believe you," Craine said when she'd continued to say she didn't know anything about what had happened that night. Innocent people had opinions. They had something to say.

"I wasn't there," she said repeatedly. "I don't know what you're talking about," she said when he kept pressing.

There were times you coerced and times you blackmailed. But it was easier to let people relieve themselves of the burdens of secrecy in their own time. He continued to ask her questions until a waitress brought them their coffee. Joyce used the opportunity to break the tension.

"I used to come here all the time when I was broke. They let you have soup for next to nothing. I hear the guy that owns it is retiring. I guess all good things come to an end, right?" When neither of them said anything, she said, "You like it here?"

Clifton's was on old Broadway and the large cafeteria was decorated in noisy jungle motifs and giant palm trees that towered over their tables. It looked like something out of a children's storybook.

Abe looked around. "I don't like it here. Not one bit," he said matter-of-factly.

Craine ignored him. "Joyce, I don't want to push you and I don't want to threaten you either, but we both know there are things you're not admitting to us. We know because we spoke to Charlie Hill an hour ago and he told us you were with him the night Siegel died."

She stared at her coffee. "You've spoken to Charlie?"

"Yeah."

"Is he alright?"

Craine noticed Joyce was staring at Abe's fists.

"He's okay," he said, knowing that wasn't really the case. "Tell me why you didn't come forward. Tell me why you've been hiding."

"We spoke to the F.B.I.," she said defensively. "We didn't want any trouble."

"But the press and the police are denying you were ever there. Which means someone asked you to lie. Who? The F.B.I.?"

Abe stuck his chin out, then ran his palm over it. "Was it Virginia Hill asked you to? She was the one who did it?"

"No."

"Who then?"

"Why should I tell you?"

Abe didn't raise his voice but he threw his good arm on the table in front of her and brought his face down so it was barely a few inches from her face.

"Because we're asking."

Craine put a hand out. Direct confrontation wouldn't work with Joyce. For some reason, denial had set in. Craine needed to set traps.

"When I called you from outside your apartment you said, 'I did everything you asked.' What did you mean by that?"

"Nothing."

He asked her again to no response, and then Abe started exhaling loudly. He was running out of patience.

Joyce looked around to the other tables as if someone might be able to help her. Craine knew the feeling.

"There's no one here, Joyce. This is between us."

Joyce began to cry and he let her. There was no one to tell this girl it was alright. No one to pass her a handkerchief. She was in a dangerous scenario and she had to feel it.

"There was a man," she began, likely knowing when she did that their conversation would end with her telling them everything. "There was a man came to see me."

"Who?" Abe asked.

"I don't know who. I promise I don't."

Craine put his hand out for Abe to let her talk. She was unraveling and he didn't want to scare her away. "Keep going. What did he want?"

"He said Virginia would need a flight to Paris and I should book it for her. That's it. He said she needed to leave as soon as possible."

Abe said, "Did he give you money?"

When Joyce didn't answer Abe's question, Craine softened for the first time: "Joyce, it's best you answer the man."

"A little." It came out as a whimper.

"How much?"

"Flights are expensive."

"How much?"

Her eyes flicked around. Her shoulders tensed. "Two thousand."

Abe slurped his coffee. "You buy the whole plane?"

Any money this girl made from it was of no interest to Craine. He kept on with his questions. "So you bought Virginia the ticket?"

She nodded. "I called up the airline."

"Did Siegel know?"

"I think so. No, not at first, but then she told him she was going to Paris. Said she needed a break."

"From Siegel?"

A tilt of the chin said yes. "He was stressed about the hotel. They were arguing. She wanted a few weeks to cool off."

"When was this?"

Joyce thought about it. The answer didn't come to her. "Hard to say. A few weeks ago. Maybe a month."

"You think Virginia had him killed?"

"No, never. She loved him. Loved him with all her heart."

Craine had investigated countless murders where husbands had killed their wives and vice versa. They were almost always sorry and they almost always said they still loved them. But Joyce seemed adamant.

"She was a little intense at times. But only because she wore her heart on her sleeve. I could never imagine her ever asking somebody to kill Benny."

"Did you see the man again? The man who came to visit you?"

"I never met him but he called me. I'd almost forgotten about the whole thing. Or tried to. Then he calls me at home."

"When was this?"

"Last week. Wednesday, I think. He said they knew Siegel was going to be out with friends on Friday. I should ask Charlie if we could go along, then make sure Mr. Siegel got home after."

"He say what they were going to do?"

Her face was impassive. "I thought he wanted to come and talk to him."

"You thought that? You really thought that?"

"Who knew? He seemed nice enough."

"The man who called. He threaten you?"

"Not exactly."

"Why not tell Charlie about him?"

Joyce had an injured look on her face. "I–I had been for dinner with another guy. This man . . . he had seen us together. I didn't want Charlie to find out."

"Who was the guy?"

"He was a writer for the studios. I thought maybe . . . I only wanted a screen test. It was dinner, that's all. I didn't stay with him. He turned out to be a creep anyway—"

"The man who called you. He saw you out with him?"

"This writer, he dropped me off. Tried to come up but I said I wasn't that type of girl. Then when I got inside the telephone rang like they knew I was home. He was calling from a pay phone outside my apartment. Same thing as you guys."

"You get sight of him?"

"It was dark. He was wearing a hat."

"Can you describe the car?"

"Not really. I wasn't really paying attention to the car."

"Because he said he'd tell Charlie?"

A nod. "You have to understand. I have nothing. I used to live with three other girls, then I got my own place, but really it's just a tiny room. That money, I didn't spend it. It's in a bank account—"

Joyce's eyes were damp. Her voice wasn't soft anymore. "Don't tell Charlie. I like him. He's a nice boy. I think, me and him, we could be something."

Joyce began sobbing. "Please. I don't want to be in trouble. I can't go to sleep at night thinking they could be coming for me at any moment. Every time I go near a window I keep thinking they're gonna shoot me. It's driving me crazy."

The check came and Abe put several notes on the table. Far more than it had cost. Craine could see this girl's terror had had an effect on him.

"Joyce," Craine said, "I'm going to give your address to someone who can help you."

"No, please," she said through tears. "Don't tell anyone."

"Her name is Tilda Conroy and she's a reporter."

Abe folded his arms, unhappy about this, but Craine went on anyway. "You tell her your story and she can help you. But if I were you I'd think about leaving Los Angeles for a few days until this blows over."

Driving back to the hotel, Craine and Abe discussed what Joyce had told them. Their instincts had been right. Whether she did it unwittingly or not, she *had* helped set up Siegel to be murdered.

"The thing I don't understand," Abe mused, "is why the F.B.I. were protecting her. Surely that tells us it was them."

"Maybe," Craine said. "Or does it only tell us that they know who did it? That they're protecting someone else's secret? Or does it tell us nothing? That they want to keep Siegel's murder contained—stop the conspiracies before they start because no one wants Siegel's murder investigation to be in the headlines. They want the focus to be on the Hollywood red scare."

He ran through different possibilities but all of them had flaws. There was a certain victory in finding Joyce, but a part of Craine felt frustrated that she hadn't brought them any closer to the killer. She was a minor player in a much larger game. She didn't pull the trigger and she didn't send the shooter.

When they got to the hotel, the manager waved them over from the reception desk. Craine was starting to worry that there might be another "package," but when he came over he had a piece of paper in his hand.

"Mr. Craine," he said politely, "a Mrs Conroy called from the *Herald.* She left an urgent message."

"Thanks. She leave a number?"

"She left this address."

The manager handed Craine a piece of paper with the hotel's logo on the letterhead. '*JOE'S AUTO SALVAGE, 3 P.M.*' had been scribbled in Birome ballpoint.

CHAPTER 26

"Our usual price is five dollars, but that depends entirely on condition. If you've got usable parts we can sell on then we'll look to go for ten. I got a good eye for value."

Conroy was making small talk at Joe's Auto Salvage. They were walking through a vast yard of cars in various stages of decay, like a ghostly parade of a lost Armored Division. It seemed to go on for miles.

"So I can leave it here whenever I want?" asked Conroy, playing the role of interested customer.

Joe was fifty or so, with thick arms and a torso that seemed to have molded itself on the surrounding tires.

"If the paperwork's clear. Needs to be off the books and cleared with the D.M.V."

"And if it's not?" Conroy probed. She didn't wink, but she might as well have.

Joe rubbed a greasy finger up his nose. "We can probably come to a cash arrangement."

The answer was what she was looking for but the two Dobermans running around the yard put her on edge.

"What will you do with it?"

"Depends how old they are. Your car? May look like junk but the parts are probably valuable." Joe pointed to the crane in the background, where Conroy saw a man pulling levers. The metal claws had been lifting up automobiles and dropping them onto the car heap since she got here. "Only the worst get scrapped completely."

Conroy said, "What if I want my car crushed?"

Joe shrugged. "Yeah. We do that. We have a shredder, too. Thing can clean disappear off the map."

That last statement was said quietly but pointedly. It was something they did. *A special service.*

"Interesting." Conroy smiled. "Joe, I was hoping you might be able to help me. It would be really helpful."

"With your car?"

"Actually I was hoping you could answer a few questions for me. It relates to a car that was involved in a homicide a few days ago."

Conroy took out a notepad and Joe shrank visibly. The dogs kept barking.

"Wait a second."

"Few questions, that's all. Then I'll leave you in peace."

"You from the police?"

There were reporters who impersonated detectives or officials. Despite the fact that there were no female detectives she knew of, Conroy had never felt comfortable being an impostor.

"No. I'm a reporter. I was after some information about a car that might have been brought here late Friday night or Saturday morning."

"We get lots of cars on lots of days."

"So you might have had someone here on Friday?"

"Possibly."

Joe's answers were close to monosyllabic. Maybe, he said. Maybe not, he said. It went on like this for several minutes.

"The car I'm referring to was a 1938 dark blue Nash. Do you remember it? I've got the license tags here we can compare."

"What if I did? Why should I tell you?"

"Because if you don't I'm going to tell my friends at the Detective Bureau that you're crushing cars illegally."

"I never said that."

"Yes you did." She scribbled on her pad and held it up for him to see. 'Thing can clean disappear off the map.' They were your words, weren't they?"

Joe seemed annoyed with Conroy, but more annoyed with himself. He looked away when he spoke to her, as if doing so meant he could deny this conversation.

"A fella came by Friday."

"What time was it?"

"Late, I guess."

"Midnight late? Are you open then?"

He didn't say anything. Conroy smiled but let the question hang in the air. People hated silences. You had to be patient and wait for them to fill them.

"It was pre-agreed. Said he had a car he wanted to get rid of."

"Did he tell you why?"

The dogs were barking and Joe waited for them to stop. It took a while.

"I didn't ask."

"Did you know the man?"

"Never saw him before in my life. And no, before you ask I didn't get his name."

A plea of ignorance was common but he seemed genuine. "Could you try to describe him for me?"

"Not that tall. Dressed in a suit. Had some scars on his face from the war, but a lot of men do. Oh, he had some kind of accent, like he was from out of town."

She stopped writing and looked at him as he spoke. "Could you say where his accent was from?"

"Hard to say. Maybe East Coast. Seemed like a city boy. But not from L.A. At least, not born here."

"Everything alright, Joe?" a voice said.

Which was when Conroy realized that the crane had stopped. The driver was walking toward them. He stopped a few yards behind Joe and took his gloves off. The Dobermans ran over, licking his fingers.

Joe didn't reply. The crane driver was big, even bigger than Joe. She looked at the two men and then at the dogs and felt suddenly vulnerable. She wondered if she'd feel the same if she were a man.

Conroy said, "I'm not trying to get you in trouble, Joe. I'm not going to call the police."

"You still going to write about us?"

"Joe?" the crane driver called, to no response. The dogs ran past Conroy, making her shiver. "Everything good?"

"Nothing so far implicates you in any crime," she said to Joe with as much confidence she could muster.

There was the sound of tires on gravel and all three of them turned around to see a dusty Mercury pull up outside Joe's office trailer. The window was down and Abe saluted two fingers in their direction. Conroy had never expected to be so happy to see that man.

Joe backed up a step. "They with you?"

Conroy nodded. She spoke quickly. "Joe, if you tell me you had no idea that the car was stolen then I'll print that exactly." When he didn't reply, she said, "*Say it.* Say you had no idea the car was stolen."

"I had no idea the car was stolen," Joe muttered, slightly confused.

"Good. Then that's what I'll write and that's what the police will believe if they ever find out."

Joe visibly relaxed, but by now Craine and Abe were walking toward them. Conroy turned back and gave them a look that told them to stay put.

"Joe, can somebody tell me what's going on?" This from the crane driver.

"Hold it a second," said Joe, raising his hand. "We're talking."

"And if you tell me you want to say something off the record, I won't print it." There was a time when Conroy didn't have such scruples, but that only made her value them more now. "There's a code of ethics," she said. "I take it seriously."

"What about this whole conversation?"

"Conroy," said Abe.

"*Hold on.*"

Conroy was standing in the center of four men with her hands out, like they'd crossed onto an ice pond. If any one of them moved too quickly this whole situation could fall through. She looked at Joe and spoke slowly and clearly, knowing that what she said next could determine whether they ever found the shooter's car.

"We can't do it after, Joe. That's not how it works. But if there was something else you wanted to tell me now, that can be between you and me. You won't see it printed. For example." She took a breath. "What I'd really like to know is where the car is now."

Joe moved from one foot to the other, his eyes shifting in all directions. Dear Joe wasn't well versed in the art of lying.

"Off the record . . . we didn't crush it," he said. "Most of the cars here, it costs more to fix 'em up than buy another. With that car, it looked fine. We figured it was in good condition so we sold it on. I told you, I got a good eye for value."

"I totally understand," Conroy said, holding her pad up. "Now can you tell me who you sold it to?"

CHAPTER 27

No two people have matching fingerprints. The loops, whorls and arches that make up our fingerprint patterns are unique to every individual. When a person touches glass or a similarly nonporous surface, they leave proof of their identity behind. Often a single fingerprint left on a crime scene has been the entire basis for a court conviction.

Even after tracking down the missing witness, Craine had yet to gather any viable suspects or plausible theories. Which meant that the car parked in the center of Conroy's basement parking lot was now the only piece of evidence that could potentially identify the man who murdered Benjamin Siegel.

It was a blue '38 Nash, and the three of them stood looking at it like a naval mine swept ashore that might explode any minute.

The Nash was in many ways unremarkable to look at. Craine thought there was something strangely innocent about it. A family vehicle kidnapped and dragged into this mess no different from the rest of them.

Like three envoys to a dead man they never knew, they had driven from Joe's straight to the person who had bought the car secondhand and Abe had paid the owner there and then in cash. Abe was so eager he'd taken out one of his thick rolls of notes and handed over the whole thing without ever asking the owner how much he wanted for it.

The man had seemed nervous. It was more than enough to buy three brand new cars. "What if I ask for more?"

"You really don't want to do that," Abe had said, taking the keys from his hands.

The car had been towed to Conroy's apartment building and Craine had explained how important it was that they not touch anything. It was a mobile crime scene, liable to be contaminated.

Retrieving as many table lamps as Conroy could carry down from her apartment, Abe and Conroy had positioned them around the car so that the surfaces were illuminated. To anyone in the building who might have walked past it would have looked like a bizarre automobile séance.

For thirty minutes they stood watching as Craine examined the car inside and out. It was methodical work. No one pretended they knew how to help—Craine was the only one of them remotely qualified.

After surveying the entire car from the outside, Craine put on gloves and examined the interior. He was thorough in his search but found no traces of blood, no clothes and no ammunition. No physical evidence whatsoever to connect the car to the killing.

Which left only the prints.

The car's metallic coachwork and glass windows made it ideal for fingerprint-lifting, even if it had changed hands several times over a period of five days.

Craine examined the door handle on the outside of the driver's side, but it was covered in dust and dirt. Retrieving prints would be close to impossible. But when he examined the handle on the inside of the door, he made out the unmistakable papillary lines of a series of fingerprints.

"We have prints," he said. "Pass me the brush."

Craine had already explained the process to the others and Conroy approached with the bowl of powder mix and one of her rouge brushes. Typically, a crime scene examiner would lift latent prints using metallic powder and adhesive strips. Given the circumstances, Craine had to make do without. He'd mixed soot with cornstarch taken from Conroy's kitchen. The combined powder mix wouldn't be as effective as the aluminum powder the police techs used, but it would be sufficient given the circumstances.

Without being asked, Abe twisted the lamplight to give Craine a better view as he lightly brushed the fine powder over the metal handle. He gave it a minute to settle and then took out a roll of clear Scotch tape.

It had been almost two decades since Craine had done this kind of police work. Taking several deep breaths to steady his hand, he placed a piece of tape firmly over the largest and clearest fingerprint. He made sure the pressure was even and then slowly peeled it off.

Conroy was behind him, biting her nails. Abe stood back, smoking one cigarette after another. Everyone was tense. No one said a word.

Craine took a step back and held it up to the light. His eyes adjusted focus. Yes, he could make out the unmistakable raised ridges of a fingerprint.

"I've got one," he said.

An hour later, and he had several fingerprints identified and taped onto blank card; different prints from different fingers of different men. But one of them belonged to his shooter, he was sure of it.

Their entire investigation rested on the trace of these lines.

CHAPTER 28

The lights were dimmed in the offices of the *Herald*, the air cool and static. The newspaper typically went "off stone" at 5 P.M. and the office emptied soon after, transferring gossip and debate to local drinking holes.

But Conroy had only recently returned, typing up her notes from the afternoon as Craine tried to figure out what to do with the latent prints pulled off the car. Besides, she wrote best late at night. It was the only time the office was quiet enough that she could hear herself think. One of the upsides of never being invited to drinks. Probably the only upside.

"Tilda?" This from Alice, standing over her desk.

"You off?" she said without looking up. "I'll see you tomorrow morning."

Alice didn't say anything. In fact, Alice didn't move at all.

"Tilda."

She lost her train of thought. "What? You're hovering. What is it?"

"Wire Editor told me he got something that came through the teletype yesterday."

Alice waited for Conroy's eyes to show she was listening.

"Uh-uh. I'm with you."

"Some Italian mobster released from prison in Chicago. It rang a bell from my days at Associated Press, so I called my old editor long-distance. He said that Paul Ricca, head of the Chicago Outfit, was released early this week."

It took a few seconds for Conroy to process this. When Frank Nitti, former head of the Chicago Outfit, was arrested in 1943 for extorting Hollywood studios, Nitti killed himself rather than go to prison. His successor, Paul Ricca, had been sentenced to fifteen years, but it was well known he still controlled the Chicago Outfit from inside.

"Did he say why?"

"Only that the parole board approved it."

"This was earlier this week? Has anyone else picked this up?" Conroy was annoyed with herself; she'd been so focused on Siegel she'd missed a major story. More than that, she'd missed a viable connection to Benjamin Siegel. She should try to contact Craine.

"No," Alice said, checking over both shoulders. "No one."

Conroy frowned.

"I thought it was odd, too," Alice said. "But my old editor says they've been told not to print it. Orders from above. Then I checked with a friend of mine at the *Examiner*. Same thing."

Conroy leaned back in her chair. There were higher forces in play here.

"You know you're too smart to be a clerk, Alice."

"Oh, I know."

"We have a photo of this guy Ricca?"

"Not to hand. Can try the morgue in the morning."

The "morgue" was slang for the archives department. It would have rolls of microfilm of both old newspapers and court photographs.

Conroy stood up and grabbed her bag. "Let's head down now. I want to find out about this guy."

A man's voice stopped her. "Conroy."

Tilda looked up to see the City Editor leaning out of his office, "Tilda, you got a second?"

Conroy followed the City Editor into his office, making polite small talk until they were both sitting down.

"I'm not exactly sure where this has come from, but our publisher spoke to me today."

The owner. The oil heir turned newspaper mogul.

"This should come as no surprise, given what happened with Henson and Redhill, but the line of enquiry you're pursuing has ruffled feathers."

Conroy could already see the direction this conversation was heading. There was no steering it away. She spoke quickly, desperate to share her story.

"Sir, William Wilson invested in The Flamingo before Siegel bought out his shares. And major studios have been paying off Siegel's Extras Union to stop strikes. This story is national."

The City Editor didn't share her urgency. He spoke slowly, delivering a eulogy. "Billy Wilson and Louis Mayer are two important people in this city. Major donors. And M.G.M. is an important corporate client for this paper."

There had been a journalism "code of ethics" for decades, but in Conroy's experience, there had been misuse of power for even longer. Owners of newspapers swayed headlines as favors for their allies. At times it felt like the whole city was a giant chess game that a handful of men in penthouse offices were playing to amuse themselves.

"The owner should push back," she said, trying to sound controlled.

"Tilda, we sell advertising to M.G.M. at twenty dollars an inch. We can't afford to be pointing fingers at the largest studio in Hollywood."

Conroy stared at her shorthand pad. She didn't want him to see the frustration on her face. She had always known the City Editor to be gutsy and hawkish. He'd earned a reputation as a hard-hitting journalist. It was unlike him to shy away from controversy.

"Sir, we're the only paper who has the trust of our readers. We owe it to the public to tell these types of stories."

He lowered his voice. "You can't go out there with a story that involves some of the most powerful figures on the West Coast and not expect repercussions."

"How can you believe in the freedom of the press if you're bowing to their demands?"

He didn't like being spoken to like that. "My hands are tied. The decision's made."

"So you're pulling the story?"

"I'm putting it on hold until we can figure out a way forward."

He was trying to placate her but she could see right through it. There would be no way forward. It would end here, never to come up again.

"I can't believe this."

"Go home, Tilda. Take a break if you need to. I'm sorry, but it's done."

Tilda Conroy wasn't prone to crying. It wasn't something she did often and she never used it to her advantage. But in the City Editor's office, after five exhausting days investigating Siegel's murder, those tears found their way to her eyes without permission.

Some of the other reporters at the *Herald* had private members' clubs, but most of them excluded women, Jews and Negroes, so Conroy took Alice to a cocktail bar off Little Tokyo that didn't have a Whites Only policy. During the war, there were a series of attacks by sailors on Latinos and Negroes in nearby neighborhoods but Little Toyko was usually safe from that kind of trouble.

"We're waiting for our husbands," Conroy said to the waitress when they'd entered, her usual excuse to let her come in unaccompanied.

The bar wasn't segregated and they were sitting in a booth not far from the counter, sipping at highballs. Alice would offer to pay, but Conroy would cover it. She knew Alice's salary was a third less than the white girls' in the steno pool, despite her being overqualified for her role in the first place.

After Conroy had explained what had happened with the City Editor, Alice lit up a cigarette and thought it over. Even though she was her senior, Conroy didn't ask for deference and didn't expect it either. Alice had always had a knack for getting details that eluded other reporters, and Conroy respected her opinion more than most.

"What smarts is that he was so behind it, then changed his mind," Alice said, reaching for the ashtray.

"He didn't change his mind, it was changed for him by the D.A.'s office. Wilson and Mayer spoke to City Hall."

"When you intend to publicly accuse someone of a crime, that's usually what happens."

"Now you're on their side?"

Alice pulled a face. "'Course not, Tilda. I'm only saying it's the way it is."

Conroy noticed the waitress kept looking over. Maybe she frowned upon two women drinking, but Conroy didn't care. She took several gulps. Tonight she was drinking with ambition. "We finally have a story and he pulls it. Like grabbing defeat from victory."

"Sorry, Tilda. I know how hard you worked on it."

"So did you, Alice." Conroy exhaled into her glass. The alcohol wasn't calming her down. "I'm so angry about the whole thing. He has no earthly idea how close we are to blowing the lid off this. *So close.* It's one of the biggest crime stories of the decade, and he's shut it down because he's worried about his ad revenue for the next quarter." She finished her cocktail, then put her palm against her head as if remembering something. "Craine. Dammit. I need to call him. He needs to know about this too."

"What is this with you and Craine?" Alice said, stirring the ice in her Gin Rickey.

"How do you mean?"

"Feels personal. Do you know him?"

"No, not really," Conroy said vaguely. She didn't want Alice to know that she and Craine shared a past. She changed the subject. "You want another drink?"

"No, I'm good."

Conroy knew Alice wouldn't probe her any further. People often assumed women gathered together to gossip about their love lives, but Alice and Tilda rarely talked about anything but work. Tilda knew Alice was married to a black police officer she'd met in Chicago, but she knew nothing about "Mr. Hickerson" other than his dislike of California's climate and that she was always on at him to buy them a new car.

"The problem with this whole thing," Alice mused, "is that no one is going to let you run the story if it involves upsetting people. You need to get the studios and Wilson onside."

"How? They're never going to support this story, Alice."

Conroy had never had a lot of faith in America's institutions. The entire establishment seemed to be run by men of a certain type, and they didn't respond well to women who had their own point of view. She'd always lacked the apple pie wholesomeness men liked.

"No. No more," Conroy said. "I'm sick of it. Why is it that ten times a day I find myself running around after all these middle-aged men with their corner offices and their boys' club mentality?"

Alice pursed her lips. "It's the way things are," she said in a low but direct voice.

Alice had never once complained about her lot in life. Conroy was well aware how she sounded when she moaned about her situation. "Sorry, it's been a bad few days. I'm not coming in the rest of the week, or I'll say something that'll get me in trouble. If the City Editor comes over tomorrow, tell him I'm off sick."

"He's not going to come over. City Editor ain't never spoken to me. Doesn't even know I exist."

"Oh Alice, that's not true." It was entirely true. Several times he'd referred to her as "that woman." Or, for some reason, "Mrs. Jones."

The waitress came over and picked up both their glasses. Alice's wasn't nearly empty.

"Wait, we're not done," Conroy said.

The waitress seemed flustered. "Your husbands aren't coming, are they?"

Conroy gave an exaggerated shrug. "They can't make it. Is that a problem?"

"If you don't mind, the owner would like you to finish your drinks and leave."

Alice seemed embarrassed but not surprised.

"I do mind," Conroy said. "We're not going anywhere."

"Please. Don't make a scene." Her voice was polite, but the waitress put a small wooden sign on the table with 'WE HAVE THE RIGHT TO REFUSE SERVICE' painted across it.

"You're the one making a scene," Conroy said with a raised voice.

The waitress leaned closer. "We have servicemen in the corner and they're getting rowdy. I don't want any trouble."

Christ, even Little Tokyo wasn't safe anymore. She was worried about more zoot suit riots kicking off because a black woman was in her bar.

"No trouble, I'm leaving," Alice said, gathering her things.

"No, wait a second. We're staying put. They should be the ones to leave."

"Tilda," Alice said to her directly. "This is not your fight. You don't get to get involved."

Alice picked up her bag and stormed out. Conroy threw a dollar on the table and ran after her. She caught her on the street walking toward the bus stop.

"Alice, wait—Alice, I'm sorry."

Alice turned around without stopping. "It's alright, I'm not annoyed with you. But honestly, Tilda, why do you think you keep getting people riled up? It's because you're intent on fighting everything head-on."

The bus to Central Avenue came and Alice waved it down. It was crammed to the doors with factory workers heading home. "Choose your battles," Alice called back. "Sometimes there's a smarter way."

CHAPTER 29

Craine knew that wartime vigilance led to the F.B.I. collecting millions of fingerprints from U.S. government staff, military servicemen and criminal suspects.

The L.A.P.D. had their own fingerprint cards in individual criminal files, but copies were also stored and managed centrally at the Fingerprint Factory, a vast repository the size of a stock warehouse. The Factory had tens of thousands of employees with access to almost half the national population, most of them male. It would be the best and fastest way Craine could identify the fingerprints taken from the shooter's car.

The first problem was that it was located in Washington. The second problem was that it was run by the F.B.I. Only a senior police figure could access the archive at short notice. So naturally both Conroy and Craine had thought of Captain Henson.

It was Conroy who seemed to know Henson best, but she'd demurred. They had some kind of history she didn't want to share. She suggested Craine meet him, wrongly assuming that as a former detective Craine and Henson were old pals. Despite years working together, Henson and Craine were anything but good friends.

Most policemen had local bars. It meant they were easy to track down in an emergency. If your wife said you weren't home and had called to say you were working late, usually someone knew where you really were.

Henson's bar of choice was Dave's Blue Room on the Sunset Strip. Popular with the movie crowd, it was more of a white tablecloth restaurant than a police drinking hole. But Henson was a Captain now, head of Homicide and clearly enjoying all the trappings that came with it.

He stood to shake his hand when Craine entered, but while there was warmth in his voice, he wasn't exactly pleased to see him. At best surprised.

They were former peers about the same age. Henson was always known as an honest cop and Craine felt he could trust him. He had the same earnest face he'd always had, but with his thinning hair and saggy frame turning prematurely to fat, Henson looked like he'd aged twenty years in ten.

They sat at the bar counter. Craine ordered soda water; Henson ordered Craine's old cocktail of choice, a French 75. The tuxedo-clad bartender hovered in front of them, so the two men watched him silently as he shook the gin, lemon juice and sugar in a cocktail shaker, then strained it into a glass, topping it up with champagne. He had a mechanical hook prosthesis where his hand should be. On his farm Craine could pretend that the war hadn't happened, but seeing this man was a reminder that he hadn't served. He wondered what he was doing when this soldier lost his hand. Painting his house, maybe. Feeding his horses.

"I didn't know I'd see you again," Henson said when their drinks had been placed on silver coasters and the bartender was out of earshot.

In truth, it was a decision Abe was none too happy about but Craine had convinced him that Henson was the only possible route to getting fingerprint identification and, more importantly, that he could do so without the F.B.I.'s knowledge. The police were irrelevant to this investigation and didn't have the impetus or manpower to get involved in Lansky's affairs, he told him. It was a punt but Abe had gone for it. Craine took advantage of how desperate he was to find the shooter now, too.

"It's a short visit," was Craine's only reply.

"Where you living now? New York?" Henson asked, feigning pleasantries.

Craine was still staring at the bartender's metal hook. "No," he said. "Upstate. I have a farm."

"Well, how about that," Henson said.

It felt odd for the two of them to be making small talk. Craine didn't have many friends in the Detective Bureau when he worked there. It was part and parcel of his being married to a movie star. People never knew how to act around him.

"How are things at the precinct?" Craine asked.

"Busy. People are intent on killing each other, that much remains the same. Although seems to be more people now than ever." He took a sip from his flute, then looked away. Clearly, it was on his mind. "I wonder about the war. What it did to all these young guys with malleable minds trained to become savages. Used to be you kill somebody, you get locked up. Then suddenly you kill a man and they give you a medal for it."

Henson waved his hand in the air. They'd both seen enough crime scenes to know you could never comprehend man's aptitude for cruelty. "So," he said, "I assume you're not looking to move back?"

"No." Craine took small sips from his soda water. "I was hoping I could ask you a few questions about Benjamin Siegel."

Henson nodded. "Tilda Conroy said you were asking questions."

"We're sharing information."

"You be careful you don't get her in trouble," Henson said.

"Conroy knows what she's doing."

Henson's features hardened. It was clear he felt protective over her. "I had Agent Redhill asking questions about you, too," he said. "Says you're disrupting the Siegel investigation. Thinks you may have been involved with a shooting at the Bradbury Building last night."

When Craine didn't say anything—didn't deny it—he gave him an enquiring look. "Are you working for the studios? Because nothing suggests they're involved. George Raft, he's not a suspect. That's tabloid fodder."

"I'm not working for the studios."

"Who, then?"

Craine didn't answer, so Henson said, "The Craine I knew didn't care about justice. He left and disappeared. So why now? Who are you working for?"

Craine lowered his voice. "Friends of Siegel."

Henson was so annoyed he almost snapped the flute stem. "The *mob*? So Redhill was right. And to think I told him it was bullshit."

Craine looked around. There was no point lying now. "They have my son," he said.

Craine didn't go into specifics, but he told Henson enough for him to understand. Murder was a high-pitched noise homicide detectives learned to get used to. But in the L.A.P.D., a man's family life was sacred.

Speaking as quietly as he could, Craine told him about the men coming to his farm; he told him about what had been asked of him under threat and he told him exactly what had happened at the Bradbury Building.

"We can help you," Henson said when he'd finished.

"No," he replied. "You can't."

"What about the F.B.I.?"

Craine shook his head. "I can't trust them. And neither should you."

"I don't think you—" Henson paused, trying to find the right words. "You're talking about a national government agency."

"Have they taken over the investigation?"

Henson seemed defensive. "I've always found the Federal Bureau cooperative and easy to deal with. We're working together on this."

"Since when did the F.B.I. get involved in local murders?"

"It was clear from the start that this homicide was related to organized crime. That's a major area of oversight for the F.B.I., even if they do seem preoccupied with the red scare. Besides, the average radio car takes 250 calls a month. Our Homicide guys pick up a murder every three days. You remember the pressure we're put under by senior personnel. We've got no problem with somebody else coming in to share resources we don't have."

Siegel's death wasn't hugely important for Henson. The Captain of Homicide simply wanted Siegel's name off his blackboard so he could focus on making sure L.A. wasn't the crime capital of the U.S. That honor could belong to any other city but his.

Craine spoke cautiously. "They've been lying to you, Henson. You know they have."

Henson's lack of answer was an affirmative.

"You arrived at the scene a little after Conroy. I know Redhill was already on-site. Who else was at the house when you got there?" he asked.

Henson took a large gulp of his champagne cocktail, then wiped his top lip. "Only Smiley, Siegel's friend. And Charlie Hill. Virginia Hill's brother. He'd been put in a car."

Craine said, "There was another witness. A girl Charlie Hill brought with him."

Henson shook his head. "I know you've been telling Tilda the same thing."

"Because it's true. Both Allen Smiley and Charlie Hill confirmed it."

Henson lowered his voice. "You spoke to them?"

"I didn't only speak to them. I spoke to the girl."

Henson seemed confused. He stared at the bottles behind the bar. Dom Perignon champagne. Hennessy cognac. Bordeaux wines. It was like he suddenly became embarrassed to be there.

"You said it yourself," Craine went on. "You arrived after Redhill. There could have been at least ten minutes, if not more, before Homicide got there when the F.B.I. were on the scene."

"Uniforms were there."

"Uniforms can be bought. They can be manipulated."

Henson was scrambling for an explanation. "Maybe they were confused. They're there around midnight, the four-to-twelve is on changeover. Uniforms heading home, fresh cars coming in."

"You think that's likely? Or that someone told them to change their report not to include the other witness?"

Henson swilled the remains of his glass. It was like he felt the need to exit this conversation. "I'll look into it," he shrugged. "But not because you're asking."

"Since the F.B.I. have been involved, have they shared their process?"

The Captain rubbed his jaw. Craine was guiding him toward the answer he already knew.

"Not exactly."

"Not exactly, or not at all?"

Henson blushed and then he sighed, but it took another round of cocktails before the Captain admitted to Craine that the Federal Bureau of Investigation hadn't shared any leads with the L.A.P.D.

"They're not cooperating," he said finally. "Haven't been from the start. And from what you're telling me it sounds like they've hidden a key witness."

"A witness paid to make sure Siegel went home that night. Paid to make sure Siegel's girlfriend left town that week."

Henson was staring at the bar again. "What is it you're accusing them of, Craine?" he asked.

"I think the F.B.I. know who did it. I don't know why but I think they're protecting someone."

Henson took another large mouthful of his champagne cocktail. "And what do you want from me?"

"If I got you latent prints from the shooter's car, could you cross-compare them against the national fingerprint archive?"

Henson thought about this before nodding. "In theory. But you'd have to find the car, and that's—"

Henson stopped talking when Craine slid over an envelope containing the latent prints.

"Conroy has access to the *Herald*'s Soundphoto machine. It'll make it faster and save you sending from your office. No one will need to know."

Henson smirked, almost to himself. "So you and Tilda *are* working together on this," he said.

"As I said, we're sharing resources where useful."

Henson stared at the envelope. “Craine, I can’t help you.”

“Henson—”

“Listen to me,” he said firmly. “Aside from the fact that I can’t be seen to be using a newspaper’s resources to accelerate a police investigation, I can’t be seen to be going up against the F.B.I. The Factory is a federal facility—”

“They don’t need to know—”

Henson knocked the champagne flute hard on the counter. Craine thought he heard the potash glass crack. “Trust me,” he said with finality. “Redhill will find out.”

Henson finished his drink, then excused himself to go to the bathroom. Craine was left alone at the bar, tired and discouraged.

He looked around, the place full now, different celebrities he’d long forgotten about hiding in different corner booths. He noticed Ava Gardner was drinking martinis with Lana Turner. Gardner used to be married to Mickey Rooney, but the man sitting between the two women was that actor-singer, Sinatra. It was unclear which of the women he was more interested in but what was clear was the shock on his face when a gossip columnist with a camera came over to their table and snapped a picture.

It was a familiar scene in places like this, but Sinatra stood up and pulled the reporter to one side before he could leave. The singer whispered in his ear and Craine knew he was cutting a deal. The gossip industry relied on a barter system. You traded dirt for a more sordid story about someone else.

This was how it had always worked. It was why Craine had never had much time for Hollywood reporters. He found their ethics lacking. Conroy was about the only one he’d ever trusted.

CHAPTER 30

Tilda Conroy drove home feeling deflated, almost colliding with a Hudson coupe as she was pulling out of the newspaper's parking lot.

A part of her wondered whether the City Editor would have pulled the story if she wasn't female. But another part asked herself if she'd have stood back and accepted his decision so easily if she were a man.

A mile from home she came to a stop sign and noticed that the car behind her was the same Hudson she'd almost nudged coming out of the office.

She waited apprehensively for the lights to change and followed the traffic onto Melrose Avenue.

She slowed down and stared at the rearview mirror. She wasn't sure what she was expecting, but within a few seconds the Hudson had turned onto the same road. *Was somebody following her?*

The car was speeding up now, steadily closing the distance between them. *Thirty yards. Twenty. Ten.*

Conroy felt a surge of nervous energy and pushed down on the gas, putting thirty yards between them. Her hands were clammy and she gripped the wheel tightly.

At the next block Conroy pulled a late left, narrowly missing a surge of vehicles coming across the junction. She saw the Hudson follow but soon it was lost in a thicket of cars. She kept an eye on the rearview but the Hudson was gone.

Conroy reached Sierra Bonita but the barrier to the basement parking lot was down, so she parked the car awkwardly on the street. Her heart was pounding and she was frantic to get inside her building and into the refuge of her apartment.

Rushing toward the entrance doors, she began to rummage in her bag for her keys, wishing she'd done this in the safety of her car. The bag dropped on the floor and Conroy suddenly found herself on her knees, scrabbling for her purse in the dark.

The building door opened and Conroy almost jumped out of her skin.

"Tilda? How are you?" A whiff of floral perfume. She looked up to see her neighbor, a fellow war widow with two children always dropping gum in the hallway.

"Thank you, Mrs. Hadley, couldn't find my keys."

"Are we seeing you at book club? We didn't see you last time."

Conroy's eyes darted behind her and back again. She was desperate to get upstairs.

"Yes. Looking forward to it."

Mrs. Hadley sensed her unease. "Is everything alright? You look a little—"

"Absolutely. Long day at work."

Mrs. Hadley wrinkled her eyes. "You poor dear. I'm having a hell of a time of it, too. Bobby has strep throat again, poor thing."

Conroy ignored her, heading inside and shutting the door between them. "Good night, Mrs. Hadley."

They had an elevator but she didn't want to wait. Conroy ran up two flights to her apartment. Once inside, she bolted the door and stood at the peephole.

The hallway was empty.

Conroy felt sick to her stomach. She ran to the window but it was dark outside and she couldn't make out the different car models under the streetlight. The sound of an engine froze her to the spot, but no car came.

Glancing back at the front door every few seconds, she backed into the kitchen, pulling at knives from the drawer. Twice she picked up the bread knife and then put it down again, settling for something smaller and sharper and wholly less ridiculous.

When the telephone rang beside her Conroy's heart thumped so hard against her chest she backed into the wall.

It rang several times. Conroy checked the peephole again before coming back to the living room and picking up the phone.

The voice on the end was a man's voice. "Tilda?"

She didn't react at first. Stayed staring at the door.

"Tilda. It's Craine."

Not relief as much as a distraction. Her heart was still beating fast. "Hi. Yes."

"Is everything okay?"

"I–I'm not sure. My editor. He's not happy with the story. Wilson and Mayer—they've put pressure on the paper to cut the article. Where did you get to with Henson?"

"I'm with him now. He'll be back any second. Says he can't get them to Washington. He's not going to help us." She heard him say that with a sigh. She could sense his frustration.

"Can't or won't?"

"I'm not even sure."

There was a drinks trolley beside the phone, and Conroy poured herself an inch of bourbon with one hand. Her fingers were shaking as she brought it to her lips.

Craine must have said something because after a while she heard him say, "Tilda, are you there?"

"Sorry. Yes, I'm here."

"Is everything alright?"

She stretched the cord and went over to the window again. She looked up and down the street.

"Yes. I thought—never mind."

And then she paused. Something was different: the Hudson was parked twenty yards or so down the road. The back wheels were a little away from the curb. Like they'd parked quickly.

"Craine, I need you to come over."

"What's happening?"

Conroy moved closer to the window to get a better look. There was the sound of glass cracking and then a loud pop outside like a car engine.

She jumped the slightest amount before noticing that there was a hole in her window, little bits of glass on the carpet.

It was strange how long it took to register; she realized too late they were firing at her. Before she could scream or dive for cover more glass flew inward, her wall pictures cracking as she heard another series of loud pops.

The phone receiver, the tumbler and Conroy dropped at the same time.

They say that when you're shot, it's not the bullet that makes you fall to the floor. It's the sheer surprise. Conroy put her hand to her chest. Her entire rib cage was numb but there was no blood. She hadn't been hit.

More pops came and she began screaming. Not for help and not for Craine. Simply screaming.

The room felt hot and airless. Conroy could see the phone receiver on the carpet a few feet away. Managing the smallest of breaths, she groped for it but more bullets came and she stopped, frozen still.

She could hear the voice through the receiver. "Conroy, what's happening? Tilda, are you there?"

Conroy tried to shout but she couldn't summon the words.

They drove in separate cars, arriving at Conroy's a little after 9 P.M. Abe looked at the uniforms moving in and out of the house and told Craine he'd wait outside. "I'll keep an eye out," he said, to excuse himself.

Henson took Craine up to the third floor, where Conroy sat crouched over in a dusky stairwell with no windows. There were two police officers stationed at the door behind her and several more in the corridor: uniforms interviewing the neighbors, filling out incident reports, bagging things for the evidence control unit. He could see that the forms they were using were the same they'd always been.

The crime desk's colored clerk was sitting with one arm around Conroy. Alice, he thought her name was. She stood up when they entered.

"I'll go bring the car upfront," she said to Conroy soothingly. "Take your time."

"Are you alright, Tilda?" Henson asked, passing Alice with a curt nod.

"No. Not really."

Craine looked at the police captain. "Henson, would you mind if I speak to Tilda for a minute?"

Henson was less than enthused. "I'm going to see the crime scene. When I'm back in five minutes I want you gone."

He left and Craine went two steps up so his face was level with Conroy's. There was blood on the sleeves of her blouse. "Are you hurt?"

"It's only glass."

"You going to the precinct?"

She shook her head. "I'm staying with Alice. They've taken my statement already. Nothing left to do."

"If you saw the car again, could you identify it?"

She shook her head. "A Hudson. Could be anyone's."

"Color?"

"There's a reason why no one can ever remember license tags and car colors. It's because it's not what you're thinking about in a shooting."

"You're angry."

"I'm upset. And don't patronize me, Craine. I have a right to be angry. You've got me involved with something . . ."

Uniformed officers behind her were too busy putting pen to paper to listen in. Or they simply didn't care. Most beat cops had seen more than enough drama to ignore a man and a woman arguing on the stairs.

"Why am I being targeted?" Conroy asked.

"We were, too."

"First it's the mob, then it's Wilson. Then it's the Hollywood studios. Anyone in this entire city could be responsible for Siegel's death. All you've done is put our lives—*my* life—at risk." She rolled her head from side to side quickly, as if shaking off bad memories. "I'm an idiot. Why would I put myself in that position?"

"You're asking the wrong question. The question you should be asking is, 'Why do they want to stop us? What is it that we already know?'"

"No. I should never have agreed to work with you. I gave you the benefit of the doubt because of what you did with the extortion rings. But I should have believed people when they told me not to trust you. Your reputation as a corrupt cop precedes you."

Craine was stung by the remark. "I thought you were the type of reporter that looked beyond the surface of things."

She stared at him. No, not at him. Right through him. He was speared.

"You don't know me at all." She took a deep breath and stood up. "My job is not to help you and whichever mobster you work for. For all I know, it's your employers who are doing this."

"Tilda, as far as it concerns you, I can only assure you that it isn't."

"Of course this concerns me!" she said, using her fists to punch fresh tears aside. "You think because I haven't caught you lying that you're telling me the truth? Well, I think you are lying, Craine. I think you're hiding things."

Craine gripped the railing. He wanted to tell her about Lansky. About mobsters abducting his son and holding him for ransom. But he'd told too many people already. She was a reporter; he'd already revealed too much.

"Tilda. I can't tell you anything that might put me—"

"So it's okay for me to get shot at, but not you? Who are you working for? Who *are* they?"

"Tilda." He tried to placate her but it only made her angrier.

"Why was Paul Ricca released from prison this week?"

The statement threw him. "Paul Ricca?"

"The Chicago boss. Is that who you're working for?"

Craine knew who he was. He was Frank Nitti's successor. Sentenced to fifteen years as part of the Hollywood extortion ring. *Why had he been released early? And why did Conroy think he was relevant?*

Henson appeared in the door to the corridor.

"Craine. F.B.I. are enroute. I suggest you get out of here."

"You tell them?"

"No. But someone did."

Craine went down the stairs. He turned with one arm on the railing. "Tilda, I know you blame me for this . . ." He paused. She was right to blame him. She was lucky to be alive. Not for the first time, people were suffering because of his actions. "I'm sorry," he said.

Abe was waiting for him in the Mercury, smoking cigarettes with the window down. He had the Savage on his lap.

As they drove down the street they passed two black sedans pulling in at speed. Craine was sure he could see the shaded form of Emmett Redhill inside.

"Where to?" Abe asked.

There was nowhere else they could go.

"Hotel."

Evidence was disappearing in front of his own eyes. Without the fingerprints, this investigation would fail to yield a single suspect. They had nothing. Not even a blind alley to run down.

As they drove toward the hotel, Craine felt like he'd been cut adrift. Now all he could do was wait for the storm to roll his boat over so he could let the ocean swallow him whole.

Captain Henson had let Conroy into her apartment so she could pack an overnight bag. She felt a little numb, but she went through the motions of opening drawers and taking out clothes like she was going away for a weekend rather than fleeing the scene of an attempted murder—*her* murder.

Conroy had been to hundreds of crime scenes, but usually when she was there she felt a certain distance. Whatever the circumstances, the victim was in some way involved in the events that led to their death; whether it was a gun in their hand or a knife in their back, they'd driven someone to kill them and to that end they were culpable.

So in a strange way Conroy felt like she was at fault for what happened tonight, too. And that sense of guilt made her feel angry, and that anger was directed at the people around her. Her editor. Craine. Henson.

As soon as she'd said his name in her head the police captain tapped on her bedroom door. She almost jumped out of her skin.

"Jesus," she said.

It felt awkward having him in her room. It wasn't the first time, and they were both aware of it. *Different circumstances.*

"Sorry," he said. "I wanted to ask if you have somewhere to stay."

Conroy put a toothbrush and her makeup in an old washbag she hadn't used in most of a decade. Since her honeymoon.

"With Alice. We work together."

"You know you're welcome to stay with me," he said a little too tentatively.

Conroy looked at him and exhaled.

"I'm offering as a friend. *Christ*, Tilda."

Henson picked up her overnight bag off the bed and carried it into the living room. She followed him but the second she stepped inside, Conroy felt oddly exposed. There wasn't a breeze but you could feel the warm air coming through the open window.

She looked around and noticed a picture of her late husband had cracked where it had fallen off the wall. The photograph looked damaged and she felt a sudden wave of emotion about it. *Oh Henry, why aren't you here when I need you?*

She looked at Henson as he issued instructions to uniforms in the corridor. She tried to remember their date. She remembered he was a good listener, which she liked. But it would never have worked out between them.

"Look at this place," he said to her. "Can't believe it. I always liked that clock you had. I'll get the uniforms to throw the rest of it away."

Conroy felt a surge of irritation. At the situation. At a lot of things.

"No," she snapped suddenly. "They're not throwing anything away. Don't think because you've been in my apartment before that somehow you can understand what it feels like. You can't."

"I'm not jousting with you, Tilda, I'm trying to help."

She'd raised her voice and it was clear he didn't want anyone else to overhear.

"I don't even want them in here. This is my my *home*."

"Okay, don't get upset. They're only doing their job."

"Don't you tell me how I should be feeling right now. This is a hazard you created when you refused to recognize that Siegel's killer is still out there. That was a military carbine shooting at me, wasn't it?"

"Tilda," he said quietly. "They probably wanted to scare you. That's all."

"No, they tried to kill me because you won't do your goddamn job."

"That's not fair. I'm trying to do the right thing. There's a lot of pressure on this."

"Oh, God. *Pressure*. Poor you."

She started to get angry but rather than let her, he took her shoulder. "Tilda, you need to calm down."

She pushed him away. "Don't you dare touch me. Get off."

There was nothing more to say. She went into the kitchen and poured herself a glass of water. It was several minutes before her hands stopped shaking.

Not long after, she heard the sound of boots mounting the stairs outside and then two uniformed officers came in.

"Got a Negro fella here," the elder of the two muttered suspiciously to Henson. "Says he's L.A.P.D."

Conroy looked out into the corridor and could see Alice and her patrolman husband in strained conversation with a large uniformed officer. They didn't have their arms on him but they might as well have done.

She addressed Henson. "That's Alice and her husband. 'Course he's L.A.P.D. He's wearing uniform, for God's sake."

At Henson's signal, the other men stepped away. He gave Conroy a look that was meant to be reassuring. "Sure you'll be alright with these people? I can arrange a hotel."

"I'll be fine."

"I'll have an escort take you down. Anything you need, you call my office."

A young man in a black suit was hovering in the doorway, too. A junior F.B.I. agent.

"Captain Henson. Agent Redhill would like a word. Right now."

The tone wasn't lost on anybody.

"I'll be there right away."

This was Captain Henson. He was the job. The grind. The box-ticker. Like his predecessor, he was a robust survivor of the police department's bureaucracy. He was never going to go against the grain.

When the agent left, Conroy took her bag from Henson and went to go.

"David," she said, using his first name. "I'm done with this investigation. But you should know that you're not only letting Redhill walk all over you, you're letting him make a mockery of the L.A.P.D."

CHAPTER 31

The hotel manager had long since left, but the young woman at reception told them they had a guest waiting for them in their suite. This seemed to hold Abe in place.

"Let's take the stairs," he said.

Figuring an ambush, Craine let Abe lead. When they reached the building's stairwell, Abe leaned cautiously over the balustrade and stared up and down the staircase. Nothing. No sound anywhere.

His Savage now stretched out ahead, he took the steps two at a time, pausing only when he thought he saw movement. Craine followed close behind as they reached their floor and sidled into the corridor.

The door to their suite was ajar. When Abe pushed it open, Craine half-expected gunfire to knock him off his feet.

Instead a voice said, "There you are."

Kastel was idling in their suite with a glass of something in his hand. The phone was off its cradle like he was in the middle of a call. Craine quailed when he saw him.

"Don't look so shocked, Craine."

Kastel's face was twitching. It was something Craine had noticed before. But this time he realized: Kastel had withdrawal symptoms. Psychostimulants. It was what they gave soldiers in the war.

Abe seemed surprised to see him, "What are you doing here?"

"Lansky sent me to check on you," Kastel said as if he were visiting an elderly grandma. "I hope you don't mind, I had them bring up some ice. This heat."

Abe holstered his pistol but Craine saw him glance sideways to check no one else was here. "When did you get here?" he asked. "No one warned me you were coming."

Kastel poured them all drinks, but it looked like he'd had several already. He was jittery and kept touching his face.

"Flew in a few hours ago. Won't be here long. I have to be fueled and ready to fly by midnight."

Kastel held out a drink for each of them in turn. When neither of them took the glass, Kastel dropped it hard on the side table. "Suit yourself."

Abe and Craine waited expectantly.

"What's going on, Kastel?" Abe asked.

"The situation has changed somewhat," Kastel said. "It's a box-up. New dice."

The terms meant nothing to Craine. "I don't follow."

"You can put a stop to this. All of this."

When neither man said anything, Kastel said, "The investigation. It's going nowhere. Harvey tells me you're convinced Charlie Hill didn't do it, and Dragna is getting annoyed with the attention you're bringing the organization. Even says you've been talking to the press."

Kastel let out a series of exaggerated tutting noises and Craine and Abe shared a subtle exchange of glances.

"We've found several leads," Craine said. "The F.B.I. have been withholding information from the public. We tracked down a missing witness. She was asked to set Siegel up that night."

"But are you any closer to finding out who actually *killed* Ben Siegel?"

Craine was nervous, unsure where Kastel was going with this.

"I told you, we have leads we're investigating. I still have two more days."

"It's a cold table, Craine. Ask yourself, are you really going to solve all this in two days?"

Craine thought of Michael. *No*, he thought to himself. *I don't think I am. Not now.*

Abe said, "Does Lansky know about this?"

"Of course. His orders."

Craine didn't move. He didn't know what to say.

Abe rubbed his jaw. "You want us to drop the investigation?" A glance in Craine's direction. "Send him home?"

Kastel shook his head. "This isn't a dispensation. We have a new offer."

The room went still. Abe was riled. "Why wasn't I told about this?"

"There wasn't time, Abe. The F.B.I. are probably tapping the phones. We're not risking sending a telegram. Mr. Lansky sent me here to tell you in person."

Craine said, "If you're not letting me go, what is the offer?"

Kastel sipped from his tumbler. "You can go on as previously agreed. You have two days. If you don't find out who killed Siegel, we kill you. And your boy."

It was said with such a lack of formality Craine almost had to ask him to say it again.

Kastel tilted the glass, casually setting the wager: "*Or* what you're doing—this investigation—it ends today. Your son will go free. I'll have a plane collect my men and leave him be. Your boy will go about his life as if it never happened."

Craine frowned, confused. He noticed Abe lower his head and rub his fingers through his eyebrows.

"You'll let us go?"

"I'll let *him* go."

"What about me?"

Kastel held his hands out with an easy grin. "You know too much, Craine. The people you've spoken to. The press. The FBI. It adds up to too much if there's no win. Stakes are too high."

Craine felt his cheeks burn but he wasn't ready to believe what Kastel was telling him. "That doesn't make sense. You told me I had five days—"

"And now I'm offering you an out. Be a man. Do the right thing and take it."

Craine didn't look at Abe but he could hear his heavy breathing. Kastel couldn't suppress a smile, gauging Craine's reaction with satisfaction.

"This—there has to be another way."

"There's not." He sipped his drink. "All you have to do is decide."

"You're asking me to give up my life."

Kastel nodded. "My country asked the same of me and I took it willingly. I'm asking you to give up your life for your son. If he means as much to you as you make out, this shouldn't be a difficult decision."

Craine wasn't sure what to say. Michael meant everything to him. But surely Kastel couldn't expect him to willingly choose death?

"If I can't persuade you, maybe he can." Kastel picked up the receiver that had been resting on the table since they'd entered the room. "He's here," he said into the telephone. "Put the boy on."

Kastel held out the phone and Craine took it. There was a rush of static, then a muffled sobbing. "Pa?"

Michael.

The sound of his son's voice ran down Craine's spine. "Where are you? Are you alright?"

"They drove us to a phone in town." The boy broke down crying.

"What about your hand?"

"They took me to a doctor." He whimpered. "What's going on? They won't tell me anything."

Kastel tried to take the phone away but Craine grabbed it off him. Through the receiver he could hear his son's voice calling after him. He clung to every word.

Kastel ripped the phone from his hands and dropped it on the hook. Craine launched himself at him, landing several closed fists on Kastel's face before Abe pulled the two of them apart.

"Enough," Abe said. But Kastel took a step and swung his foot into Craine's stomach so hard that he slumped to the floor on all fours, his stomach in spasm. He couldn't stand; he couldn't breathe.

Kastel went to kick him again but this time Abe pushed Kastel back with his good arm.

Kastel's cheek had already begun swelling like a balloon. He touched a bloody lip.

"Surprised me, Craine. Didn't think you had it in you." He spat on the carpet through hard breaths. "This is the offer on the table," he said. "Don't take it personally. It's business."

Craine's stomach muscles were still cramping and he struggled to suck in air. "If I can have more time," he said, his voice pleading even though he knew it was pointless.

"I've told you, the original offer stands. Mr. Lansky is a fair man. But if you fail, if you can't meet the terms on which you agreed, you'll lose everything. Are you willing to do that? Bet the house. Go all in on a martingale."

Martingale. Bettor's slang. Doubling down. *Risking everything.*

Craine was still struggling to breathe. He tried to make sense of Kastel's terms. *If I go forward with the investigation, I risk my son's life. If I end this now, he goes free but I die.*

Never in his life had Craine been handed a choice that felt so final.

"If I accept, how can I trust you to do right by him?" he asked.

Abe spoke up. "I'll make sure of it."

No one said anything for a long time. Craine didn't cry, but a part of him wanted that purge.

"How will you do it?"

Abe answered before Kastel could. "We'll go for a drive. Do it right. You won't feel anything." He spoke to him like a caring doctor putting him out of his misery. Craine was reminded of his dog.

"Your choice, Craine."

There wasn't a choice so much as a decision in front of him he had to take. Craine knew two more days wouldn't make any difference. They were no closer to finding Siegel's killer than they were three days ago. He thought of Michael, his fingers being severed from the knuckle. Of him screaming. That was nothing compared to what they would do to him if Craine failed to solve Siegel's murder.

His voice was thin. "You see to it my boy is safe."

Abe answered for both of them. "You have my word."

Craine felt a chill on his shoulders. There was nothing left to say.

They say the hardest part of making any decision is choosing in the first place. Once you've made your choice your brain tells you it was the right one. Stops you regretting it as a way of coping. But this was different. Craine was choosing death. There was no part of him that was at peace with this situation.

Their danse macabre was three men driving to a place of Abe's choosing where Craine could be executed. Kastel sat in the back as Abe drove. Craine was in the front passenger seat, but he could see Kastel's pistol pointing directly at him the entire time. He had insisted on coming. Craine half got the impression he was worried Abe might let him go.

"You did the right thing," Abe said. His eyes were fixed on the road ahead. He hadn't looked at Craine properly since the hotel. He was distancing himself.

Craine's senses were benumbed, as if a strange palsy had overtaken his body. He had never been a brave man. That awareness had sat with him all his life. He hadn't served in the war. Had avoided it. He was too old to be drafted, but he wasn't so old he couldn't have signed up. Maybe other people didn't know that, but he did. Michael did, too.

Hide from the world and it will come back and find you. He'd been a coward. And now he was getting his dues.

"Where are we going?" he asked, staring into the middle distance. Speaking was difficult.

"I know a place. Near here."

It felt strange to be driving without knowing where you were going but still knowing how that journey would end.

Craine had never been a religious man. He wasn't convinced heaven existed. Didn't think he'd get there even if it did. But in that moment he couldn't help but remember what his priest had taught him at boarding school. "Memento mori"—*Remember that you have to die.*

It was little consolation.

They came off before the Colorado Street Bridge. His mind must have drifted because when the car tires rolled to a stop on the gravel he had to remind himself where he was. There were no streetlamps, but when Craine looked around he realized they were at the Arroyo Seco. He knew this place. They used to find bodies dumped here every few weeks. They even put a chain-link fence up once but it only got torn down.

They stepped out of the car but left the engine running. Abe kept the headlights on to give them a little light.

"We're heading down there," Abe said, pointing in the direction of the beams. The riverbed was dry for the summer months. But when the September rains did finally come, whatever the coyotes hadn't eaten the water would wash away. He'd disappear.

Kastel wagged his pistol at Craine for him to follow. It was dark away from the headlights, and twice Craine lost his footing as he sidled down the steep embankments.

Kastel stretched the pistol toward a hidden spot beneath the bridge. "Here will do," he said with a flinty streak in his voice. "Let's get on with it."

Craine stared up at the sky. The air was thick and humid and he had to dab his eyes with the sleeve of his shirt.

He turned to Abe. "You'll leave me here?"

Abe nodded gravely.

"Don't tell my boy anything. You tell him it was quick and that I didn't suffer. You don't tell him why."

Abe exhaled. A sigh. He stood there with his arms by his sides, thoughtful and withdrawn. Kastel took the opportunity to light a fresh cigarette and draw in a lungful of smoke.

Craine wondered who would tell Michael and what they'd say. Was it dying that upset him, or was it not saying goodbye? Despite the bridges that they'd built, so much remained unsaid between father and son. So many times he'd wanted to tell Michael how much he loved him. What was it that prevented him from really expressing how he felt? What was it that held him back?

He took a deep breath. There was so much he'd wished he'd told him, and the things he regretted came out now in a sudden gush. "Tell my son I'm sorry," he said to Abe. "Tell him he needs to do what he wants with his life. I was trying to protect him, but I was wrong."

At first Craine's words didn't look as if they made any sense to Abe, but something seemed to strike a chord when Craine said finally, "And tell him I'm proud of him. That I wished I could have had the courage to tell him myself."

"I'll tell him," Abe said quietly. "I'll make sure he knows."

Craine focused on the task at hand. He felt nauseous, wondering whether Abe might pull his gun and shoot him at any second.

"You have something heavy-caliber?" he asked with a feeble energy. "I don't want to bleed to death. I want it quick."

"You want, I'll let you do it yourself. If not, I can."

Abe touched the back of his head as if to indicate how he'd do it. Craine knew that was one of the fastest deaths. Like cattle.

Wanting some control over his last moments, Craine whispered, "I'll do it myself."

Kastel waved his pistol. "Wait, don't give him a gun."

"He's not going anywhere."

Abe removed the clip, then made a show of loading a single bullet into the chamber. He put the working parts forward and handed it to Craine.

Craine looked around at the surrounding hills in different shades. He could hear cicadas.

Michael was sixteen. He'd be okay without him. He was almost a man now. Thinking that made Craine realize that he'd been overprotective of his son before. Cosseted him. He'd been so busy turning his back on the world he hadn't accepted that Michael needed to go out and explore it for himself. Maybe Craine dying would set him free.

There was nothing left to say. He felt empty. It didn't feel real. Like the situation was happening to someone else.

Kastel looked around. "Get this over with. I got a flight to Chicago."

Sweat starting dripping off Craine. He couldn't even hold the pistol grip without it slipping out of his hand.

And then a thought came to him suddenly, like a bee sting.

Chicago.

Craine had an abrupt moment of paralysis. He looked up. "Wait."

Kastel raised his pistol. "I told you, we should have done it for him."

"No," said Craine, instinctively raising his hands. "Wait a minute."

But it wasn't cowardice that was stopping Craine. If it was, he'd recognize it like an old friend. The feeling he had now was different. A feeling that something wasn't right. That he'd failed to pursue a line of enquiry. It was the beam of light to a man drowning in darkness. He pushed his way to the surface.

He looked at Kastel, then Abe. "I changed my mind."

Kastel pulled his hammer back. "There's no use stalling. The decision is made. I'll do it for you if you're too yellow."

"No. I want more time. I want until Friday."

"It's his choice," Abe said.

"He's on a tile," Kastel said. "He doesn't know what he's doing."

"You understand what you're agreeing to here?" Abe asked Craine quietly. "What this means for your son? I won't be able to protect him."

On the fringes of Craine's mind came an image of Michael. He tried to push it away, hoping he wasn't making a mistake.

"I understand."

"No," Kastel said, angry now. He shut one eye and took aim. "It's done. We're finishing him off here."

Abe stepped toward him, into the firing line. "You gave him a choice. As far as I'm concerned that choice is still his to make."

Kastel gave him a hateful look. "If Lansky—"

"Then I'll vouch for him. We give him forty-eight hours as agreed."

They stood there, the three of them, for a long time. Kastel was aiming directly at Abe now but the big man didn't move an inch. Craine could see Kastel's mind moving. Working out what to do next.

After what seemed like an age, Kastel lowered his pistol. "Forty-eight hours," he said, looking at Craine. "After that I'll kill you myself."

They walked back up the concrete riverbed. When they got to the car, Kastel muttered to Abe, something about dropping him off at the hotel. Something about his flight to Chicago again.

Kastel slammed the car door shut. The moonlight made his red face blue. It was like Celia told him once after one of their arguments; the most infuriating thing about Craine was that he didn't lose his temper, he made you lose yours.

When Craine got into the back seat, Kastel looked at him in the rearview mirror. "You're either a fool or a coward, Craine."

Craine was too exhausted to feel resentful. Besides, a part of him thought Kastel might be right. If he was wrong about his hunch, his son's life was forfeit.

The ante was set.

CHAPTER 32

After Kastel left them to get his flight, the two men returned to their suite.

They took the elevator in silence, but in their own strange way their silences had become more comfortable for both men.

The dull shock of survival didn't have time to really sink in. Craine's thoughts were only forward-facing. But when the elevator opened on to their floor, something in Craine's stomach dropped and he found himself rushing to a small garbage bin and retching in great heaves of relief.

"It's okay," Abe said. "It's done with."

But despite Abe's compassion they both knew his words didn't ring true. It wasn't nearly over. The decision Craine had made was based on a strange hunch. And while he knew that there was a new lead they had to pursue, he also knew that he'd had an opportunity to save his son and he'd turned it down. What kind of father did that make him?

Inside their suite, Craine went to his bathroom, drinking from the faucet and splashing water on his face. He glanced at himself in the mirror. His face was bleached white and a shadow of stubble had formed on his jaw. He couldn't bring himself to look into his own eyes. He wondered what Celia would have done if she were in the same position. But then again, there wasn't much to consider. She would have taken Kastel's offer without a moment's hesitation.

On the chair in the bathroom were his farm clothes. The hotel had seen to it that they were washed and pressed but it didn't matter. He brought them to his face and breathed them in. Somewhere within them was home. It was the only thing driving him.

Craine showered, turning up the hot water and getting out only when he'd stopped shaking. Abe had ordered room service and when he came back in there was a trolley of food waiting. A hunger had overtaken Craine and both men ate readily, like two old colleagues sharing a dinner platter on a business trip.

Afterward, Abe sat in his slacks and a sleeveless vest, trying to change the gauze on his shoulder. The bruising was fierce, a purple swelling that covered most of his arm and back. It looked painful and Abe helped himself to several inches of whiskey from the bottle Kastel had left out.

When he was finished cleaning the wound, Craine looked at him levelly and asked him the question that had been bothering him for the last hour.

"Why is Kastel flying to Chicago, Abe?"

Abe was taping the gauze over. He looked well-practiced. "It doesn't concern you."

This time Craine was resolute. "It does. You told me there's a meeting on Friday in Las Vegas. That other investors in The Flamingo are meeting Lansky. Is one of them Paul Ricca? The head of the Chicago Outfit?"

Abe closed his eyes and Craine was starting to think he'd fallen asleep. He needed Abe to tell him. Knew that somehow Chicago were involved in all of this. He just didn't know how.

"Paul Ricca was released recently," Abe said finally. "As I told you before, the syndicates work on a national level. Separate organizations for separate territories. Now that Siegel is gone, Lansky is worried that Vegas will fail. He's looking to sell his shares to Chicago so he can pay back the other New York investors."

"And this is happening on Friday?"

Abe coughed. "Senior members of the Chicago Outfit are flying in to Vegas. Kastel has gone up so he can make arrangements and escort them down. On Friday they will be buying Siegel's shares in the hotel at a price to be agreed."

"And what does this have to do with finding Siegel's killers?"

"Chicago showed interest in buying shares in The Flamingo before this trouble with Siegel. Now they're hesitant to go forward until the issue is resolved. It shows a lack of control. A lack of power."

"What if they did it?"

Abe shook his head. "They would never risk starting a war. Frank Nitti killed himself. Ricca has only just been released and needs to consolidate. They'd be starting from a weak position."

"Not if they had someone inside. Someone working for Lansky."

Abe was never going to agree with Craine, but he could see him thinking it over. "Who told you about the Chicago release? It didn't make the press."

"Conroy. She found out. We need to talk to her to see what else she knows. She might have files on Ricca."

Craine remembered hearing that Conroy was staying with that colored girl she worked with. He tried to recall her name. *Alice.*

Craine didn't know her surname but he knew how he could find out. He went to the coffee table and picked up the newspapers he'd bought on Monday.

"They're old," Abe said.

"Doesn't matter."

Craine picked up the *Herald* and skimmed through the pages until he found the obituaries column. Conroy was a lead crime reporter. She got the headlines and the front pages. But the crime desk had always overseen all aspects of city law enforcement: court reports, police statistics and obituaries. Craine tapped his finger on the name of the author.

Alice Hickerson.

There were several Hickersons in the directory and married women were often listed under their husband's name, which didn't help them. But what was germane to their search was that only one Hickerson lived in South Los Angeles.

* * *

Angelenos were tribal. Your address said what person you were: Malibu and Beverly Hills housed the white Hollywood elite; the Chinese lived in Chinatown; Mexicans in the Flats of Boyle Heights; the Japanese in Little Tokyo until they were relocated to internment camps after Pearl Harbor.

Even before the war the Negro areas had congregated around the factories south of Downtown. Residential segregation wasn't surprising in a city where black children could only swim in public pools the day before they were due to be cleaned. The Hickersons' address was a residential area north of Slauson Avenue and west of Main Street. It made sense because the Westside was home to middle-class Negroes. For people like Alice who worked in offices instead of on factory floors.

Their house was a single-story plywood with a prewar Plymouth in the driveway. Abe kept looking over his shoulder as they walked up to the front door. It was the first time Craine had seen him fully on edge. And then he realized: he'd never been in a black neighborhood before.

Craine knocked several times before anyone answered. There was the sound of locks turning, then a sliver of face appeared behind a chain.

"Robert Hickerson?"

"Yes."

"Husband of Alice?"

"What of it?" His voice took on a new edge. Very few men enjoyed strangers calling in the middle of the night to enquire about their wives.

"Mr. Hickerson, my name is Jonathan Craine. I work with Alice. This is my colleague, Abe. I'm afraid there's been a work emergency and I need to speak to her."

The eyes glanced away like he was checking his watch. "It's the middle of the night."

"I can only apologize. As I said, it's an emergency."

"You're from the paper?"

A pause, then, "It's about her job at the paper."

"She done something?" And then, as if Craine didn't hear him before, he repeated it for emphasis: "It's the middle of the night."

"No, sir. She's not in trouble. But this is an emergency. It involves Tilda Conroy, who I understand is staying with you."

Hearing Conroy's name changed the conversation.

The door closed; there was a metallic rustle as the chain came off. Then Mr. Hickerson opened the door. He had a billy club in his hand and he held it up for them to see.

"What the hell do you want, knocking on my door in the middle of the night asking about my wife and Mrs Conroy?"

Craine looked around. The streets were quiet. It didn't look like there was an official curfew here—not uncommon in black neighborhoods—but nevertheless loud conversations at street level would bring them undue attention.

Hickerson pointed the end of the cudgel toward them. Craine noticed it was police issued. "You better back up off my porch," he said.

"Are you L.A.P.D.?" Craine asked.

"Damn right, I'm police. You don't get back, I'll arrest you. Don't think because you're white I can't have you cuffed."

Abe stepped back, swearing under his breath. A Negro policeman was probably about the scariest combination for a man like Abe.

"I used to work for the L.A.P.D. Name is Craine."

There was a voice from behind the door. Craine heard a few harsh marital words shared, then a woman in a nightcap pushed her head round the door. *Alice.*

"Mr. Craine, why are you here?" And then, as if Craine hadn't heard her husband before, "It's the middle of the night."

"Alice, I need to speak with Tilda."

"She doesn't want to talk to you."

"If we could come inside, I can explain."

There was the sound of dogs barking in the background. A few doors opened further down the street, porch lights coming on. Several black figures in dressing gowns stood in doorways and looked at them, putting Abe on edge. He probably didn't realize that he was the intimidating figure in this scenario. A matter of perspective.

"Alice, I wouldn't be here if it wasn't important. If I could only explain—"

Craine could hear someone else inside. The door opened wider and a square of light came down the porch. Conroy was standing there in a borrowed pink dressing gown. She seemed much smaller now.

"Craine? What are you doing here?"

"Tilda, I'm sorry, but it's important."

A long sigh. "Oh, for God's sake. Alice, let him in before the whole neighborhood wakes up."

Craine had never sought pity. Not after his wife had died and not now. He was a private man and not prone to discussing his personal issues. Besides, he was well aware that the situation he'd found himself in was his to deal with and his alone. But he knew too that there was a time for discretion and a time for honesty. Tonight it was the latter.

So, in the blackest hours of Wednesday night, huddled in the Hickersons' small kitchen, Jonathan Craine told three virtual strangers everything that had happened to him since Sunday night. He told them about the men coming to his farm. About his son being taken. About being ordered to find the killers of Benjamin Siegel and the repercussions if he didn't.

At no point did he ask for their sympathy; at no point did he beg for help. But he made it clear that the task ahead was daunting. And that he had less than forty-eight hours to secure the safety of his only child.

Throughout all of this, no one said a word. Abe, aware of his role in this narrative, sat at the back of the kitchen staring at nothing but the floor.

"This isn't your burden, I'm aware of that," Craine said, taking several deep breaths as he reached the end of what he had to say. "I don't want any of you to put yourselves at risk . . ." He realized his hands were shaking. It was difficult for him to share what he was feeling right now. A man who had spent so long shutting himself off from the world only to come back to its doorstep, cap in hand, begging to be taken back.

He gripped the edge of the table and went on. "But I'm asking you if you'll consider helping me. Because I can't do this alone. And I don't have very long."

When he finished his plaintive appeal, Alice was wiping at her eyes. At different times different eyes looked over to Abe.

"It's true," the gruff man said. He wasn't embarrassed but he wasn't defensive either. "All of it is true."

When he was a policeman, Craine often used to interview Negroes in their homes. They'd be sitting in their nightwear, sipping weak coffee and trying to persuade Craine to believe the validity of their story. So it felt odd to be in here with the roles reversed. Deep down he knew he didn't deserve their help.

"Can't you stop them?" Alice asked Abe, saying what everyone else was thinking. "How can you let them—"

"Nothing I can do about it," he said matter-of-factly. "Really. There's nothing. These decisions are made by people much more senior than me."

For a while no one spoke, and Craine's mind began drifting to Michael. Thinking about what would happen to him if he failed was hard. But not knowing what was happening to him right now was even harder. Every time he was left alone, every time a clock struck or a shadow shifted in the changing light, his mind asked where Michael was. *Who was with him? Were they hurting him? Was he even alive?* It was like living on the cusp of grief. He couldn't move forward and mourn for his son, but he couldn't give up hope of keeping him alive either.

It was Alice who broke the silence. "What do you need from us, Mr. Craine?" she asked.

He was still thinking about Michael and he had to untangle his thoughts. "I believe that the Chicago Outfit may have something to do with Siegel's murder. And what I need is access to the photographs of Paul Ricca's trial taken four years ago. Photos stored at your newspaper. After that, I'm not sure what else I'll have to do. But the resources you have will make all the difference."

"I can take you to the archives," Alice said. "I'm not sure what else I can do to help but I know I can do that."

Mr. Hickerson put his hands up. "Wait, I can't let you do this."

"I'll take him with or without your permission."

"Woman, don't argue with me. You're not putting your life in danger. These men are killers."

"He needs our help."

"You don't owe this man a damn thing."

"Don't you tell me what I can and can't do. They have his son. Think of Thomas and Arthur."

Those last words sounded like she'd dredged them from a hidden place inside her.

"Don't drag them into this," Mr. Hickerson muttered.

The blood pressure in the room rose and Alice got upset. Her husband came over and put his arms around her.

"We lost our boys in Europe," Mr. Hickerson said to the wall. "Two months apart."

Abe hadn't moved much since they'd been here, but when the Hickersons spoke he started taking in deep breaths. Craine knew he shared that pain. He didn't want to take advantage of it but he was grateful that they could understand the threat hanging over him.

Alice was pressing her thumbs against her eyelids. "I'm going with them," she said. "We need to help his boy."

Craine didn't know whether he was won over or whether he was simply resigned to his wife's resolve, but Mr. Hickerson nodded.

"Alright then. Alright."

A chair leg scraped across the floor as Conroy stood up.

"No," she said shakily. "I wish I could help, but I can't be part of this. They've already tried to kill me. My interest was only ever in the story." The words caught in her throat. "Everything else has nothing to do with me. I'm sorry about your son, but I can't help you."

Conroy left the room without looking at Craine again.

He couldn't blame her. He knew too well what it was like to have men try to hunt you down. It left you sick with fear.

CHAPTER 33

Alice called the newspaper library "the morgue," and it was situated in the basement of the *Herald*'s building, adjacent to the printing room. A colored couple, a mobster and a farmer walked in like the beginnings of a bad joke, each wondering how they came to be in each other's company.

They followed Alice down several long walls of metal cabinet drawers laid out like an underground bank vault. The room was cool and dry, the microfilm stored in specially designed, water-safe boxes.

Microfilm held photographic images greatly reduced in size from the originals. It was a low-cost way of preserving thousands of photos on a single spool of film. There must have been over a million images in this basement, a record of decades of work.

Alice examined a 3-by-5 index card on top of a cabinet marked '*43*, then located the drawer she was looking for. The microfilm box said 'CHICAGO EXTORTION TRIAL—DEC 1943.'

At the far end of the library was a small office; it had a workbench with two Recordak readers mounted on it. Craine watched as Alice placed the 16-millimeter microfilm on a spindle and manually threaded it through the gate of the reader. Microfilm readers enlarged the micro-images to a legible size, projecting them onto a 9-by-12-inch screen. It was like sitting in front of a television set.

"These are the photographs you asked for," she said. "December forty-three. Taken over the course of the trial by our court photographer."

The Recordak was manually operated, with sundry controls on either side that Alice used to scroll through the pictures. Another handle allowed her to magnify the image.

The photographs were as varied as they were numerous. There must have been hundreds of photographs here. The task ahead was tedious to anyone else but Craine.

"Start by locating photos of Ricca," he said as Alice managed the controls.

When it became clear this would take some time, Mr. Hickerson and Abe moved to the back of the room and pulled up chairs. Craine noticed Hickerson—or Bob, as he told them to call him—pat his pockets, looking for a cigarette. Abe handed him one and the two men wordlessly shared a lighter.

Some of the images were distorted where the film had buckled or was blemished, but mostly they were clear, even if there were small hairs or grain on the negatives. When Alice located photographs of Ricca, Craine asked her to focus on wide shots taken of Ricca in court.

There were photographs of Redhill testifying. Photographs of Craine on the stand. But the pictures Craine was interested in were of Ricca's associates: the Chicago Outfit. Names and faces Craine had got to know over the trial. Key members of Chicago's Hollywood extortion racket.

It crossed his mind that he was looking for a needle in a haystack. Although that would imply he knew what he was looking for. Instead he was delving though a haystack in search of *anything* that might not belong there.

Thirty minutes must have passed before he asked Alice to stop scrolling.

"There," he said. "Can you get closer?"

"Magnification range is limited but I'll try."

Using the rotation control to zoom in, Craine asked her to focus on a young man at Ricca's shoulder as he was leaving court. From the way he was holding his arm out to shield Ricca from photographers, it was clear that he was some kind of bodyguard.

Blown up to this size, the images were grainy but Alice used the levers to harden the lines until the features were clear.

A strange sensation.

Ever since he'd begun to place Chicago in this narrative, something had niggled inside Craine's head. *Was someone secretly working for the Chicago Outfit? Had they orchestrated Siegel's murder to force Lansky's hand in selling The Flamingo?*

"You know him?" Alice asked.

"Yeah," Craine said. "I know him."

Abe came over, intrigued at first, and then the look of something else. Shock. Disappointment maybe, but dressed up as dissent.

There was a flicker in his eyes. "So what if it's him?" he said, extending his fingers toward the image. "It doesn't mean anything."

"Abe," Craine said, trying to calm him down. "We need to look at all possibilities. And right now this one is the priority."

Abe's low register put Alice on edge. "This idea you have in your head. It doesn't make sense."

He began pacing round the room, rubbing his face like he was kneading dough until he picked up his jacket and left the room. The Hickersons didn't say anything but Craine could tell they were confused.

The man in the photograph was Harvey Sterling.

Craine left Abe to calm down, cycling back and forth through the photographs in case there was anyone else he recognized.

Another forty minutes passed. It must have been almost five in the morning by the time he'd checked and double-checked, sure now that this was the best lead at hand.

Behind him Bob yawned and Craine and Alice yawned too.

An idea formed. There were several magnifying glasses on the side and Craine took one.

"Bob, what precinct do you work for?"

"Newton Street Division."

Craine knew it well. Not only a predominantly black precinct, but one of the first to have black lieutenants giving white officers orders.

"You have any friends at Central Headquarters?"

"Bunch of them," he replied, clearly curious as to where this was going.

"Any who work security?"

They both knew that unless they were patrolling colored neighborhoods, black recruits were often given low-level jobs in the police force, like security detail. Mr. Hickerson closed his eyes. He looked at Alice. When she nodded, he half-swore to himself.

"Yeah," he said.

"Anyone who might be on Dragna's pad?"

He scratched his chin. *Yes*, his body language said. "That's some risk you're talking about, even for bread on the table."

"No one's getting hurt. No one needs to know. And we have money."

"You get caught, they'll ask questions. Negroes on security will be their first stop. Any indictment means a departmental trial. That's enough to end a career."

"Bob, do you know somebody or not?"

"Yeah, Craine," Mr. Hickerson said. "I know somebody."

Abe was on the printing floor, smoking cigarettes. None of the workers seemed to mind him being there. A man moving a giant roll of paper as large as a tractor wheel came past.

Abe held a cigarette out for Craine and for the first time in over ten years Craine took one. A peace offering.

The smoke burned his throat. He took a few drags but it made him feel lightheaded. From somewhere there was the sound of machinery running.

"Abe—" he said.

"That photograph doesn't mean anything."

"I think it might."

"You're wrong," Abe said, turning to Craine again now. "I know this man, Craine. He wouldn't do this. I grew up with his father. He was friends with my son. He's like blood to me. You're making a mistake."

"What type of car does he drive, Abe?"

Abe didn't reply. He knew why he was asking. Conroy had seen a Hudson following her before she was shot at.

Abe raised his voice. "What's it matter what car he has? There are thousands of Hudsons. It means nothing."

"I'm not jumping to any conclusions. But it's a lead and I need to follow it up. We can talk to Dragna."

"I'm not taking this to Dragna."

"Why not?"

"Because you'll open up a can of worms that can never be closed. You even give Dragna the slightest suggestion that he's not loyal, Harvey will disappear. He has a wife, a *family*."

Those last words were pointed. A reminder that Craine wasn't the only one with something to lose.

"Then we'll need to confirm it another way."

"How?"

"You told me before, all those guys have priors. If Harvey has a record, his file will have his tenprints. I still have copies of the fingerprints from the car. All I need to do is cross-compare."

"To what?"

"To his police records."

Craine dropped the cigarette on the floor. Above them a folded stream of newspapers began snaking across the ceiling, running down the twisting conveyor like a paper waterfall before coming off the belt to be bundled into trucks.

"You got a plan, Craine?"

"Yeah," Craine said. "You coming?"

Abe dropped his cigarette under his heel. He nodded reluctantly.

It was the early hours of the morning now, and trucks were exiting onto the street. Craine could see the first glimpses of morning light. He checked his watch. It was five o'clock on Thursday morning.

He had only one more day.

THURSDAY

CHAPTER 34

The plan, if you could call it that, was to access the L.A.P.D.'s Research and Identification unit. Chiefly managing prior arrest and prosecution sheets, R&I maintained over fifty thousand criminal history files. And one of them would have the fingerprint records Craine needed.

Abe had taken a little convincing of the merits of Craine's idea. Particularly after Craine told him that R&I was located on the second floor of the L.A.P.D.'s Central Headquarters.

Craine circled the Civic Center a few times until there was no putting it off. It was 7 A.M. now. Early enough that there would be minimal witnesses, late enough that their presence wouldn't raise eyebrows. Archivists and the secretary pool didn't typically start this early. Only the cleaning staff and the 12 A.M. to 8 A.M. police shift would be working.

They drove down the ramp to the basement entrance toward the security barriers. Craine went through the plan in his head again, mapmaking the corridors of the police department from memory as best he could.

Both men were dressed in suits like it was any other day, and as long as they could get past security at the main gate, support staff wouldn't bat an eyelid at them walking through. Craine's former peers were another matter. The homicide unit functioned with a small core team, and any of his old colleagues would realize something was askew the second they caught sight of him.

At the gate a portly uniformed guard with a gray brush mustache waved and approached.

Craine wound down the window half-way. The guard leaned down and lifted the rim of his police-style cap.

"Lieutenant Craine. Forgot my badge."

"Sir, I can't let you in without some form of identification."

Craine was sweating with nervous anticipation. Abe wore his usual bovine stare but there was an audible metallic scratching sound from his seat. His elbow was crooked across his chest and Craine could tell his hand was on the butt of his Savage.

"Officer Ridley working tonight? He saw me come in last night. Must have left my badge in Homicide."

The man glanced back. "He's one of the Negroes."

"Got a memory, hasn't he?"

The officer turned away and Craine quickly wiped his brow with his cuff.

The older man barked at someone in the security shed and a young black officer came out.

"Lieutentant Craine. I didn't know you were working today."

The lines were rehearsed. Officer Ridley was being paid a hundred dollars for this small charade, the money left with the Hickersons.

"Needed to finish up a few things." Craine gestured to Abe. "You remember Detective Vine from the Beverly Hills precinct?"

"Sure, sure," he said before turning to his superior. "Lieutenant Craine, suh."

"You sure, boy?"

"Sure, suh, absolutely," Ridley said as deferentially as Craine had ever heard.

The elder officer shrugged. He lifted the security gate and waved them down the ramp toward the basement parking lot. "Go through."

They parked opposite two police trucks and Craine ushered them up the narrow ramp that led into the building. It crossed his mind that from the minute they entered, they'd be breaking several state laws. Something throbbed in Craine's chest but it wasn't fear. He was excited, despite himself.

Once inside, Craine tried to remind himself of the layout of the police department. R&I was two floors up. Craine would locate Harvey Sterling's file, take the tenprint records but leave the folder otherwise untouched. There was no reason for anyone to know they were ever there.

Little had changed since he was last here. Institutional green walls. Fluorescent tubes on the ceiling. Corridors snaking off on to more corridors. He hadn't missed it.

They passed cleaners with mops and buckets. "Careful, there. Don't slip," one of them said without even looking up.

Craine escorted Abe at speed; their feet seemed to make a lot of noise on the linoleum. He wasn't expecting trouble immediately. But while they weren't in the main organs of the police precinct, there were plenty of officers floating around these floors. And almost all of them would be armed. They didn't want to be in the building any longer than they needed to.

Craine pushed through double doors and he could see the sign to the elevators, the same sign in the same corridor as it had always been. It was less than thirty yards away but seemed to stretch on for twice that.

Up ahead they could see two uniformed officers chatting as they exited an open elevator. One of them looked over momentarily and Abe put his hand in his pocket. Craine held his arm out ever so slightly. *There was no need for anyone to get hurt.*

The uniforms returned to their conversation and the two men entered the compact elevator.

Exiting on the second floor, they entered a long corridor lined with doors. Craine found the one with 'Arrests and Prosecutions' painted in white across frosted glass.

The door opened on to a small square foyer and beyond it an open archway led to the archives. There was no one at reception.

The archives room had few windows and no direct sunlight. It had been repainted in the years since Craine had been there but was otherwise the same.

The shelves were arranged in alphabetical order, endless files of Arrest and Prosecution records for every perpetrator in Los Angeles. Each folder contained mug shots, prior arrest and conviction sheets and, most importantly, a fingerprint identification card.

When you had a fingerprint, cross-referencing them against all registered felons was a time-consuming exercise. That was why they built the Fingerprint Factory. But when you had one particular person to compare against, all it took was finding the right file.

Craine found the shelf he was looking for and walked his fingers across the spines. He reached 'S' and found the one marked 'Sterling, Harvey.' His fingers were shaking. Any investigation hinged on this folder.

He levered out the file. Craine could hear the hum of the ceiling fans but otherwise the room was silent. Abe didn't say a word.

There were no mug shots, but the description was accurate. The summary report highlighted a minor conviction dating back to 1940: a Chicago misdemeanor. Craine was already moving on, thumbing through the pages. The tenprint card was attached with a paperclip. The names and dates were correct. Craine took it out and placed it in his inside jacket pocket. He was tingling.

They traveled at speed toward the elevators. From outside came the faint sound of sirens like the police were already waiting for them and it only added to the tension.

The elevator opened out into the lower-ground corridor where the two uniformed cops from before were still standing. But this time they were talking to a man in a charcoal-gray suit. The man turned and Craine realized it was Agent Redhill.

Craine stopped and Abe stopped with him. It was abrupt enough to draw Redhill's attention.

"Craine?"

Craine didn't bother watching Redhill put the pieces together. There were times for consideration and times for reaction, and Craine went with the latter.

Seizing on his confusion, Craine pushed Redhill back against the wall and rammed his left forearm against his throat. With the other he slid his hand into Redhill's inner jacket and wrestled his service pistol from his shoulder holster.

Abe was galvanized into action. He stepped around one of the uniformed officers and pushed his Savage deep into his neck.

Craine watched the remaining police officer's face cave in with dead-eyed dread. He reached for his gun belt but Craine waved Redhill's pistol in his direction.

"Don't," he said, taking control of the situation. "Take your hands away from your belt."

The young patrol cop was in his early twenties, too young to have even served in the war. He registered the weapon and raised his hands in front of his face as if his chubby fingers would stop the bullets.

Redhill had slid to the floor, looking like someone had pulled a chair from under him. "Don't let them go anywhere," he said, coughing his hands round his neck.

Adrenaline usually arrived late with Craine but it was with him now. He motioned his pistol toward Redhill.

"Do it," Redhill said, daring him. "You're not leaving here otherwise."

Craine straightened his arm so that the barrel was sighted directly at his face. Redhill was an obstacle to him saving Michael, and there was some part of him goading him to pull the trigger. He scared himself.

"We need to go," said Abe, his Savage still pressed into the officer's jugular.

"Redhill," Craine said firmly. "This is happening, with or without your permission. But slowing us down is only going to mean people will get hurt."

The two packs remained in standoff. The F.B.I. agent sat there, nostrils flaring.

"*Tell them*," Craine said, his finger instinctively squeezing the trigger.

Redhill took several long, heavy breaths, then batted his head against the wall, resigned.

"Let them pass," he said.

CHAPTER 35

Abe changed lanes, swerving the wheel without dropping speed. The car tilted and Craine pushed one hand against the roof to steady himself.

For twenty minutes they'd pushed their way north without any sight or sound of a police car. The few minutes' advantage they had was enough to exit the building, but the dispatch call would have gone out almost immediately.

The hotel was off limits. If Redhill didn't know where they were staying already it wouldn't take him long to find out. So after several miles without spotting a police car, Craine directed them off the main roads and Abe pulled onto a side street that led to the edges of the L.A. River. He parked up on the berm beside a trash dumpster where the car was out of sight.

When he turned the engine off, Abe looked over at the fingerprints Craine was trying to examine.

"Do they match, or what?"

"There were several sets on the car, Abe. I need more time."

Abe got out and slammed the door shut. He pushed through the wire fence and walked down to the empty riverbed. There were bottles on the concrete where vagrants came down at night. Abe kicked one and the glass skittered across the concrete before rolling to a slow stop. Craine saw him shake out a cigarette and light it, deep in thought.

Comparing fingerprints was straightforward in theory but infinitely time-consuming in practice. It was made harder now with only the magnifier Craine had taken from the newspaper archive. He felt like a surgeon handed a pair of pliers and a carving knife and asked to perform heart surgery.

The first step was to thoroughly examine the tenprint records taken from Harvey Sterling's file and compare the basic elements to the ones lifted from the stolen car.

At the core of any fingerprint were the ridges—the fine papillary lines that curved and bent around the surface of the fingertip. These typically fell into one of three categories: arches, loops and whorls, each denoting different ridge patterns.

Craine was looking for arches, since they were rarer than whorls or loops. In Harvey's case, the prints on his index finger were arches, lines that went up in one direction and then curved down.

Good, thought Craine. Only one of the latent prints taken from the shooter's car was also made up of arches. This was the fingerprint he needed to compare.

Craine didn't have a pad or pen but after familiarizing himself with the R&I print in detail, he moved the magnifying glass back over to the latent prints selected.

Given the makeshift tools he'd used to lift the prints from the car, the clarity was poor. However, he could see that in both prints the ridges arched in the same place. Looking closer, he saw that both also had a single papillary line that split into two. And on both prints another ridge converged.

He began looking back and forth between the two prints, looking for matching points, comparing minute characteristics and locations until he was certain that everything lined up.

An image formed of Siegel's killer and now that image had a face.

Harvey Sterling.

Craine took several deep breaths, knowing that what he had here was enough to save his son.

He got out of the car and slipped down the embankment until he was standing in the dry culvert with Abe. It was after 8 A.M. now, and the morning sun pressed down so hard he had to shield his eyes with his hand.

Abe was smoking a fresh cigarette. He didn't look at Craine when he said, "Is it him?"

"Yeah, Abe," Craine said. "It's him."

The heat glazed both their faces. It lent both urgency and vexation. "How sure can you be? How accurate—"

"It's difficult. The prints aren't perfect. I don't have a light box."

They heard sirens behind them, and both of them looked over, but the sound had stretched and thinned before they could even make out a patrol car.

"I'm only going to ask you one more time. *Is it him?*" Abe said when it had gone.

"Yes," Craine replied. "It's definitely Harvey."

Abe threw his cigarette butt on the floor and let out something resembling a growl. He looked like he wanted to punch someone. Craine had expected resistance. But maybe he didn't realize how personally Abe would take it.

"I'm sorry," Craine said. "But I need you to call Dragna. We can't simply accuse Harvey, we need to get him to tell us why he did it. I don't think he was working alone, and I'm not even sure he did this of his own volition."

Abe was still shaking his head. It was almost like it was unscrewing, ready to fall off. "There's been a mistake."

"There hasn't, Abe. We need to find out why he killed Siegel but we don't have a lot of time. It has to be today. It has to be this morning."

Abe looked around like he was scrutinizing the air. "He wouldn't have done this. He's got a good heart. He was a war hero." His voice was strained and he beat a fist against his chest. "He was friends with my son, for God's sake. My *son*."

Craine moved back up the concrete sides to where the car was. He was sympathetic but firm. "Abe, I'm sorry but we don't have the time. I need you to arrange a meeting with Dragna."

Abe began moving around in wide circles, anything to shake off his frustration. It took ten minutes before he was calm enough to head back toward the car.

CHAPTER 36

Jack Dragna arranged to meet them at the warehouse in Pasadena. The wire service operated nationally and since horse racing began late morning in New York, Dragna's operations ran almost twenty-four hours a day.

They didn't tell Dragna in advance why they were coming, so when Harvey met them in the parking lot to take them through, both men had to make awkward small talk until they were taken up to Dragna's office, a small glass-partitioned room that looked over the entire floor.

After almost a week without sleep, it was hard for Craine to speak as clearly as he wanted. He took his time explaining to the mob boss the events of the previous few days. He couldn't simply put on him that he believed Harvey had killed Ben Siegel; he had to guide him to that conclusion himself.

Once he showed him the fingerprints and explained that they'd been cross-compared to those found on the shooter's car, Dragna sat back in his chair. His shoulders sank and he turned his head to the factory floor.

Craine followed his eyes. Harvey was laughing with another man from Dragna's security detail. Around them employees were scribbling on dockets, tellers taking calls. In another world this might have been a respectable place to work.

Craine looked back at Dragna, gauging his reaction.

"To be clear, we're not accusing you of anything."

Dragna didn't reply immediately but Craine could see he was relieved. "You think he did this alone?"

Craine clarified: "I think he was sponsored by the Chicago Outfit."

This seemed to take Dragna a long time to process. "Why would they want Siegel dead?"

"To get a better price on The Flamingo Hotel in Las Vegas."

"Lansky is selling The Flamingo to Chicago," Abe said, more forthcoming than Craine expected. "They might have been using Harvey. Manipulating him."

"What about the F.B.I.? You said they've been hiding things."

"Yes, but we don't know why. To make the case blow over, maybe."

Dragna stopped staring at the window and looked back at them. "Is anyone else in Los Angeles involved?"

Abe said, "We don't know."

"There's no way of knowing if anyone else is in on this," Craine added. "Not yet. But what we can do is talk to Harvey. We can find out what he knows and who set him up."

"In exchange for what?" Dragna asked. "*Clemency?*" The Italian folded his arms. "This is not the way I conduct business."

Craine was beginning to get fed up with liars and murderers dressing up in suits and calling themselves businessmen.

Abe looked uncomfortable. It was clear that mercy was what he was hoping for. "We don't know they hadn't threatened him. Or his family."

"Or if he's turned any of my other men," Dragna huffed.

Craine's voice was tight and raspy. "Which of your men do you trust wholeheartedly? With your life?"

Dragna looked down across the entire floor. There were men at the door. Men idling by desks. Half a dozen of them, and all with pistols in their jacket pockets. Probably a few shotguns or Thompsons locked up somewhere, too.

The mob boss sighed. "Until ten minutes ago, I would have said Harvey Sterling."

* * *

The three of them crossed the floor toward where Harvey was standing. He was staring at ticker tape where horse race results had come through the teleprinter. He looked up when he saw them coming toward him.

"Harvey," Dragna said casually. "Can we have a word?"

"Of course, sir," he said, standing to attention.

He noticed Craine and Abe behind him. His eyes moved a fraction.

"Everything okay, Mr. Dragna?"

Harvey looked at the three of them in turn but it was Craine he stared at. Harvey saw Craine and Craine saw Harvey.

"Come up to my office," Dragna said. "We need to talk."

Both men were smiling with their mouths but not with their eyes. Abe squared off, his arms folded. Craine knew his fingers were wrapped around his pistol grip.

"What about, Mr. Dragna?"

"I'll tell you upstairs."

"Harvey," Abe said. "Listen to the man. We have a few questions."

"What's this about?"

Dragna said, "Harvey. Come into my office and let's talk. There is a civilized way of doing this. And there is another way."

Harvey looked at Abe. "What's going on?"

Abe said, "You know."

Harvey's smile bent slowly until all his features were upside down. "Sir, whatever they told you is bullshit."

Their plan to keep this low-key wasn't working. The rest of Dragna's men began looking over. They seemed confused. Craine had no idea if they were working with Harvey. Every one of them was a potential threat.

"Harvey," Craine said, trying to defuse the situation. "I know it's not what it looks like."

Harvey's hand came up to his neck like he had an itch. And then his fingers moved down toward his inside jacket pocket. "It's not. It's not what it looks like," he repeated like a child's echolalia.

Abe dropped one hand so Harvey could see the other was on his pistol grip. He didn't draw it.

"Harvey," Abe said. "Don't do anything foolish, now. There's a way out of this where no one gets hurt."

Harvey's eyes were darting in different directions but when he looked at Abe he couldn't make eye contact. Or maybe he was too focused on the Savage.

Abe raised his voice. "Is it true, Harvey?"

Harvey was shaking his head but managed to whisper, "I'm sorry."

Harvey pulled out his pistol in one motion. Abe matched his movements until both men had their pistols out and were aiming at each other.

There was a gasp from one of the telephone operators and people started to shout and curse. The sound of phones being dropped and chairs scraping back. More voices and noises came from behind Craine but he had no intention of turning around.

"I'm sorry," Harvey said. "I didn't have a choice."

Craine saw Harvey swing the pistol in his direction and fully expected him to pull the trigger. On the few occasions men had pointed guns at him, it was usually with one intention.

"It wasn't what you think. I didn't choose this—"

"Whatever happened," Craine said gently, stretching his palms slowly outward to show he wasn't armed, "we can help you."

Harvey's lack of response was unnerving.

"Harvey, put the gun down." This from Abe. Dragna had stopped talking entirely.

Craine spoke again, his hands still spreading away from his body. "Tell us what happened, Harvey. Tell us so we can help you."

Harvey stared back intently but said nothing. Craine knew he was scared and he knew he was angry. In many ways they were in the same position.

"Harvey, stop pointing the gun at Craine."

Craine blinked hard, hoping that when he opened his eyes Harvey might simply disappear. He didn't.

"Tell him, Harvey," Craine said gently. "Tell Abe why you killed Siegel. Who sent you? Who made you do it?"

Harvey didn't answer. His hands were shaking. Twitching, even. You didn't want people with guns in their hands to twitch.

Around them telephones were ringing but nobody was answering them. Any thoughts of laying wagers on outcomes had turned toward this drama. And odds in favor of this scene turning bloody were increasing moment to moment.

Craine glanced in all directions. There were five other men who worked for Lansky. *Where were they?*

"Talk to us, Harvey."

Harvey frowned, then shook his head. "He said he'd kill Lucy." A deep breath. Choking. "And the kids. They're all I got."

"Who did, Harvey? Who did this?"

"I can't—"

Deepening his voice, Abe said, "Put your gun down. Let's talk about what happened."

It went this way, back and forth and back again, each man talking over the other.

For a second it looked like Harvey might lower his pistol and then one of Dragna's security guards came striding out through Craine's periphery with his pistol raised.

Craine blinked. An inward sigh. Some situations seemed determined to escalate.

Harvey spun to face him and both men fired. Harvey shot the man clean in the chest before he too was injured. He keeled forward, clutching his arm. By now the room was full of screaming.

Different bodyguards threw themselves in front of Dragna.

In the melee, Harvey ran to the exit door. There were more shots fired and people running this way and that but it was the screaming that rang in Craine's ears more than anything else. There was nothing as distinctive as the sounds of people being completely terrified.

He thought of Michael.

CHAPTER 37

The F.B.I.'s Field Office was how Captain Henson imagined a Wall Street corporation to be. The homicide department didn't even have a boardroom, but this one had a polished table with twelve leather seats spaced evenly around it. There was a framed photograph of Hoover at one end of the room and a matching one of Redhill at the other. It was a reminder that he, a lowly police captain, was talking to the Federal Bureau's head of the Los Angeles office.

When they sat down, Henson looked at Redhill's well-coiffed hair and his oversized watch and thought he looked more like an advertising executive or a bank chairman than an investigator. He was the type of person you met and didn't really like for some reason, and then when you got to know him you realized your first instincts were completely correct.

"Thanks for your call," Redhill began, taking control of the meeting. "You're absolutely right, it's time we talked. I was just about to ask my secretary to set up a meeting myself."

"But you're alright? You weren't hurt?"

Redhill touched his collar. "Nothing I can't handle."

"I wanted to talk to you about what happened with Jonathan Craine. The two uniforms you were with are giving conflicting accounts of what they saw. But what I also want to know is, why were you at the L.A.P.D. offices at all?"

Redhill smiled plainly. "I needed to collect a few things from the evidence room."

"You could have asked and I would have had them sent straight over. Or you could have sent someone . . . more junior."

"I like to keep across these things myself. You know how it is."

"Did Craine give you any indication of what he was doing there or how he got inside the building in the first place?"

"No. Although clearly L.A.P.D. security isn't what it used to be. Perhaps you need an internal review."

"We're looking into exactly how it happened. I can't be sure, but we believe he was after fingerprint records."

"Whose?" Redhill seemed keen to know.

"We don't know. I was hoping you might be able to tell me."

"How do you mean?"

Henson had no intention of telling Redhill about his clandestine meeting with Craine. If anything it was Redhill who had been hiding things from Henson. He probed him without giving his cards away.

"Craine has been asking questions about Benjamin Siegel. I was hoping you could update me on your investigation. As part of this *combined* effort."

"Hey," Redhill said, holding up shiny palms, "I get it: street crime is your business. But you know, when it links to national concerns . . ." He brought the palms inward, gesturing to yours truly.

Henson tried to be affable. "You're supposed to update me on progress. That's how it works, right?"

"Absolutely. Except here's the thing." Redhill leaned forward like he was sharing something secret: "There is no worthwhile evidence."

Henson was surprised and yet inwardly not so. "Nothing has shown up? What about the cartridges on the lawn we located? Or the ballistics tests from projectiles located during the autopsy? The projectiles were whole."

"No, nothing."

"The Fingerprint Factory in Washington has collected over ten million records since the war. Are you telling me there's no match to a single print?"

Redhill didn't answer.

"What about the car? I know the neighbors were interviewed. Reports were sent to your office."

"No usable description, Henson."

"What about this third witness—"

"I don't believe it for a second." Then before the Captain could query it further, he said, "Look, Henson, we're doing all we can here. Given limited resources."

"Limited resources? You're the F.B.I.—"

"I absolutely understand why you're upset—"

"We cultivated the press. Assured them that together we were going to invest all necessary resources to find Siegel's killer."

"We're not."

"Excuse me?"

"We're not going to find Siegel's killers. That's a fact. I'm not trying to embarrass anybody, least of all the work of the homicide unit, but I know Director Hoover has spoken to the Chief of Police and they're going to recommend we change the flow of information to the newspapers."

"Meaning?"

Redhill was holding several sheaves of paper in his hand when he entered the room and now he handed Henson one from the top. The Captain would never know what was on the other pages.

"Tomorrow morning you're going to release the following statement to the press. You can read it out or share it directly, that's completely up to you."

Henson picked up the statement and read the first two paragraphs.

"*Despite poring through files and records of federal, state and local agencies, all indications are now that Siegel's murder will likely go unsolved.*

"*A meeting of law enforcement chiefs has been called and the F.B.I. and the L.A.P.D. have agreed the necessity of broadening the sphere of this investigation. Resources will now focus on examining the enterprises and associations of Benjamin Siegel in order to compile a comprehensive catalog of organized racketeering in America, specifically East Coast crime syndicates.*"

"What is this? You're dropping Siegel to focus on organized crime in New York?"

"Correct."

"When was this agreed? What meeting of law enforcement?"

"This one. The conversation we're having right now."

Despite the look Henson gave him, Redhill's face was inscrutable. "We both know that the New York mob are responsible for Siegel's death. So rather than waste hundreds of man hours on a wild goose chase locating the individual responsible for pulling the trigger, we're going to focus our efforts on Meyer Lansky."

Henson dropped the press release on the table.

"And this is Hoover's request?"

Redhill replied to the question without answering the question at all. "Hoover has deemed me responsible. He's preoccupied with the H.U.A.C. hearings, understandably."

The timing seemed too much of a coincidence, but a junior agent knocked on the door and Redhill gestured him over.

The young man was wearing the same suit and tie as Redhill. Everyone in the building had his hair cropped the same way. Henson heard him mutter something about Jonathan Craine, but the rest was out of earshot. He hadn't even finished when Redhill stood up.

"Apologies, Captain. I'm afraid I have to go."

"Something come up? Is it about Craine?"

"Thanks for your time," he said, ignoring the question. "I'll be in touch."

And when Redhill left the room something important dawned on Henson. The L.A.P.D. didn't really have its own agency. It was a government department built to react to one thing and one thing only: the human condition. The F.B.I., on the other hand, was an independent organization with an ability to self-serve. Redill was a corporate strategist with a vision to shape America. To turn the F.B.I. into an establishment no different from the Hollywood studio system or the press.

Henson thought about what Conroy had said to him last night. She was right. Unless the L.A.P.D. adapted, they were never going to survive.

After the shooting, there was shouting, and threats, accusations and denials. The man Harvey had shot had been whisked away to an unseen room, likely to die before Dr. Fulton even got his phone call. There was blood all over Dragna's factory floor and workers had gathered around it in shock like it held the key to making this situation disappear.

Abe told Dragna that he and Craine should go and find Harvey alone. Craine thought Dragna might take some convincing, but the older man was preoccupied with taking control of the situation in front of him and almost seemed relieved to see them go.

"Tell Lansky I had no idea," he said repeatedly. "Make sure he knows I'm loyal to the end."

Jack Dragna sounded desperate.

Craine knew the address Dragna gave him well enough and directed Abe to the edges of the borough limits, where they pulled onto Harvey's road in Glendale. He had that sinking feeling of being too late.

As they counted down the houses, Abe confessed, "I told him we were going to the Bradbury that night. And I told him about Conroy helping us."

"You think—"

Abe nodded: *it was him.* He sighed, then said, "Joseph, my son, he and Harvey were in a hole together. He came home once, briefly, didn't even have to tell me. I could see it in the look in his eyes that they'd done things. *Seen* things. Whatever happened to them in the Pacific, maybe it made him do this. Like a madness."

What Abe said made sense in many ways. You didn't see men coming back from the war crying. Rarely did you see outward displays of hurt and frustration. Rather it expressed itself inward, spilling over only occasionally into anger or aggression. He'd seen farmhands back from Europe beating each other to a pulp over a horseshoe toss.

But Harvey wasn't like Kastel or the other men. He wasn't a drug addict, either. He seemed in control.

"Abe, I'm not convinced he chose to do this. I think someone was forcing his hand."

"He's a good kid," Abe said, trying to make sense of it all. "I knew him since he was a little boy."

There was a Hudson parked askew in one of the driveways and Craine knew immediately that this was Harvey's house. He wondered if Abe knew he drove a Hudson all along.

Neither man had any intention of kicking down the front door when it faced two neighboring houses across the street. Instead, they followed a flagged pathway that led from the driveway to the side of the house.

Abe had his Savage out now, aiming at anything they could spot through the side windows. Craine was wondering if they might be better smashing a window to enter but the rear door was already ajar.

The two men went inside. Hot air and the smell of something burning.

Bacon rashers were smoking on the hob and Craine used his cuff to lift the pan off and drop it into the sink.

Abe ignored him, moving deeper into the house, his pistol already tilting in each direction like a dowsing rod. But they didn't discover water. Only blood.

Harvey's wife was the first one they found.

She was lying prone, and from the way her body was splayed Craine could see that she'd been pursued through the house. Bullet holes in the corridor between the kitchen and the living room told them the shooter had missed twice. The third shot had taken the back of her skull away completely. Some of her brains were still sitting inside her head but most was on the carpet or, perversely, in her outstretched hands.

It was horrific to look at and worse to ponder. Gouts of blood had spread across the carpet and Craine could tell from its color that it was fresh. She'd died in the last hour or so.

The rest of the downstairs was untouched. But upstairs was a different matter.

The children's drawings tacked to the door at the top of the stairs were enough for Craine and Abe to both take a series of breaths before entering.

The room was powder blue. For the most part it appeared undisturbed. Twin children's beds. Tin train set and soldiers. A doll. No corpses.

Craine might have felt more hopeful but the coppery smell of blood hinted otherwise. Harvey's pistol on the bedroom carpet all but confirmed it.

There was a closet door and it was half-open. Open enough.

Years ago, when Michael was a little boy, men with guns had come into Craine's house. He'd found Michael alive in his bedroom. He'd survived because he'd hidden in his toy chest.

But Harvey's little boy and his smaller sister weren't so lucky. Craine didn't look long enough to see what exactly had taken place but he could see they were both dead, that wasn't in question. The boy's head was intact. The little girl's wasn't. The rest his imagination would be digesting for years to come.

Man's ability to do something like this had never ceased to stagger Craine. He felt suddenly hot and wanted to take off his jacket but this was a crime scene and they would already be considered suspects. All he could do was leave the room. When Abe came out they couldn't even look at each other.

They found Harvey last. He'd chosen his own bedroom to kill himself and a military carbine to do it with, but there didn't seem to be much in the way of ceremony.

He was lying straight on his back. Everything above his eyebrows was gone. His blood was crimson, fresh and everywhere. The carbine and several loose cartridges were next to him on the carpet at different angles.

Craine had seen enough suicides to know that this wasn't staged. Shots under the chin sometimes failed to kill people effectively. People flinch when they fire. Harvey knew exactly what he was doing. From the looks of the corpse he'd put the rifle barrel in his mouth, using one hand to hold it in place and the other to pull the trigger.

Craine didn't say anything. He didn't look at Abe but he heard a soft groan that might have been sobbing, or might have been something else entirely.

Craine wondered why he didn't feel more relieved that they'd found Siegel's killer, but by then there were red and blue lights in the driveway and the sounds of car doors opening and men shouting.

In another situation, Abe would have run and Craine might have followed, but what they'd seen was so shocking that neither man could muster the effort.

FRIDAY

CHAPTER 38

Conroy had taken Thursday off work. She returned to her apartment to have the windows replaced and new locks fitted. She spent most of the day petrified the shooter would return to finish the job. It wasn't until late that evening that Alice called her to say that there had been a shooting in Glendale and Craine had been involved.

She went out and bought a copy of the *Examiner* as soon as it hit the streets on Friday morning and flipped through until she found an article half-way down page eight:

> LOCAL HOODLUM COMMITS SUICIDE
> AFTER FAMILY MURDERED
> When police were called to the house of small-time crook Harvey Sterling yesterday afternoon, he was found dead alongside his wife and two baby children. Police say they have no known motives for the tragedy but two men have been taken into custody in connection with the killings.

The key facts matched what Alice had told her. Conroy didn't know who Harvey Sterling was but she remembered his name being mentioned. Alice had explained to Conroy about the microfilm. She couldn't remember the exact name Craine had wanted to look into but she'd said it was Henry or Harry or Harvey. Alice was coy about Craine's intentions, but mentioned he'd been keen to know about security at the L.A.P.D.'s Central Headquarters.

Conroy went straight to a drugstore pay phone and started making calls to local contacts. Captain Henson's secretary was wary of going into detail but told Conroy she'd heard rumors that two men had been caught breaking into the building early yesterday morning. Another rumor said they even held two uniformed officers and an F.B.I. agent hostage before fleeing the scene.

Why Agent Redhill was talking to two uniforms in the basement of the L.A.P.D. was something the secretary couldn't answer, but when Conroy asked her for the two officers' names, Conroy cross-referenced them against her own notes. Yes, both officers had been at the scene of the crime the night Siegel died. *So what did Redhill want to speak to them about? Was he buying their silence?*

Henson's secretary couldn't share any details of what happened at Harvey Sterling's house, so Conroy made several more calls, coming up short until she contacted an old friend who manned the lines in dispatch; her friend couldn't confirm whether it was Craine and Abe who had been arrested. What she did know, however, was that it wasn't the L.A.P.D. that had taken the two men into custody, but the F.B.I.

Over breakfast in a diner near the office, Conroy and Alice tried to piece together the narrative of the previous twenty-four hours.

Craine had taken a strong interest in Harvey Sterling and had broken into the L.A.P.D. for what they could only assume was an attempt to locate his criminal file. Later that day, they were found at Harvey Sterling's house. Sterling's wife and young children were dead and Sterling looked to have taken his own life.

Was Harvey Sterling responsible for killing Ben Siegel? Had Craine managed to find the killer? And what role did he have in these deaths?

Inside, Conroy knew Craine wasn't capable of killing a child. He was a father himself; no matter what the police or F.B.I. said about his mob ties, she knew he wouldn't have murdered that man's family.

"Alice, I need you to find out who Harvey Sterling was," she said when they walked to the office. "Find out who he worked for, if he served in the military and who with. See if you can speak to his platoon commander. Then get background on his connection to the Chicago and New York syndicates, specifically Paul Ricca."

They were still discussing whether Harvey Sterling might have been Siegel's killer when they reached the City Room. As the two women entered the office a row of eyes looked up at them from their desks. They moved from her to Alice and then craned backward to the City Editor's office. She noticed the City Editor was already standing in his doorway waiting for her. Captain Henson was sitting behind him.

"Glad to see you're doing well, Tilda," her editor said when she entered. "It must have been a terrible shock for you."

He didn't waste time on asking after her well-being. When they'd all sat down, he said, "Captain Henson has filled me in on everything that's happened. But he has some questions we're both hoping you can answer."

Henson didn't waste any time. It was like he wanted to leave as soon as possible.

"Were you aware that yesterday morning Jonathan Craine illegally entered the L.A.P.D.'s Central Headquarters?" he asked.

"No." A half truth.

"Do you know why he might have had reason to be there?"

"No." Another half truth.

"Have you spoken to him?"

Her first genuine lie: "Not since after the shooting at my apartment."

"Yesterday afternoon, Jonathan Craine and an associate of his were taken into custody by the F.B.I. There's no formal indictment yet, but he's facing a murder charge."

She knew the answer but she asked the question anyway: "Murder of who? Harvey Sterling's family?"

He nodded. "The F.B.I. have taken over the crime scene but my primary detective has suggested there's a possibility that Sterling himself is responsible. If that's the case, Craine will be questioned but not necessarily charged."

The City Editor asked, "If the F.B.I. are involved can we assume this is related to Ben Siegel?"

"I'm afraid I can't confirm that."

"Does this man Harvey Sterling have a record?"

"Yes. For a few minor misdemeanors. He was originally in New York but spent some time in Chicago. We believe he now works for Jack Dragna as part of L.A.'s criminal element."

There was one word that stuck out when he spoke. *Chicago.*

The police can hold you for up to twenty-four hours before they have to charge you with a crime or release you. Conroy didn't know if the same rules applied for the F.B.I. "When will Craine be released?"

"It's difficult to say," Henson said. "If he's not charged, twenty-four hours, unless they apply for an extension. If he is, indefinitely until a court date is set."

She didn't need him to translate: too late for Craine to save his son. It was Friday morning now. Even if he'd discovered that Harvey Sterling was the killer, was his son safe if he couldn't tell the men who hired him?

Conroy spoke to Henson as a friend. "David, we were wrong to turn our backs on Craine. He's figured out who killed Siegel, I know he has. And I don't know for certain it was Harvey Sterling, but I do know Craine didn't kill that man's family. You know that too."

Henson rolled his shoulders forward. He looked uncomfortable. "He hasn't done himself any favors."

"Is there anything you can do to get him out?"

"I don't have that kind of influence. Not with the F.B.I. I'm sorry, Tilda. And for the record, neither myself nor anyone at the L.A.P.D. will be commenting on accusations regarding the person responsible for Benjamin Siegel's murder—"

"—Forget who killed Siegel for a second," Conroy said. "I know Craine spoke to you. Surely you realize that you're being manipulated by Agent Redhill?"

There was a long pause before Captain Henson nodded, speaking freely for the first time. "If even a fraction of what Craine told us is true, then the F.B.I. have abused their position of power and withheld key information from the beginning."

The City Editor chimed in. "You can stop him—we can't. Redhill has sway over City Hall. As do the studios and key figures in the industry."

"Our hands are tied too," Henson said. "For me to go up against the Federal Bureau without the support of City Hall would be not only a gamble but a dangerous leap of faith."

As they spoke, Conroy couldn't help but find these debates absurd. Yes, there were blips and tiffs and scandals and conspiracies, but these were few and far between. In the big picture, there was little conflict of interest between the press, the police and the motion picture industry. L.A.'s pillars of power had been crooning from the same song sheet for decades. Now they needed a reminder.

Conroy spoke up to her foremen: "Gentlemen, are we in agreement that Redhill has overstepped his post?"

When they both tilted their chins in agreement, Conroy said, "There is a way of moving forward that can satisfy all parties."

"How do you mean?"

"There's an unofficial quorum call in Los Angeles. You need all the estates on the same side: police, studios and press. Then you have control of City Hall."

"So what are you saying?"

Her voice was measured. She spoke clearly: "I'm saying let's get everyone on the same side. Then we make a motion to remove Redhill from office."

Conroy didn't know if Henson would try to shut down her plan, but he didn't. Instead he nodded and sat contemplatively and then nodded again each time Conroy outlined how she hoped to turn this situation around.

In a zero-sum game, all gains have to be offset equally by losses. In Conroy's proposal, if all went as planned, there would be only one losing party. The person who was the thorn in all their sides: Agent Emmett Redhill.

"What you're proposing—"

"Is the right thing to do," Conroy said. It was difficult being so forthright with two men in senior positions, but to their credit they'd listened intently.

Afterward, Captain Henson left the City Editor's office. At the door he said, "I'll deny ever being here. And anything that I've agreed to is explicitly off the record and nonattributable."

"Agreed," Conroy said once the City Editor nodded.

When he'd gone, the City Editor went to the liquor cabinet in the corner and began to pour them both drinks.

"Sir, it's nine A.M."

"Doesn't matter. You'll need it. You realize, Conroy, that City Hall will have to persuade Hoover of this. I don't need to remind you that this plan of yours amounts to a coup."

"A bloodless coup." She paused. "More or less."

"Tilda Conroy." He smiled. "A wolf in Red Riding Hood's clothing."

He handed her a glass and raised his own to his lips without toasting. Conroy couldn't pretend it didn't feel special to be treated like an equal by the City Editor. To have his respect. But his mood seemed more apprehensive than congratulatory. He went to the glass partition of his office and stared out across the floor.

"Tilda, word of warning. This investigation won't end with tomorrow's edition, you know that, don't you? You'll be reporting on this for years. There are dangerous elements ... you're chumming for sharks, here. Not only the mob—the Federal Bureau will go after you. Tapping your phones, going through your mail. Every time you go home you'll find the door unlocked. Little things inside moved around. It's how they get to you. It's how they drive you insane."

Conroy didn't respond; there was nothing to say. Yes, she was aware of the risks. But no, she didn't want to drop the story. She'd been shaken up before, but now she'd rediscovered her resolve.

"If I can get City Hall to back the story, you'll print it?"

The City Editor turned around to face her.

"Tilda," he said, "you get City Hall onside, I won't only print it. I'll put it all over the front page."

CHAPTER 39

The interrogation cell in the F.B.I.'s Field Office was windowless. The door was welded steel with mineral wool insulation. It had a cross-barred Fox lock, too: two metal bars across the width of the door held by brackets. No getting in or out.

Unlike the homicide department's old interview rooms, there was a tape recorder mounted on the edge of the table and a long two-way mirror the length of one wall. But Craine ignored his reflection; instead he focused his attention on the large clock mounted above the door. He was counting down the hours until Lansky's Friday deadline. He couldn't trust Dragna to inform him about Harvey. There were too many reasons for him not to. Craine had to do it himself. This was his final labor.

Since he'd been taken into custody by the Federal Bureau, Craine had endured sixteen hours of talking to junior agents. They all looked the same to Craine: Anglo-Protestants adhering to Hoover's strict dress code—black business suits with a white shirt and plain dark tie. Different casts of the same mold, asking question after question he didn't answer.

Although he was being held on suspicion of murdering Harvey Sterling and his young family, this was a custodial interrogation and Craine knew his rights. He'd not been charged with anything and the F.B.I. could keep him detained and held incommunicado for a maximum of twenty-four hours. Like the police, the F.B.I. needed to provide the District Attorney's office with sufficient evidence against him before they could issue an indictment for felony murder.

But Craine knew that the physical evidence against him was thin. Which meant that he would be relentlessly interrogated for the full twenty-four hours under electric lights, with the sole aim being for him to confess. That was the only way they'd get him, and Craine had no intention of confessing to a crime he didn't commit. All he had to do now was survive in silence. Eight hours to go.

All of the agents who questioned Craine had been trained at the F.B.I. Laboratory. Each of them began with a monologue, a different version of the same opening speech they'd learned by rote. They were actors in a play hoping Craine would come on stage to play the villain. But Craine knew that the second he even opened his mouth about his involvement, his words could be twisted.

Instead, well aware of his right to the Fifth Amendment, he parried questions only with long chapters of silence. Sometimes he said "no comment," but only because he knew it irritated them enough that they'd leave the room more quickly. Occasionally he made sure to highlight, "I was not responsible for those murders," before he sat back in his chair and saved his energy.

He counted down the hours. It was five in the morning, and then it was six and then it was seven. Craine's eyes moved between the clock and the painted cinderblock walls he was starting to know in detail. It was an old adage in Homicide that innocent men don't sleep, and it was true. Craine barely even shut his eyes. He was so tired he was drunk with it. When was the last time he'd slept? *Tuesday?*

Throughout it all he thought about his son. Finally allowed himself to. He reflected on their argument the night Kastel's plane landed. Understood now that he needed to let that boy live his own life. If Michael wanted to join the army, so be it. As his father, he had to allow him to make his own mistakes and have his own successes. If only he could see him to tell him face to face. It was all he wanted.

Night came and went, with several rotations of junior agents. Mostly they lectured him on the range and magnitude of their evidence against him. His guilt in the massacre of Harvey Sterling's family was established and guaranteed, they all said in different ways.

A couple outright lied to him, telling him they had his prints on the murder weapon. Several told him Abraham Levine had already been released because he stated he saw Craine murder Harvey Sterling's family in cold blood.

They were the warm-up act, of course. Their bluffs were an effort to wear him down until his mind was so fragile that when Agent Redhill walked in with a confession sheet, he'd sign his life away willingly in exchange for a good night's sleep.

Around 10 A.M., Redhill finally entered with two junior agents. They filed in like pallbearers, the two youths positioning themselves in different corners as Redhill moved to the table where Craine sat.

"Let me explain the situation we've found ourselves in," said Redhill, draping his jacket on the back of the chair before he sat down. "I've got two dead minors, aged between two and four years old. I've got a dead female, Lucy Sterling, aged twenty-six. And a dead male, Harvey Sterling, twenty-eight. Husband and father."

Craine didn't say anything.

"All this ignorance. It's an incredible charade. But I've got you located at the scene of the crime with a known killer wanted in the murder of a dozen other cases. I've got your fingerprints in the house. On top of that, I've got a dead security guard at the Bradbury Building, also with your prints all over the place."

The junior agent standing by the door was another good church boy dressed in government attire. When Redhill glanced over he snapped to and handed him a wedge of manila case folders.

Redhill opened the top file and twisted it so Craine could see the face sheet. It was on F.B.I. stationery but was otherwise a duplicate of a police 56/47 form. Craine scanned the charges without leaning forward: ... *evading arrest* ... *fleeing scene of the crime* ... *breaking and entry* ... *assaulting a Federal Agent* ... *murder in the first degree.*

"It's a long list," said Redhill. He made a show of rolling up his sleeves.

This was the technique: tire you out, demonstrate to you that your guilt is indisputable and then try to wear you down to confession. It was frighteningly reminiscent of his own interrogations. The words varied but the script remained the same.

Redhill jabbed at the manila folder between them. "You set it up to look like suicide. Something you're more than familiar with, wouldn't you say?"

The F.B.I. agent paused, looking into Craine's eyes. He was reading him.

"We've got plenty here. You and Abe both. Ballistics tests will take longer to confirm, but I'm pretty certain we can link Abraham Levine's Savage pistol to the Bradbury Building, too. Juries like that. Judges do, too."

When Craine didn't reply, he said: "People who are innocent protest. Guilty people stay silent."

No, Craine thought. *I'm silent because I'm thinking this through.*

Craine looked at the stack of folders. Case files were usually pretty lean: a twenty-four-hour crime report; evidence lists; autopsy and ballistics results; a few memoranda and missives outlining witness testimonies.

Something about this interview was off-kilter. The files here were bloated. Too much documentation for a homicide. Which told Craine it was probably full of blank pages. Redhill was trying to intimidate him.

"I know you've been stalling," Redhill went on. "We're both aware that we're after a confession. But we've worked through the night and we have enough right here. I'll be taking this to the Assistant D.A. the minute I leave this room."

From underneath the folder, Redhill removed a red envelope and tipped a dozen 5-by-8 glossies into his hand. He spread them across the table. The photographs were crime scene prints of Harvey's house. Harvey. Then his wife. Then several pictures of Harvey's young children Craine wished he hadn't seen. He pondered dismal thoughts. His clothes smelt of death. His mind smelt of it, too.

"Take a good look. This is your handiwork. Or was it Abraham? Maybe you're protecting him. You think a man like that, a thug who butchers people for a living, deserves your protection?"

Craine gave nothing. No reaction. Redhill changed direction. "What about your friend Tilda Conroy? She involved in this at all? Because we can bring her in too. Maybe she's not capable of *this*," he said, prodding the atrocities in the photographs, "but we could get her on a conspiracy to murder charge."

Craine felt his eyes flicker and Redhill seized on it with a gimcrack smile. "You know, I'm surprised you've taken such a shine to her. She was the one who wrote about your wife before she died. Wrote the initial story about drugs in Hollywood, about your wife being fired by M.G.M. because she was an addict. Conroy named and shamed her. Might even be responsible for your wife's . . . *accident*."

If Redhill was trying to throw Craine off balance, it worked. Craine's wife had died of an oxycodone overdose a few days after M.G.M. had canceled her contract. The idea that Tilda Conroy might somehow have been responsible caught him off guard. He'd wondered why she'd seemed so thrown when he first told her his name. It all made sense now. All this time he'd been working with someone who helped push his wife over the edge.

Craine was so tired now, but he tried not to get upset. He reminded himself that Redhill was intentionally driving him to an emotional response. He closed his eyes when he spoke. "I didn't kill Harvey Sterling. Or his family."

"What happened then, Craine? Because you can keep repeating that, but if you don't tell me exactly what happened I'll go straight to the D.A.'s office and return with a federal murder charge."

Redhill leaned forward and pressed something under the table. The roll of tape at the end of the table began spooling. It made a wet, slippery sound like a cat washing its back. That seemed odd to Craine. It hadn't been on before. He was being recorded for the first time only now.

"I found Harvey Sterling like that."

"What do you think happened?"

"He killed his family and then shot himself."

"Sterling killed his family?"

"Yes." Craine gestured at the photographs. "It's clear from the position of the carbine that he placed it in his mouth and pulled the trigger. A suicide is difficult to fake and almost impossible to force. If he'd have shot himself against his will there would be signs of stress on his body. Bruises. Cuts. There aren't any."

"That obvious?" Redhill said with a smirk.

But the thing was, it *was* obvious. Any homicide detective would have concluded the same. The only thing strange about it was that Harvey used a different weapon to shoot his family than he used on himself. Maybe he was worried the pistol was too low-caliber.

Redhill caught him looking at the photographs. "And the Bradbury Building? The security guard?"

Craine's mind was slow and trudging. He was so tired he had to dredge the words out.

"It was Harvey," he croaked. It hurt to speak. "It was an ambush. He was hoping to kill us once he knew we were getting closer. Killing us at our hotel would have been too obvious. The Bradbury was safe ground. And then afterward he tried to convince us that Charlie Hill was responsible. Conroy was shot at with a rifle. I suspect if you compare the projectiles they'll be the same as his carbine."

Redhill listened carefully. He appeared remarkably sanguine.

"So you had nothing to do with these murders?"

"Absolutely not."

Redhill mulled this over like it was a realization. And yet something about his bearing bothered Craine.

"Why do you think he did what he did?" the agent asked.

"I think he panicked. We had confronted him about killing Siegel and he knew there would be repercussions. He worried for his family."

"You think he killed Siegel?"

"Yes."

Redhill nodded his head slowly. "And then he killed his family, why? Mercy killings?"

"Possibly," said Craine, although in truth he wasn't sure why.

Redhill kept nodding, like it was making sense. "I've seen enough veterans go on murder sprees to know there was probably nothing rational about any of it. But Siegel was planned. Who sent Harvey to do it? It must have been on Dragna's orders."

Craine shook his head. "I don't believe that."

"Jack Dragna is a murderer, Craine. He's already been associated with four killings, and that doesn't count his history on the streets of Brooklyn. We know he runs illegal gambling in Los Angeles. He has a heroin-smuggling operation, too."

Craine's mind was a fug. He began questioning his own assumptions. "Dragna didn't have anything to do with this," he said with less enthusiasm than he'd intended.

"Yes. He. Did." Redhill tapped his hand in time on the desk. "I've had a few run-ins with Dragna before. And he's a liar like the rest of them. Pathological. It's almost like they believe themselves. When all they really believe in is money."

Redhill's logic might be sound but Craine had always believed in his ability to tell liars apart.

"Thumb your nose at it, but his motive isn't elusive. Dragna's reason was good old-fashioned greed. Personal gain. Those Trans-American race wire services—you think I don't know about them? Allows him to control horse betting across the country. That's millions of dollars he gets his hands on with Siegel out of the way."

Craine's mind was slow to digest this. He'd believed Dragna when he said he wasn't involved. But was Redhill on to something? *Was Chicago merely a red herring?*

"You know, when I was a kid," Redhill went on, "we went to the circus. I remember my dad asked the lion tamer how he trained the lions. The guy said, 'You don't train lions, you feed them.'" Craine looked at him and Redhill held two hands up. "Lansky was foolish to think he could ever control Dragna. He should have given Dragna what he wanted years ago. Instead, Dragna killed Siegel so he could take over the West Coast crime syndicate."

Craine wanted to refute this idea. But fatigue made things more difficult. Like solving a math problem drunk. "Maybe," he said. "But either way, I'm not responsible."

And that was all that mattered. Leaving custody. Being released. Because whether Dragna was behind all this didn't matter. Craine could prove to Lansky that Harvey Sterling was the triggerman. After that, it was up to him.

"Here's what I'm going to do, Craine," Redhill said, as if he'd come to a major turning point. "I'm going to believe you. I'm going to trust what you're saying is true because years ago you and I worked together to bring down an extortion ring. And that counts for something."

Craine felt his heart beat. "You'll let me go?"

"Yes. I'm going to leave you here while I type this up and then I'm going to get you to sign your statement. Then we're going to release you."

It was all Craine cared about. Only when Redhill stood up to go did he remember Joyce.

"Why did you lie about the third witness?"

Redhill paused before he answered. "She was worried for her safety, so we agreed to withhold her identity. She'd been harassed by the mob and we have duty of care."

When Craine didn't seem satisfied he added, "There are no bow-tie endings, Craine. You must remember that from your days in Homicide. It doesn't end with headlines and sentences. It ends with delayed court hearings and suicides in jail. Not everything adds up all the time."

Craine didn't say anything. Redhill was right.

"You'll get your head around it. Or you won't. But either way, in a few weeks, when you're back home with your boy, you'll stop caring."

The answer seemed thin, but Craine was so tired now his thoughts were muddled and unclear. It didn't matter anymore. All that mattered was that he could get to Lansky.

He thought of Michael. Home had taken on a holy sanctity.

CHAPTER 40

"Are you a member of the Communist Party, Dalton?" Louis Mayer asked his most highly paid screenwriter after Whitey Hendry had brought him into his office.

Trumbo lifted his chin. "Congress doesn't have a right to know my political beliefs. Besides, this is simply a publicity stunt. The Committee isn't conducting a fair investigation—"

"Answer the question."

"You're starting to sound like them."

There was quiet, as Mayer didn't answer. Trumbo had a point.

"Mr. Mayer," Trumbo went on, "you and I both know that there isn't a communist plot to take over the motion picture industry."

Mayer banged his small fists on his desk. "They'll accuse you of being un-American. And then they'll accuse our *pictures* of being un-American."

The stakes were high. Mayer was well aware that if any of his writers or actors were accused of being communist, the government might well shut down their entire studio.

The writer was flippant in his reply. "They talk to us like we're radicals. Terrorists. We can't allow it. *You* can't allow it. It's our art, Louis. We have rights."

Dalton Trumbo spoke with a tone Mayer wasn't used to: like a paintbrush being cross-examined by the paint. But he was still M.G.M.'s best writer. Given the difficult year they'd been having, a part of Mayer wasn't sure if he could afford to let him go. "Dalton, we can work together to find a solution."

Trumbo took off his glasses and wiped them with his handkerchief. "What do you suggest, L.B.?"

"There's going to be a congressional hearing. And if you don't comply, you'll be blacklisted. I want you to declare to them that you're not a communist."

Trumbo stood up and raised his chin so he was looking down at him. "I told you, Mr. Mayer. They have no right to make me answer that question. It violates the First Amendment. It threatens freedom of speech. And as far as I'm concerned, that's the end of it."

When Trumbo left, Mayer felt annoyed with himself. Not because he'd let Trumbo speak to him like that but because he'd let himself feel guilty. It had been happening a lot recently. Judy Garland attempting suicide. His divorce. All that business with Jonathan Craine and his son.

He was considering how best to resolve this issue with H.U.A.C. when his secretary Ida tapped on the door. He had an unscheduled meeting request from a reporter from the *Herald.* Some reporter called Tilda Conroy.

"Send her away."

"Yes, Mr. Mayer."

"Wait—" Mayer paused. "Did she say what about?"

Ida seemed hesitant to say it. "She said it was about Jonathan Craine."

Mayer drummed his fingers on his desk. It would have been so easy to send this woman away. In most moods, he would have done.

And yet something told him not to.

After she'd reached an agreement with the head of M.G.M., Tilda Conroy drove across town to the offices of *The Hollywood Enquirer* on Sunset Boulevard.

Conroy had never been in Wilson's office before. It was the same layout as the City Editor's but the desk was bigger, the wallpaper was fresh and the windows had a view that looked like something from a picture postcard young ingénues would send their parents when they got off the bus.

William Wilson was a powerful figure in Los Angeles. A lot of his ventures—not only his paper but hotels, nightclubs and casinos—served the industry. He was and would always remain protected by the establishment he'd helped create.

So it was intimidating sitting less than three feet away from the man, persuading him of the benefits of her proposal. It was a pitch, in essence, to undermine the Federal Bureau of Investigation. The stakes were high, but his buy-in was critical. Wilson and Mayer had enough influence in City Hall to shut down her investigation. Which meant they had enough influence to open it up again. So when she spoke, Conroy appealed not to his humanity, but to his reason. Helping her was helping him.

After speaking for several minutes uninterrupted, she summarized: "You'll provide me a full interview on everything you know about Siegel's involvement with the New York and Chicago syndicates. With attributable quotes. And in return I will not release any information that alludes to your role in their ambitions in Las Vegas. No one will ever read that you were an investor in The Flamingo. That's the offer. Quid pro quo."

When she'd finished, Wilson pressed a button underneath his desk and his secretary came in carrying a tray of colas where one might expect coffee or tea. Wilson took several Coke bottles off the tray. He lowered one to the edge of his desk, where a hidden bottle opener snapped it off with a pop.

"What you're asking is very bold, Mrs Conroy," he said after taking a sip. "I'm surprised Louis Mayer has agreed to this. Unless of course you're fabricating . . ."

"I made my agenda clear," Conroy said. Her confidence was surprising even to herself. "He benefits the same way you do. Information for anonymity. If you thought I was lying then why would you agree to this meeting?"

"You're a well-respected reporter working for an esteemed broadsheet. My door is always open."

Nothing in his words sounded sincere. Wilson's reputation as a petty tyrant had been well earned.

When his secretary left, Conroy asked, "Is that really why?"

"No," he said bluntly. "You're good but not that good. You write almost as well as a man." He gulped from the bottle and Conroy could hear the cola froth in his mouth. "But not quite."

He smiled, then smiled again. This was the real Wilson.

Conroy wasn't going to get upset. If she wanted to help her negotiating leverage, she had to remain cool and distant. "But you'll agree to participate in my article?"

He responded with a question of his own. "It seems to me your plan is in part motivated by helping Jonathan Craine. Why? If my memory serves me correctly, you reported on his dead wife like the rest of us. A social conscience piece, wasn't it? Drugs in Hollywood."

"I reported on it, that's all," Conroy said as if it was an excuse, when in fact it had bothered her for years.

"You were *complicit.* We both were. You see, you say this isn't personal. And yet your actions speak to the contrary."

Her poise wavered. "My interest is satisfying public interest . . . Proving that a national crime syndicate dominates major American industries. For that I need Craine's release. His inside knowledge is critical."

"Such self-assurance. *Making a difference. Doing the right thing.* I applaud you, Mrs Conroy. But you should know, the syndicates operate through large-scale intimidation and corruption. The cost of paying off enforcement officials is simply absorbed as a necessary expense. No one is going to stop America being the biggest roulette wheel on earth simply because you write about it in your little paper."

Wilson was patronizing her. She wanted to lash out. To get angry. But she didn't. She remembered what Alice had said. *Choose your battles.*

"Mr. Wilson," she said as coolly as she could, "I've laid out my offer. Now do we have an agreement or not?"

The mogul put the bottle on his desk and rotated it. "Let me liaise with Louis Mayer. If he's onside, as you say, we can speak to City Hall. We've had our differences in the past but there's mutual interest here. And we're stronger together."

"And the article?"

Wilson ran a finger along his pencil mustache, like a gambler counting his chips. "I'll tell you everything I know," he said. "I'll show you how the sausage is made: account details, contracts, whatever you want."

"And you'll let me quote you by name on condition that I do not mention your own investment?"

"That is *the* condition. Don't forget it."

"One thing is keeping that information from the general public. But the F.B.I. are a different matter. They might use this as an excuse to come at you."

"They won't."

Something in his voice said he was hiding something.

"They already know about your mob connections?"

He nodded. "Hoover's priority is communism, not crime syndicates. He's going to launch a crusade against the red beachhead, a blacklist across the industry for anyone with communist sympathies."

"And you are part of that plan?"

Wilson spoke proudly, ever the patriot: "What was once gold has tarnished. It's my duty as an American to purge the industry of the red threat and return it to the halcyon days before it's too late."

For all his flag-waving, Conroy was under no illusions: the elite worked for naked self-interest. She was trying to assemble his reasoning as he spoke. "No," she said. "Hoover has agreed he won't touch you so long as you support his anti-union purge. You've made a deal with the devil."

Wilson smiled that Cheshire cat grin of his. “Oh, Mrs Conroy, don’t be surprised,” he said. “I signed so long ago the ink’s already fading.”

There was a hiss and a pop as he opened another cola.

CHAPTER 41

After the agents left the room, Craine allowed himself to fall asleep. He'd done his duty and the rest was simply protocol. He hadn't been charged. Any minute now he'd be released and this ordeal would almost be over.

His mind wandered, dropping deeper into unconsciousness. They weren't dreams as much as fleeting images. First Michael. Always Michael. A vision of the night guard. But then Harvey's wife, dead on the carpet. The horror of his two young children. The pistol on the bedroom floor. Harvey's rifle.

And soon Craine found himself opening his eyes with five words on his lips. "*Why would Harvey kill them?*"

Not his motive for killing Siegel. His *family*. As a father, Craine couldn't understand how Harvey could ever kill his own children. Couldn't imagine it. Couldn't picture it.

Redhill had taken his case folders with him but the photographs remained spread out like a tablecloth of horror. No doubt Redhill's intention was to instill disgust, so Craine didn't change his mind.

Using one finger, Craine began grazing over the photos. The bodies of the children were hard to look at but also hard to analyze. Blood pools and body positions had been distorted by their location in the closet.

He circled round to the glossies of Harvey's wife. Not the gore but the body. Something about the photographs bothered him. *This is something*, Craine thought, looking again at the pictures and trying to commit them to memory. *This is something that doesn't make sense.*

Redhill's technique had been no different from Craine's when he was a detective. He'd proposed two alternative explanations for the crime, one incriminating and one giving him an exit. And yet even in his tired and confused mind, Craine couldn't help but ask why Redhill would have an army of agents spend sixteen hours trying to get him to confess to a crime he inwardly knew Craine didn't commit.

Something subtler was in play. This interrogation wasn't about getting Craine to confess to Harvey's murder. It was about wearing him down. To guide his attention away from the circumstances surrounding Harvey Sterling's death. *A smokescreen.*

Craine was still running through the photographs when Redhill entered with one of his juniors.

"Horrific," Redhill said when he saw Craine staring at them. "Makes you wonder what kind of cruelty man is capable of, doesn't it?"

Redhill moved the photographs to one side and placed down green discharge papers and a two-page statement with elements of Craine's interview, a formal declaration that needed to be signed by Craine in order for him to be released.

Coding in the left corner corresponding to the case file. A stamp on the top said 'AUTHORIZED PERSONS ONLY.' An appendix included the full transcript from the tape recording. Thumbing through the pages, Craine noticed that it only began with him explaining that Harvey Sterling was guilty. The endless interviews where Craine had been accused were omitted, as if that was never even posited.

Redhill held up the face sheet and put it down on the table with a pen. He took a seat. "Sign here. Initial the other pages."

Craine looked at the pen and hesitated.

"It's over, Craine. I appreciate you've found yourself in some kind of predicament but now that's come to an end. I don't know your stake in this, but you wanted to find Siegel's killer and you found him."

"Are you going to release this to the press?"

"We'll do our due diligence and follow the necessary protocol. But we'll take care of this quietly."

A bureaucrat's answer. Noncommittal.

"What about Abe?"

"He's going to be held. Conspiracy to murder."

"Wait—why?"

"If it's not this, it'll be something else. Doesn't exactly have your pedigree. As far as the Bureau is concerned, Ballistics matched the bullets from his Savage to the Bradbury Building. I'm Old Testament, Craine. I'll be happy only when he's in San Quentin facing the rope."

"I don't have to sign this," Craine said. "I've not been charged. You have to release me within twenty-four hours. That's in forty minutes' time."

"District Attorney has given me an extension on both of you due to Abe's previous arrests. Thirty-six hours. You won't be out until after midnight tonight."

Craine's heart sank. He looked at Redhill intently.

"Don't make this harder than it needs to be. You want to keep me as an ally, you'll sign the fucking papers, Craine."

Craine noted the profanity. Redhill had never sworn or lost his temper before. Something Craine was doing bothered him immensely.

Redhill collected the photographs and had begun slipping them back into their red envelope when there was a tap at the door and the junior agent opened it a crack.

The voice from outside wasn't clear but the word 'urgent' came through. So did the words 'District Attorney.'

The young agent stepped into the corridor to find out what was going on. The door shut with a metallic click.

Craine and Redhill both turned as they heard raised voices. The door opened and the junior agent returned. He leaned down and whispered something in Redhill's ear.

"Who?"

Craine saw him mouth the D.A.'s name.

"Stay here."

Redhill's chair scraped back as he went outside.

"You," Craine said to the junior agent when the door had shut. "When were these photographs taken?"

The junior agent didn't reply. Craine couldn't hear much from outside the room. But he could make out the back of Redhill's head through the narrow mesh-glass hatch in the door.

"It's a straightforward question. All I'm asking is when these photographs were taken. You need to check with your boss for a straightforward question?"

The young agent looked at the door, then at Craine. "About twenty minutes after we arrived."

"And the techs took all of these photographs at the same time? Within, say, an hour of each other?"

He glanced at the door again, then nodded. A second later, and Redhill entered.

"Get his cuffs off," Redhill ordered the young agent testily. To Craine he said, "Looks like you still have friends in the right places. Your lawyer is outside."

Craine didn't reply. *His lawyer?*

"I can't stop Dragna from paying off the right people. But as far as I'm concerned, you're done here. I don't want to see you in Los Angeles again." He held up Craine's statement. "You want your boy out of danger, you'll sign it."

Even though Craine's mind was leaden, his memory wasn't so hazy that he'd forgotten whether he'd told Redhill about Michael. The inquisitor had made one crucial mistake.

"How did you know my son was in danger?" he asked.

Redhill's face tipped downward. The air went out of him.

"I'm not signing anything."

Before Craine could say anything else he was escorted out of his cell. As he was led down the long corridor, he wondered who his benefactor was and if he was striding into quicksand. But with less than twelve hours left to reach Lansky, he didn't have time to think about it. Besides, something else was playing on his mind. Because if what he saw in the photographs was true, then his son's life was still at risk. And there was no way he was going to survive this without more people being killed.

The sun hurt his eyes when he went outside to see the man calling himself his lawyer. Craine expected to see someone from Dragna's entourage, but the man waiting for him was Whitey Hendry, M.G.M.'s Head of Security.

"Craine," he said curtly. "I'm here to drive you to see Mr. Mayer. He's expecting you."

Craine wasn't sure why Louis Mayer had sponsored his exit but he was grateful nonetheless. When Hendry pointed wordlessly to a limousine, Craine asked, "What about Abe?"

"Abraham Levine remains in custody. He's yet to be formally charged, but there's nothing we can do for him."

Whitey Hendry opened the rear passenger door. Someone was sitting inside. The last person he expected to see: Tilda Conroy.

CHAPTER 42

They were heading east, but Craine wasn't sure of their destination. Only that they'd been driving for well over an hour. Following a long series of power lines, they passed through La Puente Valley. Craine looked at Conroy's watch. It was three in the afternoon. He had until midnight to reach Vegas.

"I don't have time for this." He was nervous. "I need to get to Lansky."

"Mayer said it was important. I wouldn't bring you here otherwise." Conroy leaned forward. "Is it far?" she asked Whitey Hendry in the front passenger seat.

"No," Hendry said. "Not far."

As they drove, Conroy explained to Craine that it was Louis Mayer who got him out of custody. From what he could gather, Conroy had made several visits to men in senior positions that morning. The mechanics of what had been negotiated were confusing but Conroy seemed confident in the outcome.

This was the arrangement: the *Herald* had agreed with Captain Henson that they wouldn't mention Harvey Sterling or Jonathan Craine in connection with Benjamin Siegel because City Hall wanted to push Siegel's murder under the bed. William Wilson would provide Conroy with background on the New York syndicate in exchange for not mentioning his Vegas investments, and M.G.M. would give Jonathan Craine his freedom if Conroy wouldn't make public their payments to studio unions under mob control.

Henson. Wilson. Mayer. All three of them had the ear of City Hall, but it was Mayer who'd brokered a deal with the District Attorney's office to get Craine out of custody and Mayer who they were driving to see.

"Did Harvey Sterling really kill Siegel?"

Craine nodded.

"And his family?"

"It didn't happen the way they say it did," he said.

"What then?"

"I think Harvey was set up by the Chicago Outfit to kill Siegel."

"Why?"

"So that Lansky would sell Siegel's shares in The Flamingo. I think Chicago know how valuable it is, and they're going to use the chaos surrounding Siegel's murder to strong-arm Lansky into selling at a lower price."

They drove in silence for a while as Conroy processed this. He thought of what Redhill had told him about Conroy all those years ago and wanted to be angry at her. Wanted to shout at her and ask her how she could ever forgive herself for chasing cheap headlines at the expense of someone's life. But he was too tired now. He didn't have the energy. And besides, who was he to blame someone else for his own failings as a husband? He had to take responsibility for what had happened to Celia. He couldn't push that guilt on someone else.

Craine was struggling to keep his eyes open. "How did you know I didn't kill Harvey Sterling's family?"

"It was never a doubt in my mind," Conroy said. "I knew you would never be able to kill those poor children."

"Thank you," he said. "For getting me out."

Conroy stared out the window so he couldn't see her face. "Well, I needed your help with the article," she said impassively. "City Editor says we publish tomorrow. I'll be following the story over the coming months. He wants the *Herald* at the vanguard."

She turned to him and there was a look there. Something in her eyes, perhaps. A steely determination to see this through despite the risks.

"But you're not going to connect Siegel to the studios? Isn't that part of the story?"

"I needed Mayer's help to get you out. He has leverage. That was part of the bargain." She paused, then said, "It was worth it to help you."

"I thought you only cared about your article?"

Conroy didn't reply, but Craine was too exhausted to ask her what had made her change her mind. What mattered was getting to Las Vegas by tonight.

He looked around at the surrounding fields in their various shades. Mexican workers struggling in the heat as they tended alfalfa and avocados, oranges and almonds. There were houses being built everywhere, a sprawling suburb to satisfy a booming population.

When they passed a sign to Riverdale, Conroy took out a photograph from her purse.

"I did some background on Harvey. After he left New York, he worked as one of Paul Ricca's bodyguards in the Chicago Outfit before joining the military. He was an army sniper. Served in the Pacific."

Conroy handed him a photograph of his unit.

"Most of them died. The ones that didn't were captured and tortured by the Japanese."

In the photograph, Craine saw a platoon of soldiers lined up in three rows. Harvey was there on the left, his sturdy face staring into the middle distance. Beside him, Craine recognized a face he'd seen before. In Abe's wallet. He must be Joseph Levine, Abe's son.

Craine went to put the photograph away but there was another face that stood out. The platoon commander, front and center. Even under the helmet his face was unmistakable.

Several strands fell into place. The shifting spotlight had finally come to a stop and the figure in the proscenium was illuminated. Harvey Sterling may have been the triggerman. But Craine knew who had sent him.

* * *

Every man needed a hobby and horses were Louis Mayer's.

He'd bought his ranch in Perris ten years ago, around the same time that Harry Warner built a racetrack, but Mayer had always been more interested in building a stable than an arena. Over the years, he'd become one of the leading breeders of stake winners in America; he developed his thoroughbreds like he developed his stars. And unlike actors, horses did what they were trained to do.

Mayer stroked the horse's forehead between the eyes. "Hey, Busher. Easy girl, easy."

Busher was a racing filly, one of his best, but maybe only a few seasons away from retirement. As he rubbed her chestnut neck, Mayer felt like his time was coming too. *I'm an old horse not long for the glue factory*, he thought to himself.

He opened the stable door and guided the horse outside. A jockey was waiting with his trainer and the two men took Busher out to the training field.

Mayer stood close to the stables as Busher took off round the track. There were no gates and no starting pistol—the jockey simply started slow and built the horse up to a gallop until Mayer could see clumps of mud exploding under her hooves.

There wasn't a universal approach to racehorse training, but horses needed routine. The trainer would canter it four days a week, with two fast sessions under race conditions and a hard-walk on Sunday. Training was important, but diet was as crucial. Incremental gains made all the difference. But there was a line, too. You had to let the beast rest. Allow it to graze and be happy.

It was the same with actors.

Mayer had ignored his wife's warnings, but he realized now that she was right. He'd pushed Judy Garland too hard. *Dieting. Supplements.* He'd turned a blind eye. He'd had a warning many years ago when Celia Raymond died, but he'd ignored it. He'd realized too late what happened if you pushed people too hard. They destroyed themselves.

Mayer heard a car engine. There was the sound of a door opening, of shoes on gravel and then Jonathan Craine was standing behind him, silhouetted in the doorway of the barn.

"Conroy said you wanted to meet me," Craine said. His tone had a barb to it.

"That woman can be very persuasive."

"Should I be thanking her or you for my release?"

There was the thunder of hooves as Busher galloped past. Mayer didn't answer Craine's question but he said, "I appreciate you coming out all this way. I can't be certain my telephone isn't being tapped."

Craine stepped into the light and Mayer got a look at him. He looked even worse than he did a few days go. Vexed, red-rimmed eyes kept Mayer at a distance. He didn't know what Craine might do.

Craine didn't say anything so Mayer continued: "We're talking a lot with Hoover. I have friends at the Bureau. Helping guide me through . . ." he lifted his hand briefly ". . . all this H.U.A.C. business." Mayer worded the next part carefully. "One of them mentioned something in passing—although there may be nothing to it. He said Agent Redhill and his team found a cartridge in the garden. They could trace it to the weapon. Military records."

"What are you trying to say?"

"That the F.B.I. already know who killed Siegel."

"Harvey Sterling. He's dead."

Mayer shook his head. "More than that. They've known all along," he explained. "They knew even before Siegel was murdered."

Mayer could see Craine processing this.

"Why?"

"I don't know and I don't care enough to find out. That's up to you."

Craine looked like he wanted to leave.

"There's something else. When you came to me, you didn't ask about Virginia Hill. Why is that?"

"She loved Siegel," Craine said. "I didn't consider her a suspect. And no one has seen her."

Mayer nodded. "The F.B.I. know where Virginia Hill is." When Craine looked surprised, he said, "I don't know what she knows but I believe they've known where she is all along."

"How?"

"I have a plane at Hughes Airport south of Culver City. Howard Hughes is keeping his Spruce Goose there but he lets the F.B.I. use the same airfield for clandestine operations. Part of his effort to get the War Committee off his back. Hughes told me they're flying someone in tonight. *Virginia Hill.*"

This seemed to take Craine aback. Mayer saw his face look away and process what this meant.

"I need to talk to her. As soon as possible."

Mayer said, "Don't worry. I've made arrangements with Hughes. My car will take you there. Is there anything else you need?"

Behind them the horse slowed. Mayer could hear her heavy breathing.

"I have an associate," Craine said. "Abraham Levine. He's still being held by the F.B.I."

"A man with his connections isn't so easily pried away from federal jurisdiction. But I'll speak to the District Attorney and do what I can."

Craine was also breathing hard. "Why are you helping me?" he asked. "Because of Conroy? You could have used your influence to make sure your involvement with the mob was never made public. I don't understand why you agreed to meet her at the negotiation table."

Mayer had wondered when Craine would ask this. The question was still something he hadn't fully answered himself.

"I haven't always lived up to the values of my pictures," Mayer said. "Many years ago, I did you a disservice. It's not easy for me to say that."

Craine and Mayer had never spoken about what had happened when Craine's wife had died. Craine had agreed to work with the studio to frame his wife's suicide as a tragic accident. It was a secret created by three men. And the third man was dead.

Their lives were so entwined in many ways, but you can't find kinship in guilt. It only makes you resent each other more. When Mayer saw Craine he saw the hurt he had caused. The disappointment his wife had in him. But being here now, he realized he couldn't hate this man any longer. He had to do what was right.

"You lost a wife," he said. "And your boy—he lost his mother."

"It wasn't only her." There was a hard edge to Craine's voice. Mayer could see the anger simmering in him. "There were other people. People we didn't do right by. I worked for you for years, thanklessly helping you as we went about destroying lives." He took a breath. "I would have done anything you wanted."

"And now you're angry. Why? Because you think I didn't appreciate what you did? You were the best. The devil's miracle worker." He let the words sink in before saying with the same strained breath, "But I was the devil and it was hard for me to feel good about that."

"What do you want from me?" Craine asked. "What is it you want in return?"

"There's no second act for me. But there is for you. Jonathan, you can accomplish something in this world. More than digging ditches in Bridgeport."

"And do what? Work for you?"

"No. The opposite. Be the person you would have been if you'd never met me."

It would take a long time for Craine to realize what Mayer really meant by that. It wasn't something he could understand at that moment.

The jockey came to the edge of the track and Mayer leaned over the gate to pat his favorite horse's neck.

He waited until the jockey had taken her for a slow walk before he said: "You asked me why I'm helping you." He looked at Craine with a look that wasn't an apology but that showed understanding of his situation. "I have a lot of things. There's very little I could want for. But I lost my family. And I've learned, far too late, that a man is nothing without his family."

CHAPTER 43

There were two guards in the hutch beside the gate to the Hughes airfield. Hendry left the engine running and spoke to them, but no money was handed over—whatever message they'd been given from above had been relayed and the very sight of Louis Mayer's limousine seemed to have an impact. The guards picked up their weapons and left, with the barriers down and locked.

Hendry turned around and faced the back seat. He held out a small revolver with tape wrapped around the grip. "Take it," he said. "It's clean."

Craine took the pistol without saying thank you.

Hendry turned to face forward. "Good luck," Craine heard him mutter.

Conroy wasn't staying, despite arguing in favor of it. What Craine was doing was highly illegal and he wouldn't let her drag herself any further into it.

When he got out of the car, Craine said: "Thank you, Tilda. For everything."

He knew she wanted to ask if he'd come back to help with her story. Her exposé on organized crime. But she couldn't bring herself to say it, knowing that his mind was focused on Michael.

"If I speak to her, I'll make sure Virginia Hill comes straight to you. Get the story out there. People need to know."

Conroy's voice was shaking. "What about you?"

He didn't say anything, and she said: "After the Chicago trial, you left Los Angeles. What you know . . . you could help us—"

"I'm not sure I'm the right person."

"You are. You're a braver man than you think you are."

He didn't think it was true. But hearing it was what he needed right now. To be brave. To keep going. To see this through.

He went to go but she leaned over. "Jonathan, wait. There's something else I need to tell you. Something that happened a long time ago." Her eyes were wet and she seemed upset. Or ashamed. "*About your wife.*"

"I know," Craine said. "Redhill told me."

Her face fell. He saw tears in her eyes. "I was younger then," she tried to explain. "Trying to make my name. I'm so sorry."

Craine looked at Tilda and thought about everything she'd done for him. There was no part of him that felt anything but appreciation.

"We've all done things we're not proud of, Tilda," he said. "I know I have."

Craine shut the car door and a minute later the car pulled away.

He wasn't sure he'd see Conroy again but he knew how much he owed her. He thought about what Mayer had said, too. About having a second act. He knew then that if he came through this alive, he needed to come back. To finish what the two of them had started.

It was time to turn to face the world he'd ignored for much too long.

The airstrip had a single runway a little over a mile long. Craine waited in a hangar filled with fuel tankers and a dozen military aircraft in various states of disassembly. It was unmanned, but that wasn't unexpected for a covert handover. There was all-weather landing equipment in an unlocked storage cupboard and he took from it what he was looking for: a landing flare.

The last of the day dissolved into dusk. Craine had been exhausted before but now he felt wired, almost sick with how awake he was. A part of him was surprised the F.B.I. weren't here already, but maybe they wanted to be discreet, in and out as quickly as they could.

It was a strange feeling, waiting there. He had taken Mayer's word that this plane would arrive. And every minute it didn't was less time to get to Vegas. Even if he got into a car and left right now he still wouldn't make it. He had put Michael's life in the hands of the man he once held responsible for killing his wife.

And yet faith was all he had now.

He'd been waiting for over an hour when he heard the distant drone of an engine. Up above he saw the small wing lights of an aircraft descending through the clouds.

The runway was poorly lit and when the twin-engine turboprop landed, the wheels hit the tarmac hard, the plane snaking sideways slightly before the pilot gained control. It taxied toward the hangar's apron and arced to a standstill fifty or so yards away. The propellers stopped.

The door opened and a man stepped off. He didn't see Craine until he came out from behind the fuel tanker.

"Don't," Craine shouted when the man reached for his shoulder holster. He had Hendry's pistol outstretched and was close enough now not to miss.

He gestured for the man to drop his revolver. "I'm not here to hurt you. But I will if I have to. Toss it."

The man did as he was told.

"Empty your pockets," Craine ordered him. When the man did so he said, "Get running. If I see you slow down I'll shoot you in the back."

Whoever he was he didn't need telling twice. He took off down the runway, swallowed by the darkness.

Unaware of what was happening, a woman came out of the plane and made her way down the air-stair. Her hair was blowing in the breeze and it covered her eyes. She was on the tarmac before she saw Craine.

Craine put the pistol in his pocket. "Virginia? Virginia Hill?"

The woman held her hands together in front of her, one wringing the other. She had brown hair and a round face. "Are you from the F.B.I.?"

"No. My name is Jonathan Craine." She didn't say anything, but Craine could tell his name meant something to her. "You know who I am, don't you?"

"Benny mentioned you before."

"So you know you can trust me."

She went to say yes, then didn't. "I'm not sure who to trust anymore."

"I know you didn't kill him. I know you loved him. But I need your help to find out who did. And I promise you, you won't be involved. Whatever you tell me is strictly between us."

She looked around but there was no one there. Only the plane behind her and the pilot watching on in confusion.

"I can't help you. I don't know why you're here—"

"I'm here because any minute now a car is going to arrive to pick you up. And inside that car will be men from the Federal Bureau. But you know that, don't you?"

She nodded.

"When did they approach you?"

She paused before saying, "About a month ago."

"What did they say?"

She didn't respond, so Craine answered for her. "They told you that they knew you'd been stealing money from the New York mob. They had pictures of you. Evidence. You'd stolen thousands of dollars and put it in bank accounts in Europe, and they threatened to tell Lansky. It was blackmail."

She was shaking. "They would have killed me. And they would have killed Benny."

Craine stepped forward. He spoke loudly.

"Did they ask for information on Siegel? Did they ask you about The Flamingo?"

"I never knew anything about Ben's business," she said quickly. "He didn't speak about it. That was all—"

Craine held up his hand and she stopped talking. "What did they ask you to do?"

"To go to Europe. And to tell them where Joyce lived. That's all."

"Joyce who worked for you?"

She nodded again.

"Did Benny know about the money?"

She looked away. He didn't need to push her to know the answer was no.

"I never wanted him to go to Vegas. That hotel . . . it ruined everything. Ever since he first went to the desert, I knew it would end badly." Virginia looked down, wiping her eyes with a trembling hand. Death was crossing off a list and her name was somewhere on it.

"The man from the F.B.I. His name was Redhill."

She swallowed. "Yes."

Redhill. A part of Craine knew Redhill had been involved in Siegel's murder from the beginning.

"We don't have very long. I need you to tell me what he wanted."

Her eyes widened and she considered Craine.

"Hurry," he said.

"He told me Benny was in danger and I should leave town."

"You didn't try to warn Siegel?"

She shook her head. "I . . . I didn't know what they'd do." She started crying. "I loved him. I still love him."

"But you left him to get murdered?"

She didn't answer at first. Maybe she'd tried to convince herself otherwise.

Virginia was in tears. "You men, with your accusations. You think I'm a traitor. Like one of those vamps in the pictures. Well, you have no idea about me. I'm a survivor. I loved Benny. But I did what I had to do to survive."

Headlights reflected off the propeller. Craine turned to see the first glimpses of three black sedans stalling at the gate. Any minute now they'd figure out how to lift the boom and be on the tarmac. After that he'd be trapped. He knew what he had to do.

"You want protection," he said quickly but clearly, "you tell your story to the press. Speak to Tilda Conroy at the *Herald*." He said her name again slowly: "Tilda Conroy."

She nodded but he made her repeat it back until he was sure she'd committed it to memory.

"She'll be able to help you. You'll need her. Now stand back until I tell you to move."

Craine went over to one of the fuel tankers parked by the hangar. There was a series of butterfly valves and he pulled all of them in turn. He heard a hiss as the rubber gaskets came loose, then he unscrewed the end caps. Jet fuel came flowing out over the tarmac.

Without air in the tank, the flow was controllable. But the fuel was inches deep and quickly covered his ankles.

When the cars were maybe fifty yards away he closed the taps half-way so that fuel was only coming out in dribbles. By now it had spread across the tarmac in wide pools. He could see Virginia standing beside the plane watching on, dumbstruck.

Craine walked toward the cars with his hands held out. Jet fuel wasn't flammable in the way that gasoline was. It had a much higher flashpoint. It would need more than a spark to ignite. But when it did, it was explosive.

He stopped when he reached the fringes of the fuel spill.

The three sedans slewed in different directions before pulling to a heavy stop twenty yards in front of him. The headlights were blinding but he saw figures moving in across the tarmac, shouting orders he ignored.

Craine's eyes adjusted and he could make out F.B.I. agents sighting over car roofs with shotguns and rifles like they'd been trained. He put his hand in his pocket and gripped the landing flare.

"F.B.I.," he heard Redhill's voice shout through the air. "Stay where you are, Craine."

Craine gestured to the fuel on the tarmac and held out the flare sideways for Redhill to see. "Be careful, Redhill."

In one movement, Craine took a step forward and struck the end of the flare with the flint strike. In the bright red light, he saw Redhill's eyes widen as he realized what was happening.

"Stand back," Redhill shouted to his men with his hand up. "No one fire. There's gas everywhere."

Redhill slowly came forward until they were within speaking distance. Within shooting distance, too.

"Keep your hands where I can see them, Craine."

Craine saw he had a pistol in his hand. His hair was tousled. He looked on edge.

"I'm getting on this plane."

"You're not going anywhere. Mayer can't protect you forever."

"Did you bring him with you?"

"Who?"

"You know who. Abraham Levine."

"I'm not giving you anything."

"You have him?"

Redhill looked back and signaled to one of his men. A passenger door opened and Abe was brought out, his hands cuffed in front of him. He looked like he'd taken a long day of beatings.

"You wouldn't have brought him if you weren't willing to hand him over."

Redhill exhaled. Craine had read the situation as it was.

Craine nodded in the direction of Virginia. "You give me Abe, I'll give you her."

"You don't get to negotiate."

He held up the flare. "I'll kill her if I have to."

Redhill's eyes were manic. "You'd never do it," he said without conviction.

Craine held the flare up and to the side as if he was going to drop it.

The two men stood there, chests rising and falling, until Redhill turned and beckoned a hand toward the men holding Abe. The big man held his cuffs out to be unlocked, then started striding toward the plane, rubbing his wrists.

"Everyone stand down," Redhill ordered.

Abe picked up the revolver left on the tarmac and went up the airstair into the belly of the plane. Craine didn't know what he said to the pilot, but almost immediately the engine began turning with the door half-open. The plane began arcing round until it was facing the runway.

The F.B.I. agents were startled. They looked to Redhill for fire orders.

"No one move," he shouted back to them.

Craine looked back at Virginia and signaled to her. She began walking toward the F.B.I. cars. She gave him a look as she passed but it was hard to know what it meant.

The propeller noise was loud. Craine knew no one else could hear.

"Why did you sanction it?" he shouted to Redhill.

No answer.

Craine had been turning everything over in his mind for the past few hours, but there was one piece left.

He said: "I know you saw the crime scene photographs. Harvey Sterling's wife was killed hours before he was. You knew that, even if you'd have the autopsy report redacted for the L.A.P.D. records. Harvey came home and found them dead so he shot himself. And I think you know who killed them."

Redhill didn't reply, but in the light of the flare Craine could see in his eyes it was true.

Craine went on: "You've been involved in this since the beginning. The F.B.I. had the Chicago Outfit do the hit and in response you had Paul Ricca released early from prison. What I want to know is, why?"

Again, Redhill didn't say anything but Craine knew he had the measure of the situation. He pointed the dying flare in Redhill's direction.

"I can keep asking questions or you can tell me and you'll never hear from me again. I'm only in this for my son."

Redhill was watching the plane as he spoke. The propeller was so loud Craine almost had to lip-read to hear him. "Hoover and H.U.A.C.

are so focused on the red scare in Hollywood that they've completely forgotten that Chicago and New York are battling it out for Las Vegas. I had to do what was necessary."

The plane wheels edged forward as the aircraft began aiming toward the runway. It was close now, barely twenty yards away. The noise was deafening.

"So you picked a side," Craine shouted.

"Siegel was uncontrollable," Redhill said, barely loud enough for Craine to hear.

"And you think you can control Chicago?"

"I told you before. You don't tame a lion. You feed it. I give them Vegas, they help me take down New York."

"So you're going to allow one crime syndicate to take power across America? This whole time, Siegel's death has been about taking down Lansky. Taking down New York."

"People gamble. People whore. People get high. We'll never win. One syndicate gives us stability."

"Does Hoover even know you're doing this?"

"Hoover is myopic. He doesn't even realize national crime syndicates exist. There's an entire subgovernment of organized crime in America and his refusal to acknowledge its existence will be his undoing."

"And you'll be ready to take his place when he goes."

Redhill didn't respond. He didn't have to.

The plane was barely a few yards away, and their jackets began flapping behind the propeller. Redhill put a hand on his head and gripped his hat.

The flare went out and Craine threw it sideways onto the tarmac. "I'm getting on this plane," he said again.

But this time Redhill didn't argue with him.

Seconds later, Craine had climbed up the steps and closed the aircraft door.

As the plane taxied forward, he looked out of the window, watching Virginia get into one of the sedans, her dress blowing in the engine efflux. The plane began to accelerate down the runway, and he thought for a second he could see Redhill screaming at his men, but that might have been his imagination.

Their wheels left the tarmac.

CHAPTER 44

The Flamingo had booked Frank Sinatra to entertain their Chicago guests.

Meyer Lansky's table was to one side of the stage, Sinatra barely ten feet away. Dotted around other tables were movie stars George Raft, Tony Curtis, Lana Turner and Ava Gardner. The biggest names in show business.

Flying in celebrities came at some expense, but they were worth the money. Besides, Sinatra always worked for scale for his New York friends. He'd even flown out to Havana before Christmas to entertain them at the Hotel Nacional at the last meeting of the syndicate families.

Sitting on Lansky's table were Kastel and their guests from Chicago, namely Paul Ricca. Like him, Ricca was an inconspicuous man of around fifty, who in his tapered suit looked more like a Wall Street banker than an underworld figure. But unlike Lansky, Ricca's cheeks were slack and colorless, his hair turning white at the temples. He looked like an aging dotard. Prison did that to a man.

Sinatra began singing "The House I Live In," a rousing tune Lansky had specifically requested for this evening.

As Sinatra reached the chorus, Lansky sipped at his whiskey soda, discreetly dropping in two Alka-Seltzers from a bottle in his jacket pocket. This meeting with Ricca had been planned ever since it was known he'd be released from prison. What they didn't know then was that Siegel would be dead. Whereas previously they had been invited to invest in minority shares, now Lansky was offering them majority holdings in the Nevada Projects Corporation, the shell company that owned The Flamingo.

Lansky didn't feel bad about selling his shares in the hotel. Idealists have dreams; visionaries have goals. And right now selling the hotel was the most prudent financial move. He could pay back his fellow investors and focus his attentions on Miami and Cuba.

The song finished and the room broke into applause.

Kastel leaned in. He seemed on edge. He had done for weeks. "Sir, you want me to bring everyone together to finalize the deal?"

Lansky closed his eyes for a moment. "Wait for Sinatra to finish," he said. "Then take everyone through to the conference room."

The plane climbed quickly so that soon the city was barely visible. Craine wondered whether this was the last he'd see of Los Angeles. He suspected not.

Their tense pilot told them repeatedly that they were going at the Twin Beech's top speed, 170 knots, which meant they'd land within the hour. They'd make it to Lansky in time, but that wasn't what worried Craine now. It was what Lansky would say when they got there.

There were eight chairs in the cabin but Abe and Craine sat in the only two facing each other. They passed the first ten minutes in silence, staring out the small round windows.

The cabin was soundproofed and quiet. They could hear themselves speak.

"You alright?" Craine said to Abe when the plane had reached cruising altitude.

"I'll get by." Abe smiled but his right cheek was so swollen only one side of his mouth curled up.

The plane juddered as they bounced through the clouds and Abe gripped his armrest nervously. Craine felt strangely relaxed. In control.

"You could have left me there," Abe said. "You had what you needed."

Craine shrugged. "I'll need your help when I get to Vegas."

Maybe it was true, maybe it wasn't. He wasn't sure why he'd saved Abe. Loyalty, maybe. The past few days had been brutal, but the fact was that without Abe's help, Craine never would have made it this far.

Craine leaned forward. "There's something you should know," he said. "Harvey didn't kill his family. He was set up."

Abe looked confused. "I don't understand. We saw—"

"I saw the F.B.I. photographs of Harvey's wife's body. She was killed before Harvey."

Abe frowned, so Craine explained. "When someone dies, the blood in their body stops moving and settles. We call it lividity. It's a way of estimating time of death."

"So what?" Abe asked.

Craine didn't have time to explain postmortem suggillation but he laid it out as simply as he could. "The blood had drained to the bottom of her body. The bruising suggested that she died hours before he did. Before Harvey had even got home."

Abe followed what he was saying without speaking or nodding.

"Harvey told us that someone had threatened to kill his family," Craine went on. "I think that same person followed through with it. They killed his wife and they killed his children. And when Harvey got home and found them dead, he shot himself."

Abe's eyes narrowed. It seemed to come as some surprise.

"Who would do that?" he asked finally.

"The person who tasked Harvey to kill Ben Siegel in the first place," Craine said. "The man working on behalf of the Chicago Outfit and the F.B.I."

Abe frowned, trying to absorb everything.

"Abe," Craine said. "You have a photograph of your son, don't you? You keep it in your pocket."

Abe took it out. It was a photograph of a group of soldiers cleaning their rifles.

"That's your boy?"

"Yes," he said. "That's Joseph."

Craine pointed to the young man next to him. "And that? That's Harvey Sterling, isn't it?"

Abe nodded. "A lot of the boys enlisted together. They could go through basic together, serve in the same company."

"And who is that in the background? You recognize him?"

The figure wasn't clear. He was half turned away.

"I can't tell."

Craine showed Abe the photograph Conroy had given him of their whole unit.

"What if I told you it was his platoon commander? The same man in the center of *this* photograph. Do you recognize him?"

Abe held the print under the small cabin light. His eyes roamed the picture until he found what he was looking for. His face held at different times a look of confusion, a look of recognition and a look of anger.

Yes, Harvey Sterling had shot Bugsy Siegel. But Craine had found the man responsible for making him do it.

Craine held his hands clasped in front of him like he was praying. It took a while for him to get the words out.

"When I give Lansky what I promised, will he be good on his word?"

Abe was certain of it. "Mr. Lansky is an honest man. I've never known him to renege on a deal."

"Abe, I need to know that you'll back up what I'm going to tell him." He found the expression he knew Abe would understand. "That you'll *vouch* for me."

Abe reached into his pocket and held out the pistol he'd picked up off the tarmac. A symbolic gesture.

"Keep it," Craine said. *I trust you to do what's right*, he might have said.

"We got to be sure before we say anything to Lansky. We got to be one hundred percent."

"Is there a telephone at the airfield?"

"There's one nearby."

"I'm going to need to use it."

Abe went quiet again. He was digesting everything. What Craine had found out threatened his entire belief system.

"Abe, what I have here, what this means . . . I can't promise this won't come back on you. You know that, don't you?"

Abe looked at him and nodded soberly. Far back in his eyes was some kind of resignation.

"I am fifty-four years old," he said slowly. "For guys like me, doing what I do, it's like living on borrowed time. Whatever way I go, it's been coming down the pike for a long time."

The plane rocked sideways. They didn't speak again until they landed.

CHAPTER 45

Shortly after 8 P.M., a security officer led F.B.I. Agent Emmett Redhill from the Hall of Justice's arched and pedimented entrance doors, through the lobby and into the elevators situated at the rear of the building.

Within its fourteen stories, the Hall of Justice housed the County Courts, the Sheriff's office and the District Attorney's offices. The top five floors housed a jail facility but Redhill wasn't going that far up. He was advised by the officer to take the elevator to the fourth floor, where he would be met by a representative from the D.A.'s office.

Redhill stood in silence beside the Negro elevator attendant and gathered his thoughts. He'd tried calling Hoover's office several times, but it was late in Washington and no one answered. Instead, if Louis Mayer had used his influence to have Craine released from custody, Redhill would have to go directly to the District Attorney. As a government representative and the highest officeholder in the state's legal department, the D.A. could have Craine arrested as soon as he landed in Vegas.

The elevator doors opened into an overscaled corridor with crystal chandeliers and polished marble flooring. Redhill pushed through a white lacquer door into a large foyer with vaulted ceilings and elegant office furniture. He found what he was looking for: beside a life-sized statue of Julius Caesar was a door with DISTRICT ATTORNEY'S DEPARTMENT garlanded into the woodwork.

"Can I help you, sir?" a woman asked when he entered. Her voice was faint, almost a whisper.

"Yes, I'm Agent Redhill from the F.B.I. I called a half hour ago. I have an appointment with the District Attorney."

She smiled sympathetically, as if the very notion that anyone could have booked an appointment with the District Attorney at such late notice could be anything more than a practical joke.

"A half hour ago? Are you sure?"

"Yes, I was told to come straight over—"

A door opened to their right and a cadaverous man in a slim-fitted suit came out with his arm extended. He looked at Redhill and smiled warmly.

"Thomas Manning, Assistant District Attorney. You must be Agent Redhill." The Assistant D.A. looked twenty years his junior but his grinning confidence implied otherwise.

"Don't worry, Sandra, he's with us."

The Assistant D.A.'s L-shaped room served as an antechamber to the District Attorney's own offices. Through it Redhill could see a ten-foot door along the back wall with the D.A.'s name hand-painted onto a brass nameplate.

"I'm here to talk to the D.A. It's a federal issue."

"Apologies, Agent Redhill. The District Attorney is in a meeting. I'm afraid we're going to have to reschedule."

But the words were already plowing past him. Redhill was pushing through Manning's office toward the D.A.'s door. He saw movement reflected in the brass plaque. Manning was scurrying for his phone. "Sandra, get security up here now."

The door opened with a twist of the handle. A glimpse of a corner office. Parquet flooring underfoot, paintings of presidents on the wall, the Distict Attorney a sandy-haired man sunk behind his desk. There were three figures across from him, their backs to Redhill. There wasn't time for introductions.

"District Attorney—"

There were heavy footsteps in the doorway. "Sir, I do apologize, he came barging in here—"

"It's not a problem," said the D.A. from his chair with absolute equanimity. "Agent Redhill, I'm sorry, I'm not going to be able to make our appointment."

"District Attorney, it's urgent I speak with you right away. It's about Jonathan Craine."

The D.A. pushed himself away from his desk. "Agent Redhill, I've spoken to Director Hoover and we've come to a mutual understanding. It seems there are elements of your work in Los Angeles that he's been unaware of. I think you and I should have a little chat. Let me walk you out."

As the District Attorney stood up, the three men sitting opposite turned in their seats to face him.

On the left was Captain Henson of the Homicide Division. Beside him was William Wilson, owner of *The Hollywood Enquirer.* And to his right was Louis Mayer, head of M.G.M.

The police. The papers. The studio.

Redhill already knew what had happened. The three pillars of Los Angeles had conspired together to push him out.

Like the rest of the hotel, The Flamingo's conference room was luxuriously appointed. A vast circular table was arranged in the center of the room, complemented by wood-paneled walls, deep carpets and low-hanging bulbs.

Once everyone was seated, Lansky gave the order and waiters served snifters of brandy and opened boxes of Montecristo cigars.

They'd hedged around the main purpose of their visit for long enough. Rising to his feet, Lansky said: "Gentlemen, I hope you've enjoyed yourselves. If there's anything we can do to improve your stay, please do let myself or our staff know. But I hope you won't mind if we can now turn our attentions to your proposed acquisition of The Flamingo Hotel and Casino."

Bound purchasing agreements were distributed alongside details of The Flamingo's financial and business history, its valuation based on five-year projections and the Nevada Projects Corporation's selling requirements. Both parties had a mergers and acquisitions lawyer present, but broadly speaking the number-crunching and tire-kicking had already occurred. They were convening to agree final terms of sale and then sign.

"The hotel has been operating at a loss," Ricca said once Lansky had gone through the finance plan.

"The Flamingo has been open six months. As you know, this is common in the first year of trading. However, you'll see on the preceding graph that the hotel operated at a loss only in the first quarter after it was opened prematurely. In the first three-quarters of *this* financial year, The Flamingo is projected to generate over one million dollars in net profits."

Ricca wasn't so easily impressed. "Your entertainment costs are extraordinarily high. The Sinatras of this world don't come cheap."

"Entertainment is a necessary expense far outweighed by its gains. We also have ties to the motion picture industry going back decades. Accessing the best talent in Hollywood won't be difficult."

"Will they continue to support Vegas?"

"The heads of the major motion picture studios—men like Cohn, Mayer and Warner—are our friends. We share tables at the races. Our children go to the same summer camps. Besides, every studio has problems keeping their contract players in check. In Nevada, prostitution and gambling are entirely legal. It suits them as it suits us."

"And the authorities?"

"Police interference in Nevada is rare. Payoffs are typically unnecessary. The risk profile here is minimal. And the overall economics of the deal are strong."

Paul Ricca spoke plainly. "With all due respect, Mr. Lansky. If it makes such good business sense, why sell?"

Lansky knew that his frankness was part of his appeal. He didn't browbeat his peers. He was completely transparent: "Banks have restricted lending, credit markets have frozen. We're looking to focus our resources in other areas. But to remind you, this is a new frontier in America and it can be yours to own."

They listened impassively as he continued to go over the finances in minute detail, explaining movements in forecasts at different points. In another life, in an America with equal opportunity, Lansky had no doubt he would have been a major New York financier or Washington political figure.

When he'd finished, Ricca looked at his lawyer and then at Lansky. His balding head reflected the lights above.

"What about the F.B.I.? This Siegel business has led to unwanted attention."

Sometimes, when Lansky lay awake at night, he wished he'd never let Benny enter the hotel casino game. His personality wasn't suited to it. He was too fiery. He lacked diplomacy where it was needed. It was a lapse in judgment Lansky was now paying for.

"Earlier today," he explained, "I spoke to our colleague Jack Dragna in Los Angeles. A man has been found guilty of murdering our good friend and business partner, Benjamin Siegel. He has since been dealt with. The F.B.I.'s interests have been assuaged."

A murmur of skepticism.

"We're all wise enough not to trust the newspapers," Ricca said, "but the suggestion was that you and your New York investors were involved—"

Lansky shook his head. "Like we long suspected, his murder was a purely personal matter. It was a vendetta, pure and simple. More importantly, it has no bearing on our plans here."

Ricca rocked forward and back in his chair but didn't say anything.

That's good, Lansky thought. He seemed appeased.

"And Jack Dragna?"

"A separate matter. But nothing indicates his involvement."

"Given our role in Vegas would require us to work closely with connections in Hollywood, we would be more comfortable with someone we can trust."

Lansky felt hot. There was a sheen of sweat on the backs of his hands like dew. Dragna's apology had appeared genuine. But clearly it wouldn't suffice. Lansky had another man, Mickey Cohen, in mind to take over Dragna's Los Angeles assets. After all, a man who didn't have the loyalty of his men had no place in this business.

"Understood. You have my word this will be the case. Unfortunately, I hope you can appreciate that I can say no more at this time."

Ricca watched him steadily. There was a prolonged silence. Lansky was the one who broke it.

"Mr. Ricca, are you satisfied with the main points on today's agenda?"

Ricca leaned toward his lawyer. They spoke between themselves for what seemed like a long time. Finally Ricca said: "We're satisfied."

Lansky tried his best to hide his relief. "Gentlemen," he said, standing, "may I suggest we take a break as our legal representatives discuss the small print, and reconvene shortly for final signature? As a gesture of appreciation, I thought you might enjoy a flutter at the tables."

Staff on hand began distributing betting plaques worth thousands of dollars. "For those who'd like a tip, avoid roulette and craps. Play blackjack, where the house edge is marginal. Although I can promise you," Lansky said with a smile, "in the end the house always wins."

His guests laughed. They stood up and filed out of the room with their chips. Lansky had agreed a considerable cash fee with Columbia Pictures to have Rita Hayworth flown in. She was a surprise guest, and had agreed to hover around the roulette tables making small talk and then sing for them. All of it designed to convince these men from Chicago to sign when the moment called for it.

Paul Ricca came over and kissed Lansky on both cheeks.

"I've always known you were a good man to do business with, Mr. Lansky."

"The feeling is mutual," Lansky replied with an earnest smile.

After Ricca left the room, Kastel took Lansky to one side.

"Abe is in Vegas. Plane landed a few minutes ago."

"And Craine?"

"He's with him."

"Keep everyone here. Bring them to my suite."

"Sir, I strongly advise you don't meet with Craine. Given the circumstances, he may well pose a risk to your security—"

"There are three dozen security guards on-site. I'm sure we can manage."

"Sir—"

"I told you, we'll manage," he said firmly, putting an end to the matter.

CHAPTER 46

The paper had gone off stone hours ago, but the Chief Printer had held the front page and was waiting on Conroy's copy. A dozen staff were working late, including Alice, who seemed to be there out of a sense of duty more than anything else.

The City Editor was standing above her, muttering under his breath for Conroy to hurry up.

"Almost there." *Tap tap.* "Two minutes, sir." *Tap tap.*

They'd already called down five times to delay the print, but she knew that the minute she saw the Chief Printer coming down the corridor to take her copy away from her, it was over. If she wasn't finished then, there would be no headline tomorrow. And another paper might beat her to the story.

The City Editor was jittery. "I'll get you a coffee," he said, picking up her mug. "Mrs Hickerson, coffee?"

Alice's mouth opened like a fish. "Uh, yes sir. Please."

Conroy was obsessing now, proofreading her own copy time and time again. The story was written, she knew that; the headlines agreed. The front page would be emblazoned with a photograph of Siegel alongside a rare promotional image of The Flamingo Hotel Wilson had given to her.

She went through it once more, telling herself *no more amendments. It's done.*

NATIONAL CRIME SYNDICATE
TAKES CONTROL OF AMERICA
Written by T.L Conroy
Benjamin Siegel, a New York racketeer, owned several Los Angeles

gambling rackets and more recently ran The Flamingo Hotel and Casino in Las Vegas, Nevada. Siegel, however, also had connections to several East Coast crime figures, notably hotel and casino owner Meyer Lansky, sources close to the deceased have confirmed. Investigations into Siegel's death have revealed information that indicates a national crime syndicate is gaining control of key American cities. According to William Wilson, entrepreneur and owner of *The Hollywood Enquirer*, "The mob's intention is to turn Las Vegas into a gambling mecca, a city of sin and corruption. They have the right influence across the political and judicial establishment to keep their businesses protected."

The public have long been in the dark over the issue of interstate crime, but sources in City Hall have stated that it is time the Federal Bureau takes its attention off communism in California to focus on the expanding influence of organized crime rings across America. Representatives from the District Attorney's office have indicated that they will petition the federal government to create a special committee to investigate the issue.

As she read it through one last time, Teddy Kahn, the political correspondent, came by her desk. He'd been working late on his article blaming the F.B.I. for the Senate's dissolution of the unions.

For the first time since she'd worked there, he addressed her politely. "City Editor told me about your story, Tilda. Very impressive. Congratulations. I'd love to talk to you about how we might join the dots on the F.B.I.'s involvement with the unions and the mob."

"Absolutely. Let's sit down next week."

When he left, Conroy suppressed a smile.

Conroy had no intention of writing about Harvey Sterling's role in Siegel's death. She knew now that the murder would officially remain unsolved, and nothing she could do would stop that. Most of the other newspapers had already stated that the investigation would likely stay open and unsolved indefinitely. There was too much sensitivity at stake and, in truth, she felt no responsibility to Siegel. His comeuppance was timely, if not overdue.

No, victory wouldn't come in solving Siegel's murder; it would be in the long road to shining a light on the criminal underworld. It was time people understood the breadth and depth of the mob, and Tilda Conroy wanted to be the one holding the torch.

A part of her had wondered if she'd given away too many chips at the table in her dealings with Louis Mayer and William Wilson. Helping Craine, for example. But a long time ago she'd done something for personal gain that had played on her conscience ever since. Taking advantage of a movie star's addiction had helped her career, but she'd never got over the shame of what had happened to Celia Raymond. She needed to right the wrongs that had troubled her conscience for so long.

Power. Greed. Money. These had never been her talismans. No; all she'd ever wanted was to be a reporter with integrity and be treated as an equal among her peers. Helping Craine was a chance to achieve the former. She hoped to hear from him again. She hoped he could save his son.

And the latter? Conroy thought about that. As she read through her proof copy, she glanced at her name in the byline. *T. L. Conroy.*

The Chief Printer finally arrived, bounding down the office with his wristwatch held out like it was a time bomb.

"Mrs Conroy, I hate to rush you, but—"

"So sorry," she said. "One second, then it's done, I promise."

Conroy rolled the paper through the platen, then pressed the backspace key over the byline. She struck through her name and typed it again in capitals so the copy editor wouldn't miss it: *TILDA CONROY.*

CHAPTER 47

The Flamingo was heaving, busier still than last week. There was an undercurrent of hysteria and it only served to put him on edge. Craine couldn't believe it had been only five days since he was last here.

They were led through the casino floor, where Craine spotted Rita Hayworth on stage with Frank Sinatra. They were singing a duet. People would have paid hundreds of dollars to be in that room right now. But all he could think about was how desperate he was to end this ordeal and go home. It was difficult not to feel overwhelmed by everything he'd gone through to get here. But here he was. Minutes away from release. Hours away from seeing Michael.

All he needed to do was stay calm and focus on what he was about to tell Lansky. And pray that Abe had his corner. If not, there was no telling what might happen.

Security was always tight in casinos, but Craine thought there was an unusually high number of bodyguards here tonight. Men in doorways wearing dinner jackets over visible shoulder holsters. Outside, he saw a dozen men with slung rifles dotted around the gardens.

At the narrow door off a quiet corridor, one of Lansky's personal bodyguards frisked Craine and removed his weapon. His bruises ached.

The man looked at Craine with porcine features and smirked. Craine took a second to recognize him: he was the man who had held him down when Kastel had cut Michael's fingers off. He remembered his wet breath in his ear.

"You look even worse than when I last saw you."

Craine looked at his reflection in the mirror opposite and eyed his clothes and his demeanor. The man was right—he'd sweated through his shirt so many times it could practically stand up by itself. His suit—new at the start of the week—looked like it had been thrown away by vagrants.

"Then at least you won't have to see me again," Craine replied.

Kastel opened the door from the inside and waved for them to enter. He was wearing a dinner jacket and looked like he was preoccupied with guests, as if this meeting was an inconvenience. He barely looked Craine in the eye when he came in.

"Lansky will be here shortly," Kastel said.

Craine looked around. Although there was one entrance door, the suite had a second paneled door the other side of the room. It was always like this in casinos. In the illegal gambling ships anchored off Los Angeles, suicides were so commonplace they were honeycombed with passages full of anterooms so that people could be discreetly removed or resuscitated without drawing attention.

Lansky entered wearing a white tuxedo jacket with a black bow tie. Formalwear for a high-stakes evening.

He shook hands with both men and asked them politely to take a seat. Kastel sat at the far end of the table; the bodyguard remained standing.

"Abe," he began. "Thank you for everything you've done. You and I will have a separate conversation, but I want to convey my gratitude—you've done a great service to our organization and your efforts will be rewarded accordingly."

He turned his attention to Craine.

"I appreciate you rushing here but I've already spoken to Jack Dragna, who has told me everything I need to know. The man who murdered my friend is dead. A coward who killed his family and then himself rather than face justice. But it's over now, and I have you to thank."

Lansky put his hands on the table, knuckles down. "I want to reassure you that your son is safe. I spoke to my men only this morning and no harm has come to him." He glanced at Kastel. "Your boy has seen a doctor. He's been well taken care of."

Craine could feel his heart beating faster. He was sick with the anticipation of seeing Michael.

"In a minute you'll be put back in a car and driven home. You'll never hear from me again, you have my word."

Lansky nodded to Kastel, who put a bag on the table. The zip was open far enough for Craine to see bundled notes inside.

"I beg you not to refuse this gesture of thanks. And if there's anything I can ever do for you, anything at all, my door is always open."

"Mr. Lansky," Craine began. His voice was hoarse, barely loud enough to hear. "You asked me to find the man who killed Benjamin Siegel, and I did."

Lansky nodded. "Harvey Sterling, Dragna's man."

"But Harvey Sterling didn't work alone. I believe that he was sent by someone."

Lansky held up his palms. "Dragna is adamant it wasn't him. I don't know whether I believe him or not, but that's an issue for our organization. It isn't your concern."

Craine and Abe shared a reassuring look, each trying to steady the nerves of the other.

"It wasn't Dragna," Abe said. "Somebody else set Siegel up to be killed."

Lansky lowered his hands. This wasn't something he was expecting.

"You wondered why the F.B.I. had their spotlight on you from the beginning," Craine said. "Well, they knew who killed Ben Siegel. They knew because they arranged for it to happen."

"The F.B.I. did this?"

"No. They would never do it themselves." Craine took a breath, knowing the next part would be hard for Lansky to accept. "Chicago did."

Lansky froze. *It wasn't possible.*

Craine explained as clearly and quickly as he could manage. "Siegel's murder was to get him out of the picture and to guarantee Chicago a better price for the hotel. Paul Ricca's release was part of the deal. The timing wasn't a coincidence. The F.B.I. released him from prison on the proviso that the Chicago Outfit would buy your shares in The Flamingo."

Lansky shook his head at the logic. "Ricca was released early after millions of dollars were contributed to the Democratic Party's election campaign."

"That was only part of it. The F.B.I. wants to replace different crime organizations with one single national syndicate run from Chicago. Their entire aim has been to undermine you and your New York organization."

Lansky didn't flinch, but Craine could see him going red.

Kastel said, "He's seeing things that aren't there."

Craine spoke up. "I see things that other people choose to ignore because that used to be me. I was the smoke and mirrors."

"Let him finish," Lansky said with his hand held up.

Meyer Lansky listened carefully as Craine detailed what had happened with Virginia Hill and Agent Redhill before they left L.A. When he was finished, Lansky poured himself a glass of water.

"Craine, this is a lot for me to take in," he said. "I'm not sure of your motive here, but if it's conjecture on your part . . ."

Abe said, "Sir, everything he's telling you is true. I've been with him the whole time."

"Ricca—*Chicago*—a move like that would be risky. They couldn't be sure how I would react."

Craine was staring at Kastel. Not at his face—at the pistol grip he could see under his jacket. Abe was staring at him too, watching his every move.

"Which is why they didn't do it alone," Craine said. "Harvey Sterling worked for Paul Ricca before he was drafted into the army."

"So they approached Harvey Sterling directly," Lansky mused.

"Did you know Harvey Sterling?" Craine asked him.

"No. Maybe in passing."

"Abe, you knew him, right?"

"Since he was a kid."

"You think he was loyal?"

"To a fault."

"What about you, Kastel?"

Kastel shrugged. "I only knew him a little."

"A little? Because you got him the job with Dragna, didn't you?"

"No."

"Yes, you did. Dragna confirmed it twenty minutes ago when I called him from the airfield."

Kastel's mistake was distancing himself from Harvey. It was obvious to all of them now that they'd known each other and Kastel had lied about it.

"Maybe I put in a good word." He tried to laugh it off. "Everyone knows each other."

Craine studied him, knowing that Kastel's reaction would give more away than his answers.

"You didn't know each other in New York but you were pals from Chicago. You both worked for Paul Ricca. Then you joined up together. Served together in the Pacific."

"We both served. So what? Most men did. Only fucking cowards like you escaped the draft."

Craine placed the photograph of Harvey Sterling's platoon on the table. In the very center was a man with two vertical bars on his helmet. *Kastel.*

"Why didn't you tell anyone you were in the same company as Harvey Sterling? Not even the same company. The same platoon," he said, to no response. "Given Siegel was shot with a long-range carbine, why wouldn't you mention that Harvey Sterling was a sniper? You didn't think it was relevant?"

Lansky looked at Kastel and the color left his face.

"Mr. Lansky, I'm not taking this from him."

Lansky narrowed his eyes. "Let Craine speak."

Craine had never been much of an investigator. Never had much of an instinct for these things. But what he did have was a surety that Kastel was responsible for Siegel's murder. Not because of the weight of the evidence. But because of Kastel's reaction to it.

For a long time he seemed unable to speak, but then Kastel drew breath.

"Sir, this man is deluded. He's not even a real detective. He's a sham."

"That's what you were hoping. That I wouldn't be able to handle the investigation, or at most that I'd discover Harvey. But no further than that. I'm sorry I've disappointed you."

"He's twisting things. He's got no proof."

"This is the proof," Craine said, ignoring the interruption. "Your ultimatum on Wednesday. Delivered on behalf of Mr. Lansky. That I should shoot myself and give up the investigation or my son would be killed."

Meyer Lansky frowned. "I never gave that order."

When Kastel's expression didn't change, Craine said: "It was a risky move, but you were worried. I suspect Harvey had called and told you we were getting closer. That we hadn't believed Charlie Hill was responsible and had tracked down Joyce Mills, a woman the F.B.I. used to set Siegel up. So you were hoping I'd take the easy option and kill myself. And then I suspect you were going to shoot Abe too, in case he ever said anything. Wouldn't be hard. It would look like we killed each other."

Kastel began to rub his arm.

"Sir, I had to. They were drawing too much attention to—"

"People think homicide detectives care about motive in a murder case. That's not true. There's who, there's what and there's how. Who cares *why*?" Craine continued, delivering Kastel's confession for him. "Maybe you did it because Ricca paid you. Maybe it was part of your deal with the F.B.I. when Ricca went to jail and you didn't. I couldn't care less. But I suspect if Mr. Lansky looks into your finances he'll find the money trail."

Kastel didn't say anything.

"And I'm not sure if you paid Harvey Sterling or if you threatened him. Maybe it's both. He's got two young children and you know he's vulnerable. In fact, you know how his mind works—you were his platoon commander. So when the deal is done with the F.B.I. and Chicago, you need a triggerman who can't be traced back to you. So you call your old army pal Harvey. You explain to him that Siegel needs to be killed. Maybe you make up a reason but you make sure no one else knows. And when he wavers, you remind him you're his senior. In the army and in the syndicate. And when he wavers again, you threaten his family."

"You're making this up. Harvey Sterling murdered them."

Abe spoke up. "When we confronted Harvey, he told us, 'He said he'd kill Lucy and the kids.' "

"Chicago," Kastel said. "Paul Ricca."

"No, not Chicago. Someone else. Someone capable of murdering Harvey's family before he got home."

Kastel's eyes unconsciously moved to Lansky. The older man was glaring at him.

"And that's what you did, Kastel. You went to his house and murdered them."

Kastel was scratching the back of his wrist. He shrugged in his suit, like it was ridden with bed bugs. *Withdrawal symptoms.*

"How did it feel to kill his children?" Craine asked. "Or were you so pumped up on bennies you didn't care?"

Lansky looked back at Craine. He knew he was right.

"Impossible," Kastel said, sinking now. "I wasn't even there."

What time did your plane leave for Chicago?"

"I don't have to answer—"

Lansky's voice cut him short. "What time, Kastel?"

"You saw me leave. Midnight."

"And yet there are no night flights to Chicago," Craine said. "It's too dangerous."

"You're bullshitting," Kastel said, coming out of his chair.

"No, I'm not. I even checked with your pilot at the airfield when we arrived. I wanted to be sure and he confirmed it."

Craine looked to Abe. "It's true," the big man said.

Lansky sat paralyzed in his place, staring at Kastel. Like he was waiting for some kind of explanation. There was none forthcoming.

Kastel dropped back in his chair, managing to say, "It doesn't mean anything."

"It means everything. Because you knew you weren't leaving until the morning. So you waited until you were certain we were on to something, then you killed Harvey's children and his wife. The F.B.I. have been protecting you, Kastel, but I won't."

There was a shriek from outside, then a cheer. Someone celebrating. Beating the house. Craine realized the music had stopped.

Kastel didn't say anything, staring at Craine in mute protest. His mouth was open and he was trying to shout but his lips moved soundlessly.

Lansky stood to face the man who'd so carefully maneuvered his best friend's murder, then looked away in disgust. He turned to his bodyguard and nodded before leaving the room.

CHAPTER 48

When Lansky exited stage left, his bodyguard took out his pistol and aimed it at Kastel.

There were words muttered but Craine couldn't remember them. He was watching Kastel intently, who stared back at him with a hatred so intense Craine wondered how he could stand it.

Lansky hadn't told them what he was going to do next, but it was obvious that whatever deal he had set up wasn't going through. Craine half-expected to hear shouting and gunfire, but he didn't know what the etiquette was with this new generation of entrepreneurs.

Abe seemed familiar with the protocol and perhaps Kastel did, too, because with the bodyguard leading the way, they left through the suite's second door and took a hidden elevator down to the basement parking lot.

There were fifty cars in neat rows down there but no one else. They idled under the fluorescent lights in silence and Craine realized that this exercise had been about removing Kastel from sight as much as anything else.

Kastel kept touching his face, then running his fingers over each other. He was frantic. Craine had been in his position only two nights earlier, except without the edge of drug withdrawal that Kastel was experiencing right now.

Craine was wondering how long they would have to wait and what for when several men in dinner jackets exited another elevator across the parking lot. The years didn't make a difference. He recognized them immediately: Paul Ricca and several members of the Chicago Outfit.

Ricca stared in their direction. He noticed Kastel, confused at first and then incensed, his arms dropping to his sides as if his presence alluded to something else. He was escorted quickly into a waiting limousine and the car drove up the exit ramp at speed before the doors had even been shut.

Craine understood now. Lansky was smart enough not to accuse Ricca and his Chicago Outfit directly. A brutal battle in the Flamingo Hotel and Casino wasn't what any of them would have wanted. Instead, in their own strange custom, he'd have shaken hands and made apologies that now wasn't the right time to complete their business deal. He'd have bid them farewell and safe travels and then promptly made himself scarce.

And now they'd take separate planes to separate cities to begin a proxy war from the comfort of their penthouses. What had just occurred was Lansky's way of showing Ricca that he *knew*. It was presenting a doomed man on the scaffold as a presage of what was to come.

When the limousine left, Lansky's bodyguard took Kastel to one side and they exchanged a few words. Craine wasn't sure what they were saying and neither did he care. Kastel was out of his life and they didn't need a final face-off to trade barbs.

A feeling of otherness had overtaken Craine. Abe turned to him but he seemed both near and very far away. He was speaking to Craine, holding out the bag of money. "Take it."

"I don't want it."

"Lansky will be offended."

"Keep it, or bury it out in the desert," Craine said with a glance at Kastel that said he knew where they were taking him.

Abe nodded and pointed toward a line of cars.

"Pick any one you want. Keys are in the ignition. We can share the driving."

"You're coming with me?"

"There are men at your farm. I'll need to speak with them. They had his support," he said, cocking his head toward Kastel. "But I'm not expecting any difficulties."

Craine swallowed hard and said, "Thank you."

The two men looked at each other. They didn't shake hands but there was an acknowledgment of what they'd gone through.

Craine began moving to the driver's side of a Chevrolet when he noticed Kastel step very deliberately away from the bodyguard.

"I'll be seeing you in Bridgeport," Kastel said.

"Shut your mouth and get in the car," Abe said, but Kastel was ignoring him.

Craine thought he'd misheard him. "What did you say?"

He wasn't sure what he meant. Something in his tone or manner had thrown him. It wasn't said bitterly. It was said in triumph.

"I said, I'll see you in Bridgeport."

Craine couldn't see Kastel's expression in this light but he thought he was grinning. Or at least, unafraid.

Abe seemed no more edified. For a moment, nothing else happened. It wasn't until he saw the bodyguard nod to Kastel that Craine realized with sudden dread that he was in on it too.

"Abe—" His name caught in Craine's throat like phlegm.

As though reading his mind, the big man stepped in front of Craine so that he was between them. He took his revolver out from his jacket but his telegraphed movements were too slow.

The bodyguard lifted his gun and squeezed the trigger; under a low ceiling the shot was momentarily deafening and then Abe dropped his gun and grabbed his stomach. He stepped back until a car propped him up, his blood smearing across the car window as he tried to stay upright.

After that, everything happened very quickly.

Craine watched Kastel run across the parking lot. He moved swiftly out of his field of vision, running through cars, his body protected by the coachwork.

Abe's revolver had skittered across the floor. Craine scrambled to pick it up but as he reached for it the bodyguard began firing at him, his .45 pistol hammering thumb-sized holes into the car door beside him.

Craine fell to the ground and crawled sideways, using the back wheels as a bulwark. More pistol shots followed, deafening, the sparks closer each time. Craine heard the squeal of tires as Kastel drove out of the parking lot but by now the volume and noise of fire was almost unthinkable, rounds pinging off the metal and criss-crossing in different directions. Something plucked at his pants and then his thigh stung. A bullet had ricocheted and caught the top of his leg.

Craine didn't scream but his body jolted like he'd had an electric shock. Lansky's betrayer fired two more shots in his direction until the pistol clicked empty.

The man swore. He came around the car and reloaded without taking his eyes off Craine. It was all strangely awkward, like an executioner fixing his hood before swinging his axe.

Craine's leg was numb. He couldn't stand up. He pushed himself up onto his elbows and began to shuffle backward but it was no use. He saw the bodyguard slide a new clip into the butt of his pistol.

Craine waited for the bullet. He didn't close his eyes but he was half looking away when he caught the man pirouetting in the air, only then realizing that it was Abe who had lunged at him and now had a hand around the man's throat.

Craine watched as Abe threw him sideways onto the hood of a car. In a fraction of a second, the wounded man was grabbing the bodyguard by the hair and forcing his head back into the windshield several times until he dropped the pistol. The glass starred behind him.

With his other hand, Abe got the length of his forearm underneath the man's chin so it was pressing against his windpipe, strangling him.

Craine saw the man's feet come off the ground but then he had his hand clutching at the small of his back; he brought his fist back round and there was a knife in it. Craine shouted at Abe but it was too late; the man swung the blade round Abe's barrel chest and into his side like Ahab spearing the whale.

The bodyguard's hand writhed, bringing the knife in and out again frantically. Abe howled in pain, ragged, uncontrolled gasps that only stopped when he gritted his teeth and butted the man so hard with his forehead that his entire body went limp.

Abe loosened his grip and stepped back before falling sideways to the ground.

Craine scrabbled for the bodyguard's pistol and aimed it at the man but by now he was immobile on the car hood, choking, barely able to breathe.

Craine turned his attention to Abe. He was lying on the asphalt, one hand held out toward the exit as if reaching for the ghost of Kastel's car.

Craine dragged him away and propped him up against a car wheel, pressing his hands into his sides to stop the bleeding. It was no use: blood was starfishing across the floor.

"Abe, look at me. Abe, please."

He said his name several times to no response, and then suddenly Abe gripped Craine's hand. He leaned closer until his ear was inches above Craine's mouth. But Abe didn't have any last words. There would be no eulogy. Instead he shook his head. Not like he couldn't talk. But like he was answering an unsaid question. *No*, his face said. *I'm not going to make it through.*

And then his head stopped moving and his chest stopped rising and his face looked very placid, swallowed by life's maw. Gone.

"Abe," Craine said, shaking him. But he didn't say it again. There was no point. He touched the big man's shoulder with one hand. A strange recognition of what this stranger had done for him. Futile, perhaps. But a gesture nonetheless. It didn't matter what people said about Abraham Levine. This man had saved his life.

Craine had experienced death in many forms but there was nothing quite so intimate as watching someone die at close quarters. Not for the first time this week he had accompanied someone on that most personal of paths. He wondered if it would be the last.

Craine looked away. There wasn't time to think about Abe being dead. He groaned as he tried to stand up. He looked at the pistol in his hand and remembered what Kastel said. *I'll see you in Bridgeport.* It meant only one thing: Kastel would go to kill his son.

Craine took the filthy tie from his collar and bound it around his thigh to stop the bleeding. The pain was such that he had to prop himself against the car to keep himself upright.

There was a coughing sound; the other man was bent over now, hacking. Craine stood, unsteady on his feet. He held the pistol out so the man could see the glint of it under the fluorescents.

"Get up," he said heavily. "Get up now."

Craine pointed in the direction of the Chevrolet. "Open the door. You're driving."

CHAPTER 49

From the back seat Craine instructed the man where to go. "Take a right north and keep going until I say so."

There was no need to say anything else and besides, Craine didn't have the strength for it.

He had the bodyguard's pistol with him but only the rounds that were left in the magazine. He was tempted to take them out and count them, but didn't want his driver to use the moment to escape or, worse, turn on him. Or maybe he simply didn't have the energy.

They drove for hours, the dry desert heat replaced with something damper and richer as they got closer to the Sierra Nevada.

Craine sat slumped in the back seat. He hadn't felt searing pain like this before, and not long after they'd crossed from Nevada to California, he threw up in the footwell. Whether it was the agony of his leg or simply the adrenaline passing, he wasn't sure. A few times he wondered whether he'd make it home conscious. Or even alive.

They drove throughout the night, stopping briefly for gas without ever leaving the car. Craine had his pistol pushed into the back of the leather seat hard enough that his driver could feel it. He was pretty sure the gas attendant noticed the blood on their shirts, but he took no interest in asking them where they were from or where they were heading. Maybe a part of him already knew.

It was black outside, but the stars hinted at what was around them. Long stretches of dry plains gave way to curling hillside roads and timbered peaks. A wall of mountains welcomed him back to Mono County.

The journey seemed feverish, and Craine felt himself drift off before an image of Michael jolted him awake. He thought of Abe, too, but everything in Vegas was behind him. Now there was only what was in front.

Several times he told his driver to go faster but they never saw Kastel's car. He'd had only a few minutes' head start, but a few minutes was enough. Kastel might have gone straight into the house and killed Michael. There was no coming to terms with it, simply an awareness that it might be the case. But it felt extreme, even for someone so clearly unhinged. Besides, it was Craine he wanted. He'd told him where he was going for that very reason.

Craine was imagining Michael's fingers crawling in the sand like worms when he felt some kind of movement inside his chest. He focused his eyes and saw the driver staring at him in the rearview. The car was slowing down, drifting to the side of the road, and he realized the man was hoping to make a run for it.

"Don't you dare stop," Craine said, sitting up. "Don't you dare."

They went on north up into Mono County, Craine instructing him where to go whenever they needed to turn off.

Their headlights picked up the sign to Bridgeport maybe an hour before first light. Everything looked the same, which surprised him. Almost as if he'd expected them to have burned down the entire town.

Craine waved the muzzle of the pistol at different turns in the road until they were crawling up the pine-fringed gravel road that wound another mile to his farm.

A fifty-foot white alder on the side of the track marked the beginning of his farm compound. Michael had carved CRAINE into it when they first arrived and he could see it in the car headlights. It meant they were exactly a quarter-mile from their house.

"Stop here," he said.

The brakes squalled briefly and the car stopped. The driver sat rigidly in the front seat. He raised his hands.

"I've done everything you asked me to," he said. "I realize you're angry but there's no need to do anything foolish."

Craine ignored him. "Leave the lights on. Keep the engine running."

Craine was staring up the driveway to see if there was an ambush there, but he couldn't see anyone in the beams.

They sat in silence. He could hear the frogs in the fields. Apart from that he heard nothing.

After a long minute the bodyguard turned around to look at Craine. His words were casual; his tone was panicked.

"I was here all week. Your son, he'll be alright. He'll recover. Just shocked, you know. Scared. He's got a mouth on him but I didn't hit him, none of the boys did either."

Craine was trying to ignore him, concentrating on his next steps. "Stop talking."

"You know, Kastel will be here. He already said he was going to come back here, we both know that. Now he's going to make you give yourself up for your boy. I can help you negotiate. He listens to me."

"I said, stop talking."

Like most people who feel trapped, the man became aggressive. "You should listen to what I'm saying," he said with more urgency. "I can get you out of this situation. You don't have to shoot me. That stuff before. All that with your kid. It didn't mean anything."

Craine no longer ignored him. He angled the gun directly at his mouth. "You held me down as Kastel mutilated my son," he said matter-of-factly.

There was no buffer. There was less than a foot between them. They were eyeball to eyeball. The man's hard stare dissolved into desperation.

"You're taking it all way too personally, Craine. For God's sake, it was only busine—"

But Craine had pulled the trigger and if the driver ever finished his sentence, neither man heard it.

The birds in the trees scattered.

* * *

There was no plan. Only a sense of urgency.

Craine left the man's body in the driver's seat and moved behind the headlights into the treeline. He'd expected his blood to freeze when he'd shot the driver but instead a bolt of energy surged through him like he'd been slapped in the face. He didn't feel nauseous. Only satisfied.

He wasn't sure what the next hour held, but he knew that at the end of it he and Michael could both be dead. But between now and then there was no horror he wouldn't act on to keep him safe. He'd turn the sky red if he had to.

Craine went twenty yards or so into the pine trees. His eyes adjusted to the dark. He couldn't see the house from here but there was no way they wouldn't have heard the pistol shot. It was the call to action he wanted.

The nights were cool here but he was too nervy to feel it. The barrel of the pistol was warm and Craine clasped it tightly in one hand, using the other to sweep his hair out of his eyes. It was matted with blood, some his, most of it not.

The gunfire had ruined his hearing but he strained his ears for sounds of movement. Voices. *Anything.*

He waited.

Finally he heard shouts and not long after saw flashlights dancing through the trees. The lights would ruin their night vision. They'd barely be able to see him, let alone aim. Besides, the sugar pines were thick enough to take the fire if they started shooting blind. That was a second advantage. He clung on to both of them.

They switched the flashlights off as they got closer to the car. The headlights were still on and they flickered as they crossed the beams. It meant they were close.

He rocked his head, trying to get a better line of sight. From where he was standing there looked to be two of them idling around the headlights. They both had Thompson machine guns.

He'd never been a good shot and accuracy with a pistol was difficult at twenty feet, let alone twenty yards in pitch-black. He might have the upper hand for a few seconds but the moment he fired it was open season.

He heard their voices again, more urgent this time. The engine went off and with it the car lights. It meant they'd found the body.

Craine was trusting that the light would speckle their eyesight. But the longer he took the sooner they'd get their night vision. Now was his chance.

A few quick breaths and then out he ran. His shoes seemed to make a deafening amount of noise as he scrambled down the short bank, coming out between two cottonwood trees and onto the road.

He got within ten yards of them before they sensed anything awry. Craine held the pistol out in front of him and when the first silhouette turned square, he fired without stopping into his stomach. Craine wasn't sure how many shots hit him but the man fell back onto the hood of the car with a wet wheezing noise.

The second gunman was no more than five or six paces away. He turned in different directions, looking like he might shoot, but Craine was already on him now. He came up so close to him that his Thompson was trapped between their bodies. Craine barreled into him, jammed the pistol into the man's neck like a knife and pulled the trigger twice, one round going clean through him and ricocheting off the car's coachwork like a lit match.

The sound the man emitted was guttural and inhuman. Like the sounds that butchers block out when they go to sleep. Craine felt the foul warmth of another man's insides run down his arms and soak through his shirt.

Whether it was on purpose or purely instinctive, the man pulled the trigger of his Thompson machine gun.

It was less like a sound and more like being shaken from inside.

CHAPTER 50

From the kitchen, Kastel watched as the sky strobed. The gunfire was close enough to judder the windowpanes. *Such a sound*, thought Kastel.

Machine-gun fire felt so familiar. Hearing it instinctively tensed his back muscles. Tightened his jaw. He could already feel his mind racing. Or maybe that was the bennies.

The kitchen was cluttered with food cans. From habit, his two men kept checking and rechecking their pistol clips. Since the first shot five minutes ago, they'd all been on edge, vigilant and ready. Now it was time for action.

Craine's son was sitting in the corner with his hands tied, slumped in weary despair.

"You hear that, kid?"

The boy looked up. The dressing on his hand was brown where the blood had soaked through. He looked scared.

"That's your father. He's dead."

The boy began shaking. His shoulders first but then his head too. Slowly, from side to side. "No," he said. "He'll come for me. I know it."

He said it with such assurance. It was like the boy knew something he didn't.

And maybe he did, because the gunfire they heard wasn't Craine dying. It was him killing. And when they saw two hunched figures loping toward the house, Kastel had to double-take.

He had a man by the window. He turned to Kastel in astonishment.

"It's Craine. He's got Frankie."

It was true. One of Kastel's men was gripping his stomach, walking up the driveway. Behind him was the silhouette of another man pointing a machine gun at his back. Kastel almost laughed with surprise. It was Jonathan Craine.

He had to admit, he never thought this farmer very credible. Was disappointed when he first met the man he'd heard so much about. And yet here he was, wounded and harried. His face blood-streaked. Like a soldier wandering back to the foxholes after a grueling night run with a hostage in tow.

Abe had turned soft. But Craine? No, he'd hardened. And that was Kastel's work. To have had an effect on this man was something in itself. *Yes*, he thought. *What type of man have I pried out of him?* He almost wanted to shake his shoulders and welcome him in.

Kastel flipped the safety catch to the off position. "Take the boy," he demanded. "We're going outside. No one shoots him until I do."

But Kastel didn't take his eyes away from the window as he spoke. He was too focused on Craine. Watching him stagger up the driveway, limping toward death.

He thought it was beautiful.

The sun was inching upward but the light was dim. It was the man he'd shot in the stomach who was limping in front of Craine and his blood was very red on the dusty driveway. Like dripping paint.

There was something unusual about shooting a man and then telling him to walk with you, but then unusual wasn't of concern right now. The sight of the second gunman's corpse was enough to convince Craine's hostage to do what he was told. Or maybe it was the Thompson machine gun pointing at his spine. Craine had no reason to ask him.

His hostage had taken two pistol bullets to the gut and walking was an effort. Being shot twice wasn't necessarily a death sentence, but Craine knew he'd bleed out and die if they didn't hurry.

"Keep going," he said. "Don't stop till I tell you."

His aim now was to draw the men out of the house and try to negotiate an exchange. His hostage for theirs—Michael. The rest he put down to chance.

"They'll kill you," the man croaked, spitting blood. "Even if they let the boy go, they'll still kill you."

Yes, they would. Craine had already come to terms with the fact that it wasn't a matter of if he was killed. It was a matter of when.

"We're almost there. Keep walking."

The man groaned. "I'm telling you. You're not thinking straight."

But that wasn't true. It might have been the adrenaline. It might have been his sheer will to see this through. But Craine's thoughts were clearer than they'd ever been in his life.

The two men kept at a pace until the front porch loomed ahead. A shiver ran through Craine's bones. Light was shining through the drapes on the ground floor and he could make out figures in his kitchen. Could hear their voices. He couldn't tell how many. *Three? Four?*

He was edgy.

"Stop here," Craine said to the man.

They were fifty feet away from the compound when the farmhouse door opened and light spilled out into the driveway. It was followed by three armed men. One of them was Kastel. He had Michael with him.

Craine's cheeks burned.

Michael's hand was bandaged but he was otherwise unhurt. He looked confused and shocked more than anything else. Craine couldn't believe he'd got this far. There were times this week that the thought of ever seeing his son again seemed like an impossibility. Even to know he was alive meant so much.

And then he heard Michael's voice.

"I'm sorry," his boy yelled, and it threw Craine. He used all his strength to focus on what needed to be done.

"No need to be sorry. These men are going to let you go."

Kastel's men positioned themselves in a flat line in front of his porch. They had pistols. Craine had a Thompson machine gun with a drum magazine that could fire ten rounds a second. The advantage was slight but it was his.

His throat was swollen and canker sores had formed in his mouth. It was hard to shout. "Kastel," he rasped. "I've got your man."

"I'm shot, sir," his hostage gurgled. "He got me bad."

"Goddammit, Frankie," one of Kastel's men muttered over and over.

Craine stood directly behind his hostage with the Thompson in his shoulder, Kastel in his sights. But Kastel had Michael in front of him, too, and this time it wasn't a knife to his throat but a short-barreled revolver. His son looked gripped by fear but he didn't cry. *That courage.*

"And I have your boy, Craine," Kastel yelled. He was amped up. A mania in his voice. "I'll kill him in the next two seconds if I don't see your face."

"I'm here," Craine said. He stepped to the side of his hostage so that he was visible in the open. Beams crisscrossed over his face like ghostly hands trying to reach out and grab him. Craine saw the flashlight reflect off the metal of his machine gun and his heart began beating faster. He felt alert and unafraid. It was like all of him was in his fingertips. At his disposal.

"You hurt my son, I'll shoot all of you."

"Then I guess we're at an impasse."

Craine stepped closer, nudging the hostage with his gun barrel. "I give you this man, you let my son go. That's the end of it. We go our separate ways."

Michael was imploring him. "Be careful, Pa."

Craine couldn't even look his son in the eye, knowing it would throw him. It never stopped feeling strange and incredible seeing yourself in your child. The brown circling his pupils was the same brown as his own eyes. He sometimes forgot how much they looked alike. It was like looking at the young man he saw in the mirror thirty years ago.

"Don't worry," the father said. "Everything's going to be okay."

"I'm scared," the son murmured in reply.

"I know. But it's almost over now. I promise." Then, turning slightly, he said to Kastel: "I'll ask you again. Your man for my son."

"I'm impressed, Craine. Wasn't sure you had it in you."

"Then you know I'm not bluffing."

Kastel turned to the hostage in front of Craine. "Frankie," he called out. "You remember what we said after Bataan?"

"Yessir," the gunman said, but by now he was preoccupied with the blood pouring out of his stomach like a skewered canteen.

"Tell me," Kastel said.

The man gurgled. It was difficult for him to speak. "We said, 'Better to die on your feet than get captured again.'"

"Exactly."

And with that Kastel pointed his pistol and shot the man clean through the head.

It happened very quickly. The dead gunman slumped to the floor. No one else moved an inch. Kastel's sentries were rigid. As if they'd expected it.

Craine's attention wasn't on his lost hostage but on the shift in balance this situation had taken. He was out in the open. He no longer held the upper hand.

Craine took three steps forward with his machine gun raised and several panicked voices began shouting at him to stop where he was, and he was shouting back too. "Let him go," he said. "Let him go or I'll shoot you all."

Craine turned the Thompson and aimed it directly at Kastel's face. He had his finger on the trigger guard, ready to shoot if he needed to.

"Don't do anything foolish now," Kastel said, tightening his grip on Michael. He moved directly behind him and Craine couldn't get a clear shot. "You'll kill us both if you shoot from there," he said. "And my men will shoot you anyway, so everyone will lose."

"I'm not going to shoot. Now you take that pistol away from my son."

Kastel did no such thing. "I'm going to make you the same deal as I did before," he shouted. "You for him."

"Why should I trust you?"

Kastel thrust out his chin. "Put the gun down, Craine."

"I said, why should I trust you?"

Kastel took the gun away from Michael and stepped aside. He was making himself vulnerable, but Craine himself was still a target. There were two other guns on him.

"Because I've got no interest in killing your son. If he's still bitter about it in ten years I'll be waiting, but that's between him and me. But *you*," Kastel said, "you have to go. You know that." His pistol nodded at Michael's head. "It's his life for yours."

Kastel let that sit there. As if the offer lay on the ground between them and Craine had to reach out and take it. *What would a brave man do?*

Kastel's men shifted uneasily. Michael began shaking his head. And in that moment Craine saw his own father the night he'd died. A memory. Saying goodbye. Felt the soft handshake that was shared. The words that never were.

Craine searched for his son's eyes. "Hey, look at me. Michael, look at me." When those widened pupils found his, he said, "I'm proud of you." He wasn't sure he'd ever said it. "Your mother would be too. So much."

Michael's voice strained. "Please. Don't go. There has to be another way."

Many years ago, on a night of many losses, Jonathan Craine had told his son he'd take care of him. And he wasn't about to break that promise.

"Everything's going to be just fine," he said.

Craine had risked his son's life before, but he wouldn't do it again. On some other plane, one several layers deeper, was an odd calm.

He dropped the Thompson.

CHAPTER 51

It was light outside now. The sun not visible yet but telling him it was there. There was something more reassuring about it than dying in darkness.

They took him inside the house. His son was left outside. Through the doorway Craine could see Michael was looking around, bewildered and terrified. Like he had grasped what was happening but somehow was refusing to believe it.

One of Kastel's men was out there with him. The other one came inside and shut the front door.

It was better now there wasn't uncertainty. No denial. No anger. No bargaining. Only acceptance. Craine didn't even have any anticipation of what was next. He was just here. In this moment. He almost felt uplifted.

Kastel was below the staircase; Craine saw him lift the back of his palm to his nose and inhale. His head tilted back and forward.

When he returned, his eyes were wide and he was pulsating on the spot.

"How did it feel, killing my guys? There's a dangerous excitement to it, isn't there? I struggle to explain it sometimes. People think I'm crazy for saying it but war made me happy more than it made me sad. Fear is thrilling. Everything else is so goddamn dull."

"Tell the man outside to let my son go," Craine said quietly. "He doesn't need to see this."

"And miss the show?" Kastel blinked at him. "A joke. I'm not insane, Craine."

No, not insane. But filled with a rage you can't explain.

The kitchen was in disarray. It smelled of garbage and there were empty food cans and dirty pans on all the surfaces where Kastel's men had squatted for a week. Light from the rising sun caught something metal on the side dresser: his Remington. *Out of reach.* It might as well have been a mile away.

Besides, he didn't want to fight. Dying didn't feel like failure now. Unlike Kastel's ultimatum two nights previously, he wasn't groping for alternatives. There was a realization of what was happening but also an acceptance of this new status. He was nervy only because he wanted to be sure his son went free.

Through the kitchen window, Craine could see Michael on the driveway. He was shouting for his father. Craine felt sick.

"Please," he managed to mutter. "Let him go."

"Relax, Craine. I'm a man of my word. I'll go out in a second and that'll be the end of it. You'll stay here. He'll go on his way."

"Wait until he's gone. I don't want him to see this."

Kastel lit a cigarette. It seemed to stop his jaw from gurning but not from talking. He was oddly animated.

"I wish you hadn't been involved in this, I really do. Was half-expecting Lansky to take one look at you and turn you away."

Craine no longer cared about Kastel's motives but the man seemed intent on telling him anyway.

"This has been an important milestone," he said. "You see, change is good. There's a war going on inside America and it's time to take sides. Don't look so sad, Craine. War is a good thing. War is movement, progression, development. Because this is a new America. For the young. For the men who have earned it the hard way."

The gunman with Kastel nodded. They saw themselves as Young Turks, part of a revolution.

"This is our legacy."

But Craine wasn't really listening. He was looking at his son. Feeling relieved knowing that soon he'd be free. Michael's life was his own now. His to waste and his to earn. His to enjoy and his to mourn. *I've done what I needed to do*, Craine thought. *I have been the bridge.*

He stepped back from the window and remembered the question he'd asked himself all those days ago. Yes, there was a cause he was ready to die for. Willingly. And in that moment, Craine realized he was smiling.

"What's so funny, Craine?"

He looked back at Kastel and said, "A legacy is what you give your children."

That grin of Kastel's was barely in check. "Stay here. Time to send your boy off."

Kastel went outside and left Craine alone with the last of Kastel's men. He had his hand in his jacket pocket on what Craine assumed was the butt of his pistol.

There was a grim silence, which Craine preferred. Talking seemed so unnecessary. Besides, he had to breathe deeply to keep himself from passing out.

There was no ceremony about letting Michael go. He saw Kastel walk outside and talk to the man on the porch with the pistol. He pointed and shouted, and then Craine's son turned and started running away from the house.

Craine counted the seconds, every yard he ran closer to him being safe. He saw Michael stop and stare back at the house but he willed him not to. *Run*, he said without speaking, *run as fast as you can.*

And then Kastel put his hand in his jacket pocket. It took a moment for Craine to gauge what was happening but by then Kastel had drawn his pistol.

He felt the dull tap of dread on his shoulders. Kastel was going to shoot Michael as he ran. He'd lied to him. *He had no intention of letting Michael live.*

There was the snap of gunfire, but before Craine could register what was happening he felt the man behind him move and then there was a sharp tug at his neck. Craine's arms flailed, grasping at his throat. A taut metal cord was slicing through his neck like a cheese wire. He couldn't breathe.

The man behind Craine began jerking upward and he could feel the wire cutting into his windpipe, shutting off the blood supply.

Instinctively, Craine tucked his chin down and raised his shoulders up. Air dripped into his lungs. It gave him a moment's strength and he stamped his heel into the man's shinbone twice, then three times, until it cracked.

The man shouted by his ear. Together they reeled back, tripping over and falling to the floor.

The garrote loosened enough that air rushed into his chest. Craine began choking but there wasn't time to lie there. He could see the shotgun on the dresser a few feet away.

He twisted his body to kick out at the dresser but the man rolled on top of him, his weight crushing Craine, the wire between his hands trying to find his throat like he was muzzling a wild dog.

Craine kicked out at the dresser over and over with his heel. It wobbled and shook. The sound of something falling onto the tiles: *the Remington.*

He flung an arm sideways, groping blindly for what he hoped was the shotgun. He couldn't reach it.

The garrote was around his windpipe now. Craine knew he was suffocating but had no sensation of dying, only the sight and sound of nothingness.

I must keep going, he told himself. *I can endure one moment more.*

For Kastel, it was like he was back on Palau again, shooting at Japs. *That old-time feeling.*

He'd left the military more of a menace than when he went in. Almost unrecognizable from the skinny twenty-two-year-old who'd enlisted in Chicago. People often said there was an intensity about him. That he had a temper. But he'd always been short-tempered. It followed him around, ready to get him into trouble at any minute.

Kastel shut one eye and sighted. The boy was tall but he was quick. He aimed at him and fired.

The shot missed. He'd taken too much powder and his arms were shaking.

Kastel aimed again and pulled the trigger and the boy twisted sideways in a red mist, then fell to the ground. There was fifty yards between them now. It was hard to see. *Did he kill him?*

Kastel could see the boy trying to pull himself up. There was blood on his shoulder but he was alive. He lifted the pistol and aimed again, taking in long, deep breaths.

Craine heard another shot from outside. His mind tuned to a new pitch and the last of his energy—*the last of him*—dedicated itself to thrashing out wildly. To fighting free. It was as if something had been opened in Craine. An instinct that had been suppressed.

There was nothing clean-cut or neat about his movements. The goal was destruction, pure and simple. He scratched and he clawed. He used one hand to protect his neck, then pushed his free hand up to the man's face. He pushed his thumb into his eye socket so hard that the man began squealing.

The pressure around his neck loosened. Taking advantage, Craine reached out and pulled the shotgun toward him by the barrel. His fist held it backward and upside down like a strange club. Clumsily, he brought the nose of the gun up to the man's head. Against his better instincts, Craine's other hand came away from his throat and crossed over, fingers scrambling for the trigger guard. He had less than half a second before the man would squeeze the life out of him.

There was no sense of aiming, of holding the Remington or even pulling the trigger. There was only the dying desperation of knuckles pleading the trigger to release.

Craine saw the man's good eye look sideways at the shotgun but he understood too late. There was an explosion and with it the warm shrapnel of his skull on Craine's face.

* * *

Craine emerged from the house with the Remington in both hands.

The gunman on the porch looked at him but Craine ignored him completely. Didn't even care as the man turned his pistol and shot him, he was so focused on Kastel.

There was a stinging sensation in his side but Craine's arms were steady. The forend came back, then forward as he chambered another shell. He didn't even aim, only lifted it.

Kastel saw him, or maybe he heard the door or maybe he only felt his presence. He turned ever so slightly but there was no eye contact made, no final confrontation.

There were many emotions Craine might have felt in that instant. Hatred wouldn't have been hard to draw upon. Satisfaction, perhaps. Vengeance, whatever place that came from. But in the brief moment between looking at Kastel and pulling the trigger, Craine felt absolutely nothing but relief.

He fired.

Kastel's head split open and then the shotgun explosion seemed to come after. It was like Kastel's head was there and then it wasn't. The rest of him dropped into the dust like a collapsed puppet.

Craine felt another bullet enter his gut. He turned the shotgun on the second man and fired as he was aiming. The impact of the twelve-gauge was like watching a pencil sketch be ripped in half and the man fell to the floor not far from Kastel in a bloody mess.

And that was it.

Craine gripped his waist and realized he'd been shot in his side and in his hip a few inches above the first wound. There wasn't time to care, or maybe the time made no difference. He started loping toward where his son had been running.

The morning clouds had parted. The sun caught his face and he had to squint to see. Moving blindly. He could feel blood running down his legs. *Don't fail me*, he begged them.

Tears came and he wanted to shout for Michael but couldn't. He felt a sharp pain but he kept moving. Every step made him blench, but with a gritted shout he kept going. He was gasping and groaning. And then he heard no sound at all.

Let him be alive. I would give everything. If he's dead, I want to hold him. Want us to die together.

Craine tried to go faster but his legs gave way and he fell to the floor.

He was on his knees, coughing. The flesh about his hip felt very hot now. Blood was soaking through his clothes. He was so close but his senses were failing him. When he blinked the world went dark, pulling him to the ground. Whatever had been keeping him upright, there wasn't enough.

He shook his head and tried to look for Michael. Put his hand out as if he could reach for him. But he wasn't there.

And then his own father. Calling behind him. The words gifted from the dead. *Go on, man. Get up. Never stop.*

His vision returned. Craine put his hand over the hole in his side and pushed himself back up to his feet. Forced himself to put one foot before the other.

The dry earth was steady beneath his soles. As if months of drought had been building to this one task. To keep his feet firm. To keep him afloat. A leaking ship a few final waves from shore.

Finally, when he couldn't go on a single step further he stopped and let his eyes search. The light brighter but somehow fading. Unclear.

And through the haze, a figure in the grass.

Michael. It was Michael.

He was twenty yards away. Lying there. Bloodied. Still.

He was too late.

Craine tried to call something but he wasn't sure the words came out. He fell to his knees again, knowing that soon it would be over.

He tilted his neck up, one final look at his son.

And then the boy moved. His body unfolding from the dust.

Michael Craine rose from the grass. There was blood on his

shoulder but he was standing. He was alive. He was alive, and he was going to stay alive.

Michael looked around and the look he gave his father grabbed at something deep inside Craine's chest.

Michael shouted his name. Called him Papa.

And Jonathan Craine pulled himself up, or someone did. Because he was walking again. Moving toward Michael like it was the only thing that mattered.

The sight of his son there should have stopped him in his tracks but it didn't. It carried him forward. It gave him life.

He ran.

Acknowledgements

My sincere thanks to everyone who contributed to the publication of this novel. I've been lucky to work with an incredible team at Oneworld and I couldn't have asked for a more encouraging and insightful editor than Jenny Parrott.

Although this is a work of imagination, I owe a debt of gratitude to those historians who have covered the period. I've read countless books on Hollywood, the mob and Bugsy Siegel and each helped in their own way to inform my narrative. Thank you for paving the way.

A special thank you to my agents Anna Power and Sean Gascoine for championing me. I am also indebted to Alexandra Arlango and Mark Bolton for their contributions reading early drafts of this novel.

I'm deeply grateful to my family and friends, particularly Mum and Jimmy, who provide the ideal coastal writing retreat when I need to escape the city.

And finally to Laura Andrews, whose continued encouragement and support was everything that I needed to finish *The Syndicate.* This book is dedicated to you.